The APOTHECARY

The APOTHECARY

M A R T H A   B L U M

Edited by Geoffrey Ursell.
Book and cover design by Duncan Campbell.
Cover image: Canopy Photography/Veer.
Author photo by Hans Dommasch.

Printed and bound in Canada at Tri-Graphic Printing Ltd.

Library and Archives Canada Cataloguing in Publication

Blum, Martha, 1913-
The apothecary / Martha Blum.

ISBN 1-55050-349-9

1. Title.

PS8553.L858A66 2006   c813'.54   C2006-904636-0

1   2   3   4   5   6   7   8   9   10

COTEAU
BOOKS

2517 Victoria Ave.
Regina, Saskatchewan
Canada   S4P 0T2

AVAILABLE IN CANADA & THE US FROM
Fitzhenry & Whiteside
195 Allstate Parkway
Markham, ON, Canada, L3R 4T8

The publisher gratefully acknowledges the financial assistance of the Saskatchewan Arts Board, the Canada Council for the Arts, the Government of Canada through the Book Publishing Industry Development Program (BPIDP), the Association for the Export of Canadian Books, and the City of Regina Arts Commission, for its publishing program.

To Richard, my husband,
In memoriam.

Let each one strive to emulate this love,
This love so free from every prejudice.
– GOTTHOLD EPHRAIM LESSING, *Nathan the Wise,* 1779

I would like to emphasize that this is a work of fiction. Characters in the foreground are fictitious in their entirety. Similarities to individuals living or dead are strictly coincidental. Historical events are as accurately drawn as I could recall them. Any error, historical or other, is my own.

— M.B.

TABLE OF CONTENTS

PART ONE:
CZERNOWITZ – THE FORTIES

A NIGHT, STARLESS AND MOONLESS, MADE TRULY BLACK by criss-crossing shafts of light. I had worked late. I stumbled coming out, the curb as if ripped from under my feet.

I had been punished for being my father's son by the Russian, or call them Soviet authorities. All the sons and daughters of entrepreneurs of any sort, especially learned ones thrown out of their place of work, were shuffled like cards. They shuffled me into the *Synagogengasse*, right near the Turkish fountain, to work in a small Jewish pharmacy in the Jewish-Turkish quarter where nothing changes through the centuries except stories that become legends, events growing on them like the arms of the Ahi henchman. This Ahi, the cursed Turk, grows new arms whenever he wants them to string up men, three at one time, by swinging a knotted rope around one and holding the others with his newly sprouted, powerful arms.

A new arm grown out of the wildest fears will get its stories soon. Retold through millennia, enhanced by the prophetic imagination, stories were lifeblood, flowing through the living corpus of all. Clustered into small dwellings, sharing air and breath, those who live here had stories run through them. Arteries and veins in a body stories were. In times of hunger it was the Messiah: *He is here. See and follow. Get up from your bed. Hope.* In times of comfort: *Remember the prophets. Watch out. You have forgotten God. The golden calf. Mend your ways.*

Tonight it was the Russians. A curse. One could not guess their next move and one could not see through to the next day. The future stopped, as if unpredictable, as if the next Sabbath did not exist.

The owners of the small pharmacy had been displaced. I had been put in charge. It took a while to function but I succeeded in the end, serving this pious group around me, serving this world of poverty and singing my sister so loved as a child, but which had never been the same for me. Laughter, light living, wealth, not the despair of the poor was my privilege. I learned differently now very quickly.

On the first day I entered this meagre shop – where shelves rattled as if bewitched, making mixing ingredients, powders, herbs and what not fall onto your work counter, drop into your eyes – I was about to sit down and cry. But there was nowhere to sit down: old-fashioned pharmacists did not sit down. Some dingy light coming through the door was shadowed to boot by all the houses from across the way. Men and women were waiting at the door, here and there someone held a prescription; for the rest, I was the doctor.

"An infection," the old man said.

"It is gangrene by now, I think."

"No, it is an infection," the old man insisted. "Give me something. I was here before everyone else. I was in front of this shop since five o'clock in the morning."

"I need a morphine *suppositorium*, my wife is in pain, ill with cancer," another man said.

I did not know where they were. I was new here, had just entered the place, tried to find my way, locate things.

"I'll make you a few *suppositoria*," I said, "as soon as I have found the key to the narcotics cabinet." Narcotics were always under lock and key. There was an account book to mark the quantity, purpose and name of the doctor. "Do you have a prescription?"

"No, the doctor has been displaced..."

"How am I to dispense *Morphia* without a prescription? I'll go to jail." I paused for a moment. "I'll do it anyway."

"I'll bring you the prescription as soon as some other doctor takes on his duty."

The crowd settled down on the long bench, reassured by my good will. Or simply by my presence. I would cry soon. It was too much. There was agitation in front. They all looked out to see what caused it. Horses and small men no one had ever seen before in the street. *Kalmucks*, they said. What is a *Kalmuck*? Oh, these slit-eyed little riders. Small men shouting outside. I'm in the *Synagogengasse*; are the people going to services? What day is today?

A Russian officer – or soldier, perhaps – going like any colonizer in front of the queue, asked for alcohol. Pulled rubles out of his tunic. Uncounted.

"I do not have alcohol for sale. Not as such. I need what little there is for disinfecting of wounds, tinctures or prescriptions."

"Are you all Yids?" And he pulled out his revolver and said very quietly, "I'll blow your brains out, all of you. Lock your doors, and you, Yid behind the counter, go through the place and find it."

Of course I knew the order in a pharmacy. Even if you were new, one ought to look for things in specifically designed places. I found the seventy proof *spiritus vini*, several litres in proper containers, the bottles as well, and I filled them and handed them over.

The *Kalmuck*: "Funny Jews you have here." And plunked another handful of rubles, uncounted, crinkled up like an old *Pravda*, onto the counter, put his firearm away and left without a smile, my people giving way, opening the locked door in silence.

I was startled by a face. I, born to love and comfort, was suddenly among the poor. And they assumed faces. *Poor* was not a collective noun. A face – a mother with a newborn. It was her turn. I had never held such a small human. The navel had become infected. We went into the "laboratory," if we may call it that. By regulation it had to be there. I found some peroxide, disinfected the navel, dried it with gauze and said, "Leave it open. The air will heal it, don't smother it, let it be free."

"Thank you, doctor," she said, "thank you," and hurried away, clutching her bundle. Noises. Shouts of impatience out there. Perhaps not even that. I just took too much time – I was inexperienced and I felt assaulted. Near tears. But slowly I rose, saying to myself: "Poor creatures, they want God. You're put into His costume, a white coat." And I tried to play the role with assurance and a lowered voice. Young as I was, I tried to learn the game fast: a smile, a little love.

The house was full now. The pharmacy had been closed for days. The Russians having "inventoried," or whatever they called their robbery. And I handed out numbers on little pieces of paper so they knew there would be a chance. Foremost: without order, no God. It is ordained, ordered to happen.

My poor folk. Trying so hard to live under all circumstances. I was left to serve the others, being overwhelmed partly by their pain but more by the emotion of living, mine and theirs. By the intensity of it: to alleviate pain I did not know existed. I had tears in my throat, swallowed them, and it was past midnight when the stream of people needing help relented.

The last to go, a girl, telling me that she was at a neighbour's, when – stepping out into the street – she could hardly find her way through horses, trucks and milling bodies. Trucks, full of people. Some she knew. When she recognized in one of them her father, mother – baby-in-arms; she had rushed towards them, called out, but by glance and gesture was told *You haven't seen us,* ran home, found the house locked. Turned back towards them, ran after them but couldn't reach them, hindered by uniformed men. And the trucks gaining distance, she spotted the open pharmacy and came in. Sat to recuperate like a lost fledgling bird on the corner bench. Did not rise until the last customer had left. Arms like wings tucked in, she waited. I sat beside her, listened to the tumbling words in Yiddish. Got the essence of it. "What are we to do? You and I?"

"I'll go with you," she said. "I've looked for my cousins but their doors were also locked. I'll go with you," she said.

And so we locked the pharmacy. I was in possession of the key, being put in charge by the Soviets. Darkest night. I nearly fell from the curb, which was there unexpectedly. But my young companion held onto me and said, "Be careful, I know these stones, I have scraped my knees many times on them. I won't fall, but you be careful, you're not from here. My name is Shainah," she said.

"And mine is Felix."

55555555555

Synagogengasse. From the turmoil, human birth and death, machines and horses, it turned into total silence. So we walked up to the Turkish fountain. Shainah knew every shortcut alley, leading me. Approaching the *Bahnhofstrasse*, the roar, shouts and unearthly-seeming thunder started again. A rolling of tanks or trucks – who could tell? Lights, beams of lights like bullets striking us, coming from nowhere, hit the two of us.

We fitted ourselves, flattening our bodies, into a crevice. Shainah in front. She whispering, "I know a doorway that is always open. I've played with the children there." But we couldn't make it to the doorway, stayed in the crack of the wall.

Oh, my little bird, so trembling for her life. But stronger almost than myself.

"Don't worry," she said, "they're going somewhere else. Just wait quietly." And she took over, her inborn motherliness protecting me. I smiled unseen.

And the scene changed as fast as it had begun when we, flat-bodied and hands against cold stone, watched the last truck move up the hilly *Bahnhofstrasse*, leaving the outer section light- and soundless. She pulled me across and we ran, backs bent, into lower Saint Trinity, a long, silent curved street that moved upward. This one I knew. It ended into my own *Residenzgasse*.

We hurried a little more, and coming closer we were startled by the same scene: noise, horses, trucks, light-shafts across the *Residenzgasse* facing us now. An enormous barrier. Truck on truck. Riders on both sides containing them. Across the Ahi fountain was the Evangelical church, and as we approached carefully – counting houses as a backup – we saw the sprawling of that train of trucks as far as the Archbishop's Residence.

We held our breath. I put a candy from my pocket into Shainah's mouth, felt her smile in a squeeze of her hand. And waited. Took a few more steps and heard the rumbling sound of the dragon moving with a slow start. A shaft of light, strafing, revealed my grandmother's face in an open truck among fifty or sixty or God knows how many strangers. I suddenly trembled. It couldn't be. "Why, my grandmother! How could it? She is past eighty."

"No, it couldn't be," Shainah said. "How would it be your grandma, on a truck in the middle of a night?" Shainah, comforting me, helped perhaps erase her own vision of her parents not acknowledging their child. "No, not your grandma, Felix." My name from her lips was soothing, womanly, and I felt reassured; was back home. Among women. An everyday comfort.

When we approached the old gate it was locked and I lost my hold on things again. But not showing my wet face, I said, "Shainah, do not worry, this is my grandfather's house. I know a back door leading to the cellar from the back to the *Hausmeister's* flat. Come." And I pulled her fast around the corner *Balschgasse*. It was the night of the twelfth of June to the thirteenth in the year of 1941. One or two o'clock past midnight, or thereabouts.

"Shainah, I cannot go in through the front gate, though I can open it without any noise, but God knows who will hear me and jump at us and put us in these trucks. Come my darling, we'll go through the back fence."

Through the *Balschgasse* around the corner, where the Old House swings inward, I helped Shainah over the stone fence and scaled it behind her. I smiled at her when I saw her down there, within the lilac bushes. She guessed my smile because I heard her giggle a little. So fast had I become a father that I shivered. But I

7

knew she was mine, and I came down from this fence carefully, taking hold of every crevice or uneven stone, my foot tracing back the many illegal times I had come home too late to get through the old front gate.

In the lilac bushes we caught our breath for a little moment. Consulted. She was my partner now. "We'll have to crawl through this cellar window there." It reflected some light, coming from an unidentifiable source, and I knew how to pry it open.

"Shainah, you know I was such a bad boy, you should have seen me opening this window with my Swiss army knife. Here is the love of every boy's life, a Swiss army knife." And I whispered, "Sit here still, sweetheart, and I'll just pry it open and then I'll come for you."

She snuggled for a moment into me, in response, anticipating perhaps her moment alone. But she could watch me. I crawled along the house, not crossing the yard, reached the window, and on my knees, with old, crafty, childish impishness, made a space wide enough for both of us. I crawled back to fetch her. "This is fun," she said, and we squeezed ourselves in one after the other.

My plan was to let her stay with Marusja, our *Hausmeister*. Her husband, Dmitry, was working on his father's land, thank God. Marusja was home; she took Shainah in without question. I left Shainah with her and rushed up our old staircase. To my grandmother's flat first.

To enter her flat, one had to pass by a big kitchen terrace-garden, unusual tropical big-leafed plants lining the vast eastern window. It was unlocked and I slid inside, hiding in one Sycamore tree I knew well. Of course, we had seen my grandmother, Shainah and I. The flat was in total disarray. Some of the plants turned over, Russian-sounding voices reaching my ears without carrying any meaning. I did not venture out, but waited a little longer. I heard two distinct voices from her parlour; they were rummaging through her glass collection.

I changed position to have a better view, chose an armoire I had always loved. It had secret doors of cherry wood, secret buttons giving me entrance into side doors, shelves above, almost to the ceiling. In there and through a slight slit as in a fortress, I watched the enemy. Two little men were sitting at her desk, swearing, taking "inventory" it seemed, and one more, a superior perhaps, drank grandmother's brandy and ate her fruitcake.

I had always loved this flat: across from our own it was wide open to the east and north and smelled of *Moschus*. It had plush curtains of deep blue, which she had brought from Lemberg as a young girl.

Esther, my grandmother, stood tall, just as redheaded as mother; but fierce, not gentle. A commanding presence. She loved me, but without indulgence. Glass – blue and gold – was everywhere. Up to the ceiling, on hidden shelves, or free-standing. "Let me play, let me take it down." "Yes, but carefully." Always a condition when doing this or that. And I permitted this order, because it was a feminine order. A discipline with a smile, even if a hidden one, as hers was. White lace at the neck, to her chin, and long black taffeta rustling when she moved, she had a queenly authority I did not dare disobey. This was Esther. Pious, with a mystic trend, seeking God and serving. She loved me with a kind of passion ten-year-olds understand. Our very own. Undisclosed to others. She did not take me to her rabbis. This was Süssel's territory, my sister's, who looked for signs within signs of the Hebrew, obeyed inner revelations. Certainties, not of my choosing. But I always came – a little boy still – to the woman Esther, not to the mother of my mother. I went to the woman, was at home there, wanted, played with. At home in our games.

"You're a fine looking boy, Felix," she used to say, "almost Polish." Which to her was the summit of aristocratic looks. True or not I loved to hear it. One day she slid a small ring with an opal on my finger and said, "It is a noble stone, just the way you are and always will be. Not vulgar, not a diamond, which gives itself away on first sight, refracts the lights in all facets. And even if very expensive, is still cheap! An opal is noble. True inner values, a little hidden, and always of a changing finesse." I held it now, to restrain my tears.

When suddenly all three uniformed men moved towards the crystal wine cabinet, I slid out. Across to my parents' flat. Total disaster. Everything on the floor. More Russians drinking, one asleep, sprawled drunk on the salon floor.

I had entered the darkly wainscoted vestibule, where I could hide behind the hat and umbrella coat rack and look through little anemone curtains on the glass doors at a similar scene, as that in my grandmother's flat. I could only look through the tiny holes of the Madeira-embroidered curtains I had disliked, finding them tasteless *Kitsch* or cheap bourgeois *Gemütlichkeit*. But now I was glad, as these anemone petals provided me with a magnifying glass to see clearer.

My parents deported, violence done to their things and to mine. Schubert's face staring at me from the covers of a coveted early edition of the *Winterreise* lay open, torn. Knives, pieces of kolbassa, empty bottles next to it. Enough.

I flew down the three floors, all in one jump, to look after Shainah. She had settled into Marusja's arms, deeply asleep.

"Marusja, I leave her with you. Feed her, help her as if she were your own, and in the morning if I'm not back, go and see if the pastor of the Evangelical Church will take her, or maybe Carl Glasberg's wife, Rachel. Take care of her, she is all alone. I have to look for help. It may still be early and possible. Marusjenka, God will reward you."

It was two o'clock or later that I arrived – running along sheltering house fronts, with my back against them to avoid casting a shadow – at Bunin's place. Trucks in great numbers in the *Residenzgasse*, and past the main square, horses with their riders and trucks in between revealed by flashing, criss-crossing shafts of light. I passed the old temple and jumped on its low parapet, holding on to wrought-iron arabesques, knowing every turn and angle, having climbed these walls on high holidays to avoid the boredom of the service inside. Hidden by the overhang of wild vine I came closer to the City Hall. I would be exposed now crossing the open main Square called *Ringplatz*, its name imitating Vienna with its *Ring*-this or *Ring*-that; my hometown's pride was Austrian.

To cross the *Ringplatz* I had to make a fast decision. I stepped out of the *Tempelgasse* into the open with a determined step, upright and fast, as if having private but official business, an NKVD officer in plain clothes or something of the sort, not having to account to anyone, stern face, upright back. It worked. Horses and riders made room for me, as I gestured with my arms for them to let me pass. Then into the *Russischegasse*, where a total dark silence embraced me like my mother's kiss. I ran. Knocked, a coded triple sound, at Bunin's window, which faced the street. She was fast at the gate, suspecting disaster, slid me into her flat, held me close for a moment and said, "I know, I know, they have taken your parents."

"And my grandmother," I replied. At the end of my strength but not feeling it, I kissed her hands, cried like a child. "Help us,

Luditchka, help us. You have power. All political important decisions end up on your desk. Save my people."

Ludmilla Bunin. Soviet woman. A *politruk* party member,
head of all pharmaceutical industry and retail pharmacies,
responsible for "correct proletarian behaviour," which meant
name-calling, denunciation, and all that went with a power-
machine unnatural and mad. She fell in love the day she
denounced me as a "capitalist bloodsucker," son of the same kind
of criminal – and I had to hear this perverse terminology in front
of everybody. She fell in love with me. Spotted me, declared me
"public enemy," displayed me in front of the assembled pharmacists and industrialists of the city as the worst of them all, made
me beat my breast, confess to crimes I had not committed,
declared me to be beyond rehabilitation because of the bourgeoisie I stemmed from. All new to all of us, unimaginable absurd
theatre demanded by the system, with words coined to match.
And the poor souls that fell to her hatchet, arbitrarily and innocently, got ten years, or twenty, without a trial, just shipped out,
as I learned later.

On that first day of her official function, we were made to sit
on the bench of the outcasts: my father beside me, fifteen familiar faces, colleagues all. She stood there, at the head of table.
Seated along it were six or seven uniformed faces, pieces of paper
and sparkling water in front of everyone. She stood and called my
full name out, a stern, loud Russian-sounding irrevocable command, "Felix Geller, come to my office, immediately." My father
and the other "comrades" were dismissed. She had fallen in love.
For the first time in her life, she said, to an enemy of her class.
And she changed in my hands and under my very eyes.
Transcended her monstrous, asexual exterior, loved me, with the

intensity of abandon. All through the Russian year: June, 1940, to June, 1941.

It was the night of the twelfth, now the very early morning of the thirteenth.

She dressed in all her official regalia, went to her office, medals on her huge bosom, called the minister of health for the Ukraine, took responsibility for my father's release, and his dependents, and promised that he would look for a replacement in the plant. I sat beside her in that half-dark NKVD office. She used a little flashlight to illuminate the numbers. *Who is calling? For what purpose? The secret code?* An hour it took to reach the minister. But then it was done in three minutes. Bunin put the receiver down in the dark and we were silent. I had imparted exhaustion, despair to her; we kissed without lying with one another.

It took three days to release my father, mother, and grandmother from the cattle cars waiting on rails to finish operations, and the order to move. Three desperate days! Bureaucrats shirking responsibility and Bunin shouldering it all.

THE PASTOR took Shainah out of Marusja's hands in the early hours of that morning. She had woken Shainah, who was bewildered. "I am here," Marusja said, "I love you, Shainah." And Shainah, seeing a Ukrainian peasant doll beside her, held, cuddled and talked to it. "Is your mommy on the truck, too? Your daddy, where is he?" And the doll answered in such a low voice that Shainah had to put its face close to her ear. Understanding her now, she said, "Do not cry little Marusja, do not cry. You have to be big now, grown up." And they wiped each other's tears.

"Take little Marusja, she is yours, Shainah."

"No, my mother calls me Shainale. Call me that."

"Shainale," Marusja said, "here is bread, milk and a lump of sugar. Shainale, good? Give me your hand."

Dawn had not broken yet. They went up the cellar steps, through the front old gate, crossed the *Residenzgasse,* went through the back garden of the Evangelical Church, and knocked at the pastor's door, who took Shainah and the doll from Marusja's hand without much question.

The night had been turbulent in the church. Soldiers had broken in, had desecrated the altar. Drunk, they slept it off.

He, a Christian, gave love without measure. Smiled at Shainah, who accepted it as if it were the most natural thing on earth. "Take good care of Shainah," Marusja said, hugging Shainah to say goodbye.

The pastor took Shainah's hand and said, "Come and see my daughter's room. Her name is Martina."

The pastor avoided Rosy's room, not wanting to be reminded of her. He could not recall how long it was since his wife Rosy and their daughter Martina had left *Heim ins Reich* to Germany, by the command of the Führer. He had not gone; he could not have left his church. The pastor – avoiding the scent of clothes, the sound of her voice, the memory of rejection, her immodest presence – passed her door, entering a small paradise, Martina's world. Shainah, suddenly jubilant.

In a turn of mood, of immediacy, of female pragmatism, of survival, Shainah recognized Martina's world. Dolls, dressed in Sabbath elegance. A tiny table, two candleholders, white candles, lace tablecloth, and something that looked like the Sabbath bread, a braided *Chalah* under a lace doily. Her mother's Friday night table. "Here is your bed, Shainah," the pastor said. It was right beside the window, looked out onto chestnuts in bloom. And through them the Old House shone. Its east side in the full light of the rising sun. Shainah folded her hands, said her *Baruch Atah* – and crawled into that white linen, dressed as she was.

A Theologian of the Heart: June 1940

T HE PASTOR CLOSED THE CHURCH DOORS FROM THE
inside with a bar across. He felt his aloneness surprising –
that none of the events since that day in September, 1939, could
have been predicted, that the silence or death of beloved voices
could have been pre-imagined. He closed the door tightly. No
believer in outer evil forces, he locked the gate and inspected it
several times, astonished at his own fears.

The Russians were on the move up the *Bahnhofstrasse* towards
the centre of town, *Ringplatz* and City Hall. He had not gone to
their encounter. What could be there for him, a theologian of the
humane sort who looks for faith that binds us and eschews divi-
sion? As a young man, he had loved to talk to Jews in his search
for the basic Judaic Jesus.

He had waited a long time before addressing Felix's mother,
but when she had passed one day through the *Rothkirchgasse*, the
street at the southern edge of his gardens, he did. She was with
her son; they were laughing and walking fast but had stopped at
the chestnut trees in full flower. She had broken off one of these
candlelike multiple blooms, miracles in themselves. There the

trees stood close together and the pastor felt that they were the guardian angels of his goodwill.

He had said hello to have her turn towards him to show that brilliance, an illumination from within which he had expected to be there. At other times he saw her alone. In thought. Asked her to come to his church to hear a distinguished churchman's sermon on a specific Sunday. "I'm a Jew," she had said, "and do not go to church. But I will come if you would kindly invite me." And she did come. Sometimes with her wild daughter.

He saw her across from the church, passing the road up to the Gallows Hill and down to the Holy Trinity Street that noon day just minutes before locking the gate and putting the bar across. And seating himself in a pew of his deserted church it struck him that his *angst* was for his beautiful friend. "They'll kill her," he thought. Who the "they" were did not matter. "They'll kill her – there won't be anyone of beauty to talk to."

The pastor, not just a shepherd but a human partner in finding God's purpose, liked both to walk the trodden path and go into the wilderness. He felt comfortable in early Christianity, when young Christians and Jews worshipped in the same places, not yet petrified in their respective empires. Of course with the victory of the Roman Creed the frontiers were well staked out.

He was happy to live among Jews. They read Hebrew and were the only ones to worship in this majestic tongue. "There will be no one to talk to," he said to himself, sitting in his pew, with a premonition he had not known before, so deep and so disturbing. "Had it not been for them, the living Hebrew, right off the page, read, recited and repeated, would not be with us."

He rose slowly as he remembered the potatoes his wife's relatives had thrown on the cellar floor; the last onions had been dug and the winter vegetables, carrots, beets and parsnips, had been taken in a hurry from the land not to let them rot. They had no time before leaving on Hitler's orders.

"Come into the garden at night," they said, "and pick your own apples. Do not let the Russians have everything." He would try, but he might not have the energy or might indeed not have the will. His daughter Martina and his wife Rosy had gone *Heim ins Reich*, together with all the Germans of the village Rosch and most of his parishioners. He sat in his pew with a mocking smile on his face, thinking to be the last man left to pray. "The onions too will rot if I do not rise from my inertia – Oh God, for whom?" And he suddenly felt the silence physically on his shoulders.

He sat down again for a while, thinking of the bags of flour Rosy's cousins had stacked in his backroom just before leaving *Heim ins Reich,* which was by no means *"Heim"* – or home – to any of them. Not to his wife and daughter either, caught by the spreading madness of *Deutschland Deutschland über alles.* His wife more so, who never adjusted to the small life a pastor had to offer; she longed for the excitement, the uproar and whirl illusion brings, drinking it in with every word and spewing it back to him magnified and coloured with euphoria. Very different or not so very different, but slyer, more fearful and disoriented than their daughter Martina. Looking back, he remembered being left standing in the door of the church without a goodbye. He had watched their backs bent by their rucksacks, hands full of bundles, walking through the chestnut trees to a waiting fiacre to take them down to the train station. He did not move to wave goodbye. No one waved until Martina, jumping out of the horse-driven coach, ran back to him to sob and hug. Her stone-faced mother letting it happen.

Jews were jubilant, lining the streets to greet the tanks moving up the *Bahnhofstrasse*, preferring the Russian variety of anti-Semitism, the latter not being immediately murderous. *Oh,* the pastor thought, *the Jews also have been fed illusion. But not maddened by false blood-bonds like the Germans of this land, they found themselves on the other side of the barricade.* They had embraced the communistic lie and the pastor knew what the Jews did not care to know, that there was famine and deportation across the Djnester. *Poor things, just guessing which way to turn.* The Jews too had to learn, and his heart went out to them.

The day had grown ominous, chestnut trees darkening faster when so close to one another and dense foliage forbidding the light – he had seen mother and daughter leave, had heard the horses' hoofs gaining distance, and had stood at the door a long time before entering his small one-storey rectory attached to the church.

He stumbled now over Martina's garden shoes, old broken-through slippers she used to step into when running out where she crouched to find mosses, living things, small green toads out of a water hole; bringing them up to build her world in her room, she closed her door tight. Hidden from her mother, she was his accomplice from the cradle. The pastor pushed that slipper in the dark a little, sat down to feel his loss. No tears, but a hurting presence of *never again.* Picking it up again, the pastor held the small, backless garden-slipper in his hand for another moment: *If you let it go,* he thought, *you lose it all. Then Martina had never lived; then you never held her in your arms.*

So quiet the church, a disquieting moon rising, his *Doppelgänger* – his double – from his youth. A romantic soul, the pastor had kept his longings to himself; a partner to the night, familiar if not consoling, he was accustomed to use the dark to clear his thought. It was different tonight. Pain rising with such force, the ending of things unimaginable, he held on to the little shoe to reinstill worth in existence.

A little girl so elfin and transparent was born to his Rosy. Strong and handsome when young, a Swabian Roscher woman, practical but aspiring to what she called the "better things in life," his Rosy did not see that miracle from heaven. She had no milk, or not enough, disliked to keep this elfin child close to her body, finding her too weak to suckle, and blamed her for her own empty breasts. "It is too small," she said. "It won't live." "It" – not "she" – and they baptized her fast, to make sure her soul was saved at least. So Rosy had pushed the bundle at night a little more towards the pastor in their marriage bed when the baby howled with hunger, showing a determined will to live. The pastor then took her out of her linen, laid her flat on his breast and, letting her suck his little finger, she slept. Early the next morning he rose, convinced that Rosy would not feed her, dressed, put his baby into clean swaddling clothes and ran across past the Ahi fountain to the door of the Jews, knocked at the grocer's door, and his wife Rachel answered baby in arm.

"Hello, Pastor Rempel." Seeing him holding a baby also, she smiled. "What can I do for you?"

"My wife cannot nurse, the milk does not come and –"

"Heaven-sent," Rachel Glasberg said, taking the child from him. "I have such abundance I'm flowing like a river. May I have her please, may she be permitted to sleep with us, she –"

"Martina is her name," the pastor interrupted.

"Martina is so small, she should grow fast. If my milk is too thick, I'll try to draw it off and thin it with boiled and cooled water. Wonderful, wonderful, the Lord knows what to do to bring us together." And with the pastor's Amen, Martina found a breast warm and welcoming and another little being like herself to look and wonder at.

Rosy too, released of the burden of unwelcomed motherhood inflicted on her, was a little less stern. And the pastor, seeing Martina grow, smile for the first time her toothless, grin-recognition of her father, took her home to the rectory from her nurse-mother Rachel after she had made her first steps with Rachel's hand. Martina, slightly bewildered by the stillness of her new home, looking around for her playmate Rachel and, missing the noise of the disorderly household with three more children playing, reacted by being silent, as if despondent. She called "Rachel, Rachel" at night, but it sounded very different without the Rs and the Ls – which Martina never learned to pronounce, and it became her trademark – but the pastor of course recognized the name she had given her nurse-mother.

In time Rosy adjusted to her child, who looked more like what Rosy called "human," and taking a little joy in her she called her that. "Where is my Joy?" she would call through the church when Martina took to her wanderings-off which persisted all through her youth, and "I am not here" was the reply, so the mother knew her daughter was under a pew in the church.

Martina indeed was a joy to look at, a translucent skin – the blue design of veins branching only divined – that design that every cabbage leaf, tree trunk and root has, was there beneath her skin. Skin of no colour. It allowed her inner world to be seen, just holding it all together so it would not fall apart, enclosing crown and toe. But it wasn't Rosy's kind of beauty. It seemed impractical to her, not protective enough. *Skin that fine and bones that could splinter any moment...* she thought and quarrelled with the Lord: "Why do I have to get such an eerie child with an unpredictable mood and days of not uttering a sound as if dumb?" Rosy slowly adjusted, loving her as well as she could. She served her husband and worked, cleaned and scrubbed, and there was no other like her anywhere: she renewed the flowers for every Sunday's service, washed the linen, starched and "blued" it, "to put the sky into the Lord's table" so that it shone.

The congregation, of the ascetic-evangelical sort, did not think the pastor could have a better wife. But she was cold in bed, feared the night, never showed herself undressed, hid in the closet when she changed – *not to give him any ideas* – and did "it" for him when she absolutely could not escape his begging eyes. But he grew lonely, feeling that Rosy considered it her duty, and so he spared her more and more. Relied on fantasy. On early teen days. *A Jewish child you're running around with – avoid it. I've seen you,* his father had said. *There will be trouble.*

Alexander Theodor had inherited this church from his father, a dear pastoral type of churchman very unlike his dreaming romantic son, a son whose playmate, a Jewish girl, was a wealthy merchant's daughter across from the rectory. Clandestine and forbidden, their meeting held mystery for both, and he called her his Orphea instead of Euridice because of her voice. She sang all the time. But he felt like Orpheus and sometimes Romeo, and he used the balcony – as a code. They were both fourteen years old when she stole the gate key from her mother's key bunch, undoing it skilfully and putting it back after having rushed home guilty and jubilant. They sat on the rim of the Ahi fountain – a mythical place of fear and legend – and felt protected by the pagan gods outside of both their traditions. A wonderful strangeness, a land of their own, a crossroad between the rectory and the old house.

And so the generations lived and dreamed around the fountain, the rectory, and the old house. Susanna, mother of Süssel, and Alexander, father to Martina, have leant against the powerful iron body of Ahi in the fountain for shelter, separated and threatened by a turn-of-the-century world preparing for confrontation and assault. It tore the gently-nursed flower of acceptance of one another to shreds.

They both married within their own fold, where the words "given away" were almost accurate. She, Susanna, was given to a "mighty fortress father" as their children called him later. Wealthy and of high intelligence, she learnt to contain, domesticate her dreams, and turned to big-household duties, her children and poetry: the late-nineteenth-century French or the Germans of Goethe's time. A world of her own. And Alexander of course was "given" to Rosy, who took him also, as one takes destiny.

So the pastor held Martina's little slipper, talking to it, calling her back. His daughter Martina, who would punish anyone with the silence of disapproval and would answer his call by, "I will come to talk to you but if it is something you want to say against my mosses, my tiny baby toads and my beautiful stones, I won't talk to you."

This is how you are, my Martina and this is how you were. Holding the slipper another moment, the lining and trailing threads clinging to his vest, he thought, "She gives herself to whom she chooses," and the pastor had played her game, one entirely of her making. She loved the Jews, their wild, irregular households, her nurse-mother Rachel, and she remained her child. She would go to their High Holidays, on New Year's and

the Day of Atonement in the fall, and she would sleep in the little garden house – the *Sukkah* – for the harvest festival and go for
the Sabbath meal on Friday night, and she knew the blessings for
bread and wine in Hebrew. Perhaps the pastor's own wish to learn
more about Jesus's childhood, the early message of love, came
through Martina's blessing over bread and wine.

She built her Friday night table, spreading her desk with a
white tablecloth and asked her father for two candles. There she
celebrated her own Sabbath, "the true one" as she said, and the
pastor had watched her. *It is the same root, if not altogether the
same,* he thought. And habits die hard. They grow and change.
And he thought of the Lord's table, of His transformed body in
bread and wine, as the true TABLE. *How close we all are, how deeply
related and rooted in one another. Martina knows better than
almighty adults – children know better, they cut through games about
power and see straight to the heart.*

The pastor was intrigued with a time in flux, when Christianity,
taking hold of the poor and the women, spreading slowly in a slave
world, was still not violently polarized into opposing camps. A very
rich, fertile time – but he had to contend with Rosy: "Martina is
crazy; it will only amount to trouble."

Rosy had banged her pots and pans around, pounding her
Schnitzels with a cleaver, to make them more tender, while talking
so he could hear her. "All the meat we eat here comes from people
in Rosch. We would starve without my parents and sisters. They
have all stayed at home to work the land and livestock, only I –"
and she banged her Schnitzels and cried, wiping her tears with her
sleeve. "And – everyone knows. I'm not only poor, but betrayed."
And she would sit down with her last sob, knowing full well that
her husband would soon be there to console her, as had always

been the case. And when he came this time, she quietly and cruelly said, "I will leave you and I'll take Martina with me, the way she is, poor thing. She is of my blood, and though you took her to the Jews to drink their milk she is still mine. When the time comes you'll be left alone like a dog in your last days. Alone."

The pastor put the little shoe into its place and started up the staircase towards the second floor bedroom, thinking it had come true. A non-believer in oaths and curses, he was bewildered that they would lie so heavily on his shoulders. A burden he had not expected to bear. The few steps, always easily taken, were almost insurmountable in this utter stillness. So he rested, leaning on the rail, disoriented with a distinct almost articulate sensation that all endeavour was for naught, when he was startled by an unusual, unfamiliar rumbling sound coming from the upper *Residenzgasse.* A steady rolling noise increasing slowly, making the earth tremble, seemed to come closer to the church and suddenly stop in front. Russian voices, commands, tanks on tanks lit the dark night with the reality of a dream. Jumping from these tanks, soldiers pounding on the church door frightened the pastor, but strengthened him also to defend his church from desecration. He felt what any animal would feel for her cub, and he ran from the back of the rectory to the front, to face ten or more Russian soldiers, shouting and demanding the church be opened. He understood them well, having a Ukrainian grandmother and having lived among them. He said, gaining stature, "No! This is a church. It is locked and barred from the inside, the congregation of German descent have left for the *Reich* according to an agreement between Stalin and Hitler in the summer of 1939 –"

Wild hilarity as the *soldateska* pushed the pastor with rifle butts towards the door of the church, saying, "Open the door son of a bitch, or your head will fly. Have you not heard that God died in 1917?" They were angry and impatient, but were brought to order by an officer who spoke more gently, "Open the gate, reverend. If there is a bar behind as you said, remove it, please. My men have been on the tanks for ten hours, they want to eat and drink. We have vodka for ourselves and some food you have to provide…"

"If I am under your orders I will open up and provide what I can, but remember the church is for service to God only."

"We'll show you service," the crowd shouted. And the officer, "There is only one service in the Soviet Union and this service is to the State." The pastor saw them move towards the gate, so he hurried inside through the back to remove the bar.

Breaking the lower branches from the chestnut trees to bring some tanks into the garden, besieging the church, the men entered the now open door, took the Lord's table as their own, heaping vodka bottles, sausage and bread upon Rosy's starched and blued lace, her last gift to the pastor before leaving. They rushed into his kitchen, looking for whatever there was, ran through the pews, pushing them around to suit their needs. The officer let them do as they pleased. "And where is your wife and daughters? Sons we do not need – ha, ha – we could use the women." The pastor did not reply and they sprawled – after having drunk themselves into oblivion – into some comfort on the church floor to sleep it out.

The pastor extinguished the lights in the church and slowly rose to his room. It was the end of a day.

Felix & Martina

Spring Days

ARTINA HAD GIVEN BIRTH AT SIXTEEN. IT WAS MINE. Her mother, shouting at the wicked ways of Jews, had sent her to Bucharest to hide the shame. It was mine. She was my dream child, a ball in the air to catch, a wild flower to pick, an Evangelical child of the Evangelical church. And I to her perhaps the hope, the rescue from it. She was a Jew at heart, knew more than I did about the Sabbath service from the moment of her birth through the first year on Rachel's breast, a true child of my faith while I was a loose hanging leaf. Not my sister's mystery, nor my father's Greek. I was my mother's son. An ancient primogeniture, re-enacted every time, it comes with the whole territory and the owning of it: you tread the land with ease, being the master. No one else counts. Fathers can be hated and dismissed into non-existence, sisters or brothers, younger, have no power, can be subjugated with a glance. Not even a fist is raised, just a look or tone of voice will keep them from rebellion. It is enough. I'm talented at forcing their submission, not seeking it either. I was born to wealth and ease, strutting in my yellow shirts, silk, loose and raglan-cut. I dyed them in all the sun's shades, from the citron to the dark, ominous, browned gold.

In spite of fighting, I loved my sister. Dominated her to worship me as the sovereign. Castles in the air I spun for her pleasure, taking her to silent spots down the slopes of the Archbishop's Residence where she had never been; she, enchanted, found mystery in every coloured stone of that roof or walkway. She followed me one day and said, "Let's not marry. Let's build a mansion Süssel-Felix style," and all that fantastical nonsense. She was marvellous to touch. Her skin, a velvet apricot I tried to avoid. But she responded with all her being to me. It frightened me a little. A wild thing. Hard to protect her from getting hurt. But Süssel knew her measure, kissed me and ran home.

It was then that I learned this ease with women. Not just mother, sister, maids, but this response that came my way by greeting them with a slight bow of my head, opening a door to ease entrance, or holding a coat in such a way that it poured onto their bodies.

"Watch out," I said to myself. "You'll hurt them." And finally I did, love overwhelming me.

Walking by the Evangelical gardens after our light supper, mother and I, in my early teens, spotted Martina, this pale flower among her mushrooms.

"Such a sweet thing," my mother said. But out of this pale mushroom grew the slenderest figure, otherworldly, svelte, with a miracle of a smile in her eyes. And she looked for me. I could not walk by past the church, past the University grounds, on winter days, on melting spring days, to my boys' school, or past the theatre, without her being in my way. Somewhere. Early at seven o'clock on winter days, she would be in my path. Hidden by the bare but thick intertwined branches of one of the two chestnut trees, she would emerge and say, "I'll carry your satchel."

"No," I said. "No, you won't."

"Only to the corner."

"No."

"Just let me hold your hand, the free one."

"No, you will not have my hand. Did your mother see you go out?"

"No, she did not. She does not like mornings. I take my own milk and bread and am just as delighted not to see her. She smiles sometimes, but never in the morning. So I dress fast and wait to see your old gate move. I can see it very well through my upstairs bedroom window. It is in plain view. Oh, let me carry your books just past the University grounds."

And I let her have them. Sometimes a slight, loving slap on her arm or back and she seems in heaven. I know then the chord is struck. She loves Jews, all of us, no matter who we are, good or mean. And I fear for her. For myself, too. I know I will kiss her soon – on one of these mornings, I will kiss her. She wants me to, she comes too close, she is always there on the same side on the left and leaves a little space to be able to turn her face into mine. And did on that spring morning. She was fourteen and I had just entered University. It was a womanly kiss, rich in spit and tongue, an unfinished breast against mine, so ready for love. We walked and kissed, sat down on that bench under her chestnut tree, blooms just coming.

"Martina," I started.

"No, no," she said, "don't talk, I know it all. There is no use. Some things are as they are and I am yours."

I held my body away, but she sought it and knew where it was.

We kissed every morning in the spring of that year.

The Pastor

A LITTLE BIRD FLEW IN

THE PASTOR HAD BEEN TERRIBLY LONELY SINCE THE departure of both Rosy and Martina. He missed the noises. How could a house be so still, relying on an occasional bark from neighbourhood dogs? Rosy's noises were no lilting lullabies. A harsh woman, she was not to his liking in the beginning. But he wanted a wife, and it seemed right. He missed her now, had loved to watch her dress and undress in the morning hours, before she had put on mail and armour and had fashioned a battleground. There was vociferous fighting. "So different we were," he thought, "as if sprung from an alien root." But even her shouting, demanding money and a modest new hat with a feather – not thinking of ostrich as other bourgeois women sported, or the Jews in their finery – even these ugly sounds were better than so deep a silence. It disoriented him, as did his own voice and his sermons in the empty church. Addressed to a dwindling community after the *Heim ins Reich* of September, 1939. The Lutheran world had disintegrated, Russians in boots and military caps had desecrated the altar with sausage and vodka, and he was left to his own silence. Even Rosy was better than such singleness.

The pastor rose this morning, washed his hands and face, found his hair thinning, did not mind. Brushed it back to see his face emerge with a distinct smile. Hummed a childhood tune of *"Kommt ein Vogel geflogen"* – about an imaginary bird, flying in unexpectedly to seat itself on his foot with a small letter in his beak, a greeting from his mother. Hummed, whistled, found himself scaling the steps to Martina's room without conscious intention. He wore a white shirt, open collared, an ordinary trouser, and no other insignia than a small print copy of the New Testament hidden in his shirt pocket. Just an everyday father, happy to go up to see his daughter. He knocked gently, got no reply – lazy little darling – opened the door cautiously, looked in and saw Shainah's angelic features, in total peace, in Martina's bed. "Of course," the pastor said to himself, "of course I knew this little bird had flown in," but he was not fully sure that this was true. He had expected Martina.

His Martina, his daughter, had filled his life and answered all needs. She was there for him to feed, dress and cuddle in his arms. There, all to himself. But he had to love her in defiance almost. Under Rosy's jealous, possessive, all-seeing eye, he felt guilty. Or was it that he had always felt guilty loving the tiny birds that flew in to sit on his knee.

He had been a lonely young man, loving unusual things and hating boys' rough games. His parents thought him odd, fitted only for the priesthood. He literally collected everything hurt: living things, young things. Birds unable to fly, wings broken, fallen out of their nests, cats with thorns in one paw hobbling about, a rat, still alive, looking at him with teary eyes, crushed under a horse's hoof, he brought home. In his village, Rosch, there was little time for such boys. Little patience. A hard working, early-rising-people, with obedience to the father, the all-powerful master, the rod, communion on Sunday and ten o'clock service to God in clean shirts and trousers, they shook their heads in dismay: *There is something wrong with him, no gang games, no buddies.* The only thing a good German mother in Rosch could think of was church.

The pastor looked at this dark resting face of Shainah. *Another root, fleshier,* he thought, *a more ordinary human maybe than his Martina, still unutterably beautiful – and young. Why do I love them?* And he seated himself across from her to cherish the moment, look at her clothes, and taking a small shoe into his hand, he cuddled it. To the pastor it brought Martina's slipper back again, her garden slipper that he had picked up, having for the first time faced his abandonment: his child leaving him. The little shoe, shoelaces trailing, he cuddled now.

Closing his eyes, and leaning back in Martina's hard small desk-chair, he went back many years. To when he felt that love first. That wish to help the little ones. Somewhere in the middle of his parents' hierarchical household, often forgotten and left alone, he fashioned his own routine. Avoiding conflict, fitting outwardly into the hourly mechanism of the family, he succeeded falling between the cracks to be left to his own devices. All his little brothers, younger by six or seven years, he had watched grow up, made sure he was there to help them, earned the approving smile of both his parents for being such a good boy to help out: bathe the little ones, scrub them with brushes, hard or gently, and soap them well.

But when he grew into his thirteenth, fourteenth year, to be re-baptized, fully conscious of his commitment to Christ, he felt guilty. And in spite of wanting the special attention, clothes, food, love, ceremony, he asked to be permitted a later date. He had not studied enough yet, he said. This they understood. A good, true,

Christian young man. And when one day he proclaimed he was ready, he was not. But he enjoyed the fuss and took to carrying in his shirt pocket a small-print copy, gold-embossed, of the New Testament his godfather had given him. The one he touched now to remind himself.

He put Shainah's little shoe next to the other one, into an order it had not been in before, straightened everything, and sat down overwhelmed. Shainah's one arm, the right one, was raised behind her head, losing itself in her black hair; she was beautiful beyond words or imagination. And looking through the chestnut trees into the reflection of the rising sun in the east windows of the Old House, now all aflame, he said to himself, "I won't let the devil into my house. I have resisted him, God knows, I'm a Christian." Smiling again now, he said, "But I can only love what is truly of my choosing."

Conscious now of the beauty, the uniqueness of the young, a promise to be divined and not yet come to fruition, he watched Shainah. Approached her now, gently kissing her forehead, he said, "Shainah, my child, come wash, dress, and let's have breakfast." All that they did together. Such rejuvenation, recall, such living moment! She did not mind. He brought a tub of warm water all the steps up to her room, whistling *"Kommt ein Vogel"* – "a little bird flew in." He smiled at her, and she smiled in return, not finding anything uncommon or unnatural as this man helping her with her morning toilette in another girl's bedroom. He was no stranger to her.

THE PASTOR WAS HAPPY. Since that September day when his Martina had left, he felt as if he were the last trembling chestnut leaf to hold onto the twig. With the Russians in town over the winter, his congregation disintegrated, and he was left single-handedly to keep his church from becoming a stable. When the first horses were stationed in the churchyard, he thought, "If it is God's will, my church shall be a stable, maybe there will be a Second Coming and we'll put straw on the ground for the manger."

But it was a hard winter: with no wood to burn in the ovens, pipes froze, and he celebrated mass for ten people. In total disarray. But then ten people is a holy congregation to the Jews. They always call the TEN a MINYON, a basic necessity for communal prayer. He was familiar with Jewish practice. He took Hebrew up again this "Russian Year," as he called it, when his people had gone *Heim ins Reich* – to Germany.

He missed his duty at their sickbeds, duties he always had taken very seriously. A theologian of the heart, he had to defend himself when Rosy shouted, "You're not a Catholic. Why do you rush to everyone, whenever they have a mere cold? They're not dying, and if so, they are not in need of your absolution, holy oil, and last rites. They're Lutherans, if you wish to remember. It is I that have need of you. My kindling isn't done, I can't cook a meal..." and so forth. Rosy's voice. But his true duties he knew: to look into the eyes of the dying and to comfort them.

He was humble, did not call it compassion – not to elevate himself to be Christ, but to walk in His footsteps, a teacher. The pastor knew suffering, the loneliness of the erring soul, and he was there where he could reach it. A Christian of the "early sort," God's church. He wanted to avoid man's church, which was full of plate collection, intrigue and hierarchy.

The pastor was happy: a little bird to look after. A little one that had fallen out of her nest. "There are all Martina's things, shoes and clothes, toys and books she can have." He looked at his calendar. The thirteenth of June, 1941, almost a week to the day the Russians had come in a year ago. And in spite of a sleepless night, with noises of rolling trucks and strange flashing lights all through, the pastor was happy. A duty to do good, and a hope to do right in the eyes of the Lord.

Two days passed. Two good days with Shainah. But streets were deserted, had a nervous air, with Jews and non-Jews in a state of terror and disarray – deportation, Russian-Soviet-style. He knew as he always did, where his duty lay. He kept still and waited, shared bread, stories, and games with Shainah as the world outside closed them in. A strange, suspended happiness for both Shainah and the pastor. Just a little time, the limiting time these hostile events offered, forged a love so intense…in Shainah's words: "I love you forever." Whatever "forever" means in a sixteen-year-old's mind. But love feels "forever," if it is that, and if for that moment only. The pastor brought Martina's puzzles out, and the two of them, now sitting on the church floor, put together the story of the three kings and the star. She found all the parts for a beautiful baby and she shouted: *Oh, the gold and the gems the kings brought for the baby Jesus.* It was a delight to watch her. Shainah did not know any of the Christian imagery. It was not taught in the *Synagogengasse* or any Jewish home, where all legends were Old Testament. The pastor knew, of course, of the divided worlds, and that these divisions start early with images, pictures to reinforce the faith. He knew that, but to face someone totally unaware of the Christian myth was stunning. Christianity, ubiquitous, at Christmas time or Easter – how did the Jews keep out, so determinedly, so convinced of what and who they are? A mystery of the soul. He felt it when Martina, a little one still of two or three years, took to it with such abandon, to Rosy's shouting, "She'll end up in their fold, she'll fall to their beguiling charm. They're seducers, she'll love them and marry them."

"Well, it is true," the pastor had said. "She did love Felix. But why assign it to Jews versus non-Jews, if they were just young and had seen each other and loved?"

And now Shainah. Innocent. Entertained by a puzzle of kings, real kings, crowns, jewels, gold, and a star in the heavens! The pastor was happy, with so much to teach, just as much to learn, and their time so short. But he pledged to keep Shainah. *I have all that food in the cellar my Roscher relatives have literally dumped on me. Dry beans, salt pork – oh dear!* A sudden awareness of these divisions; to live just a few streets apart and millennia in between! *Pork – of course not. She won't like it.* He did not offer it at first. But then, these were hard times. The pastor cooked a few finely cut pieces into the beans. Shainah thought it was heaven. But the pastor cautioned her, "We Christians eat it, but your people won't."

She said simply, "I'm with you now."

The third day, towards evening, he heard cautious knocks at his back garden door. It was Felix, and Shainah rushed into his arms.

"Where have you been? We had a lovely time," she said and she took the pastor's hands. "I'm his now," and then feeling perhaps Felix's rejection, she added, "and yours too."

The pastor set the table for supper, and Felix spoke incessantly.

"They are home now; two nights and three days almost, in the cattle cars on abandoned rails, waiting for the collection to be completed. All three of them, my parents and grandmother have lived through unimaginable days" Felix said. "That's all I say now. They're home." He stopped, suddenly aware of Shainah, added

"You have to wait a little for yours, sweetheart. Be good! You have more than any other girl, three fathers." She laughed.

"Yes," she said. "You two and my own. But he'll be back," she said.

The pastor had set a small table on Rosy's linen; cutlery of silver, a big *R* engraved on the handles, and napkins with crocheted lace around them. All these German virtues gave this odd little company the feeling of ordinariness and stability. But it was to no avail. The meal over, Shainah went up the steps. Singing now with a clear voice, *"Weisst Du wieviel Sternlein stehen* – Do you know how many little stars there are in Heaven –" She had learned them fast, these German folk songs meant for children. Indelibly, they stay in their truth and simplicity all one's life. Shainah loved these simple tunes, German words in them that sounded like the familiar Yiddish but were not. "Teach me, teach me," she said to the pastor. On the third day she hummed them perfectly. "The one about the little bird that flew in – that's me." She smiled going up the staircase. There was none where she had grown up. *Synagogengasse*. Small lodgings – no upstairs bedroom or kitchen living – it was one room. Beds were put up at night by pushing the dining table to the wall. She had her own bed, being an only child.

But she loved this luxury-staircase of wood; windows on both sides, looking into pink chestnut blooms. She would tell the pastor that her birthday was tomorrow, the sixteenth of June. And she took her time to investigate sunken niches under the windows. Knick-knacks, crocheted dolls, with pearls set in for eyes and red thread embroidery for an upwards-at-the-corner-mouth laughing with moveable hands and feet. They were in every niche, dressed differently, and the one in the wedding dress was taller than the others, with a train of lace behind her. A little torn. And

Shainah took it up to "her room," closed the door, looked for a sewing basket. It was right there, with neatly ordered threads forming patterns in all colours. Found the right one, sat down to mend it. "Tomorrow is my birthday," she thought, "maybe she'll be mine."

THE PASTOR sat down with Felix in the church pews. Evening falling. Shainah stayed upstairs tucked into soft down feathers of a quilt, pride and joy of every Roscher Swabian *Hausfrau,* Rosy's, her mother's, and all the way back: everyone's quilt. Shainah saw it immediately and had said, "I want it, it's cozy," and the pastor had tucked her in.

The two men sat silently for a while, not knowing where and how to begin. There was a long, unspoken history between them, and this did not seem the right moment: the immediacy of events, uprooting, and a total unpredictability of the next hour did not permit their own history to emerge easily. Though, of course unspoken, it was there. Martina. The pastor had known about their love, this adolescent, idealized impact of "the first." He had seen Felix coming by himself in the early hours of the evening, waiting to catch a glance of his elfin daughter. And he had heard their whispers in the back garden, when they fell to their ardent love.

Martina, vulnerable and poetic. The pastor had loved his daughter with this ferocious love he gave to all little birds under his care. And he saw the danger. But the loud, insufferable warnings of Rosy – her unjust vulgar accusations of Felix's Jewishness, her enormous tirades of "Look at the bastards, dressed in ostrich plumes, making money on my back." And she shouted: the

"Polish Princess" of the Old House going around behaving as if she were the "granddaughter of the Count Potozki" – a preferred idiom of hatred for Rosy. "Rabble they are, proud of their bible, denying Christ. Do something about it, you're the father."

All that made him angry, obstinate, and he would not interfere. The more she shouted, the more he resisted her. In fact, he protected Martina. She was only fifteen, younger looking than that even, finely built, a body as if she were a boy of ten. The pastor knew, and heard her when she ran in from the back garden, afraid of her mother. He did not interfere. Martina came one day to him, after mass, and said: "I'm carrying his child." It had to be covered up. She was sent to Bucharest to give birth, and she gave the child up. It changed Martina, and after even the pastor did not permit her to see Felix.

Lava flowing, the town so still, as if eruptions from the bowels of the earth had extinguished every sound, singed the air. No breath, so still a town.

Hugging the pastor, Felix rushed up to Shainah for a goodnight kiss. A radiant face, every laughing, tiny crease drawn stronger, more markedly by a burning candle, greeted him. She had not slept yet. The doll in wedding dress sitting upright against the wall, two more attendant dolls on each side, made a lugubrious party. But not to Shainah. She was in a charmed world. "It is my birthday," she said. "It is past midnight, so it is the 16th of June right now; you can congratulate me, Felix. I am sixteen – a young lady my mother would say – and these guests over there against the wall have come to my party."

Only now was he aware of the coffee cups and saucers, a neatly arranged service with silver spoons; embroidered, one-inch-square serviettes; and lace around the tablecloth. All set upon a footstool. Martina's dishes. And Felix thought, "I have kissed Martina in this bed. My eyes had wandered along her stones and mosses, to linger on the set wedding-party Martina must have given when Shainah's age. Now she is God knows where; *Heim ins Reich,* taken by her mother into a *Heim* which is no home at all, to a Hitler Germany."

"No, I did not invite the pastor," Shainah said. "I was afraid he'd be angry with me – to stay up past midnight! I would have been very happy to have him also. Still, you are here and it is a surprise to have you. A lovely surprise for my birthday, and you don't have to give me anything. It's enough that you are here, having tea."

In the middle of a scorched-earth town where no one dares or can breathe, where volcanoes of hate have extinguished the next day, we have an imaginary birthday party, Felix thought. More real and true than fifty people in a cattle car fighting over a centimetre of space near the air hole on top. *I've seen it, I've been there, Ludmilla was with me to rescue my mother and father. I have to go to be there now and I should run. But I linger a little longer in this haven of charm and illusion....*

Sing to the Lord of Joy

A GOOD HALF-HOUR OUTSIDE OF TOWN, DESERTED, unconnected rails stood waiting. They shone as if light came from within their metal heart. Shone, but did not seem to reflect. This is how black it was, or felt, to the two of us. Ludmilla knew the position, hid me in her official vehicle, an NKVD jeep, or something of that kind. She drove the car without any other light than the silver of the rails, descended a little into a low-lying hollow and waited.

We saw them come. Saw them first, then heard them. The empty cattle trains, lights flashing. Screeching sounds of the rails clicking into connected ones, they had been standing assembled but we had not spotted the locale. Now they were moving, smoke rising from the engine, moving, stopping; Russian sounds, commanding orders, metal on metal grating. *Slaughter of pigs.* I bit my tongue, so tightly clenched were my teeth that blood oozed through the corners of my mouth and trickled without being noticed by either of us.

It was the sound of screeching, when my mother's silver knives hit the porcelain so that my father almost sprang to his feet at the dinner table with a punishing look in my direction. Or in our direction. We had played innocent games, to annoy each other, my sister and I, but were turned to stone by father's nervous fury.

The rubbing, screeching, clanging and rhythmic clicking of the rails, the alien commands, horses' hooves pounding, and the Russian military coming dangerously close, made my stomach heave, bowels clench, and I half-fainted in Ludmilla's arms.

As the sun was about to break, trucks arrived. Full of our people. Fifty perhaps in each one. We saw them unloaded. My own weren't there yet. Ludmilla, in a swift move, put her headlights on, her NKVD car into gear, shouted a loud Russian command, legitimizing her presence, her authority, and stormed out of our hiding place.

PARALYSIS. A town severed at its spinal cord. Last collections. Trucks and horses disappeared, moving fast into the direction northeast. Silence took over. Shutters downed, we hid our intense dislocation. What to think? What to feel? Ludmilla drove me back to the Evangelical church, advised me not to go near the Old House which now, as the sun was flaming its way through the east windows, appeared to me so unearthly beautiful, as never before. "Go to the pastor," she said. "Wait for me. You'll hear the good news as soon as I receive it. Go, be good, eat and sleep, talk with friends. Trust me. The Minister of Health has promised to release your parents. But you must also go to the laboratories and ask the workers to back me up. Ask them to send a delegation to the NKVD headquarters because I have said that the workers cannot keep the plant going without your father. Go there as soon as you have rested to make valid what I stated."

We had arrived. A squeeze of hands, and I knocked at the back door of the parsonage. "Rush up to Shainah's room," the pastor said. "There is a small cuvette there, wash the blood off your face. What have they done to you? I'll bring you coffee and bread. Sleep."

I ran up the stairs, threw myself on Martina's bed that Shainah had slept in, looked through the blooms of the chestnut trees to the sun rising in the east windows of the Old House. Closed my eyes. It took a little for my muscles to stretch into rest. My skin tightened with the dried blood, but there was no strength or will to lift a hand to it. I felt a cool, wet towel around my mouth, chin, and down my chest and heard a sweet sound, a Jewish mother's lullaby. Soothing, lamenting, it wasn't one I knew. In the minor key. Shainah left the wet little cloth, to cover eyes and forehead. And with her Yiddish: "Sleep little baby, my own –" I gave up my soul.

All day, until nightfall, I slept. When I woke, the coffee on Martina's night table had cooled, but I was grateful for it and for a piece of black bread thick with butter. I heard the sudden roar of the diesel engine, the roar of authority – which owes no account to anyone; it made me jump, take all steps at once, crawl through the hedge, and I saw Ludmilla's car around the corner. She had stationed it on the side of the garden opposite the Ahi fountain where the hedge was high, mingled with the over-hanging chestnuts in pink bloom, and almost hid the vehicle. I slid around that corner, avoiding the ditch that skirted the church garden, to join her.

"They will come out," she said at once. "Tomorrow or the day after. The papers have been signed." And she started the jeep, roared away, and took me to her flat. It was low lying, a parterre-flat, windows and door down to the sidewalk in the lower

Russischegasse beyond the cathedral. Passing it, she said, "I went there yesterday. I went to pray. To John Chrysostomos, the Golden Mouth Saint, who sings the way you play your piano. I prayed so intently, forgetting myself, and suddenly I was aware of a pair of stern eyes looking in my direction. I was in uniform; a Communist at this critical time had no business being in a church. It's dangerous. I prayed for you. I told Chrysostomos that you are a musician and have a golden soul, golden fingers, as he has a golden mouth. So you are in his protection."

This night I kissed her. With all my heart. Slept and kissed and made love. She drove me to the plant, which stood on a beautiful piece of land, framed on three sides by beech, fir and birch facing the *Balschgasse*. Father had purchased it to build his modern pharmaceutical plant. Now I went to face his workers.

They were assembled by now, to talk. All of them. About forty, in a circle in the big *dragée*-hall, where all the newly acquired *dragée*-kettles stood, gleaming in stainless steel, with three- to four-inch leather belts – *Treibriemen* – around them. Father had gone to Leipzig, had spent the last penny on these fabulous, electricity-powered kettles. The workers sat around them. "Where is he? What will happen to him? Bring him back! We can't work without him! Let's write a petition and sign." It was all done. I had no work to do, nothing to say. He was their father. They did not fear him as I did, in my youth. They loved him. Because of his justice, and proper payment, which in Judaism is the basic law. They formed a delegation of four or five to carry the petition. Lovely German women, Ukrainian and Jews. All worked for him as if for themselves.

I looked at Fanny. She was totally still, sitting on a cardboard box by herself. I knew she had been my father's lover at one time.

Süssel and I had uncovered an anonymous letter that told of their clandestine meetings. Brown-eyed, tall as a *Bucovina* – beech tree – she sat hunched over, all to herself, not wanting to be seen. A simple woman, as only queens could be, she had a silent grace, and my heart went out to her.

After all was arranged, and the delegation had gone to the Secret Police Headquarters, I went furtively closer to her; put my hand on her shoulder, hiding it under her collar as well as I could, and said as if to myself, "He'll come out tomorrow, I was promised, Fanny." I pressed my fingers gently into her shoulder bone, leaving them there for a little. Just as a sign of complicity, and that I knew the not-to-be-told story.

I left, walked through the *Balschgasse*, along the overgrown, vine-laden fences past the Old House, whose windows, blinded and lifeless, stared at me with dark eyes. Passed our hiding places, where generations of boys have dug holes in the ground to trap the adults, for laughter and a specific wicked satisfaction.

Around the corner, on the *Residenzgasse*, I saw no angels in the old gate, only the devil above. And mourned. Went across. Fast. Past the fountain of Ahi, who did not grin in his iron mask today, but was thoughtful, and I leaned against the centre mast of this ancient well, all legends of terror stilled for a moment. The iron felt cool. Cool and consoling, in spite of the horror story it told of Ahi the Turkish henchman. Today it felt good. And I smiled at how he changed his features according to what he felt, or according to what I felt, perhaps. A face that could be so terrifying that little children shudder. The story told at nightfall about the multi-armed Turkish henchman, who grew as many arms as he needed to strangle the wicked. Not today, the day was still young, and he looked peaceful, if a little stern.

Somehow Ahi rinsed, cleared my mind, and I rose with the distinct feeling they'd be safe, my beloved people. I made my way across the ditch, through my hole-in-the-hedge to the back door of the pastor, up the steps to the shouts of joy of Shainah. "Where have you been so long, Felix? Come, I've helped the pastor bake bread." There was heaven on earth in fragrance. And I, Felix, smiled. A man of the senses, whose gods are made of sound, colour, and smell, felt life returning with unsuspected force, and I hugged her and said, "Come, Shainah, I want to taste your bread first and then we'll talk. All day."

It was a long day, but it passed. At sunset I heard the roar of Ludmilla's diesel engine under Martina's window, and I joined her by crawling through my now widened hole in the hedge. She had placed the car so the lower heavy branches of the chestnut gave us a roof of green and, looking up, we almost sat on a branch, candles lit pink for the picking. "Early tomorrow morning they'll be released. I've seen the papers. Your father is the nominee and he will name his dependents," she said.

Around noon the next day Ludmilla was again under the chestnut branches. "They're home," she said. "Approach the house slowly. Don't rush, the militia is all over. Or you'll be under suspicion.

"I had gone early, six o'clock or so. Stationed the jeep in our hollow, across from the trains, but they had shifted and I had to manoeuvre the car to get a better look. Police were everywhere, horses, trucks. Being in uniform, I decided to risk mingling among them, as if on duty. A truck arrived. An NKVD officer, who greeted me. It was my superior, papers in hand. Shouted a few names, seven or eight of them. Did obviously not pronounce them properly, or the unslept, unwashed, tightly packed, locked-up lot inside so desperately desired to hear their own names called out, that there were hundreds and hundreds of calls. 'It's my name, it is I, it is I!' It took an hour.

"A few men with their wives, some with wife and children, came out, and then a man, a woman, and a very old woman were helped down the steps from a cattle car. And I knew it was your people, though I had not seen them before. I choked on my tears, made the sign of the cross inside my mouth so God would help me live through it. She is tall, your mother, but not redhead as you said, she was rather grey, hair hanging. Your father, with an overnight-lined face, held both women, walked between them, and they were mounted on a truck and it stood for a while longer to collect the others. Ten or twelve among the ten thousand. They're home now. You can go safely, I think. Watch out. Right and left."

But I was unable to move, as if I were a tree that finally falls after years of sawing have tried to bring it down. I was a stone, inanimate matter. Could not utter a sound, trembled, my body wasn't mine, limbs disconnected, a loss-of-self made my eyes close, my head dropped onto my chest, and Ludmilla, my friend, let me rest.

NO UNIFORMS IN SIGHT. Midday or so. Existence wiped out. No life anywhere.

The Old House spun into a silence as if eons had passed over it. The old gate opened to my touch and I stood, soul open to sound. Certain of assault, I held my breath. Hostile forces all around me. My own shuffling soles against stone made me shiver as if to break a thicket or eliminate a hundreds-year-old cobweb spun around the *Dornröschen* – Sleeping Beauty – castle.

I advanced cautiously, step by step. A mirage of fear and hope: what will they look like? My beautiful mother, my great first-and-forever love, what will she look like? But I did not dare go to her.

Breaking the spell now, I took the three floors but went to my grandmother's flat. Open doors everywhere. As if into a dream, I entered. She was dressed, asleep on her couch. Better than feared. Stilled. I had never seen her house in disarray before. Orderly, majestic, singing to the Lord for His gifts, for the pleasures of living; it's from her it all stems, the magic in a meal, to taste, talk about, combining colours of the yellow turnip, the dark orange carrot, and the deep green bean. "Come," she used to say, "sit by me. I do not eat alone gladly. Look at this apple. This is where God is. In this roundness, shine, navel, and stem. Let's pray, sing and feel. Never forget, it isn't all books." And she held me on her knees, age four. So close a woman's body! It would always be with me. Her majesty. Giving me a God of my own, to live through eyes, ears, and fingertips.

She lay stretched out. I straightened her left foot to join her right one, lifted her head a little on the upholstered pillow, carefully, not to wake her. All in disarray. Prayer books leather-bound scattered, a ruby-glass splintered and wine spots everywhere. It did not matter. I kissed her like the prince his sleeping beauty, humming the ancient intervals she had sang with me:

Sing to the Lord of joy
Sound the timbale
Lyre and harp
And blow the horn –

I crossed into my parents' flat. All doors were unlocked; but having come through the dark wainscoted vestibule, I saw nothing.

Startled by the tinkly sound of the brass curtain rings, I closed the doors fast. Total chaos: my own books, chess game figures ivory-carved, I so loved – bottles of perfume among dry bread on the salon floor....

I entered the bedroom of my parents. They lay in deep sleep. My sister, Süssel, holding both of them, stretched out between my father and my mother.

I sat down across from their bed on father's easy chair, as if at the end of a long journey.

EAST. EAST.

JUST BY COMPASS AND RISING SUN, SLEEPING WHERE A
stone could serve as headrest, we went down the crevices of the
Caucasus Mountains. I, a mountain-raised child, born from the
mighty mountain mother, Cecina, our legend and mystery, always
cloud-crowned at its summit. I – and my wild teen-comrades who
thought we could scale any stone wall – was in awe. Unimagined
ranges, dark wooded tops, naked granite, and flowered slopes
descending came unsuspected upon us. Hungry, with bleeding
feet, if boots were gone, torn or taken, I came upon God's creation.
An enormous jewel, scintillating blue. Mirage, *Fata Morgana,* or
just a childhood dream. A mounted aquamarine with sapphire and
amethyst glances. Mounted in green and almost black.

We were not thirsty. We were hungry. Water comes to you out
of every crevice in the Caucasus. Wounds heal in those sources,
every speck of dirt is carried off from feet, hands or clothes by cos-
mic forces, washing it down the hills, leaving you thinking of
grace. One sleeps by these springs as they cradle and murmur.

We were six by then – road companions of sorts in the summer of '41 who joined us for a short trek to disappear into the

mountains if it suited them – and I learned the ways of the world faster than I thought possible for a young man with a *Bösendorfer* piano in his mother's salon and a father reciting Homer.

Cruelty seemed natural suddenly: "Strip! Boots! Coats! Hand me your rifle or I'll slit your throat!" And leaving us poor wretches with our mere lives, we learned fast. I was not as good as Sasha. He was a genius. He fell upon any straggling soul from behind, pinned him face down to the rock, took my Swiss army knife and stuck it through his tunic, screaming: "Strip." Boots of any denomination, mostly discarded Russian, a few rubles, matches, we took; a mother of God I occasionally left around a poor miserable neck. Pants too, army or other, we let him have; out of what people sleeping in beds or sitting by a fireplace would call compassion. A taboo forbidding total nakedness will perhaps hold you back. A fear will rise from archival atavism and you'll let them have pants. Call it compassion. But even that depends on the grade of your own descent. They may have been too much to carry or the trousers were totally useless for barter. A shirt you could barter, the oldest boots for a night's sleep in the valley. Matches would feed you, literally.

Sasha took the items casually off the ground, shook lice out of them, folded a shirt as if it were crushable silk, rolling it tight and considered how best to carry the loot. Cool, bureaucratic. He smiled at me and said, "Brother you're fabulous." Slowly two, three joined the two of us.

Sasha, who had sat beside me through eight years of *Gymnasium* classics schooling, had spotted me at the train station – the famous *Bahnhof* – and I saw soon that God had sent me a saviour. He had always been a railway nut. Knew by heart the most intricate railway-line connections and their history: when laid, how, and by whom. Every net.

In July '41 the Russians had fled east, the Germans were hard on their heels, the Romanians had come north, so we had to hurry, and it was on foot for us, mostly at night. But Sasha went along railway lines, he knew where they connected, where they parted, where small train stations were which could house us, be it against the rain, since it was yet summer. Rails are better than compasses, they shine silvery at night. Even in moonless nights they catch a glint of the stars, leading you, and planks of wood binding the rails from metre to metre make the muddy ground dry enough to sleep on.

Sasha had won every Physics prize in school competitions. Applied Physics that is. I was good at it, but better at Chemistry, because I liked surprise and not always proper predictability. Sasha, a wizard at connecting wires, had fashioned a small radio to catch sounds – fading in and out, sudden codes or Morse – to help us figure out logistics. Who was where? Were we in front of the Germans, caught from the back to be slaughtered, or were we in their back, encountering Russians?

Heavens, how fast one falls outside the law. Marauders. How simple it is to join strangers, band or thrown together, when old laws of bonding primates take over. Hierarchical. Leaders and underlings bound by a momentary purpose for cover or assault. Outside the group, no pity. A NO with big letters. None. Men powerless or attacked will beg for their lives. And we'll give it to them. But this is all they'll get and this is how Sasha and I learned it: life is cheap. Who needs it? A life was not bargainable for bread. It just messed up your army knife, and blood is sticky.

Dusk. Men were tired. We saw shadows moving fast. No noise but the rolling of stones underneath their feet. Sasha grabbed me, flattened his body and my own to fit into a crevice along the mountain rock, boots showing; two enormous men, or so they seemed in the dark, ammunition belts swung across their chest, and two other men trailing, passed us. But the *arrière-garde* turned suddenly, alarmed somehow, spotted our boots, shouted in jargons of the region, Georgian, Azeris, Chechen-Ingush maybe, sharp, short commands, and we found ourselves with rifles of the Russian variety stuck into our faces. *Strip, you sons of bitches!* They took all we had looted, our good boots still from home, and left us, God knows by what divine law or commandment, in our trousers. *Down on your knees, beg for your lives!* And I saw and heard myself beg for our lives. It was me. Invoking our own Adonai the Almighty. They must have heard of Him. The word Elohim sounded like Allah to them, perhaps, or something made them laugh. The two huge men then held fast council with the *arrière-garde* and decided to take us along to carry the stuff they had looted; they made us rise and returned our boots and shirts. Sasha and I now carried, cleaned, collected wood, made a fire, cooked what they shot. With the ammunition in their belt they shot fowl. The boars they let run. They could perfectly catch these wild sows by hand, but didn't. Pork was not for Muslims.

Sasha seared the feathers of the birds on coals, plucked them, cooked them, and we all ate. Slowly, after hours of walking the often untrodden passes, next to Sasha's fire and food, we tried to talk. Not I, but Sasha, whose parents, descending from the Russian Jews, spoke it; it was his childhood memory. And I thought of my Ludmilla Bunin. Russian sounds alone triggered it. That goodness and love made it possible to rise against a murderous state. She had come to be our saviour with that selflessness and courage of the simple heart. And saved my people. I would never forget her.

Our captors all spoke Russian, but would not do so among themselves. A ferocious political picture emerged: partisans, they fought the Russians. Chechen-Ingush had been slaughtered and the rest, deported to Siberia, were languishing and dying. They, the partisans, would fight the Russians to death, would not fight their "patriotic war" against the Germans, but would wait and willingly turn to the latter, who might win and perhaps give them a national homeland.

We parted almost friends. They left us our belongings and disappeared into the mountains. Fed on fowl, berries, drinking from cool springs, we climbed a small top to have the ranges fall at our feet and disclose a jewel of blue sky and a limitless pool: the Caspian Sea. Not a sea really. An inland lake, drinking all the waters of the Volga. We cried, embraced, and kissed and wanted to pray, but it was impossible so we sat down, silenced by the majesty. A piece of pumpkin smoked over the last fire, a few seeds to chew, chew and spit, for a treat. We crawled down to a hiding fold and huddled into each other for animal warmth, summer nights in the Caucasian mountains are cold, before deciding which way to turn.

Freedom. Holiday. Youth. We had slept. Rose to the eastern sun that made us fall to our knees. Brilliance over the Caspian Sea, mists around us lifting fully, a panorama of pictures we took with our souls to talk about forty years hence. A crown jewel. Blue in blazing gold. We laughed, looking east, washed our feet in a spring without equal, ate some more of the Chechen's pumpkin until a decision was made. No, not east. We'll go southwest towards where we assumed rescue lay: to Tiflis Tbilisi – warm spring.

Sasha caught sounds on his wireless, had some vague idea, and I consulted my compass. Down. With the sun in our backs. Still jubilant, with youth, with survival and the worth of it.

We've heard of this wonder: grapes, oranges, a valley where all waters collect into a mighty stream, the Kura river, wine and Cognac – we're already drunk just thinking *Cognac.* And following the old Russian advice to talk about Vodka, or *Vodiczka* – the little water – if there is none. *Let's talk about Cognac, tables heaped with braided bread, fruit and fowl –*

Not easy. Days becoming weeks. Boots falling apart. Not encountering anyone, and neither of us in the mood for murder. Hidden in bushes or thickets, hearing or fearing voices.

All was forgotten in this sunny world. Running, tumbling down all the hills; these Caucasian wooded hills made me think of home: Cecina, my world of ease and nonsense where pranks remained unpunished, and I grew up within a female permissiveness. I had perfected my ability to recreate this world wherever possible for my comfort, avoiding men, stricture, the unforgiving law, or the one that would single you out, you the small sinner for the exhibit of justice.

From my early days I knew my father's tall-standing law, I knew how to duck and run and flee from men. I like them only for playing, be it four-hand piano, or singing in parts, and I left male-bonded groups to those who wanted authority and rule. Mine was the female world of laughter, banter, clothes and poetry, of my mother. Desired above every sexual object and incorporated into every one.

In my Vienna student days, Jewish students behaved like Germans, wore colours across their chests, hats of *Hasmoneea* or *Hebronia*, duelling like Germans. *Idiots,* I thought even then, when twenty – thought that it was culturally foreign, betraying what they were. Indeed, not simple nonsense, but living a lie. I went to women for true living. Studies were easy for me, once I decided to follow in my father's footsteps for the study of pharmacy, which became my fascination as I delved into its chemistry. But it was easy, and I did what I had to, not to fight father all the way. But my real life was the night. In Vienna also. The Viennese maids. They made my bed, fed me, and I could go across this world, find them, love them, and live.

Running down the Caucasian hills, I saw the city before Sasha did. It lay in the valley, a bridge across the Kura. "Sasha, hurry up, we've made it." And I ran, mad with joy, to the bridge across. Tbilisi on both sides of it. Sasha had an address and wanted to get there, but I took my leave from him. A wonderful companion, the best for the road, but of male companionship I only wanted that much and not more. With a little tearful hug – I took the address to know where to find him – we parted, thinking it would be for a day or two.

A paradise. Wine on the south slopes, trees heavy with fruit that looked like golden apples, flowers in all the gardens. Except in my hometown in spring, I'd never seen such beauty. I turned towards the centre of town, dazed with sun, hunger, and the hope of female comfort.

I stood at a *Litfassaüle* – where the town news is advertised – to find accommodation and felt a hand on my shoulders. Turned to face a dark brown, elegant matron, my rucksack in her left hand, who sized me up with one look. "You're a Jew," she said, "I can see you need a night's sleep and a tub of warm water. Come."

It was an open-terraced home, sprawling towards the south. Jewish symbols were everywhere, *Chanukkah* nine-armed and *Menorah* seven-armed candleholders and the holy books, Hebrew, Aramaic, Persian. A fast glance showed all the pilgrimages since Babylon of our own people, on different routes, assembling other wisdoms and ways to look at the world. "You're an Ashkenazi

Jew," she said, over cantaloupe, coffeecake and cognac. "German-speaking, of course, perhaps also prejudiced against everybody else who has wandered different roads, like we did, who went east two thousand, five hundred years ago."

She laughed and continued, "We, my own people, have not been in the Erez Israel to be defeated by Rome, taken into slavery, or marched up the Rhine to fight or settle the German tribes along the Rhine! Oh, don't worry, I won't teach you history and my prejudices before a bath. Still, our branch of the tribe were taken into Babylon. Exiled from home and it was we who forged the yearning for – *May my right arm – if I forget ye, Oh my Jerusalem.* Yes, this is where you German Jews have it from. We in exile, between the two great rivers, the Tigris and the Euphrates, long before the might of Rome smashed Judea to pieces, we in Babylon five hundred years earlier, we coined it."

I was hungry, my feet were bleeding within boots whose provenance was marked by Caucasian earth and stones and unaccountable miles, and I couldn't care much about her famous ancestors that had "coined" our own desire of return. "Oh, Jerusalem –," she started again, interrupted herself, seeing me desperately trying to take off that scraping boot. She, now trying to help me, pulled it off with a jerk that took a piece of skin, bleeding into her hand. "Oh dear, oh dear, how long has this boot been on your foot?" she asked. Then, "Oh dear, oh dear, you certainly need a bath. I can truly smell it!" she said.

"I can't recall when I had it off last, I took the right one off here and there –"

And she broke into a wide-mouthed, throaty laugh, "Here and there," rose, ran to give me a foot bath first, to soak and rest and heal the poor skinless heel. Again broad laughter, her face a map of all these two thousand, five hundred years of pilgrimage. My feet in a tub of warm water with a spoonful of Georgian salt – and my soul was open to that comfort. She let me rest.

Shainah

The Cocoon

SHAINAH SLEPT AND ATE, BRUSHED HER BLACK-BROWN hair and listened to fairy tales. So unreal they were, so wondrous, that she invented her own magic endings or sequences for the next day. And it was a simple story in spite of its wonders, one every child knew in Christendom. But in the bosom of a Jewish motherhood, untouched until her sixteenth year, none of it had found its way to her through a shield of custom, *knishes*, chicken soup, and *Sabbath* blessings. Everything in the *Synagogengasse* breathed a life as if there were no other, though, just turning a corner, people decorated Christmas trees. *Why turning the corner? Who lived there?* To visit, to play, to be happy, angry, or mean to each other at times: she did not need anyone. With two grandmothers, her own playmate-mother, why turn a corner? Spun into ancient psalms, singing intervals as old as Babylon, Shainah was a dreamer, a poet of the everyday thing. Pots against their covers, big wooden ladles against handleless saucepans were her cymbals, and she moved among women's skirts, hid under them. Chased out and chided, "Hush, away, we have work to do, carry this, carry that, bring water from the well." She had laughed. Nothing was serious, love taking off every edge, every pain from a scraped knee or bleeding finger. She pricked herself often with scissors when trying to build a house of paper, which collapsed instantly. "Oh, well," she said, "it was not meant to stand. God knows best. If He does decide against it…it's His world. He can do with it as He pleases. We're just here to adore Him."

She hated February mornings when the embers in the ceramic stove from last night had gone down, the heated brick at her feet under the coverlet had cooled and she shivered, thinking of her cold clothes on the chair next to her. "But there will be spring," she said. "Dress fast, Shainale, so winter will sooner be over." And she slipped unwashed into her waiting woollens. "They'll wash me at night, all my mothers will, I'm sure, behind the ears, between toes, and under arms. No escape, they'll scrub until I shout stop. No one can be cleaner than clean." General hilarity.

"It's not easy though to have four mothers: two grandmothers, my own mother, and a spinster aunt. But I'm lucky, and so glad not to have sisters and brothers. All my cousins around me, with five and six and seven more cousins, have to share one mother. I have four mothers and my own private self, bread and butter, an apple when hungry, and so many playmates. Well, they also shout at me. But I know what they mean: mend your ways; you're not alone in this world. So they say. But I know better. I have a bed of my own, and my mother on her sewing machine treading it until the late hours of the night, to make my pretty Sabbath dresses.…

"So good. So simple. Until one dark night, the whole world intruded. Strangers. Small men-creatures speaking tongues of the tower of Babel turned my world, clogged the streets, piling people on trucks, or who-knows-what these were. And I saw all my four mothers, my splendid father among neighbours I knew and some I didn't in the sudden flash of moving lights upon a truck. I had slept out that night. In a small shed built for me by my uncles or more exactly built for our outdoor prayers on the festival of Sukkoth.

"This was the night that the world turned a corner, without return. I had fled my shed, awakened by these shouts of Babel, had run towards the house through the yard, found it locked, turned into the street crammed with a crazy crowd of people from another world, saw the pharmacy open across, fled into it, sat next to others I seemed to know but didn't because of their silence. Sat still and waited my turn. Until Felix sat next to me.

"How did I get to the pastor – it seems there were underground passages, a sleep in Marusja's bed, in-and-out through windows, up and down steps, on Felix's hand. Up the staircase, an inner-curled one, around the church steeple into Martina's bed. There was a smell of grasses. Leaves and tiny heaps of spongy greens, springy as the ground we picnicked on, were dry-folded into pages, a smell sweet and musty. Martina's. And now mine. I smell it when I brush my hair or curl it around the index finger of my right hand, which is my often-scolded misdemeanour. I curl and turn it, making locks all my mothers disliked. *You're ruining your hair, you're pulling it, you'll have a bald spot, we can see it where you have pulled it, then you suck it, which is not nice.* So my mothers. True. Now I do it again, pull it, taste it, smell it, and it is Martina's dry grasses I taste and smell – funny, to suddenly be someone else than oneself. And what my mother did not know, thank God, that I pulled a single hair and always looked at it before discarding it behind my bedstead. Horrors! They may have found it when cleaning but did not want to scold me for everything. So good they are! Would I be that good? No, no, I am too vengeful I think. Or maybe I'll change, being Martina now, smelling like her and having the pastor for a father, as she did. Father? No, not father. I have a father, no matter where – but, perhaps, I'll marry the pastor. I have to grow a little yet. Yes, I'll marry the pastor. I'll marry him.

"Martina likes to be like me. Jewish I mean. She has Sabbath candles of her own, for the blessing. The pastor said, 'Martina loved to light the candles like her Godmother Rachel Glasberg and secretly thought she will be Jewish when grown up but – she is Lutheran like her mother Rosy and me.'

"'What's Lutheran?'

"Not today, another time, when we're alone and no one hears us, I'll tell you all the stories I know."

THE TOWN FELL SILENT. An eerie week or two, but Shainah knew none of it. In her private heaven, between the downstairs small kitchen wrapped around the inner staircase and the one room under the steeple of the church, she rushed back and forth. A mother to the pastor, and his child all at the same time, she saw him worried but could not tell if it was her fault. And everyday she rose earlier to cut and butter his bread, which he had baked the day before and had stored in the cool pantry in a metal box lined with Rosy's embroidered linen. Saying in red and green *Kreuzstich* – a special stitching that crossed itself – "Bread is the Lord's body, don't take His name in vain." It sounded a little unusual. Not all of it. "The name in vain –" of course not. It's all in the Name. The four holy letters which she knew by heart: IHVH. "You don't utter it," her grandmother Leah had said while brushing Shainah's unmanageable hair. "What for? He knows and you know. Just think it if you are in need of Him and he'll be there –" or – she forgot now, what else?

Leah was my mother's mother, much closer than the other one, who never thought I was being brought up right: too spoiled, given no responsibility. "Just wait and see," she said. "Shainah will walk all over you, pretentious and inconsiderate as she is." But she was good too, tying my shoelaces so they wouldn't trail, did not mean all the things she said, and oh, how beautiful she was in a black lace scarf over her silver hair!

It is good to cherish His name just thinking it, so much better because of the thousand names you can give Him instead of only one. And you're the only one to know. No sharing with everyone. The *name* I know all about, and need no teaching. But *the Lord's body* is truly bewildering. A body, what body? I'll ask the pastor.

Shainah gave it no other thought, took the bread from Rosy's box, sliced it on the flat board next to it, and took it in a basket to the pastor who said, "Oh, so good of you to look after me and come, have a little of this ersatz-coffee, it's made from roasted barley and chicory. Come, keep me company, I've been up early to get fresh milk from my neighbours. I go in the dark, so no one can catch me." It is for me, Shainah thought. It is for me that he gets up early.

And they sat on the wooden stools, backless, straight little stools, which one could hide under the table, pushing them out of one's way, so small the kitchen was. And they sat across from each other for a chat like an old couple having their morning coffee, not yet totally awake. And Shainah asked suddenly, "Why *the Lord's body* on the bread box?"

"Another time. There will be lots of time to talk, tell stories, give answers. Today just let's enjoy each other. Without words." And he reached for her hand across the table, holding it a while in his. Such a happy smile on his face, Shainah thought.

He loves me. Is it me or Martina? Or both of us? No, no, even if I sleep in her bed and wear her pretty nightgown – cross-stitched *Goodnight,* embroidered in blue and white – even if I light her candles, with his permission, it is Shainah he loves. The smile is mine and mine alone. And I smile back, leaving my fingers in his until he takes them back, busying himself with the clearing of the dishes. And I rush to his side, "It's my job, it's my job." And he lets it happen.

THESE WERE THE MOST BEAUTIFUL days and nights of her young life. A cocoon of silence. Outside the door, hours slipped, changing their nature, unfelt, the sun coming and going with its ritual call for love and food, play and dream. She brushed her hair, which had grown in on the bald spot above her left brow, right at the hairline, and was lustrous now. Pulling the brush through, it shone chestnut on top and black within, and she looked up from Martina's little mirror and turned to the pastor, who sat on the edge of Martina's bed, to see his face illuminated. She could not find another word for a smile that was not one, a curl of lips and half-lowered eyelids – she had no word for it. Shining, she thought. Nothing was right. Except the surprise of what others would call a lit-up face. But with a turn of her head, it vanished.

She was left to contemplate her happiness. "How would it have been thinkable?" she mused. Such joy, having him all to herself, with no milling cousins about, mothers giving orders, the smell of fish on Friday night pervading the air, which made her ill. And all the other smells she liked – rose-confiture – and hated – onions, garlic, laurel leaves on meat. A life sweet as a walk by one-self on the river Prut.

Erasing all days in the *Synagogengasse*, as if born to the day of today, she allowed herself to love, to look forward to his footstep on the inner staircase, coming nearer or oh, turning away. The way he put one foot in front of the other in brushed and polished black shoes, even if she thought them brutish, unsuitable for his person, so elegant he was in gesture and gait – his suit was too shiny, used at the seat as the old gabardine of her uncles. She started to think, "Maybe I will later –" but suddenly aware that her sixteenth year had passed she stopped, not to think of later, to hold the moment a little longer. So sweet it was.

BUT THE COCOON WAS BROKEN by noises in the streets. German sounding. The pastor rushing up to her said, "Do not open any door; stay here until I come back. There is war. Last night Germany bombed the airport of the city. It is the twenty-third of June!"

"Don't worry, I'll be good. I have work to do." And she started cutting out a new wedding dress for her one bride-doll, who had no train and no silk roses on her neckline. She rummaged in a big footstool, which she had discovered one day and found to her amazement that it had an openable cover with the world's great-est treasures: odds and ends of silks, laces, velvets, buttons in gold and silver, needles in all sizes and for all purposes. "Oh, I do come from disorderly people; none of my mothers had anything as neat as that, though the Singer was humming day and night. Materials were rougher and they were never arranged to form patterns. It was winter-stuff, wools grey-brown-black, no fun. Oh, the Germans are definitely better than the Jews!" And she started choosing, touching textures, and smiling at her riches.

War, had he said? What is this or what will it be? Something like that Russian night or – I'll ask the pastor. But she was anxious for the first time. Fearing loss of her heaven.

The pastor was also anxious. Worried not to divulge his premonition and hoping to keep Shainah safe, he was silent. They sat with each other as before and their closeness became closer, more knowing, an intimacy of wordless response. Shainah reaching now for his hand across the small kitchen table, said, "Aren't we happy?" And she cleared the table, took household chores from his shoulders, and did not ask for all the unfamiliar, great stories she expected to hear one day. She knew he could find no words now. But these were still, inner-sounding hours, many, and at the end of nearly seven days she said one night, scrubbing unsuccessfully a burnt pot, "I'll marry you, when I'm grownup."

"Shainah!" he shouted as if cut through the heart, and he took the cornmeal *mamaliga* pot out of her hand with a gesture, a little rougher than was his custom or what she knew, to finish the stubborn spot. Then he softened his features again, turned to her who had come closer, and kissed her on the forehead. She knew she was married. Sealed by a kiss, be it above the brow. "I'll serve him, learn his faith, get up before he does, polish his ugly shoes until they shine and cook his cream of wheat as light as a feather. And I'll get up tomorrow early. What will I call him? So many things to think about." She kissed his hand like a serving girl for a goodnight and he took it fast from her, hiding it behind his back with a scolding look. She smiled and knew better.

The morrow was a different day. The pastor was up there, under the steeple before she woke, sitting by her bedside and waiting until she felt his presence. She sat up straight, fully awake, waiting for the pastor to speak. "My darling, the Germans are in town," he said. "Have you heard anything at night?" No, she shook her head. She had the sweetest dream. "They are shooting in the streets. Your people. Yesterday afternoon they had marched in, rounded them up, just pounding on their doors with *Juden raus!*" No, not really, she had heard, she thinks, some shots, or something that echoed through the walls. But, she had been up in her steeple, doing a doll's wedding dress and singing old Hebrew songs.

"Yes," the pastor said, "these are wonderful old thick walls and thank God no one has come to our gate yet."

"I have not slept all night," he continued. "Watching them, I went out to help the Jewish people from the Old House to bury their dead and then, Shainah, listen carefully: I went into the church office to falsify the register. I have entered your name as born and baptized a Christian. God will have to forgive me for my falsehood. I would not want you, Shainah, in the hands of anyone but mine, in such times as these. He will have to understand that I do not take your name or your parents' name lightly. What occurs now cries heavenwards and He will have to respond."

Shainah smiled at all of that thinking; there was nothing to forgive because it was with her permission, unspoken and under-stood, that the pastor changed her name and faith to his. Martina too, his own child, born a Christian, liked to bless Sabbath can-dles and build a *Sukkah* in the garden to sleep out at the festival of *Sukkoth*. And she said flirtatiously, "And what's my name? I have to learn it."

"You are Anna Steffanie, it is my mother's name. Wear it with pride, she was an angel. You are the daughter of my brother Paul, whom we lost a few years ago. So Shainah – a few more things. A strict order: You are not to open any door, you are not to answer any knocks, no matter how violent. I will deal with everything. You are in my charge. But you have to accept now, to stay hidden, not stray without my permission. And this is an order."

What filled her heart was inexpressible. It felt like fate, but had no words. "I'm his, I'm his. He is in charge. I'll serve him; I'll kiss his soles, fingertips, nose, and eyes. I'll cook for him and I'll clean his chamberpot." And she jumped from her bed and said smilingly, with a wicked girlish giggle, "Help me dress and I'll show you my cut-out wedding dress; the dolly's wedding dress, I mean."

Days went by. Days and days, silenced more now by the pastor's preoccupations, his own thoughts, and the running in and out, to help stricken neighbours. In these early July days of 1941, the pastor came up one day to his virtual prisoner and said, "It reeks to heaven, blood runs in the streets, imprints the sidewalks, and runs between the cobblestones. Shainah, I have to speak to you, though it is not right for one so young as you are."

"I am not so young as you think. You can say whatever you have a need to say."

And the pastor told her about a young man whom he had known, the son of one of his congregants married to a Jewish gentleman, who had knocked at the door. "Yes," she said she had heard it. Yes, she had also heard the rifle butts and *Juden raus*, "but I am Lutheran now and they could not have meant me."

"No, they couldn't," he replied. "Good, good girl to try to think of yourself that way but – the young man had to be helped.

I took him in, accommodated him in a small room on the other side of the steeple where there is a good view of the Old House, its whole east corner and the Archbishop's Residence. You see, he could watch the whole street over the Ahi fountain far into the garden of the *Habsburgs Höhe* beyond. So the young man was there a while but then he ventured out, which was not allowed, and came back for help. I rushed out to find a German officer in great despair. So I was busy, Shainah. I cannot tell you the whole tale."

"Yes, you have to. To whom else will you speak?' Smiles all around, handshakes, a timid hug, and the pastor rushed down the staircase with, "Bye, my sweet bird. Don't mind the cage. You'll fly free one day."

She heard him descend, counted the echoes of the diminishing steps, and looked at her golden cage. Like a crowning dome, it closed under the steeple; familiar objects around her had made routine possible, and the slim, tall window, reaching into the sky, brought all her dreams when she stretched out upon Martina's bed. It had remained that: Martina's. To please the pastor also, who might like to hear her pronouncing his daughter's name. The mosses, the stunted Japanese trees set into stones of varied orange colours and crooked shapes, she watered daily with an eyedropper and called them Martina's "Japanese Gardens."

But the wedding doll was hers. From the first day with Felix on her bedside, when Shainah's eyes fell on her, it was her own wedding doll. She did feel a little guilty to take her as her own so readily and without question. "But some things are mine," she said, with a human rationale of any robber, "and there is nothing I can do about it." This was hers from the beginning, and so was the magic footstool with a world of unimaginable fancy inside.

She had closed the cover after her discovery and said, as all the plunderers would, "This is mine." No questions asked. And proceeded to organize her world around it.

Cage? What cage? Home, sweet home it was; there were just a few steps from the kitchen to the staircase-in-between when the pastor called, be it for a meal, that there was no danger around, or just to give her an outing, she could easily hear him. And sometimes, he came up to help her dress. She was a little sloppy, took her time. Did not rush down to cook his cream of wheat. Forbidden to do so, she was slow, neglectful of brushing her hair or getting into clothes, Martina's clothes the pastor had set out for her.

This was the only one of Martina's things that she did not cherish. Was it the light musty smell that emanated from them, the odd cut, colour, or Rosy's eternal cross-stitch everywhere? She always seemed to postpone putting them on. Her own did not fit well either, as she seemed to have filled out a little in places or felt differently about herself looking into Martina's mirror.

"Well, I'm not perfect, you know, not like fabulous Rosy and Martina. I'm just ME. Imperfect me. Take me as I am or let me fly –"

"All right," the pastor said, "I'll open the window then," turned to it, only to be grabbed from behind.

"No, no," she said. "Who wants to fly if one lives in paradise?" And so the banter went.

Yes, this is a little woman with all the cunning and know-how about a man's heart, the pastor thought, practicing it to a high art, to bind us inextricably to each other. Oh!

There were quiet days to follow until the pastor called up the staircase that he would be absent for part of the day, something of importance had occurred: "A hostage-taking of one hundred Jews because of suspected sabotage and a missing German officer! Wait for me."

He had been absent many hours when she heard the other garden back door open, the one that led to the upper steeple. She looked across the inner stairway, which at a certain spot wound itself around a second one leading up, and saw a young man leaning against it. Breathless. She rushed down, jumping the small wooden bridge that bound the staircases, and said, "My name is Shainah. Come, I have cornmeal, I'll cook you a little *mamaliga* with butter." He did not answer; let his hand rest in hers as she led him down the remaining steps towards the kitchen. Pulling the backless stool from under the kitchen table, she made him sit down with a slight pressure of her hand and busied herself with a pot and spoon on a naphtha lamp the pastor had filled with fuel the day before. Lighting it, she took water with a measuring cup from a small barrel in the corner, and asked him his name.

"Max," he said. "I'm Max, my mother is a Lutheran congregant in this church. My father is a Jew."

"German cornmeal from Rosch," Shainah, wanting to make conversation, said to the young stranger, "is perfection. It pours like sand, one kernel the size of the other, it is a golden yellow as if it had caught all the sun and smelled the heat of it, cooks in three minutes and falls out of the pot onto a warm plate without sticking to the pot. Look, Max, at this perfection, round and yellow, like a midday sun; one almost can't look at it, not to be blinded, so beautiful it is. I burnt it only once, just missing the right moment. My fault, not the fault of the cornmeal – I am just too often in thought and time races away on me."

"Welcome," Max said, "welcome to the club of idiots that we are." And he smiled at her now, "idiots who think all the time and forget to live." He hesitated to dip the spoon into the dish, watching the blob of butter melting by its own laws. But then he went at it as any young man would with a savage hunger. Shainah had seated herself on the other backless stool, as she so many times had across from the pastor. She watched every bite he took and said to herself, "I did the right thing, though it was against the rules to talk to anyone. Well, I did not let him into the church. He lives under the steeple, being another one of the pastor's children. So he won't chide me. Because Max is a Jew like me, though he is part Christian and I am a whole Christian." She nearly burst out laughing, not really knowing what this meant to be a Christian, half or whole. Anyway, she was written into the church register. Would he be too? And she asked him that. Max replied that his mother was, but if the children were – he did not think so. He had finished his meal with a glass of milk Shainah had set aside on a little doily next to his plate, and he now looked at her for the first time.

"You're a pretty little girl," he said.

"Not so little any more, I've grown and as you saw I can cook a *mamaliga* to perfection. Come see my room –"

No, he couldn't, he replied. "Thank you for all you have done. I have lived through a rough day," he said, "and I couldn't. Forgive me." He rose from his stool, and only now she saw his earth-encrusted shoes had left puddles of muddy water where he sat. She bent down to wipe the floor and wanted to undo the laces of his shoes, which partly trailed, and Max said, "Heavens, no, I'll do them."

"No, I will," she said and before he could make a move, she had his shoes off, putting them onto a piece of old newspaper in a corner. "I'll clean them later," she said. "Go, go and rest." He let

her do it. It had been a strenuous day. "And thank you," he said,
taking his leave.

THERE WERE STRANGERS EVERYWHERE. Romanians from the
south, who had never been in the lovely valleys of the beech country, a land backed by mountains, holding the past in its darkening, wooded tops; they walked the paths as masters now and so
did foreign-sounding, German-speaking, uniform-clad men.
History had come, Jews were deported, murder was in the streets,
and a silence descended into these days to stay with a deeper
soundlessness, if that was conceivable.

It was a Sunday morning early that the pastor ascended the
staircase. Knocking his three rhythmic knocks, he opened the
door, approached her bed slowly. Stumbling over her disorderly
shoes, he woke Shainah and said, "Well, it is time." Turning to
Martina's closet, he took a few dresses from their hangers, laid
them out in front of her, and said, "I'll want you pretty! Choose
whichever you want." And she did not like any well enough. Too
big, too blue, too smelly, too many roses on all of them and she
settled on a smallish plaid Scottish-looking two-piece: pleated
skirt and top with white collar. The pastor was overjoyed. He saw
his daughter wearing it on a Sunday morning at mass. Close to
tears, he helped Shainah – so natural it was between them – and
guided her to the small sink with cold water from the tap to wash.

Dressed in the Scottish pleated green-blue skirt, she looked
grown-up. So fast, he thought, so fast. Not allowing himself anything else but this, the pastor prepared her today for mass. "I've
prayed tonight and asked for God's blessing, to teach you what
your people have taught us, and what we took a little farther." She

did not know what he meant; but went down to sit in a church pew. Sunday, eleven o'clock. A few silent congregants arrived in hats that looked like Rosy's. All ancient men and women. Shainah did not like to be introduced to these strangers, but she heard her new name, called out by the pastor. "This is my brother Paul's daughter, Anna Steffanie." And she shook hands with a few of them, paid attention, listened to his warm, silky-smooth voice and was glad it was all over. *Well, I'll be a Christian,* but it was not what she had hoped. Too formal, too sad, with a murdered, to-the-cross-nailed beautiful man as God, there between the church pillars. *I'll learn,* she thought, *I'll take my time. I am his,* she thought, *so all is well.*

They went out for the first time in so many days. Together. He wore his parson's garb, "A bullet-proof defence system," he said and laughed, and so did she. They walked through the wildering-now grasses and flowerbeds of the church park. Benches, their wood unstained, pebbles unrenewed, a weedy growth, as if nature knew better than man. Down the Schiller Park he took her, the statue of the poet nowhere to be seen, slopes thickly overgrown, a year under Russian rule having annulled all trodden lovers' steps. The paths still showing undergrowth here and there, the earth was terraced-down on the slopes, and the pastor and Shainah took them in a tumbling dash to fall at the foot of the hill into each other's arms laughing. They rose to brush them-selves off, with the sudden guilt of having kissed and felt the other so close. They took a silent march up the Cecina, through sum-mer wild grasses, bluebells, and buttercups; rested near the springs. They shared a piece of bread and butter out of an old newspaper the pastor had grabbed on the way out and they start-ed down the hill again. The war non-existent, a breath of air to nourish them, they returned, avoiding possible encounters with the uniformed or any others, sheltering themselves between whitewashed fences of the village Rosch.

The sun moving westward camouflaged darkening houses, and the eerie absence of life – most of the villagers having gone *Heim ins Reich* September, 1939 – made them shiver and accelerate their steps. In the dark portico of the back entrance to the rectory they stood a moment longer, with a trembling desire for each other and at the end of their strength.

THE JEWS HAD GONE. The pastor had lived all his life among them and did what was in his Christian heart to do when the young man Max, son of one of his congregants, had knocked at his door and asked for help, telling him that a German officer was lying unconscious in the lower labyrinth whorehouse of Rebecca and Mitzi, and one hundred Jews were taken hostage for him. Without hesitation, the pastor had followed Max to find the officer, and Rebecca and Mitzi had dressed, steadied, and brought Gerhard Schneider up the rickety steps into the *Heinegasse*. It was a rainy late day and the pastor let the young officer rest on the upper steps of this underworld vault to consider his next move. The pastor had a vague idea of the location of the headquarters of the German army. "Yes," said Gerhard Schneider, "that sounds right." They rose, started hesitantly along the bourgeois houses of the *Theaterplatz* and down the *Ringplatz* where the pastor recognized the hooked cross flags flying in the misty air. Thinking, *It really is an Indian symbol, nothing German about it, with the hooks going the other way;* he smiled at his own irrationality, having real things before him.

Both were slow to arrive there, resting on the curb of the *Theaterplatz* for innumerable minutes, walking as sleepwalkers would. Gerhard Schneider closed his eyes, stumbled over a displaced curbstone, then sat on one, pulled the pastor gently down next to him and said, "Come sit by me so I can speak to you. I have thrown a baby out of the window in the *Residenzgasse*." He said it as if it were an ordinary everyday thing. "It was just a bundle, a doll, well wrapped, and did not cry. I had done it before I knew, pushed a little by my superior, but in fact I had done it with not much thought." He then took the pastor's right hand to lead it to his little finger to let him touch a small cool ring and said, "I stole this from a night table. Just picked it up in passing. But I won't part with it. I do not know yet – no, I have to face it all. Let me keep it. It's the one thing I took, but I have watched the other comrades fill their pockets." Gerhard Schneider rose, steadier now, not in tears but trembling, legs refusing to remember the next step, arms dangling as if disconnected, he took the pastor's arm. They moved a little faster now but walking across the *Ringplatz* was almost not feasible, his whole body stalled. "Forgive me," Schneider said, putting all his weight unto the pastor's arm, "forgive me," he said. "I've always feared open places." And with an unnoticeable smile, "As a child I hid, disappeared in the bushes to the mockery of everybody when facing an open boyish battlefield."

Sweat ran from his forehead, his palm was hot, the pastor felt the young man's angst and whispered into his ear in pastoral fashion, "I'm with you and so is God," slapping lightly the officer's left foot with his left hand and adding sternly, "Move your left foot and now the other." And foot by foot the body of the young man settled into the automation of motion that brought him, on the arm of the pastor, across the *Ringplatz* and into the front of the four-floor building with the flying colours.

"I'll go in," said the pastor, "I'll go in with you to tell the story truthfully, as I cannot do otherwise. Not only because of my conscience, but mainly because it is the simplest, the most believable thing to do. We have to be fast now, every minute counts. Do you know that your army will shoot every tenth of the hundred Jewish hostages at dawn and then every fifth, if you're not found? Let's go in to look after it speedily and God bless!"

The two of them passed the sentry, a pastor and a German officer having no problem. Up the three steps to the gate. The pastor took his arm again to steady him, and both were let in instantly by two officers in charge at the desk. They seated Gerhard Schneider, offered a chair to the pastor, who refused and told in very few words that he was called to the brothel to help the unconscious officer and how he had brought him to this door. They thanked the pastor civilly, took name and address down, and let him leave. A last look at the officer assured the pastor that Gerhard Schneider was recuperating, though looking pale as chalk in the one-bulb light.

I Will Never Leave Her

March 4th, 1944. This morning, Shainah looked back at the first day. She had come as a sixteen-year-old Jewish child and grew to be a Christian woman in barely three years. The calendar showed the fourth of March, 1944, and she forever printed the date of her own commitment on her soul. The sun was high now. It had gone out of the eastern upper windows of the Old House across the street, but she would not rise.

Let it trickle red. It is not abundant. Just a fine red thread, it was slowly staining the linen, and a slight morning sickness down in the lower belly made her muscles stall and her memory roam through these last three years. She felt in total shelter. Untouched by occasional Jewish derogatory remarks she may have heard around her when she was young, she had remained innocent: from the star above, gold and myrrh, to the family and donkey on the way to Egypt – miracle is simple. It's joyous, anticipated, and wanted. And Shainah desired it with a woman's heart. All is possible if God is in the fragrance of the blue-green hyacinth in early February.

Many a still evening passed between pastor and Shainah, with the symbols of bread and wine becoming easily hers. Wine she had drunk, drop by drop on a Passover night, when all the plagues were counted in drops of red-blood wine, lifted with her little finger from the glass into a bystanding dish, and bread she knew as *Mazzah* unleavened, broken, blessed, one-two-three times, lying in layers in a special ceremonial embroidered bag. White-blue Hebrew cross-stitch on top. Passover was her favourite feast of the year, with Elijah coming to each door, wherever the Exodus was told. Shainah had watched the prepared-for-Elijah wineglass: "Had he sipped from it?" "Of course, he had." She remembers vividly measuring it with her eyes: the wine was up there and now it is down here – and all my cousins saw it too. And then bargaining time for a piece of the hidden *afikoiman*, a piece of cherished *Mazzah* given special importance, to be chased, found, and re-bought by the children in bazaar-style bartering, by the patriarch at the head of the table. Oh, the three intimate years of cooking, eating, fairy tales, and a truth emerging: of a love beyond expectation or rule.

She dressed slowly, waiting for the pastor, who delayed coming. Looking through the window, through the chestnut trees, she saw people emerging from some of the *Residenzgasse* houses – agitation, running or walking. Some alone. She ran to the north window to look beyond the Ahi fountain and into the Holy Trinity Street where a stream of people seemed to be moving down in the direction of the train station.

Contemplative this morning, she had trouble bringing herself back into the world, but had to. Going down to look for the pastor who had just returned, she said with an enigmatic smile, "I have something beautiful to tell you, but I won't yet. I'll wait until evening."

"Good," said the pastor, "I'm a little hurried, people are leaving in droves. Romanians it seems. The news is that the Russians are near. The front has moved closer to town and it perhaps is a matter of two weeks or three and they'll occupy the town. I see a Jewish face emerging here and there. Some I know had taken their yellow star off. I saw them last night sitting undisturbed by police, who looked the other way, on the rim of the old Turkish fountain at the entrance to the *Synagogengasse*." And the pastor stopped for a moment. "I went in response to a call for help. A few people squatting in the empty doorways of former Jewish houses. They were hungry, after days of walking, they had to be fed. I ran back and forth with clothing and food. Not really familiar faces, just one or two returnees from Transnistrian camps I thought looked local. But no one looks like anything one has seen before. Faces, haggard and drawn, have no inner life to show." *And*, the pastor thought, *in rags there lies no personal touch.*

But he tired of explaining the morning events to Shainah, who seemed slow to comprehend today, as if sleepwalking. Yet, she was beautiful when still. It was a new face. So still. He could not contain himself, took her hand, pulling her a little to himself and said, "Oh, let me sit down by you, Shainah." She busied herself but sleepily – as all her morning had been making a cup of tea. She did not want to hear of anyone but herself. It was the fourth of March, her day.

THIS WAS OUR WEDDING NIGHT. It was late night. I had watched the daily dressing or undressing; it nourished weeks of daily dreams; her recalcitrant yet giving vicious womanhood made me want to beat her, but I resisted, calling on God. He responds to me always, so I can discipline my ways and go on with my work. But her deep knowledge of my heart left me vulnerable, uncovered, exposed to her will. I feared it, its unexpectedness above all, its earthy non-Martina behaviour, with her feet on the ground, to stand on her own, getting what she wanted.

She had something to say to me, she said. I had seen that day more than there was in my power to bear and I wasn't ready to listen. Neither was she. But her face, enigmatic, still and new, urged me to take her hand, pulling her towards me, and I said, "Sit by me, Shainah." She fell onto her knees before me with her head in my lap.

"Alexander, we'll be married, after...is over."

I helped her up from the floor. It was in our little kitchen, and I sat on the backless stool, leaning against the wall slightly, and said, "Let's make it the ninth or the tenth of March."

"Yes, this will perhaps be right." Her cheek against mine was not close enough for me to sense its silk, but I felt her breath and we sat quietly a moment longer. She sprang to her feet then, saying she had things to think about, work to do, and pointing to her lower belly said, "It hurts there." And away. Not fast, but away, to leave me stricken. She had called me by my full name, Alex or any variety of Alexander – it made me shudder – how will this be? A bride with a false name, a presumed niece. She looked Turkish I thought then, or Turkmenish from the inner steppes of the Russian southern rim, a pale olive skin, shiny black hair, here and there a curl or two.

My Martina was more subtle. Less earthy, more inward, fables of all sorts roaming her elfin mind. But a little ready-made woman she was too. Not as provocative – *let the male victim show love* – and she would wait a while before fully responding. Response or provocation, it is all one. And so Martina fell to Felix, to his young but experienced maleness.

Three years. To protect, feed, help and cuddle, a father-lover will heighten every moment, recall the one past, and predict, pre-imagine the one to follow. "It's easy to see her wicked ways, it's easy if you're stung by provocation as old as Eve and almost see yourself hitting both pale-olive cheeks – one feels justified, if one knows her intent. But all this, only rarely. She is helpless, I'll protect her and I will never leave her."

Shainah disappeared from my view for the next four, five days. Told me not to call her, let her rest or work. She wished to be alone. I heard Rosy's sewing machine going, the heating of the big water cauldron in the bathroom, and I guessed her throwing herself on Martina's bed, which screeched, as old metal springs do. They needed repair but I never found time for it. I heard the water run, the shoe drop, her idiosyncratic grunts if things did not adjust to her will or liking. Intensified by her absence, I lived by the sounds she made, sometimes through the walls a tra-la-la echoing I could not identify, thought it to be a Romanian Colinda, but wasn't, and the silences in between taught me more about her than cooking and eating *mamaliga* together in the kitchen.

I had no congregation. Practically none. Part of the church served as a magazine and I kept the front gate closed. The rifle butts against the door, the *Juden raus* of the first murderous madness had given way to an eerie disquieting quiet, where every noise multiplies itself, open to the interpretation of danger for Shainah. These strange intense four days of denial – carrying fulfillment were to come to my Christian habit as the four advent candles to heighten His Coming would. Compressed into four days living and listening to noises familiar yet removed, tensions building in every muscle, I could hardly swallow. And I groomed myself more, looked into the mirror to watch a receding hairline, brushed my cleric's coat and thought I should wear civic clothes. But rejected it. A pastor is set apart from the mob. I would not part with separateness and elevated status.

The altar was free. I served mass – I think I would die without it – to a very few straggling practitioners, often old or having entered by chance. After Stalingrad, in the summer of 1943, Jewish faces, reappearing in the streets, entered the church for help, rest, food or a night's shelter, having survived this or that. It was good to be still here for them. Yes, charity. I think it to be higher than justice: no balancing act and all for barter. Straight giving, uncounted. Whatever else is in me that I cannot account for, I hope I will be forgiven.

I looked leaner, Shainah said, after her four days, calling from her "tower," as she called it – her own kingdom under the steeple – that she will be down in no time. And she was. Storming into the kitchen she said, "I'm ravenous, feed me."

"Pretentious, immodest scoundrel," I replied. "You feed me." And we laughed, feeding each other. Not lightly and unguiltily, but a laughter to cover premonition, making room for whatever was to come.

Then silence fell and we prepared for the night. "You will come to me," she said. "Come late. Don't tell me when. I will wait. And when you come my wedding dress will be spread across the big armchair next to my wedding doll."

As the evening descended into night I still waited. Obeying her orders, I waited for the sun to set behind the Archbishop's Residence; then I slowly walked up the steps.

She had changed her mind. It was not spread across the armchair. Shainah wore her wedding dress, train on her left arm, standing against the window. Two candles in Martina's silver candleholder lit stood low on the floor – camouflage still severely enforced – to throw an ivory shine upon the white satin sheath, sleeveless and long down to her ankle. She stood tall with her nineteen years; her young breasts moving just a little, shadowing the ivory silk around them, made me tremble. With my back against the closed door I watched her as she walked towards me. She was barefoot. Toes and soles hugging the floor, a slightly lifted heel gave her an air of flying, and I divined a smile when she said with husk in her voice, "Let us go to the church now." Arm in arm we walked down, lightly crowded by the walls of the steeple. There was no light anywhere except some coming from the lengthy slit cut in the side of the "tower," making the twin staircase and the small bridge leading towards it eerily visible. We walked slowly down, Shainah leading my steps. Sure-footed like a donkey, she had run these two staircases, jumped its linking bridge, played in the dark light of its mysterious corners, and she guided my steps now. Whispered unto my ears, with female superiority, "You're the pastor and I have to lead you –"

"Right," I said, "I submit."

Small, giggly sounds, and we had arrived through the side door into the church. Two candles under the cover of the altar she lit and pulling me towards her, so I would face her fully, she extended her two hands and said simply, "Give me your hands, Alexander, and we'll commit our lives – I to you and you to me." There we stood, hands grasped, bound by the ivory silk train, which she had thrown across them. We stood in silence, each one with words of our own unuttered. An empty church unrecognizable, the flickering shadow of my Saviour against the ceiling gave our wedding the "forever" of death. I will never leave her.

Thanatos. Eternal sleep. Love. Eros. All one. We waited for the
sweat to moisten the inside palms of our joined hands, and taking her train onto her left arm Shainah urged me to come and sit
in a pew somewhere. With Christ above losing its shadows, the
candles burning into their pewter sockets, we sat until the greying hours of morning. When we slowly rose to walk up the
staircase.

We did not move at first. Silenced, we lay alongside each other
with an awareness simple and sweet, a savouring of the morning
hour – until she slowly covered all my face, her fingers stopping
only to take the air back that I took from her lips. And she
rested for a little, waited, smiled, warmed by my love. I did not
see that smile. Eyes do not see what one knows. I will never leave
her. The palm of her hand – its taste on my tongue – a little sour,
just a little, but sweeter than manna from heaven. There is no
food like it. "Kiss me," she said, "kiss me." And it wasn't a kiss. It
was to learn with skin and lips the shape of her curled hair. Not
just all the hair. But one, drawn between teeth and lips, to savour
colour and shape. Curling, self-curling around my tongue. And
down her navel. She said kiss me, kiss, kiss me. And it wasn't a
kiss. It was a falling into oneself, expected and self-inflicted. And
I stayed as if arrested; but it was simple, so simple, just invited to
descend, guided. I did not fear that dark, unexpected world.
Sweet and sour and herring tasting, as if marinated. I will never
leave her.

IT IS SPRING, or not yet, just early spring, the pastor thought,
stepping out into the Evangelical gardens to find Martina's hidden
treasures: early mosses, not yet fragrant violets, and the snowdrop.

Picking one, "Yes, this is the proper name for you," he smiled, holding it tenderly by its stem – "wagging your whitish snowy head as if you will drop any minute." Gathering a few young grasses coming from bulbs underneath, he thought of his daughter Martina as a four-year-old marking the long lines on a lily leaf. A lily of the valley. Not yet. Not until late April. Not yet. Having risen early, after a night of love, he longed for a lonely moment. He walked fast across the lawn, overgrown now for lack of attention, avoiding the pebbled paths; the misty cool held him captive like a chestnut in its shell and he smiled, seating himself to rest under the chestnut trees guarding his pastoral mission.

Pre-dawn and dewy-cool, he shivered a little in his cottony garb, accustomed as he was to the black, heavy-textured pastor's cloth. March. *Still March, tenth – eleventh perhaps.* He gave thanks to his Creator for such undeserved abundance of love. To give and to take. Felt the cool suddenly penetrate to chill his bones, and his heart turned to stone. A premonition, a knowing about *End* had returned with an intensity unerring and absolute. He had seen troop movement the night before, knew the Russians were near but could not identify friend from foe. Wilfully ignoring the world, he was not ready to tear his cocoon to look out – *Are the Romanians and the Germans running, are the Russians so close?*

Living within a fancied world, a fairy tale of banter, games, and a love of extraordinary dimension, living it with his bride, wicked and just as innocent, he had shut the doors, had refused to look through windows. But it had registered somewhere. Disturbed now, he rose from his bench, gathering the little flowers, careful not to crush them. He stepped out nervously through the gate between the chestnut trees into the street facing *Residenzgasse* having heard scuffling noises, isolated machine gun fire, sudden shouts in Russian, a roar of diesel engines, a cry and a shout for help. He ran around the corner, facing the Ahi fountain, saw a local Romanian boy bleeding on the ground, his rucksack scattered; the pastor ran towards him, as he always would when God's work was to be done, and was hit by a straggling bullet in the back. He saw Russian faces suddenly bending over him; he asked them haltingly in local Ukrainian to help him to the back door of the Rectory. They carried him there, pushed the door open with their rifles, laid him flat onto the kitchen floor and left. Only now he bled from the wound, but he would not call Shainah as he heard her descending the staircase. Humming a Hebrew blessing as she always did in the morning, a *Baruch Atah,* she entered to put the kettle on and to polish his shoes, as she had promised in her silent commitment in church. She jumped to his side, could not lift him, but turned him to one side to watch the blood now spurting as if it were a spring.

"Shainah, turn me onto my back." She ran for kitchen towels, holding them pressed against the wound to stop the bleeding. "Do not lose time. Take my head in your lap." Cradling it, she listened carefully. "In the rectory you will find a shoe box, with your name on it, bound with a string. Your Christian birth certificate, a deed that entitles you to my land in Rosch and to all my earthly possessions, a small bag with gems and goldsmithing, as well as the names of the owners: the parents of Felix whom you knew. In the ghetto – for safekeeping – you will have to return –"

She shut his lips with hers and waited for him to die. Carefully bedding his head in more kitchen towels, she went out to the shed to find a spade and sat down to mourn, barefoot. She remained with him for twenty-four hours. The blood had darkened; thickened, it would not flow. She did not eat, sleep, or ponder her next step. She sat next to her lover, to live these moments of loss, permitting herself no tears. Rose to go to the registry to mark in her own handwriting the 11th of March 1944, the hour of 10 a.m., and signed her name. Felt hunger, cut a slice of rye bread he had baked two days ago, took a glass of water from the corner barrel, and with a hard, determined grip, she grasped the shovel and went to find a spot in the garden.

She started digging, but couldn't. The earth was wet from melting snow; misty air holding her hidden, she forced her foot against the spade into the ground, but couldn't lift the earth. Went back. Waited another day. Sat by him on the floor. Heard trucks in the garden, Russian trucks, soldiers jumping down, beating at the church door. Food they wanted, water to drink and to wash. Shainah, showing no fear, proud as the prioress of a *confrère* abbey, said she would let them in, if they would help her bury her husband the pastor. Her commanding presence made her sound and look the part and she said in strong terms, he had been hit in the back. *Fast,* they said, *let's do it.* They carried him out and she followed as his true widow. Covering the grave with young moss, she went back into the kitchen to feed the eight men. She hurried into the church to take a small, sculpted oak-cross from one side of the altar and with the pastor's own pocket-knife she scratched A.R. into the centre of the cross and went to mount it on his grave. It lay away from the street beside a small path along the back hedges that they had walked together at the end of the day.

Sitting at its side a little longer, she finally rose to resolutely walk up the steps to her room to pack a small rucksack, grab Martina's winter coat, two books she took as they fell into her hands. She went into the registry for the bound shoe box, into the kitchen for the pastor's rye bread and Roscher sausage, smiled at the roaring soldiers, and left to the Russians' call of "Come back pretty child."

She took Holy Trinity Street, turning back once more to look at the slit window below the steeple, to take along her three years of love, but for a short glance only. It was noon, the sun shone, warming the Ahi fountain; not lingering, she had directed her steps towards the train station. Walking faster now, downhill *Bahnhofstrasse*, and approaching it, she thought she'd never make it. It seemed to be the last train going south. Romanian-speaking mainly, soldiers, officers, wives, children already on the roof of the train. Shainah pushed through the crowd, assaulting the train steps, brutally using her elbows, recognized a CFR man, a railway conductor, who had rented a room once in the *Synagogengasse*. She shouted his name, and he grabbed her, lifted her above the crowd like a child. He held her in his arms, her rucksack and coat, shoved the crowd away from the door of the train toilet, opened the door with key in hand, pushing the pressing multitude aside, and said in Romanian, "Stay here, my child, until I come." And he locked her in. A toilet seat of her own, a small window across, pounding boots on the roof above and a desperate lot at her locked door – Shainah put the bottom of Martina's coat on the toilet cover, wrapped the rest around her shoulders, and cuddled her head into the rabbit collar.

A Toilet Seat of Her Own

S HE DID NOT KNOW HOW LONG SHE HAD SLEPT — SHE HAD left behind the golden watch-bracelet she had found on her night table one morning — but knew it was evening. She had wakened, startled by the sudden bumps of switched rails, and heard the locomotive sounding. Dreamless, she had slept many hours. Perhaps six or eight.

She saw fireflies running furiously across the lightless window in the direction contrary to the moving train. Silence had overtaken the anonymous crowd outside her door. She bent down in the half dark to look for bread and sausage. Took a little. Tried a drop of water from the small toilet sink in the corner, which came drop by drop, enough to refresh eyes and face, and she swallowed a little. Not willing to read or look into her books, she held one for a moment when a not yet dry snowdrop flower fell into her hand. She had rescued it from her lover's tight fingers and recalled saving it to dry between the pages of a book.

Oh, she thought, all that is true, but wanting to forget, she pushed it, with a stronger gesture than was warranted for a little perishable thing, back between two pages. *It hasn't happened,* she said. *Not now, I won't have it.* She chewed slowly, savouring every bite: too much garlic. The Roscher are crazy about garlic in sausage. I did not like it in the *Synagogengasse* either, when the Sabbath *cholent* had so much garlic and onion that the whole body reeked and it oozed from every drop of pee. I like sweet smelling things. Herbs; rosemary I grew in my pot on the windowsill, facing south. Oh, wonderful, how wonderful. God is everywhere. Even in rosemary, not just hyacinth, and I walked with that pot from window to front door to catch a few more rays. In the *Synagogengasse*, there was not much light. Really too sad! I loved sunny spots between the tight houses, which seemed glued to each other as if they couldn't live alone, would fall apart or break with their beams rotting.

I do not remember anymore. Oh, don't look back. Enjoy the rocking sound, such cradle for a kitten! I was young then. But not as young as I told Felix in the pharmacy. Heavens, I lied. I'm sure I was – What does it matter? Why did I lie? Something I rarely do. I felt so young, helpless, and perhaps looking for shelter. So it may not be a true lie. Just a stray kitten. Lost. Yes, I've always loved stray things. My teachers in Hebrew school said we are the image of God, He made us in His image. How did God know His image? Did He look into the water – mirroring Himself, or, being God, He knows all there is to know. But I see Him everywhere. Even in the firefly rushing against my small window. Do I see myself? – Oh, nonsense, God is God. Oh, I hope He is with me now.

She held her rucksack for a little longer on her knees, wondering what she had taken along almost thoughtlessly. Putting it down now in front of herself, she stretched her legs onto it for support. *Oh, good.* But sleep wouldn't come. She cuddled her head into the rabbit skin as if it were her kitten who used to creep into the hollow of her nape after sundown.

Her parents returning with the power of the unforgettable, she saw her father sitting on top of the table, his mouth full of pins, and Shainah looking up from under it, wondering if or fearing he would swallow them. He laughed: a gentleman's tailor has to learn how to handle pins, albeit between his teeth. She was so small then. His shoes, especially seen from under the table with her crouching between his two dangling feet, looked enormous; man's shoes – she did not like them. They did not smell right.

And all came back. The train sang Hebrew lullabies in a rhythm from one to four with a slight bend towards the third beat. *Just to throw you off,* she thought. And all the ones her mother sang at her bedside, she could tell apart: four different versions, depending on the lessons they seemed to be teaching her. The best were her father's, but he did not come at night. Shainah had to sit under the table to hear him. And he was funny, with his mouth full of pins. *How can you sing with clenched teeth and needles in your mouth?* Well, he could.

Her father, a Jewish tailor, worked for the *uptown people* who came to try on things, making their way through narrow cobbled streets in fiacres with two horses and a coachman. And people appeared in the windows for the event of the day: "The rich Jews have come to town." So my father said. "They pay me well and I do not have to run and beg for my money, as I have to from my *Synagogengasse* customers. But not all the rich behave well. They sometimes come with their stuck-up wives, knowing everything better than I do: 'This seam is crooked,' and they tear it apart with their dainty fingers full of rings or 'This lapel is too smooth, don't you have any proper stiffening?' – and so on."

Oh, I'll punch them with my tight fists – sitting under the table I knew my father was suffering, and I held the pins, ready to stick them into their fine ankles showing below fancy cloth. I nearly did it; hoping I had done it, so they would scream at the unexpected assault from under the table. But I did not do it, for fear they would never return, and he needed their money. Revenge is perhaps the sweetest thing, but I didn't take it.

He always interrupted his work for prayer. A few short moments, but as true as the sun would rise. And he took his tea in a glass with a cube of sugar. It had to be hot or he would say to all his women serving him: "Why don't *you* drink this tea?" – never a curse word or something stronger – as I heard in the street.

In the *Synagogengasse* everyone lived in the others' houses; knew the hours, all the turns and twists of their lives. Through common walls, or from across the street, windows looking into windows, cooking, spicing was inhaled by all; and because the killing of their chickens was done by the same slaughterers, they knew what one ate. The Mikvah ritual bath, just next to the ancient Turkish bath, was a true registry of what women knew about women: namely everything. Shainah, like all girls her age, young yet still to be initiated, heard their talk without grasping all of it, but intuitively knew it was about what they did with their husbands.

So everyone lived in everyone's marriage-bed and, knowing the forbidden days, the women laughed, chatted with one another in that conspiratorial air of a secret society. Women. Providing, giving life, and keeping it going. *This is what I am now, one of them.*

A signal-knock at her toilet door shook Shainah out of her childhood existence. She heard a key inserted. It was still night but an almost greying morning when the good Petru, her winged saviour who made her fly through the air into her private palace, came to tell her that the train would stop for an unknown number of hours after crossing the border of what he knew was Romanian territory. This would permit the crowd from the roof, hallway, and densely packed compartments to get out, relieve themselves somewhere, and stretch their legs. What would she like to do? "Nothing," she said. "I'll stay here until you come again. I am so grateful, I could kiss your hands." But he waved her away, put a huge apple into her hand, and said with inimitable Romanian sweetness, "Sleep, my child." He went out and locked the door. The train continued into a green-greying morning, fireflies changing into water drops which drew streaks of dirt on the window.

Good. Rain. I've always loved that sound. There is just such freedom in it, from doing, going anywhere. A coat it is, a shield, a crawling into a sweet corner, a tearing of the web of obligation and even seeing beloved faces. I would sit under father's table with a child's sewing machine, making it turn, competing with the storm of rattling, miserable, loose windows or doors. And I would smile, listen to my father sing and sew, my mother walking about on felt slippers so as not to be heard. A respect for the heavens having opened and peace descended. Such a shelter for a little girl. And this enormous table-roof over my head, it filled the room, almost wall to wall. A walking space was left around so father could place the big rolls of cloth, unwhirl them onto the table in a very specific way. Take as much as he wanted, fitting it on pre-cut, designed paper-patterns, and standing always at a certain angle to the table he would raise his huge scissors or a sharp-edged knife to cut the cloth. His face, beautiful but worried. An intensity I will never forget, and a great smile when he liked what he saw; or redesigning with little chalky pieces, marking the cloth if he was dissatisfied. So good not to have brothers or sisters, so good to be his alone –

Shainah fell into her rabbit collar and slept a deep, undisturbed sleep until the jolt of stopping woke her, the repeated ugly sound of metal, screeching of rails, the final puff from the locomotive. Now she heard the boots rumbling to get down for their desperate human needs and others stretching to occupy, if for a moment, their places. She heard it all. And the peace that followed. The rains had stopped but the day remained cool and dark, a true March day. She had lost count. Perhaps the seventeenth. She rose from the toilet seat to relieve herself, to find a few more water drops in the corner sink for an eyes-and-mouth wash. She stood for a little against the door, lifted the rucksack upon the toilet seat, opened it: to have the shoebox stare at her with all the immediacy of recognition of the last lived-through days.

"I'll look," she said, "it's good for me. I can't live under my father's table forever. I'll undo the string and see." It fell off effortlessly, and she approached cautiously to lift it. Tenderly holding the box open she slid slowly to the floor. And now she looked. Simply and without apprehension she undid a lovely leather pouch to glance inside, but closed it just as fast. Gold, gems, Jewish people's precious things, rings, diamonds. *No, not now. Another time.* She picked a leather wallet, opened it. She had never seen American dollars. By ones, by tens, by twenties, she counted two hundred and eighteen American dollars. Green bills that looked greener in that obtuse morning light, a face staring at her. A poem in the pastor's handwriting, a tiny-print booklet in red leather, a cross in gold print on the front, and all papers and deeds across the bottom of the box. Fake birth certificate and name. She smiled at all the lies. Did not wonder how she'd live! No thought of any tomorrow, Shainah just thought how in heaven did one lie feed the other. *I am Anna Steffanie Rempel now, past nineteen.*

She closed the box, holding it on her lap a little longer, and slowly all the tears there rose to her throat, shaking her. She sat and wept until there were no more, dried her eyes with the back of her hand, rose carefully to bind the string around the box, fitting it into the bottom of the rucksack to free her bread and sausage. She took a few carefully chewed and swallowed bites, then removed the rucksack to cuddle into Martina's coat and wait for the train to move.

It didn't for a long time. But peace, the absence of the steady beat and cadence brought to half-consciousness a benevolent and sweet memory. Finding herself in her own quarters, the ones where she knew every crevice in the fir wood floor under her father's table. Collecting the ends of thread in all colours, winding them into balls or strands she threw them to Miz, who was trained to find and return them. She tried not to hear her mother's voice. Had to be called again and again. "Oh, dear! Buttonholes, so hard to do: the hole one makes with an ivory piercer is always crooked; the repeated winding of the thread around the needle knotted itself into totally unpredictable skeins. Oh, yes, I had to crawl out from under and sit by my four mothers to learn what I wouldn't want ever to do: buttonholes."

Father never did the lowly work. The women did, Shainah mused. Women, that is what we do, the lowly work. But then, what would we be without men's mastery, expertise and – well, their love; yet, if you think about it, theirs is the absolute dependence. On us. Miserable masters. Nothing they are, without us. Well, all buttons big and small, square, round, two-four-six holes and the wonderful stems, which had to be wound around and sewn onto the trousers. They were there – on stems. We did it for my father. A skill of its very own. If you sewed them too close to the cloth, one could not put the buttons easily into their buttonholes, and the heavier the material, the heavier the stem. All four women were experts, daughters of tailors themselves. A long line of tailors. Doing it for my father's clients now, for the rich from uptown. Yes, Felix comes from there. His mother was once in my father's shop. I was under the table and saw her stepping in. I could tell, by stance and step, shoe and ankle above it, if it was uptown or low-town. This was definitely uptown. As if unburdened by weight, she flew across the floor, crevices seemed to avoid her so as not to scratch or sting a silky sole. The voice above fitted the shoe, dark yet light, heaviness taken out; it was a bird song of a voice. I looked up. And there she was: life to suit her, not the other way around as my mother, aunts or grandmother would have to do. Everything bending to please her, smiles to ease the how-do-you-do, money almost uncounted, coming out of a silver-thread knitted bag gently hanging on her left arm, handed over to be counted by the other. My father in this case, who said, it was too much.

"Let it be," she said, "my husband was very satisfied, the suit was pressed to perfection and oh, the buttons and buttonholes, handmade each one of them, of course."

"Yes," my father said, "my wife is an artist. She had in her early youth learned the craft from her father and they sewed uniforms in the Great War for the Emperor Franz Joseph II! One has to be clever to be so honoured!"

"Yes," the lady said, smiled to ease her parting, leaving an air of perfume – my mother, inhaling it, said: "Oh, the rich, with their *Houbigant*." And this is what I called them forever: the *Houbigant* people. So different from garlic and onion in hair and woollen cloth.

So my mother as a little girl had worked for the Emperor – such excitement. "Tell me about it. I do not want a story," I often insisted at bedtime. "Tell me about the Great War and how young you were when, just a little girl, you crossed the Prut, to run from the Russians. Was it 1914 – 15? And how grandmother carried you, possessions across the bridge – and how in the Vienna train station, you, your two sisters and mother, all strangers, did not know where to turn."

"Enough, enough," she would say. "I won't. Sleep, my sweet. I'm tired of it, you have your own life to live, not mine." She kissed me, pulled the covers up, and left.

Such peace. The train is still. I'm warmer now. I always warm towards the morning, cool and chill before the night. I'm warmer now, I feel it in the tip of my nose or little finger. Oh, to close my eyes, to stretch my legs onto the rucksack, head curled into Miz's pelt. Oh – and to wake to face the future. One not thought about for over three years. *Dornröschen* – Sleeping Beauty – years, the little thorny rose. Three years like a hundred with my prince on the other side. Yes, wrapped into the pastor's life and his fairy tale of love and a second coming. Of what, exactly? What is the first? He is not here to tell me.

The pastor. Was he real or my Sleeping Beauty dream? Thorns as on the stem of a rose, that is what the gate of the Evangelical church had become. He made it the outer end of my world, thorns that would kill, dared I step out. So he said.

Fiercer and wilder, as only my imagination could conjure, I lived in my castle, hearing the shuffling feet going past the Ahi fountain down Holy Trinity Street in the fall, 1941. It is the street I took three years later, knowing it led to the train station. I heard thousands of silent-sounds. People pulling themselves and their weights throughout these years – as I know now – going down into my own streets, the *Synagogengasse* – *Judengasse* – Turkish quarter. How many had slept on my father's table, how many under? I heard the silence that followed after they had gone; just from little stories I gleaned it all: the pastor's, Max's, the German officer's. It bound me hard and fast to my bedstead, Martina's that is, and fed me with nightmares of my own, of the life unimaginable, which is worse than seeing it. But, warming to the rising sun in the eastern window of the Old House across, to bread and milk and the pastor's goodness, I grew up. But not easily. Not living like Felix's mother: flying, not touching the ground. I woke every morning having to fashion my day, working it out by the moment. A hundred years to live with: they are killing the Jews and who am I to be a Christian? Besides not knowing what this is and certainly not wanting to know about any "tomorrow."

The German officer – all the things I knew without ever having laid eyes on him. That he was handsome, young, soft-spoken, had done something atrocious – Max not telling what it was – that he had gone through the *Heinegasse*, close to the opera house, had fallen ill or fainted and had to be rescued with the help of the pastor. And I have said to Max, "The pastor will rise to heaven on a ladder of his own construction. It will be so high that he will hear the angels sing. They will lift him from the uppermost rung to rest in God's arms." "Yes, that is him." Max smiling. A little derisive or a mocking smile, but sweet: "Yes," he said, "a true Christian." So, this is what it seems to mean – but the danger was that the German occupation forces had taken one hundred Jewish men hostage, and would kill every tenth, then every fifth, and so forth until the German officer was found – and so the pastor acted fast. And I remember him coming in, running out again, Max coming in and out, and I remember the meal I gave him the first time he came through the back door of the rectory. What had the German officer done? What terrible thing? And why did he faint, young and handsome as he was – Did he lie, did he confess?

What kind of Christian? The pastor said there are different kinds. Good and bad or what? It's too complicated for a Jewish girl. Being Jewish is just so simple. You do what you are supposed to do or you'll be scolded or chided a little. So you'll improve next time. Maybe you'll wash your hands before meals, get to your work faster, or stop dreaming – there is work to be done. One day the lad who apprenticed at my father's – lazy Abe – did not come to sweep the atelier, as my mother called father's workroom proudly. "Shainah," she called, "we have to gather all the pins. Come out from under there, here is a broom, fold materials, do this, do that – what will become of you?" – and so on. It's easy to be Jewish. Count on your fingers, every one of these Commandments. It's easy, just count till ten and do as you're told! There is always a moment's dream to be had, an apple or a hug. Christian? I guess one has to go out, rescue German officers to save one hundred Jewish lives. Of course, there are all the wonder stories, water to wine, lovely weddings, and all of that! Jesus's death – Why did he have to die for me? I can die for myself. But that is what he did, the pastor said. So it must be true. Our stories are beautiful too, I think, maybe not all of them. Some are just as awful as Jesus's death, but I won't think now which. I have a life to figure out. Such peace, a stopping train, a sound of locomotive here and there to remind us – Where are all the people? So good to be alone.

Oh, I must chuckle or giggle or just have a good laugh, even if it hurts right here under the breast bone. Oh, no belly laugh. Nothing is that funny. Though it is, if you consider or just think, having come from one church-castle-prison, lock on the gate, except an evening stroll with my good pastor, to a toilet-seat fortress-jail in a moving train. If this not be funny! Oh, no, it isn't. I've cradled his head in my lap. I've sealed his eyes and lips. No, it isn't. The wonderful, wonderful church years. The slow growing, the daily bread. The one he baked and the one he blessed. Stealing myself down, while he slept, into the church pews, to learn to feel something and not knowing where I could find it. To hear him scold me, as if he were my father, but then no, as if he were someone or something else, mysterious, promising, not yet imagined. Contradictory, all at once. He caught me at my nightly expeditions, down the staircase, or up the double staircase to the tower. I just wanted to find the secrets that seemed to elude me. The inner world of his magic stories. I was not built from my childhood to put meaning to his words, to so many new ones. "Saviour" is one of them. Or "to save." Save was a word my father used and my mother hated. "Don't spend on foolish things, I have to save for a new cutting machine," he said. "Nowadays, tailors have new tools."

"There is nothing wrong with time-honoured scissors, and I don't know anymore where I could save," she would reply. "Shainah needs –" and so forth.

Secrets were everywhere. I understood and then I didn't. I asked and he always answered, but the words again were his, not mine. I had to fill them on my own. So I took liberties. The one thing I did not do was venture out. I knew I'd be murdered. I just knew. As 1942 to '43 proceeded, I could not go out that front door. Unless in dusk or darkness and with him. I loved the strolls through magic spots he knew so well, having walked all over the Evangelical gardens with his Martina, and I took on my role to be her: sleeping under her covers, eating from her R-embossed dishes and walking through dewy mosses in her sweaters. And he held me tenderly, barely touching my arm, and taught me the family of plants, took samples home, looked into books to put names to everything.

He had a charmed crystal in a silver ring, which, when held at the right distance would show the finest inner workings of a leaf, the parallel streaks or layers in a stone. It hung on a leather string above Martina's desk. Her perfection and diligence, her orderly mind I did not have. I loved to see her stones arranged in shaded colours, size, and forms, through the looking glass, and hear the pastor's silky tones calling them this or that, registering, but not everything. I just looked at him sometimes, thinking *It is too good to be his own*, while he elaborated on granite or silicate, as he called them. I felt his breath when he spoke. He needed names I did not. He would say, "Why don't you write the categories in orderly fashion?"

"I have my own order, in my head. It's very orderly in there, even if I am sure to have forgotten it already." So he smiled, shook his head and left, behaving like my mother. My writing improved, accustomed as I was to Hebrew, which had to be correct, but German and Romanian were secondary. Now, I had to work for

him. Spell correctly, read books. Greeks and Romans. Goethe and
Schiller by heart. And he taught me and fed me and tucked me
in at night. Lullabies from Rosch at my bedside he sang, the
German song of the people. They're mine now. *Weisst du wieviel
Sternlein stehen?* – Can you count the little stars in the blue of
heaven?

It's good to sing, with words to match, so simple for a Jewish
girl. Going to the heart, straight, avoiding the head with all the
meaning. Still, I was disobedient and I lied about everything. Oh,
I can explain everything that does not seem to suit me! I certainly
lied about my secret forays after dark or even daytime, the ones
into the upper steeple of the church to have another view from a
slit window facing south and not west. It was so high and looked
straight into the sun. When the pastor went out to comfort the
few remaining German friends or parishioners, I rushed up,
jumping the bridge to the second stairway. The steeple attic was
full of old books, a hundred years old in a script called Gothic,
old Lutheran Bibles which did not say nice things about Jews, but
it did not concern me. I found a big picture of Martin Luther,
damaged a little, but one could see in his face how clever he was,
and wicked too. But the pastor said he was a great man who
played the flute, wrote songs called hymns. And this is why all
Lutherans sing. I like that. This is lovely to sing in church, not in
Hebrew, which one does not always understand, but in German
or in Yiddish, maybe – perhaps not. Oh dear! And I looked
through the slit windows. There were three hugging the corner;
and though not being allowed to walk out, I saw the life out
there. People coming for water to the Ahi fountain, sitting on the
rim, women chatting, and then suddenly, one day at high noon,
I saw hundreds or a big crowd around the fountain, not well

dressed, not good looking, gesticulating. Are they Jews? What is happening? They were a strange lot, but they left as they came and I was thoughtful all day. The pastor, returning, looked into my face and said, "Shainah..." I brushed him away, saying I was hungry. But he did not allow me to interrupt him: "The Jews are returning. Some. It worries my parishioners. It shouldn't, unless they have robbed their houses, eaten their food, and worn their clothes...and they perhaps have done all that. They're worried: what will the Jews do to us? Revenge? And I have to say to them: pray; that they are back, or that at least some are back, return what you have taken; do penance and help them readjust. But they're sick with worry."

So, this is what I have seen, Jews returning. My heart stopped. But this time I must ask him, "My parents maybe too?"

"No, no, they were not taken by the Germans who deported the Jews to Transnistria and that is not so far, just on the other side of the river Djnester. Your people were taken by the Russians, far, far away to Siberia perhaps, up north. Sweet Shainah – maybe one day, after the war is over they'll return. Not yet. Perhaps soon. Let's pray, the two of us, whichever way you want, yours or mine."

I said, "Yours, so we can do it together."

I'm hungry but can't stand the garlic of the Polish sausage. It makes me thirsty. My stomach turns. I am jolted by a sudden switch of rails, an inexplicable jarring sound and a deeper silence to follow, I jump to my feet as if demented, run to the window, which smeared with soot and streaked with rain encloses me even more. I scream, turn to pound the door with fists, kick it with my boots. An ungiving door, wood echoing my despair. I hear a key turn and fall into the arms of the railway man, the kind Romanian who had lifted me like a child at the train station to carry me now through the empty corridors to find a spot of comfort.

He looked around himself, having to tip-toe or walk over bundles, suitcases, desperate knotted-on-four-corners bed sheets, decided to sit on the step, to have some fresh air. "Praise be to God," he says, "do not worry so much, another day or two and we're home. You'll come to us. My wife will receive you and you'll stay as long as you have to."

He propped her up like a doll against the open train door, put a CFR railway man's thermos bottle with cold tea next to her and a dry piece of corn bread. She couldn't eat, but it was good to see it there. The sudden fresh air, the exhilarating change of scene, meadows, hills, a palette of spring flowers mixing with the green of a Moldavian countryside in March, made her giggle. The good man beside her, slapping her thigh, said, "Good girl, you can sit here until I return to put you back in your safe private room. And for God's sake do not go anywhere because I won't be able to get you in again over the heads of all these people." And only now she sees them all, between the grasses, in the hollows, in twos, threes or alone, asleep or just resting. Solitude under the sky. Relief from the pressing presence of so many people in corridors, compartments or on the roof, they slept stretching their bodies into all the room they could get; as if one were able to accumulate, hoard, store air, space, or the absence of the other. And Shainah's heart grew full of gratitude for a little room of her very own, with a seat, a window, and a drop of water in the corner. Looking at him, who rose to do his duty, she took his bottle to drink but couldn't open it easily. He lent a hand. Just to show him love without using words, because there weren't any, she took a sip and he smiled in return, accepting her thanks. Back in her secluded palace, she heard all the shuffling, the shouts – a little less violent now than before, it seemed to her – still, people scrambling for an inch of space, not to have their arms stick so closely to their bodies, they fought. Silence settled and the train took over, the screeching rails, motion, and a sounding locomotive assured her she was on the last leg of her journey, no matter where they were going.

I better think a little, or it will be over soon and I'll regret not having thought things through.

Sitting on her throne in comfort, she looked into her ruck-sack: There was her wedding dress, folded safely at the bottom. Not to disturb it, she touched its silky *crêpe-soleil* surface to bring back the four days' seclusion and total devotion to her task. No other thought. Neither what for nor any other consequential one. Just doing it. Like a tailor's daughter and granddaughter, sit down at the sewing machine, see that the seams are straight, finish end-ings properly, don't let threads trail, hold on to the slippery mate-rial, which needs a very different attention than sewing heavy woollen homespun stuff. She knew. Her mother had to sew the lining of jackets, vests, and gabardines, in silk or serge or rayon even. And she had said, "Look Shainah, everything has its own laws. Treadling a sewing machine does not mean sewing. All things have their own laws. Learn them."

And so it was with her wedding dress. A simple sheet of silk, but she would do it right. And when she had put it on, the night of church and love, she thought herself her mother's daughter and a king's bride. A king of the church. The best there is. When she stood at the window – Was there a full moon, the room was so lit? – and had heard his steps sounding on the last rung, she promised to polish his shoes every morning before his rising and light the primus for tea, so he would know his servant. And walking down the tight staircase, light coming from somewhere, train on her left arm, he had held her so lovingly that she thought it could not be wrong in the eyes of the Lord. Lies or no lies. Love could not be wrong. And she had gone barefoot, which to Shainah was being in touch, beholding God's earth; taking it in, infusing soul and body up to the crown of her head. But he was dressed, smelled of soap, shoes polished and collar turned. A pastor. She a pastor's bride. A long night, with Christ's shadow falling onto the ceiling. A little nervous and fearful because of His death. But very beautiful. One single ring. His own he gave her. Now on her index finger, being too big for her ring finger. But nothing mattered. It still was too big, even there.

And she touched the silk again but wouldn't lift it. Just to think of the moment he took it off. *Let me do it. Let me.* It had to be opened on both sides of the neck. Front and back joining with the finest hooks, male-female hooks, her mother had said. You have to know how to make them invisible. And she giggled. He, my pastor, did not find them. How does one? – well, she showed him that by unhooking the five hooks on each side of the neck, the sheath would fall down to your feet and all you had to do was step out, leaving the silk curled like a rose at your ankles. And I stepped out, naked and barefoot before him. He sat down. Just to look at me in this half-light of the small hours. Slowly undressed. No haste, orderly, so I could look at him fold his trousers neatly and put his jacket around the arms of the chair. He took his time, perhaps not to frighten me, for I had never seen a man the way the Lord had made him. And he slowly approached, not to touch but just to kiss a little. We stretched out on Martina's bed in silence alongside each other. Then it was I who said, *Kiss me, kiss me.* And it did hurt, as I knew it would.

The train rolled with a steady rhythm, a hum of song, the locomotive sounding at intervals, reassuring and safe. Cornbread and the railway man's thermos at her side, Shainah crawled into Miz's fur collar, folding the rest of the coat over stretched-out legs on top of the rucksack. No sound from outside the door. As if there were no life beyond it. Magic oblivion. Shainah felt privileged. Chosen. A gypsy smile, a toilet seat, Miz's collar to tickle and warm her cheek, and the absolute truth of the last lived days – love. She had been chosen. Muscles relaxed though distended, eyes closed, a smile playing around her lips, she slept.

Night. Perhaps midnight, when the rattling, the puffing, metal sounding slowly stopped. Shainah had wakened before, felt time had reached its end. Was it the cradling rhythms diminishing in cadence, or were there newly inserted layers of harmony that made her wake, alert her to the coming end? "I will wait," she said, "to the last, until Petru comes for me." She settled into the slower tune of the train for a little after-feel of the last days. After-feel or after-dream, not to give it up so brusquely, living it to its deserved fullness, she closed her eyes to catch the outer corner of what she had half-dreamed or fathomed last. But she couldn't bring it back; as if it had lived itself out and an entirely new tune were to be followed. Awake, alert now to every sound outside the door, she sensed all the lives, shivering in the late-night March air. Pity she felt. Such pity. The poor things trying to cover chilled bones, pulling coats tighter and themselves closer to the other animal next to them for warmth, their breath, and perhaps also for – as she herself became aware of – the last moments of "the known." Be it even as passing a "known" as a train corridor. Or a toilet cabinet.

People seemed kinder out there. She heard whispers rather than shouts, and even a "thank you" reached her ear. Shainah smiled to herself: I guess they fear diffusion now. We'll all suddenly run away from each other trying to find a corner, a bed in strange streets, no one waiting for anyone on the platform of the train station. Yes, she smiled, feeling such compassion for the anonymous lot out there, when absolutely no one would be out there for her either. But she was glad that her soul could be moved for others and she had not become an unfeeling stone. So she started to prepare in the deep dark of that night, to look for her rucksack, arrange her coat, and wash her eyes with a drip-drop of water in the corner. She could reach it now without rising from her throne, so efficient had she become, accommodating her body to the given circumstance. "I'm sure I'll think of these secluded days – How could I forget my thoughts? Fears? I guess I'll never close a toilet door in my life," and she giggled, "for fear it may be locked forever, and jumping to my feet – when? – screaming, pounding the door with Martina's poor booties, being absolutely certain that this door would never open – how could I forget it?! Then settling down into Petru's eyes and arms. So a door did open! But how to forget such wild, sudden despair? I hope I will close toilet doors having learned that doors can open."

Shainah heard the people outside getting louder, more agitated, shouting at their restless children as the train shook all these creatures into a kind of frenzied action, but not against each other somehow. It was a common worried sound that came through the door; something that Shainah either read into or truly felt, as this mighty body on its rails screeched its last.

Now she sat down, holding on to the strings of the rucksack and the bottle of the railway man, coat in readiness. She had eaten the last crumb of his cornbread and now she waited. The sound of shuffling feet disappeared fast, people rolling down one on top of the other; corridors, the roof seemed suddenly empty and still. She savoured her last minute before having to step out that door and down those steps – to nowhere. And indeed he was there. Key in lock. Good Petru with a flashlight of the official, helping her to carry, talking softly with that light southern lilt she had heard for the first time. "Where are they all?"

"Gone," he said enigmatically, as if they had never existed and weren't worth the question. Ghosts one can't question. "Gone," he said again and took her arm to get her down the last step, which was unusually high. And putting her rucksack beside him on the ground, he said again, "Gone, trying to get to bed some-where."

"Call me Anna," she said simply.

PART TWO:
BUCHAREST – THE FIFTIES
AND BEYOND

CALL ME ANNA

THE NIGHT WAS COOL AND FRAGRANT FOR MARCH. Budding roses, not yet ready to give all of themselves, lined the roads. But their great abundance flowered into a scented air of promise, of enchantment, and a giddiness of being gently drunk. Limbs stretching into strides, both Petru and Anna took the three- or four-hour trek skirting Bucharest in perhaps just two-and-a-half hours. Anna, in a state of bursting anticipation, followed Petru's lead on unknown roads, marching in step, feeling nothing but her liberated body.

Morning was near when they arrived at his door. Colentina, northeast, in deep sleep. Crowded rooms, two or three, a few beds with many little ones she saw when she entered. "It's not for me," she thought, before falling asleep on the kitchen floor of a derelict house, an uneven floor with an age-old smell of onion peels.

Enormous noises waking her, dirty little noses, sweet things wanted to see her, crawling around the blankets Petru had thrown over her. Mother, aunts, or grandmothers, putting on kettles to cook cornmeal for ten or eleven of very dark, very pretty faces. One or two of stunning beauty. Eyes black, swimming within an ivory yellowish-white, nearly all of them, except one boy whose hair was red-blond and the skin so pale one could write on it with chalk and it would not show. He sat alone, if one could call it that, at the breakfast table. "No one could be alone here," Anna thought, "it's like being Jewish. Yet it is not. In fact, totally different. The air is easier, less pressure of: faster, faster, better, better, work!" Rumbling about, bare little feet with no signs of shoes anywhere, a disarray of collectibles, all unmatched, but no shouts calling to order, a soft spoken lot. There were fiddles in different sizes, dark brown or rich red, hanging on the walls on nails, with bows on strings. Some children took their dish from the table and crawled into a corner to eat, having a heap of stones around themselves. Obviously this was their little paradise and no one minded. They did not speak or smile; they ate and played with their stones. All ages, like a set of organ pipes, unpredictable how old the bigger ones were. "This is Anna," Petru, father, uncle, or grandfather – who could tell what status? – pronounced. And he mentioned a few names of the youngsters, but soon gave up. He ate heartily of *mamaliga* with milk, exchanged a few words with someone who looked like his wife and said, so Anna could hear, "No, I don't know, it's up to her." Of course she understood. One more person would just be one too many. So she turned to Petru, having sat behind him on a chair beside a small table, clean but not that clean, and said, "May I speak to you after breakfast?"

"Yes," he said, "gladly," and they went out into a March-air morning or perhaps late morning by then.

"Petru," she said, "there are no words for thanks. I will not be able to stay. Let me sleep one or two more nights. But I cannot stay. I'll have to go and find my relatives. Family of – my husband." And this is what the pastor became from now on, her husband. Anna went to fetch her shoebox, unravelled the string, and handed Petru a twenty dollar American bill from the small cache. It was bound in cloth and also had a leather string around it.

"It is too much, it is too much, I won't take it. A whole family could live a year with twenty American dollars."

But she said, "I would give you more but it is not all mine." She couldn't easily express her thoughts or even know what they were. Petru, reticent in his ways, blushed in response and said: "It was not for any reward that I helped you. No, not for money." She knew.

ON A DREARY NOVEMBER DAY she gave birth to a very tiny baby, fully nine months after Petru had lifted her out of the multitude into his train. She had left the gypsy family in Colentina a week after her arrival, had taken the bus to town, following Petru's instructions: "Go to Lipscani Street, where all the black marketeers are. You look so different that they will recognize you instantly, so you will not have to address anyone. Exchange one or two dollars. On the street. They'll give you the proper daily rate. Do not be afraid, they are mostly more correct than shopkeepers. But play it safe. Do not show your money to anyone. Rent a room and see what you can find: work, friends, family."

And suddenly: "How old are you, Anna? You're young to be married."

"I am nineteen," she said. And that is what she remained, married at nineteen and a widow at nearly the same time. Birth and marriage certificate authentic, rubber-stamped by the Lutheran church. No death certificate of her husband. "War and the like," she explained. "You know, the Russians coming back, Romanians and Germans on the run, you know."

"Yes," Petru replied. "I do, I was there, and ours was the last train to leave the Czernowitz train station. On the twentieth of March the Russians occupied the city and countryside. You're lucky," he said.

"Yes, I am," she said. "I know, Petru, you have to run, but may I please have your address and kiss you too?"

They remained friends. At a distance. On the twentieth of November, 1944, her baby was born and she had the Merciful Sisters write to him. They had picked her up one day when she worked along the river Dâmboviţa, but she had spotted them also. It was a Grace maternity station, down river from the Senate. She had knocked at the door on a Sunday afternoon in June, saying she needed help. She did not look very big but the sisters said they were willing to have her examined, whenever their doctor was able to see her. So she came again and again; was cared for, gave her name as Anna St. Rempel, husband dead from a Russian bullet in the back at their re-conquest of the city. "You were lucky to have a husband in such times," the eldest said, looking at Anna's youthful body and hardly swelling breasts.

"Yes, I was," Anna said, keeping herself to herself and not divulging what gracious but piercing eyes wanted to know.

A tiny thing it was, transparent, a sister to elfin Martina, almost blond-white and perfect. Out of Anna's small breasts came a torrent of milk. So much, she had to share it with other young mothers. And only now she looked around herself. Mothers? Children, they were all barely fifteen or sixteen, who the Merciful Sisters, combing the streets, had picked up. The one next to her – whose baby Anna took to her breast – saying thanks, wondered if

Mother Anastasia Sofia had asked her also if she would allow her baby to be baptized or "taken to the heart of Jesus" as she put it; meaning baptized into the Catholic order of the Sisters and be brought up by them. "No," Anna said, no she hadn't. But she did one day. Two weeks after giving birth, Anna let her daughter be baptized as Maria Eufrozina. She stayed another week to recover well, came every evening to give her breast to her baby, and slept the night. Took instruction, which Anna thought came with Christian charity, but did not mind. "Christian is Christian, one way or the other. It's all about Christ, and if they kneel or make the sign of the cross and say a Hail Mary or two, it makes no difference, as long as they love my little one." So she thought in her pragmatic way. Justifying what was necessary to do.

Maria grew. She was beautiful. When a year old and walking for the first time from her hand to Mother Anastasia's hand, Anna was happy beyond anything she had ever felt. A gratitude without measure, of having been allowed that miracle. Anastasia said one day, "Just make the sign of the cross dear, and I'll kneel down beside you." Anna had never knelt down. She had never seen it. Jews stood upright before their God, and the pastor had never done it. It felt very strange, but she was Anna now and this was her child that needed love so she did not mind. When Anastasia Sofia intoned *Mother of God* she made the sign of the cross for the first time.

She fed her baby in the evening and very early morning. Washed and dressed her in donated clothes, of which the sisters had an abundant supply. There were smart little dresses, with tiny booties, embroidered hand-me-downs from rich patrons of the order in all sizes and colours. The sisters sat around the elfin child, clapped their hands so Maria would move, dance a little, and know she was loved.

One winter morning, early, Anna held Maria close, breathing in the milky scent, her own mixing into the baby's skin, the eyes looking up at her, "As if to drink her mother's face," she said. "You're mine, Maria, and we'll never be apart. You're beautiful." A picture on a wall suddenly materialized in Anna's mind. It had hung opposite her bed in Martina's room. "Yes, of course, you are the pastor's child. Such a close resemblance: Maria, my own, my gentle-limbed baby. Features as if of breakable porcelain, the finest, regular, yet entirely new." What Anna had seen silver-framed on the wall lay in her arms and on her breast, had come to life, could be smelled, kissed, cherished, fed and cleaned. Waiting for a smile before parting, Anna held her a little longer and finally said, "Little one, I have to find work. I'll leave you for a short day with all the good sisters. I'll go now to work for you, clean homes, shops, even stalls on the Lipscani." Anna had met the leather dealers, foreign-money exchangers from her first week in Bucharest. It was easy and she worked well. But when the hours of the workday were over, she could not wait to return to her little one. Breasts pressing too, she stormed the door to the Sisters of Mercy.

Two or three newborns were brought in by their mothers or found at the gate almost daily. Anna took life in an hourly way. No thought of who she was, no quarrel with the Lord. A little, very little dark boy brought in one Sunday morning she took to her breast. He looked like Petru's children, round black face with the whites of eye a gentle ivory. Anna took him to her other breast to have a dark, thick-skinned counterpart to her white-transparent elfin child. "So," she said, "now I have two. The sisters will let me have him. We'll christen him, whatever Christian creed suits them. It is all the same to me. God is everywhere, so why would He prefer –" And she let it be. She looked at her breasts, small, plumper than before, veined in reddish ropes, they were unstoppable. A flood of benediction. The more she fed her two babes, the more she could feed, and she did not see where the floodgates were for she remained slim; tall now, closer to her black son than to her white daughter in colour of skin and different from both of them. When Anna dressed in good shoes – from the Sisters' immense store of charity donations – Martina's coat on her back, a smart beret over short-cut, shiny hair, no one would have suspected a lowly cleaning lady. Literate now, avid for learning, she had a book in her left hand, manipulating her breasts into the mouths of her two children with her right hand, she read. Working at the Lipscani bookstores, she bought used books about plants, the universe out there, the names of stars and constellations, and about child rearing. No thought other than living, working, and the world that she built now of her own making.

Her breasts hurt more. A boy is a powerful little thing. She smiled at him and said, "Jon, enough is enough!" Though every day brought new little lives to the door, she decided not to accept more children to put to her breast, the tips of her breasts being all raw. And she started reducing their feeding a little, so the breasts could heal, leaving both children in the care of the sisters.

She dressed smartly and looked for different employment. Walking up the Victory Road one night, she saw a sign in a University Square pharmacy looking for help cleaning and selling cosmetics. She made a note of it, but would not enter because she was after work, and having spotted herself in the shop's window, thought she did not look her best. She waited for the next day. Entered the pharmacy to present herself to the owner, a Romanian lady called Elena Gheorghiu who, seemingly enchanted with her, hired her on the spot with what seemed to Anna an adequate salary but probably was not. But seeing young pharmacists at their work mixing something in a mortar with a pestle and talking to customers she suddenly recalled the night scene in the *Synagogengasse*, which she had forgotten or pushed down to unconscious levels. It took on such presence that she supported herself a little so as not to sway or call attention to herself. She turned to Madame Gheorghiu with a smile of thanks and left. The night of loss – shafts of lights criss-crossing the sky, and father, mother, neighbours on the truck – recreated itself and it was hard to go home in spite of breasts and time pressing. Felix's face across from her in the *Synagogengasse* pharmacy was there and she sitting on a bench, waiting for all the poor to leave. So young she was and she had to grow up so fast. Running with Felix up Saint Trinity Street to the old house, down to Marusja's cellar and out again to the Evangelical church, the pastor – all of that in so little a life.

And she sat on the steps leading to the pharmacy on that chilly day in January. It was 1945. Sat a little longer until more of the silently falling snow collected on her face, melted on her lips, and she felt her breasts again. She rose and said, "I am Anna now. A Christian. I have the right to be here. I have children to feed. Tomorrow I'll go and take the job. Eight o'clock in the morning, sharp."

The Sisters came out with a straight question, "Are you or are you not? We are behind you all the way, but we do want the truth." Anna opened the shoebox, showed her birth certificate, Lutheran. It made her out to be nineteen and the Sisters accepted it grudgingly.

Anna had grown. Her beauty a disarming unawareness. A dark appearance, but highlights in skin and hair of rusty brown shades

changing in all lights, made her look playful and young. She
blushed easily, hues of chestnut moving up almost into her hairline; she had kept an innocence, a child-bride quality. Holding
her elfin and her robust child in her arms, after they were sated,
she closed her blouse to hide her breasts. Three children they
were, holding onto each other. Yet in that innocence lay power. It
was the strength to move into every moment's necessity with ease,
to be born with its knowledge. So she held her two babes, giggled,
and they cooed back. The dark one with a violent – almost –
vivacity, the white one with reserve and elegance, but responding
just as much with smiles and dimples. *Such happy times,* Anna
thought. *The happiest. There are no better times* – and she cradled
the little ones a little longer, humming ancient melodies that
came up uncalled from the depth of past lives. Inherited, resung.
"A long line of song, linking us all," she thought, from the "Can
you count the stars in heaven?" of the pastor to the Shirha Shirim,
the song of songs of old in the *Synagogengasse*. And way back: God
is everywhere. In all songs. If He is He, the heart open to be read,
He'll read it.

And sitting by the window looking into the river, she saw a
miasma full of debris, a dirty flow, but green on both banks. All
her Sunday afternoons, she sat with the white and dark little ones,
looking into the new growth sprouting from under the snow.
Small yellow buttercups came duly up, a daisy here and there. Just
being, not much thought. And these rushing waters! Sometimes
blue like the sky and sometimes brooding, grey as lead. Once, on
such a day, she saw what looked like a little body, an infant body,
carried by the river down towards the morgue, among bottles,
refuse. She saw it. But did not move. She sat with her little ones
in her own happiness and saw the river float by with all its dead

life. *Purifying,* she thought, and did not move. And when she rose for supper or to change Maria and Jon for the night, she thought of all these poor creatures, but permitted herself no more than that.

I have work to do. We'll see. And she rose at five o'clock that Monday morning to wash, pray with the sisters, wake her children to feed them. She took milk and cold *mamaliga* for breakfast, put Martina's coat on her shoulders, and the smart brown beret on her head, and hurried to reach Elena's Pharmacy by eight o'clock sharp.

M ARTINA'S S ISTER

ARIA HAD GROWN ALMOST TO HER FULL HEIGHT AT
the age of twelve. Stronger, more muscular than her long-
lost sister Martina, with leg muscles of steel hidden by her legs'
perfect form, she could outrun a wild deer. In the gym of the public schools she climbed rope ladders to the top in record time,
jumped the "horse," circling its body three times around, holding
as if lightly onto the handle with her right arm. Slender, she had
no weight, her breasts coming but slowly.

Maria grew up among women: the Sisters of Mercy, her mother,
adopted siblings, and new, unforeseen, little lives thrown at her
door, but she had become her own unmistakable person. Her
dreams were elsewhere.

Anna had moved into the two back rooms the sisters had
granted her, had registered her order properly with the City Hall,
a nondenominational order called *God Is Everywhere*. This shield
in big, black, printed letters on white enamel, she pasted to the
front gate next to the Merciful Sisters sign. And she started her
ordinations, going to the houses of the rich, villas cradled in rose
gardens, hidden behind fences of wild vine, to ring sonorous bells

that would not wake anyone but the servants. She left a hand-written or printed page with a plea for help and word that she would return the next day at a certain hour. She took Maria from her infancy to accompany her. But not always. Anna had watched her child with amazement become someone so different from herself, a wilful, self-contained little person, who no one could teach what she refused to learn.

"Let's go to the poor," Maria said one day. "I do not like the rich, they do not open their doors, the servants look through lit-tle peep-holes before opening, and then there is a chain across. But all the derelict doors of the poor open in the summer for a draught of air." True. They called mother and daughter in and gave on the spot or, if they had nothing to give, Anna left her address to come to *God Is Everywhere* for a meal.

In her twelfth year now, Maria took up a corner in the back of the back room, surrounded it with a screen she found. A Spanish screen painted red and black on wood, a folding, fanlike triptych to protect her private space. "I am not my mother, and not my older half-sister Martina of whom I have heard since birth. And I will not do God's command according to my mother and the Merciful Sisters." And she started, on Sundays, to get up early and leave without permission. The circus was in town. "I've seen the clowns in the streets," she thought, without saying anything to anyone.

But she liked the very little lives. Bathed them, fed them, wiped their running noses, spoke soothingly to still the crying spasms of the newborns. She spoke and she sang in low tones, in whispers meant solely for the one she held. They knew that voice of pity and smiled in recognition. "But I won't give you all my life, you sweet, needy things. I'll hold you for a moment, because we are so lost without one another. But I'll leave, I'll go tomorrow morning. Early."

She woke towards dawn, startled by familiar sounds at the back gate, hinges screeching, dogs barking, furtive steps, and the sharp hunger cry. Maria ran towards the window, caught a glimpse of a shadowy figure running, and heard the gate lock click. She grabbed the woollen scarf her mother had knitted for her. She had hung it onto the Spanish screen, cursed impatiently as it wouldn't come loose, at last succeeded and threw it around her shoulders. "I won't do this forever, this is my last little one. Oh, the miserable living things, I love them so. No, I won't give them all my life." But she was down in a hurry, barefoot, knotting her scarf tighter, feeling the chill of pre-morning as she stepped out of the back door. A newspaper bundle, a dirty cord to bind it, and a small two-year-old perhaps on the upper step: this is what she found. Maria could not tell how old he really was, though she had seen so many and was as expert in telling their ages as any old, wise woman would be. But this was different; she loved him instantly. Her own. A possession, as if engendered and carried. Thrown upon this corner step too close to the door. She cursed these mothers: "They always do that, these criminal mothers, they misjudge the opening of the door. I could have flung him down to the ground had I not known what they do. But here he is. I can't tell yet what he looks like with all that newsprint on his skin."

Maria rushed up to the corner sink. The water, cool to the touch, did not feel uncomfortable so she decided not to wait to heat a cauldron, but let the cool water into the sink and submerged the young body. He squealed with delight. Wrapping an old linen around him with his head on the hollow of her shoulder and neck she felt the stab of parting: "How will I leave you, little Alexander?" she said, smiling at having him christened the name of her father, the pastor. "I am a funny girl. How can I run away and be my own master if I bind myself to another one?" But it was a stab, the sharp cut of love and leaving.

She put him in the community kitchen upon a high table that her mother had begged for from a bombed-out hospital on the north side of Bucharest and had carried home with the help of unknown men who saw Anna struggling. She had smiled at them, Anna's smile. Maria thought, "It could break hearts or bind them forever. We're slaves to it. We'll do anything to see it light up her dark eyes. It has the power to force you into an obedience no fist could achieve. And when it is off her brow, God does not seem to be everywhere. For me, it resides in there; It made me helpless without it when I was a child of six or seven. Even now my mother's face, when it creases around her eyes announcing good times, thrills me, and I know the break must come soon. Every joint in my ankles yearns to run from it. And yet I stay for another day. I've seen the clowns and I will go. Alexander, my child, and Anna, my mother, I will leave you both. But first things first. I have a little work to do."

On to that high table Maria put the young body. And she looked at this most perfect human child: a crown of brown curls, a laurel wreath around the forehead, delicate features to fill your heart. With a closer look she found that the left leg was a little shorter than the right one. Stretched them both by applying gentle strength to both knees and truly found them different. "Let it not worry me," she sang for Alexander and for him alone in her seductive voice. "The world will love you the more, my limping angel."

Maria did not leave that Sunday. But she honed her skills and went out for an hour or two every day to the school gym to bend her back, fold it, and knit it until it rolled over the polished oak floor like a ball. The first time she did it, her back curved backward so that toes and fingers interlaced; the youths around her made room for her, applauded: *Do it again, do it again.* When she did, they lifted her – head safely tucked within her arms – and threw her to waiting open arms across the gym. She had an act ready! But she kept it to herself, not to wipe the smile off her mother's face. In the evenings she sat by her mother's sewing machine to watch and learn. A tailor's granddaughter, Maria learnt fast the ancient art. She sat late into the evening with her little Alexander in her arms, next to Anna treading the Singer. These were the best of their hours. And they talked to each other; the mother knew the daughter would go, "There is no binding her," because Maria would break all fetters and she would go without a kiss. "So I will, at her sixteenth birthday, tell her that I know and she may go with my blessing. I will keep Alexander for her until she retrieves him if she so wishes," Anna thought, watching her daughter.

And Maria in turn looked at her mother, at her profile and her rich black hair held by a black ribbon freeing her face. "How beautiful she is. How simply she carries herself. No need for that hair to soften her features, she can pull it all away, expose her forehead, supported by eyebrows, long, comfortable, not worried ones that cut eyes and forehead in two. A serenity." But the daughter had to go. Every muscle ached to run. "It is not for me. I can't sew white linen, wash and bleach it and beg at people's doors. I can't see birth and death from morning till night.

"It's not for me. I want colour, lime, yellow, ochre, glitter, silk, jade, jet. Not white sheets and dying babies. I'll keep Alexander.

I know she'll want him too, but no, I'll take him along. He is slow to speak but understands everything. Points with his fingers, but I have not heard one little word. Of course he'll limp. It's in the hip somewhere. The left leg being a little shorter and toes moving inward."

Every Sunday Maria went to the Martian Fields on the edge of town where the circus had set up tent, and she smiled at a stable boy who was about her age, or perhaps just a wee bit older and she offered to groom the horses for a little riding instruction. "Well," the gypsy-looking boy asked, "well, have you ever been near a horse?"

"No, never," she said. "But I can do everything – almost. I'll groom the horses, clean the stable, all Sunday, for one hour of instruction, but it has to be the right way and no other."

"Well, can you mount a horse?"

"Show me," she said. At the first try she was up there. Muscles tensed in the arch of her foot, and she swung herself onto an unbridled horse as if born to it.

"Come down," he shouted, "this is not a tame little lady. She is wild."

"So am I," Maria threw back at him, took a short gallop, but returned obediently. She was in heaven. She carried manure, lifted it, heaped it with enormous flat forks, swung the cling-ing, smelly stuff on a compost heap, running back and forth with a lightness of foot and heart that made her sing. All morn-ing until one o'clock when she said to the astonished young man, who sat against the wall of the tack room waxing and shining the leather gear, "May I mount the lady one more time? And please correct what I do wrong." He rose to help her, touched her hip lightly to push it into proper position and their eyes met. She shivered just a little, but forgot it instantly over the joy of having done it right.

"I'll be here next Sunday," she said. "And my name is Maria," she called back, turning her head for a goodbye.

The *Clowns* ARE IN TOWN

ALEXANDER WAS MUTE, OR HAD DECIDED NOT TO BOTHER with words. They just went away so fast, he thought, they did not seem to stay, and one could not look at them again. It was better to draw because one could change it the next day. He wouldn't speak, you couldn't fix it, change it, once uttered. He was worried he'd hurt Maria's feeling or Anna would not smile at him. It was too dangerous. They flew away. Once sounded, words had wings. He thought he could paint them. And oh, he would. He'd draw them hiding in thick branches, or on a dark day they'd mingle with a cloud and suddenly they would rain back at them and they'd all cry. He could think and paint much better. Anyway, he thought he did not look like people. He walked crookedly, moved sideways instead of what he saw in other children who surged forward like shot from a slingshot. He did not mind his leg. It made him think more, he did not have to hurry, get sweaty and wild. Though sometimes he'd love to catch a ball a little faster so the bullies wouldn't call him cripple. Oh, and yes, the Sisters yesterday said something – you see, because he did not speak, they thought he did not hear, so they talked to each other as if he were made of air, or did not live. They said, well not all of them but Eudoxia, who knelt all the time in front of the Virgin Mother and fed her burning candles, paper roses, and flowers – Alex always wondered why that pretty picture would want all of that and her kneeling and crying – well, where was he? Yes, Eudoxia. She said, while peeling potatoes, to the others around there, he did not recall anymore who it was, she said to them, "There is no doubt, Satan has struck that child." *Dracu* she really said, meaning just that. "Look at him, he sits like a stone, eyes cast down, his left foot turned inward, a clubfoot, I'm sure. We have to do something about it, or the devil will take us all. Devils are known to get into the weak part of children, on the left mainly, take a hold, real root and jump into others on a day perhaps one hasn't said one's prayers."

"So what are we to do?" they asked, looking at him in horror.

"Pray and exorcise," she said. A silence followed when he really sat like a stone. His dear left foot twitched, kicked the right one, hurt as it never did, the toes felt as if attached by wire and not his. He was just a little boy, why would the devil want to go into his left hip now? He heard it creak as if the hinges were rusted. But he wouldn't go to Maria, his mother, or Anna, his grandmother, they did not have a creaking left hip and left toes attached by wire as if they were someone else's. So they might not understand, worry and talk to each other in low tones, and then he would be truly alone. Yes, he felt that one day, when the two whispered to each other, knowing full well that he understood everything, particularly if it was about himself. But they lowered their voices and he wondered and tried hiding his tears, because they did not want to see them. They wanted him happy. They'd give him chalk and paper, push him to say at least Ma – perhaps Ma-ria or Ma-ma or just simply Ma. They planted themselves, Anna mostly, in front of him, closing their lips, pressing them tightly and made him say *Mmmm* – he did it for them in the throat, but then it wouldn't come out and they let him be. This was how he liked it. And he was happy for most of the time, and the other times – he kept to himself.

He drew with chalk, with crayons, or coal, even a pebble would do. Anna told him stories, which he painted on pieces of paper, on walls, on doors, on any surface that would allow it. They scolded him when they found the newly varnished door to *God is Everywhere* decorated at the base with bright yellow flowers. They were hanging from a blue sky on their green stems. A little upside down of course, houses stood on chimneys sometimes, smoke falling downwards, things on the left were often on the right. But he liked them this way – some of his letters, he didn't know many, but some turned the other way: p's were g's and d's were b's. Well, he thought they were more beautiful this way. He drew a baby Jesus in the arms of his mother, his left leg just a little shorter than the right one. My mother was Maria also, so he gave Mary flaxen hair and a black beauty spot on her left cheek.

It worried him: is it true? If God was everywhere how could there be a devil on his left side? It was hard to fall asleep with such thoughts. No, he wouldn't utter a word, it would just fly up, sit on a thick cloud for a while and then rain back, soaking them all. And then he'd cry.

Maria, looking on Alexander's countenance, saw a contemplative face; tears now and then. "He knows us all, and more than anyone that young should," she thought.

The animals had left first; the tents were folded, stakes still in the ground had to be lifted, arranged, numbered and marked to ease the successive pitching. Maria came early that Sunday, the last one in September. Leaves singly on the ground were edged in gold, and the last rays of the declining day brought a shade of amber to the still green of Martian Fields.

She had said goodbye to her mother for the day and taking her Angelus – Alexander with her for the first time, called back at the door, "Anna dear, Alex and I are having a picnic out on the Martian Fields. My basket is heaped with your goodies, and thank you for your *Sabbath* bread, your *Challah*. Don't worry, we'll be back." But she thought, *To go and not to come back would be so wonderful.* No tears, no goodbyes; no hugs, no kisses. But no, it was unthinkable. She would not leave like a thief in the night. She closed the gate gently and made her way to the bus line with Alex by her side. He was six years old now – by her estimation – and would not sit any more astride on her shoulders as he had done before.

People made room for them to get onto the first steps of Bus Number One. This was a mighty Bucharest artery, the Number One line leading from the centre of town past the huge markets where smells of green, red, and ochre peppers, and melons in green stripes and yellow stripes, mingled with seared chicken feathers. It hit one at a certain station approaching the market, and one knew without the driver announcing it where one was. It led to the Colentina; gypsy women sitting on all corners, small, lit-coal tin-ovens in front of them offering popped corn or melon seeds in season, perfectly roasted. Maria, getting down from the bus, looked at her son's eyes and knew she had to get one of those rolled newsprint cones filled with melon seeds.

She found a peasant wagon and hired the people to get them both to the Martian Fields. She had always walked that remaining distance, but realized she couldn't today with Alex and the basket on her arm. She had loved that walk. It led her over the Colentina lake: an even mirror on sunny days, it was lead-black, boiling up with foamy crests on stormy ones, and rolling back towards the centre of the lake the waves were a metre high. Maria would outrun their coming to shore; so swift, so sure of herself she was. She gauged her power, fought like a prize fighter insulting the opponent: "Don't you threaten me, I'll outrun and beat you every time" – as she used to throw herself into churning water which had lost its lustre, ancient mud having swum up to the surface. Not today. She regretted it. Maria was a true swimmer. She could swim on her back, propelled by coordinated small movements of her arm-leg-fins. "I was born in the lake, I'm sure," she thought as she emerged one Sunday – clouds hanging low, about to burst – laughing as any winner would. Not today. She passed it by, sitting with Alexander next to the sour-butter smelling peasant on the shore, regretting it a little. "Another time," she thought.

He had waited for her, that slim, brown, curly-haired boy. He had worked since daybreak, as there are no hours for circus people. The tents were down, folded and numbered and Maria, setting her basket on the ground said, "I brought my son along Mister... What is your name?"

"Daniel," he said. "Call me Dan." And he turned to Alexander to ask for his. Alex smiled, opened his mouth, and a lovely sound of Aa emerged to the joy of his mother, who said "Call him Alex," and the ice was broken. Chalk and coal, a huge piece of brown wrapping paper fastened by two stones was enough to keep him busy, but the little boy ran after Dan to hand him things and look at him. A woman's boy, Alex had seen boy-children but boy-men he had not. Trying to straighten his left foot or hide it behind the other to make a good impression made Maria proud of him, and she said to Dan, "Do not mind him, he limps a little, but he is the best boy on earth."

"Certainly he is," Dan said, showing his good nature, his white strong teeth and crow's feet around his eyes. He picked Alex up, whirling him like a baton around his right arm, circus-fashion, then sat him down saying, "Be good," and both Maria and Dan forgot all about him, getting at their work. Leather gear had to be cleaned and waxed, hemp cords braided, horseshoes freed of stones and nails, and countless paraphernalia thrown into boxes. Dan tired, sweat collected in pearls under his hairline, but not Maria. Everything was easy. Her own body of boundless energy astounded her. She did not know it. Dan sat down on a remaining footstool and said, *Do this, do that,* and Maria did it as if she had always done it. Shoulder blades of invisible strength were there to carry iron junk without aching. And ankles, knees, and hips unconnected, seemed free of the earth when she ran across the Field.

Last Sunday, when the tents still stood, she had climbed up the rope ladder to the trapeze. And without any instruction had grabbed the bar with the assurance of a gorilla in the trees and thrown her body to the dangling trapeze across, caught it, swung herself into its seat to the horror of everyone on the ground. They had scolded and shouted: *You are going to ruin us all, you'll kill yourself and we're in trouble, don't do this.* But she had sat, clapped her hands, showing them the strength and balance in her thigh muscles, before finally obeying and waiting for "the princess" to come to take her on her back ladder, which she climbed down backwards. They had never seen anything like it. And the "princess" said, "If you want to apprentice with me, you can join. With very little money, mind you, we're poor. You'll get a share from the take, but only according to an apprentice's status, and not always."

"God – who is everywhere – is good to me, gracious and forgiving," she said. The princess, Claudette, giggled a little at this unctuous mention of higher powers. But she had seen everything, the praying and the cursing, so she just shook her head and said to Maria in parting, "You have a little infirm boy. Bring him too, we do not mind. Children are born and we can't help it. Bring him with you, or else you'll worry and won't be good for anything."

That was last Sunday. How to part! How to pick up this or that to take? And what to leave? She let the days pass and left with Alexander the following Sunday morning, going for a picnic only. She truly thought she'd come back at night, take a few things, winter clothes perhaps, a trinket or two, but she did not that night. Having missed the Colentina Number One bus, she decided to stay in the princess's wagon with Alex, having been invited to do so. She cuddled with Alex in the bed next to Claudette, woke in the morning to brewing coffee, black bread and butter. The small, rickety table was next to the wagon window; a sheer curtain was slightly off the hooks in a corner because of so much wear and tear. It permitted a soft eastern sun to warm the earthen cup to a gilded bronze, and Maria was happy. Claudette's lazy pajamas, shiny with old silk, trailed half-open, buttons hanging loosely. Her once magnificent breasts moved within the graceful circles of her body. Maria was happy. It was a small, enclosed quarter with a comfort of shelter, and away from the serious eyes of the sisters, whose breasts Maria had never seen.

Maria, sipping coffee slowly and holding the brown cup, hugging it like a chalice with both hands, lifted it to her lips as if she were alive for the first time. The tart-bitter taste, an aroma of spice in the air, the closeness of the wagon walls and the sensuous touch of Claudette's breasts made Maria giggle. "I'm in fairy land," she said to Claudette. "This is not real."

And Claudette, pouring her a second cup: "Oh, I wish mine were made of that stuff. Mine was all too real. My father taught us the trade, whipped us into shape, three boys, and myself the youngest, and my fabulous, inexpressibly beautiful mother. Not more beautiful than you are. No one is. You should have seen her. There is something about you, Maria, that reminds me of her. Your paper skin, lucid almost, one could think the sun looks through. You're not yet as tall as she was, but you will be. You're young yet. After the brute left with a younger circus princess, taking most of the equipment with him, we remained what you have seen. A modest outfit, with horses, clowns, and trapeze artists who come and go. My mother was content. Well, we'll talk again. If you'd like to join us, we'll be good to you."

Maria watched in astonishment. She had never experienced such freedom. Claudette stripped off her bottom pajamas, revealing a tight, light-brown body, muscles showing on calf and thigh as if drawn by brown coal, her womanly hair moving up to the navel almost. Naked now, she pulled an enamel bowl from under the bed into the middle of the room, filled it with water from the corner pail with a cup hanging from a string on a nail. Filled the small tub and, giggling, she spread her legs wide above it, striding it. Bent her knees with the elegance of a rider and proceeded to soap her rich sex with white lather. Maria had never seen anything so irresistibly beautiful. But a sudden sensation of heat streaming to her cheeks frightened her. "It's the coffee," she thought. "I should not drink coffee."

But that wasn't the answer. She had to lean back against the wall to feel her body take over as she watched through lowered eyelids Claudette rinsing the soapy lather with a fresh cup of water. Claudette, giggling and joking about all the mess she had made, threw the water from the tub through the opened door from the upper step, naked as she was. And Maria knew she would love her forever.

Coloured balls, red, green and blue on an old abacus, moving and sounding when pushed or thrown, kept Alexander busy. He seemed delighted when given the little petticoat he had discovered in the corner. It had rushes around it, patches of flowers appliquéd, of the fantastic sort: nothing one could call a rose. Just immense petals in ochre yellow on green stems. It was a trapeze artist's mini-dress, and it hung from his midriff to the floor, hiding his left leg. But it was cumbersome, and he took it off, dressed himself with his clothes from home, and spread it into a big circle; it lay there making a perfect flowerbed on the wagon floor.

He was pensive as usual. Liked it here but was not sure. Having bed, table, wash basin, and all things crowding one another left no floor for him. Where would he spread his papers to draw on? It was cozy and warm, but the floor was wet now, the drops of water hitting him he had wiped away. He felt unimportant, ignored, had watched his mother leaning against the wall, Claudette above her little tub, and it was theatre to him. Entertaining. He giggled a little. But he wouldn't want it for every day. And went on listening to the sound of the coloured balls on his abacus, a sound so different if two or three were hitting the frame than ten or twelve rolling on their metal bars. He could almost sing the difference, slight as it was. With his strong right arm, Alexander made them fall faster, louder, and throwing the abacus into the corner jumped to his feet, glad to hear his mother say, "We are going home."

THE PARTING

ANNA HAD KNOWN FOR A LONG TIME THAT HER DAUGHTER would leave her. Repeated Sunday outings, increased weekday gym training, and a certain melancholy in Maria's features made her think of her own adolescent captivity. The silence Maria kept at mealtime, the impatient anxiousness to leave the table, her angry glances at the gregarious Sisters, and the furtive goodnight kisses brought Anna's angst back, her anger at the benefactor pastor. Master-husband to be, dispenser of small comforts or praise: she had run out several times in the last few months before the wedding, had taken the other staircase, the one leading to the steeple attic that wound itself around her own, had slipped out of the back door into the garden. The night, thick with unfamiliar overgrown bushes, was black, full of fearful sound, water dripping. A stone she had pushed, a pebble only, rolling had the thunder of an avalanche. *Better,* she had thought, *better to die right here in freedom than living shackled to the walls.* But it was a passing thought. The stubbed toe, perhaps bleeding, the soil clinging to the naked sole, made her find her way back. She leant a while longer against the wall, breathing the night air with that melancholy mix of joy and despair that Anna saw now in Maria's features. She knew she couldn't hold her daughter any longer, or she'd run at night without a goodbye. So Anna stood at the window to watch for a moment's return at least. To take leave, to ask perhaps if Maria would take the little velvet pouch with her. Or was it too much to ask, at this time, to heavy a burden? She spotted her daughter and Alexander crossing the street towards her door. "Oh, how lovely she is! How grown, tall, subtle, smiling now to her son. Oh, God is everywhere, if you only see Him!" And she ran to the gate, to take them both into her arms.

"MARRY ME," the stable boy had said on that last Sunday on the Martian Fields outside of Bucharest. "Marry me," he had said. "We'll just take six of our horses, Claudette, the tent, and all the horse paraphernalia, now that the big animals and their trainers have left us. Marry me, I'll adopt your boy, mute and crippled as he is. I like him. Marry me and we'll be a company of three. I'll do the clowning, all the stable work and we'll set out. We'll hire help on the road as we need it. You'll be the queen. Claudette is getting older. She can repair, sew costumes, clean – you know."

"No," she replied, "I can't marry anyone. I have to be chaste like my mother. In different ways, but chaste. I've seen too much."

"And what is it you've seen?"

"Look, you're a sweet boy, but I've seen too many tiny bodies in bloody wrappings thrown at our door."

"And why – why would this –?"

"Well, you'll laugh at this. But my body is for myself. I won't have anyone – well, I'll be chaste. I do not even kiss Claudette, though she can't give me any babies. I'd rather stand on my head, climb ladders, swim three miles, or run. No, it's not for me."

But Maria accepted the company. It was time to leave. She had stayed two more years with her mother after that first Sunday, and when Dan had appeared at her door one day, she knew it was time. Grown to nearly six feet, a dancer, she could not take a cup from a cupboard without standing on one leg and stretching the other. Of sunny disposition, she did not expect trouble; met others, their opinions or malice, with a shrug or "Oh dear," and didn't take them on for a fight. She still did all the work required of her in *God Is Everywhere* to earn her keep, but when Dan was at the door she said yes to the small company – one or two more had swelled it – she was ready to go. "I'll come tomorrow. Eight o'clock in the morning. I need one day more for my mother."

They sat all day with each other. Anna had not aged much in those sixteen years since Maria's birth. Dark skinned, she had remained young; just a few lines across her forehead to parallel her Jewish almond eyes, her "oriental traits" as she laughingly called them. They sat together, this dark, ripe woman and her long-legged, light-coloured child, held hands and talked. "I'm always here for you. I'll hear your call. Come back or not, but know that I'll come if you can't."

"I know," the daughter, "I know."

"Maria, there is a duty to fulfill. Your father went to the ghetto and was entrusted with a piece of jewellery." And Anna brought the shoe box out into the front room, undid the string, the same one the pastor had tied secure, and opened it to show Maria her papers, baptism, fake birth certificate, and marriage. "These were times," she said smilingly, "you could not easily comprehend, but Maria –" And she took the gems out of their wrappings to show them to Maria, "To blind one's eyes," Maria said. There were three times eighteen diamonds in increasing sizes, all set in gold, on a heavy chain. The mother put them back and said, "They belong to Felix and Süssel's mother. This has to be returned, if not to her, to her heirs, and time does not matter, Maria."

Both women sat silently near the window a little longer, and as the day progressed, with mealtimes, children crying, running in and out of Maria's bedroom, they busied themselves with collecting necessities. For Alexander mainly, who had grown taller than expected. Pants needed lengthening, shirtsleeves cut into short sleeves, and holes in pockets had to be repaired. Anna, the tailor's daughter did it all, fast, painstakingly accurate. And Maria fell around her neck, saying, "You're the greatest mother there is." "It's my ancestors," she replied, "born with needle and thread in their hands, not me. So it comes to me honestly and it will to you too. One day."

Basics, the very basics assembled, an unslept night, hugs and kisses all around, Maria, as mute now as her son, took a fast leave. At eight o'clock in the morning she stood in front of the *God Is Everywhere* sign on the door and saw Dan approaching to help her carry the few bundles. And they left. Her mother at the window. No one raising a hand in farewell, and no visible tears.

THEY ARRIVED IN ITALY by way of the southern Romanian plain, across the Danube, through Belgrade. Stayed mainly in little towns and villages. The company was small and not in competition with mighty, noisy, rich outfits. The six horses had gone down to four; the princess Claudette more and more incapacitated, left Dan and two slow-minded helpers in charge of their care. But then there was Maria. A heroine now in Claudette's fringed, jet-black sequins, with gold and turquoise overlaid on a dancer's short skirt, white-gold hair held tightly by plumes of all shades, she was a star. Riding her horses, standing on one foot to use the other for a fast change onto the rope ladder and back again, she was fearless. And seeing her move from the back of the one to the back of the other and then in a frenzied succession up the ladders to the trapeze and finally back to horseback, the crowd roared.

But they did not go into the big centres. Villagers, the poor, the landless, often vagrant, and the hardworking peasants of that mixed Slavic-Latin folk were their audience. And they were given a high-class spectacle, for a few *leva*, crowns or *lira*, wherever the company stopped. A simple tent, a small manège, but a wild show. The three clowns with Dan in the centre and the two mind-less boys had been joined by Alexander. All united into a mimicry that spoke ancient tongues, had faces that showed what we know without going to school. And Alexander shone, doing nothing. Just being there. A child, knowing everything as well, from humiliation to elation. Theirs was a simple routine, with Alex-ander playing the outcast, trying desperately to get in on the jokes; being always repelled, he stood there thinking hard how "to make it." The crowd was his from the moment he set foot in the ring and from his first attempt to trick the territorial conspiracy of the three, whom the people jeered at and hooted at and hated to their heart's content.

Alexander had painted the big surfaces of the tents with a great *A*, being a little person against the world. The world of the three. And children came to see themselves versus the cruel, incompre-hensible, exclusive world of adults.

Their renown grew by word of mouth and from village to village, down the Croatian coast of the Adriatic and across to the little islands. In Krk, that Adriatic island with the funny name of three consonants, a glowing red gem of an island in a green sea, they stayed the longest. Islanders regarded them as their own tourist attraction, and when the season was over, *The Big A* became their very own. Maria had time to hone her trapeze act, which began as a more primitive flying, catching and sitting upside-down, almost the same things she had done when she first flung herself upon it. But now with a body of seemingly limitless ability, she created an act, taking Alexander with her. She would fly to the trapeze, holding him in her arms, having rescued him from his frustrating earthly existence below. Like an angel she would swoop down from her swinging heaven, pick him up into her strong arms, and no one could tell that she tied him with a fast stroke to herself to have a least one arm free for the trapeze. And then she let him run down the rope ladder, to the wild enthusiasm of the house. It was almost symbolic of his life: brought in swaddling paper to the backdoor of *God Is Everywhere,* he was rescued, cuddled, and loved. And he painted now. Larger and larger. Enormous hyper-flowers that had never seen the day except on tent sides, on pieces of brown packing paper, or any flat slate stone he could find. A cornucopia bell-tulip three metres high greeted the crowd at the ticket door on the one side and *The Big A* on the other. He often took the money in, if the two slow-witted helpers had other things to do, things that always came up in a low-budget business: a horse had eaten too much and had to be helped to release the gas or a thorn was somewhere in its flesh, or a pole in the centre had wobbled and endangered the whole show. They were a good team, their own masters, and shared the take. Not absolutely equally, but almost.

Every free moment Alexander drew. Landscapes, mountains, and rivers, and everywhere winged horses, winged Marias, spread across the sky above, to cover, to protect the earth. Having a few mild winters in Krk and a few breezy summers with hardly any packing or pulling of stakes to be done, he roamed the coast on his own. Loved and known by the villagers as "The little A," he was welcomed into their kitchens. Sat with the women, peeled their potatoes, played with their dogs, and discovered one day that he sat on a kitchen floor made of squarish stone pieces. Fish he discerned, small crosses, faces, lions perhaps; it was a mosaic-floor of the early Christian era, with silent-speaking symbols. The villagers knew what they had and kept it from the museum's hungry wolves. When Alexander with questioning eyes pointed to the fish on the floor, the woman put her fingers to her lips with a *sh-sh-sh* sound; he understood a secret and thought about it for a long time. He went home to their wagons and did not divulge anything.

They now had three very comfortable wagons: one for Claudette, Maria and him; one for Dan; and one for the two helpers. The wagons had motors attached to them, and as the troupe's fame spread by word of mouth, they could afford more modern things. But Alexander loved old things. The mosaic in the women's kitchen, broken here and there, had spiritual power to haunt his imagination. *It has been here for a long, long time, made by people mute like myself but telling of their deep conviction. A story in pictures, it was meant for me.* He thought of them all as his fathers, as he had never known his own, speaking to him, their son, of love. *They have called me to sit on their handiwork so I can hear them,* he thought. *It is my world.* And he started to draw fish, winged, enormous fish, Maria riding them, and some smaller ones with little boys on them, one leg longer than the other. He added small crosses or sweet, smiling, halved Maria faces. He spread any piece of brown paper and glued it to castaway old rags. He fitted pebbles, an odd shell – these sound-endowed, convoluted miracles – with fluted grasses to create the world, the one he listened to.

Maria and Claudette scolded him for having taken up all their room. He smiled his wickedest smile in reply and the next day in front of the tent, a half-hour before the show, he displayed his art, offering it for sale. Heaps of painted shards he showed, torn ends of shopping bags he had transformed into earth, sky, and winged creatures in orange-ochre next to a furious red, mingling or taking over. For any money and for nothing he sold them, for two eggs, a fresh loaf of bread, a sausage, or last year's calendar. But a replica of the cornucopia bell-tulip in sky-blue, a big *A* threaded through, he offered in an auction after the show with the permission of Maria, who introduced it, saying that they needed money to repair the tent, poles, and ropes. She shouted *Help* in all the Balcanic tongues available to her. And the hands went up, throwing the money into the clowns' hats as Maria called out the last bid.

Alexander had done it. He had saved them from the strictly hand-to-mouth operation. But as the money came in, the team broke apart, perhaps by coincidence, or because it had achieved its goals – in either case it crumbled. Claudette fell ill with cancer and could not be saved, the slow-witted helpers were paid off, the three other dear brown horses were sold to good people, and the tent folded. But to say goodbye to Giselle, a mare of strength, with subtle knowledge of her mistress's wishes, was the bitterest task of all;. Maria had looked after Giselle herself for a long time.

She had groomed her, braided her mane and tail with streamers, the colours of *The Big A*, ochre browns and rose pink.

Giselle was Maria's. She had acquired her somewhere near Brescia in Italy for little money, for a written contract that she would look after her lovingly, never sell her for dog food, and would put her to sleep when Giselle was old or infirm. How to part from one that was your arm, your leg, your very soul? Giselle knew all the secrets. She knew her mistress's sleepless nights, she knew her torn tendons, responding and shouldering her burden. An intimacy. A bond. The true *other* without whom one cannot live. Like God. A partner on the road. And they spoke sweetly to each other, in tongues unrecorded, ancient, and more rooted than all the ones wagged by men. But Giselle was getting older, a little slower to rise to all Maria's whims, and visibly sadder. Or so Maria thought one day when Giselle took more time in the ring than was allowed to her. Split-second timing, catching Maria on her return from the trapeze was indispensable. And in the evening of that unsuccessful turn, when Maria had torn a leg muscle in a failed effort to reach Giselle, Maria fell upon Giselle's neck in tears. And she took Maria's head into the hollow of her mighty neck in an animal union of deepest love.

But it was sealed and both knew. Parting. They worked a little longer yet, as if life was reversible, or the end not yet reached. But it was on Krk that Maria said goodbye, the last one, to Giselle. She walked with her, leading her by the bit, which Giselle loved. It had always been a sign of reward. She liked to chew Maria's fingers or touch them through the bit. Giselle pushed Maria's lower arms to make her lead holding the bit or go for walks together outside the tent through the fields. *Oh, you wicked thing*, Maria scolded her. *I know what you want. To eat me, all of me, starting with my little finger.* But she loved to feel the nudge on her lower arm and willingly gave herself to Giselle.

So on a brilliant, early summer day, when the sea was as blue-green as the sky above, Maria took her by the bit and Giselle let herself be led. Maria, for a while silent on the road, suddenly pushed Giselle to run a little because she had felt Giselle's impatient muscles trembling in the slow trot, so they both took a fast gallop. Then they halted and Maria mounted her for the last leg of the journey. Slowly riding and talking into her ear. "We'll say goodbye beloved. We'll kiss and say goodbye. And I'll be with you and the woman vet who will help us. Let's not be sad. We had the greatest love to share than any one was ever given." Her voice losing tone a little, Giselle's ears went up, and Maria didn't know if she knew.

For seven days Maria mourned. She sat in her wagon barefoot and mourned. The Jewish way. Her mother had once said to her, "If you suffer an irreplaceable loss, sit down, like my ancestors the Jews, sit down barefoot and grieve. Pray if you can or know how, and if not invent the words. God Is Everywhere. He'll hear you, comfort you, and you will live and relive your love. One can't go on to the next thing – take seven days. Sometimes life does not grant them to you. But if there are seven days that you can take out, assemble those you love or still have around you." There was Alexander and Dan, but she asked them to go to the shore, to that high rocky shore, overlooking the blue-green until it flowed into its sky. To dip into these waters that clad your skin, anointed it with salted oil, was to come out saved, was to return from it as another. "Go," she said to them. But she wouldn't. Not today. She hugged them both and said, "Go, go, go children. Here is money, I had promised Alexander a guitar. Here it is. Go out to the arm where swimming is best and then go to town."

Maria let the curtains down, seated herself on the floor against the wall, and thought back. As far back as the Merciful Sisters. But their prayers did not suit her, neither did her mother's God Is Everywhere. So she sat silently, her tears welling up. She had lost her love.

It was spring and it was summer. The town was lazy. There was little incentive to rise in the morning, and whatever wish there was to better oneself was interfered with by Tito's communism, with its lies and shabby work; but the inventive genius of the little man trying to make ends meet silently celebrated the seasons. Time standing still for a while was so good for Maria. There were two new wagons left stationed outside the town on the island; the villagers regretted the folding of the tent. Children beating the remaining drums were permitted to do so, and Alexander, who used to chase them with sticks, let them do as they wished. He sat down and drew them. Painted a monstrous contraption with lions and jaguars on its periphery and in the centre all the little ones. Derelict rubber hoses, sticks, cudgels, and soup ladles in crazy colours he attached to it. A butter churn dominated in canary yellow, huge marbles sticking to it, with very different faces at a closer look. All drawn with coloured pencils he had found or was given by the children for the gift of a piece of painted paper.

Paper in a communist country, like everything else that depended on the state, came unpredictably and disappeared fast into an unfillable, bottomless need. Wrappings were of the crudest paper, but Alexander used the ungainly, roughened texture to heighten relief, shadowing cool into the valleys, cutting the torn edges to diamond-oval or square, glued it with fish skin to a piece of wood or board, which the wind had carried, held it up, and asked for a price. Audiences swelled to his Sunday afternoon auctions and the island of Krk had found its homegrown master. He remained modest, started at a very low price, not to frighten the villagers, but when tourists, from East Germany mainly but from everywhere else, flocked to the unique event on Sunday afternoon, he became bolder.

He worked all week. As long as the tent stood, he had plenty of room to spread paper or the occasional canvas, but now he worked outside the wagon on sunny days and inside the wagon in his own corner. Shards of all kinds, earless jugs, footless candy dishes, a rusty roaster he dignified; no object was too humble for transformation, rebirth, or the acquisition of a new role. So the money rolled in, and Alexander, speechless and limping, was bread-and-joy giver. He decided, not trusting banks, the state or anyone else, to let Maria keep the money. He took all currencies, and at night on Sundays when lots of tourists had come to the auction, he poured the fortune out of a Maria-made and Alexander-painted cotton bag, pulled the top string, and the three of them marvelled at the German *Marks*, Austrian *Schillings*, Bulgarian *leva*, Romanian *lei*, Czech *korona*, *francs* Swiss and French. Marvelled and learned. Perhaps it was no fortune at all. But to these three innocents, the whole world had come. Arranging the monies in heaps, strings around the different denominations, they built their hopes around it.

And it was a summer like no other would ever be. It was divorced from the past and free from the training, the worry about health or sickness of man and animal; they rose to go swimming, the two of them, Dan and Maria. On weekdays Alexander joined them for their picnic, his hands, pants, and face in the colours available that day, to the laughter of Maria, Dan, the passing-by villagers or tourists. He was proud of it. Took the laughter for fame and notoriety: an island institution of his own making. Then he undressed in their own cove – discovered by Dan one day – and dipped into Adriatic waters. He swam well, making up for his shorter leg with his whole other side, and when he emerged, naked, tall now, he became a young Apollo to put all Greeks to shame. He was careful when climbing on the rocks to the two of them up there; then he changed into clothes Maria had brought and stretched into the sun. There was little shade at noon, or ever. Small bushes of the subtropical sort, short-clipped roots clinging to stone, if cypress or creeping evergreen.

Shores like these had suffered through the ages every kind of seafarer. From before the Phoenicians, then Greeks and Romans, Arabs, Jews and every other pirate had robbed, had plundered the woods for their ships, before setting off or staying for a while. Perhaps goats had taken the poor remaining grasses, and the shore redid itself as well and as painfully as it could. But there were cool coves to hide a sudden single – if not very high – deciduous tree to lean on. So they rested on this shore that summer, a respite welcomed and savoured.

Once more, on that Sunday, Dan and Maria went farther than they had ever swum. It was out there, in the comfort of the Adriatic waters, that Dan, swimming on his back as one would lie cradled in a hammock, had the courage to say to Maria: "I have met a local girl. Svetlana. Her parents own a small tourist shop. They all like me, and if you let me go, Maria, I will marry her."

Swimming back to shore Maria said, "Go. Blessings, beloved Dan." And now they cuddled and kissed and sat silent. They were alone, the two of them in the hollow underneath that single tree where they ate a few biscuits, drank cold tea, and packed their belongings. Alexander did not come on Sundays. He waited at home for them, holding his bag and sitting at the table when they returned. Coins made the bag heavier than usual, and he was anxious to see and count it all. But today both Dan and Maria were as mute as he. They both smiled, saying little words like, "Oh, how wonderful, let's see what our great artist has brought home."

There was no fooling anyone. Sweet little words could not change what Alexander knew. The break had come. After the death of Giselle and Maria's seven days of mourning, he knew the world had changed. It was in his body, a young man's body now. An awareness of the break, an impatience in the limbs to part, to run. And that Sunday, having counted the money and kissed good night, he cried, overcome by inexplicable sadness.

No, there was no fooling anyone. And they had all missed Claudette. It was as if a rich fabric had ripped in spots and the finest needle could not repair it. Maria missed her most. She missed her sisterhood, her broad laughter, her wise or at times scatological remarks. The fun they had.

They all missed her work. All that extra work, be it repair or the ingenious, inventive solutions to the daily problems of a nomadic existence. She was good at it. And somehow with her death, the tent was sealed.

FOR GODOT: THE POST WAR WORLD

THE 8TH OF MAY 1945 HAD COME AND GONE. AN unaccountable jubilation, a hilarity took hold of all those who had survived. The war, with its abolition of law and respect for human life, was at an end. The joy of witnessing another sunrise was immense, and a strange brotherhood emerged. Jews, suddenly without the yellow star of David, felt glad to be ordinary, with no one looking their way. People scrambling for places to live collected their property – coats, shoes, wedding rings – or couldn't find them, as they were now on other people's backs or fingers. War is good at that. Money does not smell, neither does any object bear insignia. You conquer what you can get.

Felix found himself in a strange *singleness* in that post-war world. His parents had died, his sister Süssel had joined the Czech army. And he was rootless, hanging in or on the Teodorus who had hired him to work at their Senate pharmacy and welcomed him at their table. "Real Romanian" *sărmale,* which Felix knew as cabbage rolls in Czernowitz, or as *galupzi* in the Ukraine, were hailed as truly Romanian. Well, yes they were spicier, tasting more of the south or the southeast, with memories of Turkey – and yes, *moussaka* in layers of meat and aubergine, tasting Greek with its coating of eggs and goat cheese, was also proclaimed *the real thing.* Peasant wine to wash it down. So they took on each other's tastes, these neighbours, and added a little of their own past lives. Perhaps a taste left over from barbaric invasions, a taste of horseflesh from Asia, camouflaged as *steak tartare,* or memories of Arabia with its honey dripping, nutty pastries, made it all Romanian.

Felix loved the Teodorus. They did not mind his limp, though it slowed him down during work. Generous to a fault, they climbed the ladders for him for something out of reach, or Mr. Teodoru would run down the cellar steps to fetch a solvent or a tonic wine Felix needed for a prescription. Just before entering Bucharest, Felix was caught in a crossfire of bullets between warring local bandits and "partisans" for one cause or another, which war was so good at. His leg was hit, shattered from the knee down. It had to be taken, and he was fitted with a crude prosthesis. It was cumbersome and heavy, and it changed him. He was more thoughtful now, and very much conscious of his altered gait. It made him turn inward. Punishment, reward, destiny? No answers.

It was a very fertile time, because in his leisure hours he could use his language skills; he translated Romanian poets into Russian and the Russians into Romanian. Wrote for the paper occasionally and was paid. Czernowitzers are good at it. Literary and multilingual they are, with a heart towards the poetic. Yiddish, Romanian, or German, they are at home between the cultures. Now Felix also felt free to use it. He bid goodbye to the Teodorus in order to translate a major Romanian trilogy. Everything was suddenly there for him. His early facility with German and Latin and his mother's perfect French, all came to bear fruit. He rented a damaged flat, on the fifth floor overlooking the Opera House to the left, the bridge leading to the Senate at the right, and he had the city at his feet. He installed a telephone, which was very hard to get. Tried to contact the Czernowitz poet Paul Celan, but he had gone west by then. It was 1948. Surrealism in Bucharest had a fabulous flowering and Felix translated some of it. But it was too esoteric, non-specific, and not his genre.

The years 1945–1947 were lonely and intense years, where self-assessment and the search for a personal truth were at the centre of Felix's life. He read the great poets. The Russians: Mandelstam and Babel. But he avoided the 20th century and looked for Pushkin or Dostoyevsky of the 19th. It was safer in a communist-dominated world to translate the poets of the past. The moderns were dangerous. Dictatorships stifle, distort, and ultimately destroy their talent. To survive somehow, poets work clandestinely on their own, digging up the past, as did Boris Pasternak, who translated Shakespeare for a living. So Felix too tried his hand with Pushkin. Translated *The Queen of Spades* into both Romanian and French. But was startled and a little saddened by Pushkin's archetypal treatment of the Jew in that famous work. The Jew appeared as suave, in league with demonic forces knowing the winning cards – but Felix continued assiduously. He had to learn to deal with historic anti-Semitism and remain respectful to the writer in spite of it. Russian translations did well at the time. His experience in the war years, when fleeing the German onslaught deep into Russia, left him in good stead. He read and wrote Russian now perfectly, and with the Russians as supreme masters, he earned well.

But political horizons were dimming. Everyone felt betrayed, and Felix saw no future. All of Eastern Europe had been handed over to Stalin on a silver platter, and the Iron Curtain came down with a thump. He had to go. Fast. West. Paris, perhaps, where he suspected Sasha to be. But no, Vienna first. The town of his youth, the town of his father's youth, and the aspiration of every son and daughter of the Austrian Empire. Borders were still fluid, no one had a passport. Jews, freed POWs, and an array of displaced people were moving across them. Routes were known, illegal and treacherous. Between Romania and Hungary, one had sometimes to cross the river Tisza, and the boatmen made a fortune.

Felix changed his earned Romanian *lei* into American dollars, which was the one currency everyone recognized. It cost five dollars, the greenbacks, to pass the Romanian side of the river Tisza, and the price was just as high on the Hungarian side. Felix trusted his good fortune as he had always done. He made all the preparations, but it was hard to leave. He had made friends among the Romanian writers, had for the first time since the war worked with pleasure in a field which was naturally his: poetic prose. And he discovered Yiddish. He understood it well; it had been his only link to his grandparents. But he had ignored it with the arrogance of the High German and the French of the upper-crust Jewish bourgeoisie; he had disdained the lowly Yiddish. Now he discovered its wealth. Imagery, past pain and past glory – he sought out the Yiddish poets. A past emerged. Of biblical dimension. Written in Hebrew letters, a Germanic tongue of the Middle Ages, its commentary on the *everyday* was intimately mingled with a fervent search for God. It was exhilarating. But he could not embark on something so vast as his time seemed to grow shorter. Intentionally, he stayed alone. Women smiled at him as they always had, but he looked the other way. It was a time of account taking: he was thirty-two. A slight thinning of the hairline above the brow and its moving upward uncovered a stronger forehead and diminished his prettiness. His hair still fell over the ears in waves, masking them halfway as in younger years, but it had become a very different face.

Bucharest had a southern air, with a Latin mood in language and way of life, an easy approach between selves and between the sexes. Felix may have found female company, but he did not seek it. Yes, it was being truly alone that he cherished. He stripped himself of the comfort that *Woman* had offered him, and he cooked his own meals, made his own bed. But 1947 was a summer of hunger all over Europe. Drought and the marching boots of armies across Europe had laid all fields to waste. It was worse than Russia in 1942 and 1943 in some ways, when he had still found black bread, occasionally milk or yogurt, and a runaway or stolen piglet to slaughter. Now even the Romanian peasants were hungry. The fields were burnt by the sun of the southern plain, men had not returned, and nothing was seeded or gathered. Children were sent to town in trainloads from the surrounding countryside, in the hope of a meal. Felix saw them. He could still eat. Some sunflower seed oil, bread, and sausage came his way through the Teodorus, his pharmacist friends.

But in a strange fashion, the rich, spoilt son of a beautiful mother wanted deprivation: to see himself for what he was. It was this side of his poetic imagination that had not had a chance to plumb its depths. It had always been the power of his father that demanded the sciences, the modern truths, the 19th century illusion that absolutely everything was in man's grasp; given time, endeavour and hard pursuit would solve the puzzle of life's beginnings. Of course, Felix wanted it too, discovery, the enormity of the cosmos, the beauty of its laws, he wanted it all. So he obeyed his father, but not entirely and full-heartedly; he had to choose and his art suffered. He loved the word in all its manifestations, as idiom, as revelation, and above all as expression of the inner self. Now was time for it. Not being nomadic, or on the run as in Russia, and not hunted, he was settled – if for a brief moment – and on his own truly. These were the years he did not dream of Martina, avoided sexual comfort and the easy charm-talk that had been his lifeline. And he wrote in verse, blank verse and prose, sounding the words out to himself in German and turning them for other hidden meanings into French, Romanian, or Russian. And he felt more fulfilled than having spent days at the lab table.

But freedom had come to an end, and with Stalin and Anna Pauker, his local enforcer, in command, Felix knew that there would not be either a free press or permission for him to grow. He packed his rucksack, carried some of his last writings in a small briefcase, and left at night. It was the 15th of August, 1948.

There was no use waiting for trains. *They come or they don't,* Felix thought, not seeing any schedules properly advertised in the train station of the *Gara de Nord.* People milling about with little children in their arms or on their shoulders, bags hanging on somewhere – they looked funnily monstrous in the sparse light of 40-watt bulbs. The train station, the northern entry to the city, had been heavily bombed on the 4th of April, 1944, but somehow repaired, if shoddily. Who the people were next to or across from him, he could not tell, as no one spoke except in a whisper. Now and then one heard parents calling for their children. A mother shouting "Jon, come back!" "Tibor, where are you?" Or an anguished cry of a mother in Yiddish, "I've lost Moishale."

So, Romanians are leaving the sinking ship also, not just Hungarians and Jews, Felix thought, settling down on the edge of a big wooden crate next to what he judged to be a closed ticket counter. A man had courteously made room for him and said in a heavily accented Hungarian-Romanian, "This is my crate, and I don't let anyone sit near me whom I don't like. I've been here for three days and I'm waiting for my wife and two children. They are supposed to come from the city of Iaşi in Moldova. So I can't let anyone with a family sit on it. Yesterday, a man with a pregnant woman offered me one American dollar if I let her sit by me on the crate. See how good a place it is?"

"I see," Felix said. "Thank you."

"I won't take any money from you, because you look like a decent chap who would move if my wife showed up."

"Of course I would," Felix said, wondering about the human race with its sense of territory, be it just the edge of a crate next to a wicket. It was a tall, narrow crate so there was not so much room for either of them, but it was safely out of the shoving crowd, leaning against the wall. So it was good to rest one's back. And Felix could place his rucksack and briefcase in front of him for a comfortable footrest.

"See," the man turned to Felix. "See, you could stay here for days and you wouldn't get tired, and the main thing is, you can keep your feet on your rucksack or whatever you have without having it stolen from under you. You're in control."

"Well," he added "you really should give me a dollar for all that comfort I provide for you. But no, I like you and one should definitely do something for one's fellow men. By the way, I'm not asking for it, but have you by any means got an American dollar?"

"No," Felix lied, "No, I don't." *Too dangerous to show any money or to open a briefcase,* he thought. "No," he said again, "but I can give you an apple or share with you some bread."

"No, thank you," the man replied, a little ashamed to have offered his hospitality and then intimated payment.

But Felix was touched at the man's light embarrassment. *Aren't we a funny lot?* he thought. *Man needs decorum even in so small a thing as to let you sit at the edge of a crate.*

A sudden commotion attracted the attention of the crowd, which in a sort of arrowhead formation had already assaulted the second wicket. The owner of the crate said, "Hurry, the other wicket has opened. They sell tickets to Braşov – there are no other trains to come – go fast before they sell out. Don't worry about your stuff, it's too hard to push through the crowd. I'll look after it."

"Thank you," Felix said, "that would be very kind." He got down from his high crate, felt a chill through his bones, and said again, "Thank you, that is very kind, but I'll keep my coat on my shoulders, I'm cold." And he hurried across to where he thought the wicket was. Felix was not a tall man and could not see well above the heads of the crowd. People were blindly elbowing their way to the wicket or trying to and there was no proper queue possible. But a woman ahead of him turned to him and said very quietly, "I'll let you go ahead, mister, if you buy me a ticket also. I'm just not strong enough to make it to the wicket. You're a man, you can." She put Romanian *lei* into Felix's hand, and pushed him ahead of herself, which angered the crowd; but Felix succeeded by not looking right or left, landed at the small window, and heard a voice asking, "One or two? But no more than two."

"Two," Felix said, paying with the woman's money, and he got two tickets to Braşov as there was nothing else for sale. It was just as hard to get out as it was to get in because the fear that the wicket would close increased with every minute that passed. The woman was right there when he emerged. She thanked him profusely, took the ticket, refused the change, but Felix scrambled in his pockets and paid her an approximate sum back. "I'm going onto the platform with my ticket to wait for a train," she said and was out of sight.

Suddenly stricken with angst, he turned back, but could not identify the spot where he had left his bags behind. He remembered the dark wicket. "Did you see a man just a while ago, sitting on a wooden crate?" he asked the people passing by. One said yes he had, another said no or wouldn't bother to answer. It had all vanished. *Good, I still have the coat on my shoulders, it is a chilly night.* And he touched the linen bag holding his money and finely folded birth certificate that was hanging from a shoelace around his neck under his shirt. *Oh, clever mother,* he thought, and again, *Good, I still have my coat around my shoulders,* and went out onto the platform, waving his ticket to the commissar at the door. There were many people now, standing around or sitting on the ground. Felix spotted the woman, who sat a little apart with her back against the building. And he sat down beside her.

IT WAS A LONG WAIT. But it felt familiar, not at all extraordinary, as if it were a man's destiny to sit on cold stones in railway stations, waiting. Neither did it matter, as one seemed to have forgotten what it was one had waited for. Destinations simply did not exist, and time had no end.

All seemed familiar, he had been there before. A slight regret for the printed pages in the briefcase, the poetry of his last two Bucharest years, bothered Felix. But it was just a fleeting *It's a pity.* He did not mourn the loss, or sit *Shiva* as is the Jewish way. *No one can take it from me,* he thought. *Yes, I have been here before. Train stations are where people live in times of war. There are corners to hide; toilets do work sometimes or do not, then there is the man beside you for a night's companionship and the sharing of the stone floor.*

Every wanderer knows train stations. Every man and woman made nomadic by conquering or retreating armies hopes for a train station in which to set up house for a day or a month, as the case may be. Felix knew them well. On his retreat from Tbilisi, Georgia, which he would always remember as a gift from God, he had slept many a night on these cold floors. Now sitting on one of them again, he looked around himself: a few more people with tickets had come through the platform door. But the trickle slowly stopped, and he heard the woman beside him say, "Thank you again, mister. See, there are no more tickets to be had. So we are lucky, you and I…"

"Thank you, indeed," Felix replied, "I may not have succeeded in getting a ticket, were it not for you." But he would not carry on a conversation. All the train stations of his Russian war years were with him, every one of them, and he was in no mood to talk to anyone.

They are all the same, Felix thought, *but the Russian ones are better.* A train arrives or does not, leaves or does not, rails leading to them are wider than anywhere else, with broad boards in between spread less apart, which may make a daybed on rainy days. And if one is particularly lucky and one comes upon a station after days of sleeping in the mud, one may find boiling water pouring from a samovar, with a tea-betty on top perhaps and a cube of rough-hewn crystal sugar beside it. Well this is the moment one never forgets. Life gains meaning – Russians know better than the rest of the world what happiness is.

On his retreat from Georgia, he had come as far as Sevastopol.

Sitting now with his back against the brick wall of the building, which was warming perceptibly, he recalled Romanian commands and shouts. Retreating in disarray, the Romanians threw off their uniforms to join the partisans. By then colours did not mean anything, neither did the stripes on the collar. And Felix remembered finding himself dressed in a Russian top, Romanian pants, and a coat of no identifiable provenance. Only boots were unattainable, as everyone wore them to their last heel.

He felt good. The stump of his leg had acquired a comfortable position and he pulled his right foot up to steady his back. *I am lucky,* he thought and recalled how he had joined a ragged lot that had once been part of the Romanian army. Sporadically running trains he mounted clandestinely, no matter where they went, as long as it was west, and he got down at train stations when these trains suddenly stopped, behaving as irrationally as the whole world did. Nothing was predictable, and he couldn't tell how he lived or where the next piece of bread would come from.

It was before entering Bucharest that a partisan bullet had splintered his leg. Just on the last stretch, with the city nearly in sight. His whole left side heaved now, feeling the past event in its detail with a momentary intensity, and stretching his wooden leg sideways, which he could somehow do by moving his stump, he got despondent, not knowing if his strength would last through the night.

But morning came early with its fine spray of dew to dampen his hair and wash his face. He had jumped to his "feet" to look for a corner to relieve himself, when he heard the miraculous sound of an approaching locomotive. *General assault,* Felix thought. *I won't be able to fight my way through.* But the woman who had sat next to him all night was already on the first rung, shouting, "Leo, I'm here, this is my husband, help him I beg you or we'll be separated, he is a cripple." And people made room for him, as almost all who had been on the platform had succeeded mounting the train. It was a spectacular rescue. He tired suddenly and couldn't swing his right foot up, but the woman grabbed his hand, saying to the crowd, "Help him, thank you," and then, "Leo, follow me." As the train pulled out of the station, which was in a matter of seconds, he felt her hand in his and heard her say, "Thank you for helping me get away." It was a little strange to be called a cripple when, in his mind, he had remained whole. But he squeezed her hand in reply and said quietly through the din of shuffling feet, pulling of luggage, the shouting of the conductor to get away from the train door: "It is for me to thank you, for I would never have made it." And settling next to her in a corner of the corridor that she had conquered, he wondered when and where she would have noticed his wooden limb.

The train went through Sinaia, passing mountain villages that suddenly took on a totally peaceful, everyday-life look. It stopped to let people off for some comfort, a drink of water, which women sold by the glass, as to purchase a piece of baked pumpkin or its roasted seeds. There was a sudden courtesy among the passengers, not to call it benevolence. A holiday ride it had suddenly become, through wooded mountains with springs falling over naked rocks. Forested heights, small coves of beech trees interspersed, relieving the dark spruce of its grandeur and reminding one of our own deciduousness, of the moment lived, of its intensity. Looking through the corridor windows, which were large, if coal-streaked, his own early world seemed out there. Beech country, the Bucovina, that first imprint of beauty, the oneness of God, never to leave you.

Felix rejoiced; not that one went anywhere. The train started out going west, stopped in Sinaia, squeezed in one or two people for a little while, who then got off mysteriously. It behaved as purposelessly as the days following one another do, when nothing mattered, rails shifting gear, a few wagons disconnecting themselves as if on their own, hitching back on or not. Felix could not tell; his compartment, close to the locomotive, never left it. The rich, ozone-drenched air, garlic-smelling, made them all gently tipsy, heady and unworried.

"Call me Leo," Felix said to the man next to him, having been asked for his name, and the woman smiled conspiratorially at Felix and he replied in kind. *So I am a cripple called Leo,* he thought, and it felt wonderfully liberating. To get out of one's skin, to be suddenly another with a ready-made wife to boot at one's side. Absurd, too, as neither time, the succession of day and night, or destination made any sense. The train stopped outside of Sinaia. Mountain air having changed the mood into holiday hilarity, they all stepped out of the train, the conductor assuring them that he'd blow the whistle. They ran into the grassy hills on the one side of the tracks and into a small Romanian village on the other. People disappeared as if they had never been there. Felix and the woman, a self-understood team now, chose the grassy slopes. He took her bag, as he had none. People shared their bread, a few apples; an army bottle of water made the rounds.

They heard the rails screech, the locomotive manoeuvred, but there was no whistle, no one knew how many hours had passed and no one spoke. There was peace and welcome sleep, but when the whistle sounded they rushed to the train, not as worried though, because now they all felt their territory assured. *A strange, bizarre lot we are,* Felix thought as he mounted the train, helped by others who had by now noticed his wooden leg.

As it had been like a picnic in the fields, so it was now with the reassembled vacationers. No conductors to ask for tickets, the train stood still in almost open countryside, the passengers accommodated one another with a smile or the offer to share their provisions. It broke all barriers. As if they all were on conquered land, with the enemy beaten, they organized the available space more efficiently and took care not to stumble over Felix's leg. It was a good day, with doors and windows open, and as the night approached everyone settled for it somehow.

"Braşov." The train stopped. "Terminus," the conductor announced, and the scrambling off and away happened so fast: unimaginable just a moment ago. Felix lingered a little longer. Letting them all go, and the woman did too.

"We have to part," she said now. Taking his hand for a good-bye, she pressed into it the Romanian money that he had returned after purchasing the ticket.

"No," he said, "please don't." But with a light hug and a "good luck" she was out of sight.

"I WOULD LIKE TO CHANGE one or two American dollars," Felix said to the clerk at the grand Hotel Braşov, in the centre of town. "To what bank should I go?"

"No bank, sir. We have our own bank here," the clerk replied. "Please follow me to the manager's office."

Felix was seated across from a heavy-set, good natured, beaming man, who said, "No need to go anywhere. We give you the best exchange in town." It was thousands of *lei* to the dollar and they were produced instantly, lying on top of the desk in bundles.

"That's fine," Felix said. "May I use your bathroom first? I am just off the train." There was one not far. He washed his face and hands, opened his shirt, took the birth certificate and ten dollars out of the linen bag that hung around his neck on the shoelace, and put it all into his trouser pocket.

"My luggage was stolen in the Bucharest station and I have to go to town to replace it," he said on his return.

"Oh, yes," the manager said not believing a word. "The clerk will help you with everything. Show you where to shop. You are staying at the hotel, I presume?"

"Yes, of course," Felix answered.

"May I ask for how long?"

"It depends –"

"No indiscretion intended, we just want you to know that we are at your disposal for all your needs, sir, travel – and otherwise." What the *otherwise* meant was not clear. *I will have to be cautious,* Felix thought, being suddenly aware of the danger he was in, holding American currency.

He went to town. Braşov. Old Saxon churches, people speaking a German different from his own, but pleasing to his ears. Hungarians, Romanians, and a seemingly low-class, post-war, scrambling world. But he was cautious, not as light-hearted as he had hoped. To own foreign currency was strictly forbidden, though every transaction, big or small, was in American dollars. Total corruption. From top to bottom. Every policeman on the street was available for a dollar. *Marvellous,* Felix thought. *Murky, transitory times, no one belonging anywhere, loyalties lasting one night long on a train station.* Felix bought what he needed. It was a good day, with an almost hot shower and juicy pork cutlets.

THEY APPROACHED THE INFAMOUS SPOT where the American dollar was king. Rival empires had sprung up at different crossings, which took both Romanian and Hungarian currency, competing against the dollar, guaranteeing a faster, safer crossing. How one could be safer than safe wasn't clear. None was safe. *The funny thing is that Hungarians and Romanians, who fight tooth and nail for suzerainty over one another, become Mafia brothers at night,* he thought. *It's the power of money, it builds bridges over territorial chasms, no one had thought possible.*

Communicating in both languages, both sides spoke the other: the Hungarians stressing the first syllable in their Romanian and the Romanians in their Hungarian stressing the penultimate. But what made it irresistibly charming was the instantaneous replacing of a missing word of the other with one of their own. It created a bilingual Babel, a sort of comforting chaos, reassuring in dangerous times. Demand for business was high. Groups of all sizes appeared suddenly. Some, having walked over the Bucegi Mountains to the banks of the river Tisza, others in hired, ancient Fords had come from every part of Romania, only to get out of the vehicles and be totally disoriented, unsure which way to take. *Thank God,* Felix thought, *for the middleman. They invent themselves at moment's call.* A middleman was a self-created, instinctual creature that smelled, heard, and sensed with invisible extra feelers: a certain lack here or need there. They were someone who knew someone else, whose brother...and so forth. Brotherhood having sprung up between ancestral foes, artificial boundaries were dismissed, and instinct united both banks of the river, as it always does when there is profit on both sides.

Felix had arrived with six other companions, who had hired a car in Brașov, knew where to go, and had been looking for one more passenger to reduce the cost. The hotelier clerk had found the connection – everything for a price – and Felix was on his way, but it was a silent, worried seven hours.

His love of rivers had been restricted to the aesthetic or the philosophic sort. It was more the Greek idea of *Panta re* – that all is flowing and moving and shifting – that fascinated him than the experience as such. This was his sister Süssel's way. She would throw herself into the high water of the Prut to fight the current. It was not for him. Yes, to stroll along these endless waterways, contemplate their changing with light and season, conducive to thought, that is what he liked. As a child he would go down to the Prut to watch the athletes parade their gleaming muscles, and happily sit on a bench for hours, letting time pass. He was fearful of the current and its unpredictability. And so it was now. Night crossing, over the Tisza or Tisa – according to the fighting neighbours, spelling its name differently was to show possession. Night crossing in derelict boats with lugubrious ferrymen, visions of robbery, and the cold waters of the Tisza-Tisa closing in over his head, made him not willing to share in his younger companions gallows' humour. He was not prepared to laugh at dumb jokes of the scatological variety, and they took his silence for arrogance and attacked him: "You're a stick-in-the-mud, we should never have taken you with us." Or "You're a traitor and we'll end up in jail." And they opened the car door at a certain moment telling him, "Get out, right here." But they didn't push him out, prevented perhaps by the basic bargaining system of underground honour: they had taken money and had witnesses. So who trusted whom? No one of course, and a very healthy thing it was. So they kept the deal, and Felix saw himself facing the dark river by nightfall.

It went without a hitch. Romanian-Hungarian complicity did
it, with exchange of money at the border, traditional in-jokes, and
a specified language – created for the purpose – to be understood
only by the dealers to the disadvantage of the customers. Five dollars American on this side, the Romanian side of the river, at
embarkation, and five dollars on delivery after the crossing on the
Hungarian side, and people there already waiting to guide you to
an inn for a night's sleep.

So it went without a hitch. Now it was all Hungarian. Felix
had never attempted to learn it. Hungary sat all by itself in the
heart of Europe with its history and language of Asiatic roots.
Felix had never had time for it. But money spoke, and was well
understood. And there was another wonderful accomplice: the
old Austrian-Hungarian Empire. It still showed its residual power.
Abolished, the Empire in tatters, Franz Joseph II long dead, every
neighbour pulling at the carcass had swallowed a piece of the
land, yet something had remained, unifying the diverse enemies:
a mother tongue, German. They all had heard it from their
grandmothers, in school or in songs, and Felix was understood
everywhere in Hungary. The ideal of this defeated federation of
many nations under a benevolent Emperor-King persisted at its
roots through a very powerful bond: the sound of words one had
heard when young. But nationalistic forces were dominating, and
people often replied in Hungarian.

He loved the people. Again it was a vacation. From village to
village on erratic-running trains to reach Budapest. Hurray for
the underground! The trek to the Austrian border was perfectly
organized. Illegality and getting the better of the law was master
when a world in turbulence shifted its citizens around. It was perfectly organized. Hundreds of people seeking refuge at the

Austrian border made it across at different checkpoints. So did
Felix. Such a comfort to hear familiar sounds! And how close
Czernowitz German blended with the Austrian sound of Graz or
Klagenfurth German. But Vienna was still far.

In three or four weeks Felix spoke the local dialect as if born
to it. He hired himself out as a farmhand, away from books, texts,
and scriptoria for the first time. They all liked his courteous ways
and the keeping to himself. One could still eat better at the farm
than in town, and no one asked for papers or who his grandmother had been. He stayed over a year with no pay, but he was
well-fed, had fresh linen and down-feather coverlets on his bed.
Though tired at night, he had never been so well. He stayed on,
but when one day the peasant's sons, returned from the war and
suspicious perhaps of his Jewishness, asked for his papers, he took
his leave.

PART THREE:
VIENNA – THE SIXTIES

Florindo, RED LEATHER BOUND,

BANGING THE WOODEN LEG AGAINST EACH UNEXPECTED stone, slowing the almost stalled rhythm of his walk, Felix crossed the road, his eye having caught a bookstore on the corner. A little more animated by an indefinable hope, he hurried now to avoid the few oncoming cars, which were not abundant at five o'clock in the early evening, and he stood before the window of the shop seeing his image suddenly multiplied by fractured light. Slightly bothered by the display of holy books of the commercial variety, chalices of silver plate and so forth, he turned to leave when he was startled by a sign in the shop window advertising "Rare and author-signed, gold-embossed, leather-bound books." He distinctly recognized his father's collection of Hugo von Hofmannsthal's signed series. His heart stopped, his phantom toe twitched, water ran straight down his back along the vertebrae.

It was as if his father stood before him in his grandeur and he trembled. He had always hated what his father loved. Not books in general. Jews could not do without them. But the preciousness of his collecting habits: search them out, find them all. Triumphal pursuits and homecoming, as if they were a warrior's conquest.

The new possessions then were territory to be owned, slowly savoured, categorized with numbers on shelves in precious book-cases, walnut-carved; Venetian glass to just let them glance in. Idols they were to be adored. Felix liked his own books of fun and escape when he was very young. But his father in grandiose, right-eous fury ripped those penny-books through in the middle, shouting, "You will never amount to anything with this kind of literature!" The walls shook, his sister cried in the corner and his mother appeared from nowhere, leading him away: "Let it be, please, these booklets are not his, they're in exchange, let it be." And Ileana the maid swept the paperbacks into a bin, coming closer to Felix than necessary to console him. *I read the French poets when older,* he thought. *Loved them. Distilled poetry, they were taken from life yet transformed; I read them with my mother.* Her voice was in his ear: warm, elegant. Not books for their own sake, to be owned and not fully read.

He entered the shop. Heart a beating drum now. Could not hear either his own voice, or the one of the shopclerk, but felt his stomach heave, assuming the ooze that must be pouring off his lips; servility in all of his bent back. Felix ignored him. Moving cautiously towards the shelf where his father's books were, he said, "May I please have a look at *Florindo* by Hugo von Hof-mannsthal?"

"This is a single copy, signed by the master, and we are not allowed to handle it unless you are a serious buyer."

"I would like to have it in my hand to be able to see if it is truly authentic. Also, what is the price, please? And are these four more by the same author?"

At this moment a back door opened and a small, elderly man, a face sharp as all the pencils he had handled in his life, grey hair, grey skin and suit said, "What is the gentleman's pleasure?" Felix repeated his wish and the grey little man handed him his father's author-signed copy of *Florindo*. Etched into the back of his eyes and consciousness, Felix recognized the red Morocco-leather, hand-bound copy. He held in his hand number ninety-five of three hundred and fifty copies printed, illustrated by Otto Hettner, signed by Hofmannsthal in his bold, clear, gently-to-the-right-leaning handwriting, and to the left of it a calligraphic, balanced signature of the illustrator. Avalun-Druck: the publisher. Blinded, as if a dark rain had hit the windowpanes, Felix could not decipher the titles of the other volumes adjoined to it. He saw *The Tower – Der Turm* – also by Hugo von Hofmannsthal, but was not sure it was his father's.

Having lifted *Florindo* out of its protective cover, he held the warm leather in his hands. The back was peeling slightly at the top, but with the gold design, gold-cut and embossed, the year 1923 clearly showing on its last page, the book was perfectly intact.

It was as if Felix had entered his own childhood world and stood in front of the dominating bookcase, which covered the whole east-end wall of his parents' house, and he asked his father to give him *Florindo* to look at the drawings. With stone-cut graphics and hand-printed, it was his favourite book. "Take care, it is not for children really, it is about a character who does not know right from wrong." To Felix it was a picture book. And he saw himself sitting in the corner of a formal chair in his mother's salon transported by an imaginative world that did not need words. Such a return! His little sister Süssel, an intruder into that sweet moment, wanted what he had, always. "You can't have it, you're too young, your hands are sticky and it is not for stupid little ones." *It's all there,* Felix thought. *It has all returned but my fear of him.* His heart beat against his golden pocket watch a strange and intimate duet, and he felt his shoulders, all muscles losing tension, holding his father's book. He turned to the little grey man with the sharpened-pencil face to ask for the price, and seemed to hear something like ten thousand *schillings.*

"May I please see the invoice for this book, and I would also ask for information on its provenance." His voice cool, quiet but aggressively accented, this voice he had never heard before.

Putting the book back into its protective cover then, pressing it against his breast, he looked up into a violent razor-sharp face and saw fists raised, ready to punch, and felt the book ripped out of his embrace. Pushed by both men, with shouts of "Dirty Jew, out! How dare you come to my shop to rob me of my hard-earned piece of bread! Peter," the grey man commanded the clerk, "Police, immediately."

Vienna, I won't stay here. I won't. I will not be able to. Nothing has changed since my student days. Disoriented, pushed out the door, Felix found himself in front of the shop, not knowing where to turn. *No doubt. I have held my childhood book in my hands. How did it get here? Who took it? Search? Should I? How to start? These are my father's books.* So strong a presence cannot lie: a little boy in front of a bookcase. Obsessive little boys who knew what they wanted, not to be deflected from their wishes. He wanted the book. And another one. Was it in the Meyer or the Brockhaus? That long row of Encyclopedias? It was the letter H he wanted. Hector. Defeated hero of the Trojan Wars. No, he did not want Achilles or Ajax or any of the Greeks. His heart was in Hector. "The letter H, please father."

"And what fascinates you, may I ask?"

"The letter H, please father." Undeterred, a little boy's heroes were so passionately chosen. So he faced the shelf with *Florindo*. A homecoming so strong. There was no other.

I had forgotten. Vienna had murdered its Jews, sits in their houses, eats at their tables, hangs their pictures on the wall and does illicit commerce with their art books. Loot. And looters will murder their memory; I had forgotten. He could not go to his lonely digs, and without knowing how he got there he stood in front of Martina's *Ringstrasse* flat, ringing the gate bell.

The *Hausmeister* had seen him before and let him in. He felt again his shoulders rise with tension, being aware that he was an outcast in the streets and not at home at Martina's door. Dr. Schneider led him into the dark vestibule and through the milky-edged glass door into the salon. "Martina is out, but will be back in an hour. A glass of wine, perhaps?"

"No," he said, "many thanks. I had the strangest feeling of being back at my father's house and holding one of his books in my hands. It is hand-bound in Morocco leather, red leather," he said, as if this detail would add any believable explanation for its being in Vienna. "Red Morocco leather, gold-embossed with stone-cut graphics, hand-printed in Hellerau near Dresden."

"Oh," Dr. Schneider said.

"Yes, it is a play in fact. Not just a story, a piece of theatre about a rascally young man; with beautiful drawings. Yes, all my childhood emerged; I see myself sitting at the dinner table, all of us facing the immediacy of parting from one another. My sister, father and mother were to stay, expecting the German onslaught but I – It was early July, 1941.

"'They'll kill young Jewish men first,' my father said. 'Go, my son. Go,' he said. 'Here is a small packet of ten grams of luminal and two grams of morphine. Only *in extremis,* in the absolute extreme case of torture. And two twenty-dollar bills, American. A fortune in 1941. Go, my son, go.' And he had never kissed me before. But now he takes me into his arms, holds me as if I were a tiny child, his tears wet my face. 'Go, my son. Go.' And father checked my coat pockets for a spot to hide the two little packets. Remember, it's only if you fall into murderers' hands. Don't let yourself get hurt.

"Mother and sister busied themselves to fill the rucksack with sausage, bread, an army knife and fork – the famous Swiss army knife – and God knows what." And he pulled it out of his trouser pocket, as if it mattered today. "It's always with me," he said, replacing it, "and I'm pushed out of my father's house."

Dr. Schneider, who had also seen the world, albeit from the other side of the barricade, was patient. Felix's hurried accounts, words tumbling fast, an emotional breath carrying them unhaltingly and not making immediate sense, did not induce Dr. Schneider to press for an explanation. He, Dr. Schneider, stood silently all through them. Guiding Felix to the pink pin-striped sofa, he took a down feather-filled cushion out of a heap of criss-crossing pink-ivory cushions, put it with a pat of his flat hand against the back of the sofa, and said gently, "Please, make yourself at home."

Felix let his sobs, his tears come. The little warmth from Dr. Schneider's hand, the puffing up of a feather pillow, that unuttered acceptance of his incomprehensible story, unleashed the torrent.

The late day moving into night brought its own comfort. The absence of Annie and Martina – with their female knowing-it-all readiness to do something about things – and the silence of a man friend, allowed Felix to sob. Both were silent now, and they let things run their course.

Lights went on one by one in the *Ringstrasse*, yellow globes of light, symmetrically strung along the curving road, looked like a *collier* of pearls through the balcony doors. Felix, warmed by the feathers at his back and the presence of this stranger-friend who knew without knowing, asked for a cognac. Dr. Schneider rose, moved towards the sideboard where crystal glasses, Armagnac, and wine in slender bottles caught the last light from the windows across. And Felix thought, "How beautiful he is, legs long, fashionably trousered, he seems careful to avoid corners in the half-light, and so pliable he is and slim in the middle with no hint of a paunch." Felix saw other men now with a little more envy. He watched their movements, trying to relearn or to learn a simulation, an imitation, to cover the awkwardness of his artificial limb. "How beautiful he is. I know his name is Gerhard. Or maybe Gerrard. I would like that better. He looks more like a Frenchman. Oh dear, it's all bias! Oh, the French, it may be because of their books that I love them! Or fantasy; not having lived with them in crucial times, French not being my mother tongue and there for fun only. So different from the German."

Dr. Schneider lit a dim lamp on the sideboard, which did not disturb the lightlessness and hidden objects, but revealed a single painting above the board: a woman's glinting, golden hair falling and enfolding at the ankles, both man and woman, melting into one. *Gustav Klimt, perhaps.* Felix, turning, cast a fast glance, and that one ray of light speaking of love, of union, made him say quietly, as if to himself, "I was Martina's first lover."

"I know," Dr. Schneider said, "I know." Handing him a stemware crystal glass and keeping another one for himself, he seated himself now across from Felix, into those hard-backed chairs no one expected to be comfortable, but were. And he started in a bedtime-story tone:

"I was not in the first killing unit. Not in the one that passed by the old house. I was in the second. A mobile body, that went first for the chief rabbi and the community elders. Just a few people by name. For the rest of that day it was random shooting, whomever we could get. It was the seventh or eighth of July, 1941. Hot summer days. We had been on tanks all day, across the river Prut, sweaty and angry; as the sun set we changed into smaller vehicles, motorbikes and the like. Then on foot. From house to house. Banging our rifles on your doors, shouting louder than I have ever heard myself, we made them pour out of these silent houses that felt more like a churchyard before the killing than after. A theatre set, it wasn't real. *Juden raus'* a cue. Doors, gates flying open at once by push button nearly. My unit – called the second – took men only, arranged them into marching formation of four to six, and made them run in step down to the river. We, having had mounted our motorbikes on both sides, pushed them on. No digging of ditches. No time for it. We made them line up – to save bullets. Each one got one. We were angry. I thought, *Even one is too much.* Tired, hot, and in a strange way indifferent, it seemed rifles did it on their own. *Genickschuss.* Into a kind of a ditch with the river close, they tumbled face down. A grave as good as any. Allow me to speak freely."

"Please," Felix said.

"The next day we went back. To the women and children. No time, no time for anything. All was fast done. But we had another day for the job and maybe a night to rest. The town, as paralyzed as the day we entered it, looked worse. The blood had blackened on the streets. Big splotches, some seemed to flow still, but the bodies had all disappeared. Cleared away and cleaned as if the *Heinzelmännchen* of the fairy tales had done it. Every German child knows these little elves who come at night and do the cobbler's job for him, the tailor's or the wheelwright's, until one day a cobbler's wife spotted them, curious as women are reputed to be she had overstepped the *Verbot,* the forbidden, and had looked at them. And the little *Heinzelmännchen* never ever returned. The bodies were gone. The Jewish *Heinzelmännchen* did it, this crew coming at night to clean up; another *coup de théâtre* enforcing the unreal. We entered the houses, and I do not know if they were all the same from the day before – women and children, old men gathered as if in heaps. Discarded rags they were. Or looked like inanimate mannequins. So motionless. It made us louder, our steps heavier. This strange living frieze of collective death to come, made us shout, laugh and scream at them: *Get going, move, separate, this way, that way!* Pulling the children like rubber dolls from their mother's lap, I threw them into a corner. A heap of rag dolls. No sound. The four of us went through the rooms, putting objects that looked like gold or a pearl or something that tickled our omnipotence into the tunics of our uniforms."

And Gerhard slipped a wedding ring from his little finger. In the half-dark now, Felix could not make out the initials engraved. Were they Hebrew? "This is what I had picked up, not really wanting it, walking by a night table. Now it is with me for the rest of my life and I touch it from time to time. I won't find the owner. They're gone by our hand. But who knows God's ways?"

"It was a *parterre* flat. Major Grünewald holding a little bundle, pushing towards the window, handed it to me and said: 'Here, do it, throw it through the window. Nothing to be afraid of. They're vermin.

Get rid of them. You have to better your ways. You're too timid – ha, ha.' A rocky laugh. 'You're a bleeding heart, I've looked through you. I saw your eyes coming into this room. Do it, you have to learn the trade!' And before I knew, I had done it. It flew out into that July day – out of my hands. The three men had drunk some of the Sabbath wine that was on the sideboard, laughing, banging them-selves with their rifles to frighten the women: 'It may be devil's blood that we are drinking, too sweet for real wine. But we are in the devil's business, so it might as well be sweet.' Grünewald pulled a young girl out of the heap, threw her onto something that looked like a sofa, ripped her dress, parting her thighs, trying to do it to her, groaned. She was virginal. I vomited into my hands, ran to a spot to empty my bowels and said, 'I'm sick, I'm respectfully asking to leave.' I went out into the *Residenzgasse* just for air or to walk away from men. I may have glanced to see where the baby had landed but saw none: the Jewish world is full of *Heinzelmännchen,* I thought, and continued down the street."

Putting the small wedding band back unto his finger, Gerhard bent forward towards Felix, and lifting his crystal glass with the last drop of cognac in it, said softly, "Would you care to rise so we could link arms to drink *Bruderschaft?*" And Felix rose, came close, bodily close, to cross arms, and both lifting their glasses through these linked arms to their lips, drank to the DU. The inti-mate DU of friendship for which there is no English equivalent, where God, the Queen, and the beggar are addressed with You. A light smile on both their lips. Gerhard saying, "Don't go, don't go, the night is young. I do not work tomorrow and neither do you, my *Bruder,* there is a holiday."

They heard Martina's key in the lock, a silvery, tinkling sound. Gerhard still on his feet saying, "Don't go, don't go," rushed out into the vestibule to greet Martina. Felix heard him say, "He is here – no it is not dangerous, he wears a different shirt, without the two pockets – leave us tonight Martina, we have just drunk *Bruderschaft.*" She entered, hugging Felix, a cheek-to-cheek hug, and excused herself. Gerhard, holding the Armagnac bottle in his hand, brought it closer, set it on the low Arabic coffee table and seated himself close to Felix on the silken sofa, a down feather cushion at his back.

"It was still noon or half-past, a sun overhead of killing heat when I stepped into a murdered street. Here and there a silent dog in front of a master's residence – and I passed the Old House. I know now that it was yours. Martina told me, and also that it was hers as well. She grew up at Rachel Glasberg's breast, her own mother running dry. It was her second home. She loved the Glasberg's, practiced secretly their faith, was with them until their murder. And I did notice, in spite of my – I found myself in a state of lucidity almost, non-corporeal, I did see the stucco design, different from all others around it. Above the windows, wrought-iron balconies hugged the corner. Some vine over-grown. I did see them. But all windows closed on such stifling days were ghostly, spoke of a deep angst. The town was terrified. And terrifying now to me. Driven by a nervous energy, I walked faster, past the fountain. I wanted to drink, ran to the well, but faces and horrid masks on the central statue prevented me, and I moved on.

"Now I walked on the side of the Evangelical church with the comfort of hedges hiding me. Such momentary relief from being exposed in a silent, so utterly silent street. Alone. The hedge took me in, the benches under the chestnut trees holding me for a lit-tle. But I moved on. That I wore a uniform of the conquering army depleted the rest of my strength. I opened my collar, against regulations, and walked on. Fast. Away. I was one of your prophets in the desert. A lucid ear, we would say *hellhörig* as if we could see light with our ears. A mixing of the senses, I perceived all doom as one: man is lost, there is no road left for him to take, he has passed the Styx. Felix, I felt a slipping away of the body, a hallucinatory disembodiment: a Jeremiah shouting, 'It is the end of the world!' Almost running now, I found myself around the corner, *Heine* – or *Goethegasse,* or another one named after our great poets, looking at girls standing in doorways; they seemed ready for work. I had money, *Deutschmark,* which I pulled out without thinking, and heard an elderly whore – who I know now was called Rebecca, of all names – calling me *'Liebling.'* An enormous woman's body, her warm flesh enfolding me, talking about a younger one than herself, a 'sweet thing.' I heard very little; all sheltered in her embrace I was led into what seemed the lower catacombs to that sweet thing called Mitzi. I saw a wide bed and fell onto it. From then on, oblivion.

"When I awoke I found myself in a half-light No Man's Land, unable to identify locale, time, or the women. A slender young man entering minutes later. A nightmarish picture of dolls, teacups, a Madonna lit by a candle underneath. But the faces took on voices suddenly, Mitzi shouted with joy: 'He has opened his eyes, Mother of God!' The young man disappearing fast, and the pastor, Martina's father, entered."

Felix, listening intently, took a sip of cognac, turned closer to Gerhard and said, "It was about this time that I left my father's house. I went east. Down the Holy Trinity Street, passing the fountain as you had, Gerhard, then across from the pastor's church, towards the *Bahnhofstrasse.*"

"I know the *Bahnhofstrasse*," Gerhard said, having also come closer, as if in love, or disclosing something very private. "I know the *Bahnhofstrasse*. We came up, by tank across the bridge, from the north." Both laughed.

"Everyone comes always up the *Bahnhofstrasse*. From the *Bahnhof* – the train station – rarely friends," Felix said and continued. "Rarely. But this time I went down, not up, to see if there was anything moving. To run east. You, Gerhard, were in Poland, this is north, and you were all over in the west. All I could run was east. I could not run south because the Romanian brother-in-arms of the Germans might just pull in from the south. But it's not about me. It's about you, Gerhard." And they both put their feet up on the small Arabic table, leaning back into the feather pillows.

There was such comfort between them. They had tread the same pavement stones at almost the same time, had no business being there, but were. And Gerhard said, "Do you realize I could have entered your house?"

"Don't talk like that. It could not have happened, because it didn't. But we could have crossed paths –"

"Yes, I awoke or returned to consciousness and disaster. The *Oberkommando* had taken hundreds of hostages and every tenth or every fifth were to be shot if I didn't show up. Well, jubilation in the whorehouse! I opened my eyes, and they tried, the two women and the pastor, to make me stand up. But I couldn't. I fell back into the chair. Nothing obeyed; muscles stalled, trembled, shook. No body-feel. I did not exist. 'He is hungry,' Mitzi screamed, 'he is hungry. Tea, tea. Put on the naphtha lamp. Bring water to a boil. Push the small table to him. Get bread and cheese. Find a tablecloth, he can't eat on the naked table, he is an officer.

A German.' What we in Germany would call a *Tischlein-Deck-Dich* – do you, Felix, know that fairy tale, a wish-for or what-you-want-table which comes up by magic, like in my childhood fairy world. The *Tischlein* had set itself. Well, you know us well enough, Felix. All our stories –"

"Yes, I do. I'm of your *tribe*. If life is what it is, we want lore, poetic nonsense, stories, rescue really."

"Yes, we do. I love you Felix. How I can talk to you!" It was simply said.

"We have a tongue in common. German is our childhood sound. It is the most romantic, poetic, hot with emotion…."

They were well into their cognac. Love and tears were loose; eyes ran over, the lights dimmed one by one on the collier of pearls through the glass doors. Felix started humming: *Weisst du wieviel Sternlein stehen?* – *Can you tell how many little stars?* – Gerhard joined the childhood tune and both fell silent.

THE PHANTOM LEG

F ELIX ROSE STEP BY STEP, BUT SLOWLY. STOPPED IN between to touch his shirt pockets, left and right, with a familiar slap, ensuring the stuff was there. The late afternoon was shifting, no air in the street moved, no one entered the staircase, predicting death. He smiled in recognition of a lack of discomfort at the thought he had not foreseen.

There was no one home but the maid when he knocked at the door. A lion's body type of brass knocker, wild mane on top. *India-made*, he thought. *Too cheap*. Three knocks and a not-so-pretty-as-she-thought-she-was woman of thirty, dressed in the lace-apron and cap of a pretend upper-bourgeoisie, opened the door halfway, to show the chain linking door to door post, shutting him out, and said, "No one home." She had recognized him of course. Holding the door handle – a real handle, not a knob, one that you have to press down with the palm of the hand in order to open – holding it firmly, she gave him that curtailed time in which to act, so he pushed the tip of his toe into the opened crack, said between his teeth, unvoiced but stressing each word, "I – have – to – see – her."

She let him in – removing the chain unwillingly, with the gri-mace of the knowing underling, the knowing and recording ser-vant, treacherous, but paid and powerless. He passed her, pushing her with his body, doing it without showing intent, but it was taken as intentional by the maid. He entered the vestibule, where hat stands, umbrellas, coat hangers against dark wainscoting make a lugubrious welcome to any visitor; light was dimmed fur-ther by milky glass doors, art nouveau etched in. Annie, in proper maid behaviour, went before him now, to open these doors and with "Take a seat, sir, she'll be here in around an hour," she left and he sat down facing the balcony. An open view – balcony doors both wide open towards the gardens at the back of the house. A breath of air touching his cheek now in spite of the late-afternoon stillness, nearly brought tears to his throat as he sat down on a large sofa against a straight, high back. He looked around, knew where to look for things, having been here before, but saw them for the first time. "Secession – Art Nouveau – all around me," he thought. "Secession: phony design, wilful and in humour, looking for ideals we can't have. Beautiful, though. Beautiful."

He slapped his pockets, knowing things were in order and nothing unexpected could surprise him, he tried to lean back into a comfort that was not designed. Fetched a down-filled pretty pil-low, likely meant to make up for the hard back of the sofa, but settled for the downy warmth, which made his thoughts wander to a back alley behind the old house where he had sat with Martina, having looked for a spot of dense foliage to sit under and kiss. He closed his eyes, stretching his limbs, arms, legs with a known anticipation, half-sleep, half-presence, and was startled by the opening of the glass doors. Annie's accomplice voice saying under her breath, "He is here, Madame. Watch out, he looks, well, not dangerous, well, you'll see." Felix jumped to his feet before Martina had entered to greet her with a prepared smile.

"Well, you have come Felix, you have – it seems you don't take no for an answer."

"Of course not, why should I, when I know what your thoughts are – I know your intimate wishes: You do want me here. You want me to come and beg and grovel on the ground and kiss your patent leather shoe – or is it shiny crocodile? – while you put your handbag down, coolly taking no notice, pushing me slightly away as if I was not worth your crushing blow."

"Well, no theatrics please," she said, doing just that, putting down her handbag and heading towards the balcony. "Oh, come, stop it all. Come be a good boy, take my hand, and let's sit in comfort on the balcony easy chairs, which you so love in contrast to the sofa. Come, come, my baby." Pulling him with her, she seated him in one of the life-easing, supportive chairs, which make you think you floated, having lost all bodily pull towards the centre of the earth. Just suspension. And she sat across, leaning her mature, almost but not yet middle-aged arm on a glass-covered, white iron table, an open rose underneath to support it. All iron. *Quite useless,* he thought, except for a cigar-cutting contraption, a small silver bell cut in angles he had not noticed before. And her not yet old, round arm.

"Look at the gardens," Martina said, "cut and stylized this morning. The French gardens. We have this extraordinary luck, Felix, to be able to employ a new, beautiful young man – mainly paid by *Schönbrunn,* would you believe? – on extra hours. He styles, cuts, trims, lovingly, every blade – smell the air full of cut grass – a different world from the front door. It is a world in which to find one's bearings, to remind you of home," she said, while turning to the little silver bell.

"Oh don't," he said, "don't bring Annie in."

"Don't you want a drink?" she said.

"Well, a glass of water maybe. Yes, a glass of water." He rose from his comfort, walked the length of the balcony, where the house turned towards the street, took a moment longer to avoid the silver sound of the bell and the face of Annie. When he returned, very slowly this time, Martina noticed his limp, which he hid with perfection when not stressed. A stiff leg, which made him suddenly look taller, more commanding unexpectedly. Stretching it before him, in pain perhaps, he sat down to say:

"A beautiful young man, did you say? Another one, I'm not surprised, and may I humbly ask, if your husband – ?"

"He is cutting the grass and creating a fairyland, that is all I said, don't insinuate anything. Here is your glass of water, dear," she said, handing him the crystal glass full of the coloured play of fractured light.

He pushed it away, suddenly, with a determined gesture, saying, "Not yet, the time is wrong." Smiling, touched the shirt pocket that bulged a little more than the other. "I have ten grams of barbiturate in here and that is what the water is for, but I can't vomit easily for simple *theatrics*. As for the real thing, the time is not ripe."

"Whose?" she said. He smiled enigmatically, tried to get up on the stiff leg, which made her suddenly realize it was his artificial limb. She jumped to her feet, to help him get up, holding his left arm close for support; when he turned, he embraced her with his right arm as he said *sotto voce:*

"Kiss me, Martina, kiss me."

"You're mad," she said, turning her face away. "My husband will be here for dinner in no time. Annie will come and clean up, the gardener –" and she freed herself from his grip, which made him tumble slightly. Regaining balance, his face a mask, he said, "There will be penance."

"Oh Felix, go my sweetheart, we know the scene, it has been with us uncountable times."

"Not forever though. Not today, but there will be another glass of water – you can't escape, Martina. Not my destiny." She held him firmly now, saying quiet things – "Get a taxi, go home" – she rang and Annie appeared from nowhere.

"Naturally," he said, "she stood behind the curtain."

"Annie, help him down the steps."

"No," he said, "I won't have her. You. I want you to give me a hand. All these steps down."

"Is this my penance today? Is it?" she asked.

"It may be accepted as such –" and he smiled: a small, triumphant movement around the eyes and mouth. They went down, his good leg first and the other pulled behind. Step by step. He loved her. On his arm, her touch alone – for so little, so mundane a reason – made him unutterably happy – he would have fallen to his knees, had it been possible. They went together into the airless street, but he felt just jubilation. Martina hailed a taxi, which pulled to the curb, and said, "Take the gentleman to 45 *Weingartenstrasse*, please." She watched him leave, and waited until he was out of sight.

They had been children together. Martina a pastor's daughter, Evangelical, Lutheran. The father of a mixed Czernowitz heritage, with all strains of that land. The mother German, of the Roscher Swabians. Martina, their only child, was elflike, with black eyes against a translucent skin. She moved as if free of flesh. Felix had seen her one day running up the Gallows Hill and had wondered if her parents knew. *She should not go up there, she is just a tiny little thing, someone may put a stone in front of her shoe, she may slip and fall and break those almost non-existent bones. I'll rescue her. No, no, she shouldn't go there.*

On the way home now, after having been close enough to smell the acetone from her breath – which to him, a trained scientist of the biological sciences, meant she was either fearful or hungry, and he hoped it was the former – he trembled. Recalling that breath brought it all back: the nearness of her arm when walking down the staircase, her almost leaning on his, and the light rub against his right flank. It seemed so long a walk – the time it took down the staircase – so rare for happy moments.

"Go around the *Ringstrasse*," tapping the chauffeur on the shoulder, Felix said. "Go by the *Burgtheater*."

"There is construction there," the taxi man said. Felix so longed for the memory of sitting by her. They had seen each other several years after the war, for the first time, when their eyes met over the heads of an enormous theatre crowd. A recognition so intense it wiped all the yesterdays away. They had forced their way through the protesting multitude, and fallen into each other's arms to kiss. The crowd understood, and in spite of its former anger made way, watching a reunion everyone around them had perhaps dreamed about. Holding hands, they had advanced towards the doors. Aided, smiled at, the usherette was willing for a price to reseat them and Felix and Martina found themselves to be a love-play within a love-play. Overwhelmed by the encounter, they were totally speechless, hearts beating with the poetic pulse on stage. A play pure as their own: Lessing's *Nathan der Weise* – love as wisdom – the parable of the three rings with equal worth, being played out on stage. It reached them through their trance; people sitting next to them, touching them almost to be part of it. The message of a father to his children. That was then, and he still wonders how he parted and allowed himself to lose sight of her.

"Go around the *Karlskirche* –St. Charles Church," he said now to the taxi man, "if it can't be the *Ringstrasse*, go around St. Charles's."

The taxi man, worried about his fee, said, "It will cost you, sir, an arm and a leg."

"Don't worry," Felix handing him money said, "just drive half an hour, rest by St. Charles's and then bring me home."

"All right," said the taxi man – he who knew the world in its variety almost as well as barbers and prostitutes. Pocketing the money, he said *"Geht in Ordnung,"* and stopped behind St. Charles for a cigarette.

Yes, it was here at her wedding that he had touched flathandedly his shirt pockets for the first time. *A Catholic wedding for a Lutheran girl,* he, a Jew had thought, *this tops everything.* Looking for pain it was not hard to find: he had stood among strangers in the church, where the scent of roses hanging from the pews and the hats of the elderly ladies mingled with naphthalene from the black, freshly brushed suits of Viennese men. Smelling it, Felix had felt his absent toes, shin bone and knee so vividly, so violently that he had to look down to reassure himself of their absence. *So, a taken leg is never taken. It is always there. No scalpel can take it.*

And he felt it was so with his sweetheart, who was standing there next to a still young-looking, slender man. She had tea roses in her hair and hands and wore an off-white light *voile* suit, showing her ankles above her pumps. Organ music filling the church with a rich sound had made him ask a young girl to give up her seat for him. It was the beginning of a ritual: the strains of that Mendelssohn, *Here comes the bride,* and the touching of his shirt pocket. The other pocket too, with a different stuff. "Make sure it's there," he had said to himself smilingly. "Make sure it's there."

"This is it," said the taxi man, "this is it, I'll take you home."

"Thank you," Felix said. "Thank you."

IT HAD BEEN A GOOD DAY; Felix stretching into his narrow sofa felt again her arm pressing his and her voice in his ear hailing the taxi. *How modest I have become,* he thought. *To take morsels for a meal and be grateful for it like a beggar.*

Women were his world, an exclusive territory – not walking over them, but with them, and on their hand, through a charmed landscape. They were all his to play or not to play with, to throw spoken lines across and have them come back with a throat full of laughter. He was at home in their world, in symbolic French, or comfortable in the German nursery rhyme. They sang to him, his maids of the lower classes in sorrowful minor or dance-major keys, and he walked through their world with a lightness of foot and heart as if at home. The Romanian servant Ileana first. She took him up by the age of fourteen, and opened or lowered the peasant *décolleté* to hand him her breast – pink and brown. *Give it to me. Let me* – but she pushed him down, laughing that raucous sound, and said, "Not yet, not yet, rascal."

All loved her; the girls loved her, joked, pulling apart her wrapped-around skirt. Only mother didn't, he thought. Well, not really disliked her – it may just have been a competing-female dislike – but one could not escape Ileana's charm. Not even my mother. Hard work all day, carrying wood from the cellar on her back to feed all the tile ovens, she kept her legs apart for better balance. She laughed, saying, "Thank God for my peasant square feet to hold it all." Threw the wood down with a jerk and shouted, "Felix, good for nothing, come help!" and he ran to her. "For a kiss, I'll do it, for a kiss."

And she, "Nothing, you get nothing for it, just work now!" But before bending towards his task she took his right hand and put it upon her left breast; so full a breast as if just to spill it all into his hand. But it didn't, it stayed ripe and round and he thought, *This is my breast for the rest of my days.*

Being fourteen, the rest of one's days is like tomorrow! Or yesterday. What does one know of passing, past, and what of to come? *I worked for her, we bent down to pick up the wood and I helped her in carrying it and setting it up, so the firing would be easy, sizing it, the smaller on top. I did it for Ileana. Even without reward. Just to be next to Mother Earth! Ileana. What a good day it was.*

Up the fourth floor — there were only three in my grandfather's house, the fourth was all attic. Drying linen, stiff in the winter, they dried to frozen boards, and the summers for us boys under the roof was a hothouse, but it was our world. I still dream of this first time. To have lain between her legs. Shielded by linen in a private cocoon and watched by Hans, for my pleasure and his. So he would see what I can do. The first to go dare and enter that fortress woman. And it was not so awkward as they all said it would be.

Felix rose to a beautiful Vienna morning. His back-of-the-*Ringstrasse* tenant's digs facing east gave him a feeling of a retrieved, regained youth. Stateless and totally unattached, he had run from Bucharest through Hungary, guarded by heavenly forces it seemed. *There aren't any, of course,* he smiled at that singular mixture of truth and the disbelief of it, and dressed avoiding yes-terday's shirt, the one with the two pockets, ten grams of Luminal in the one and two grams of morphine in the other. *No glass of water today. Oh, the games I play. Being on the run for so long – Run. What a word!*

"Why run now," he said, "if I can't even walk? Though as then, through war-swept frontiers, into Russia ahead of the Germans, and with or just slightly behind the Russians, I still could."

Wiener Wald

SELMA

H
E ROSE TO A BEAUTIFUL VIENNA MORNING. WIENER
Wald is bright in late May. Vienna woods are a young
green, almost golden, with the sun bringing out what hope there
is in its still unfolded foliage. Felix considered taking the tramway
in front of the *Burgtheater.* Somehow in Vienna all roads lead to
the woods. Different from his home town Czernowitz, which was
backed to the southwest by wooded, sheltering mountains, mixing pine and birch – but open to the northeast, and across to the
steppe.

Standing in front of the old theatre, Felix saw actors moving
in and out and felt again that strange attraction to the strolling
life, where masks change and one can be another, albeit for a short
few hours. Standing there, he addressed an elderly woman, in her
seventies perhaps, Scandinavian-looking. She seemed familiar,
and he remembered her name as Olafsen from the playbill and
asked her which tram to take and how to get into the green
Wiener Wald – the Vienna Woods – or any other.

"Wonderful," she said, "Mister…?"

"It is Felix Geller."

"Great, Mr. Geller," she said, "I've finished rehearsal, I'm tired of the town and of my colleagues. I know a small restaurant behind the theatre, which makes the best *Brötchen* on earth. Let's take some along with mineral water. Wait here, I'll be right back."

It did not take long and she was back, carrying a paper bag with lunch and mineral water in small bottles. She knew which tram to take, and Felix went with a total stranger to spend the day. Not a total stranger perhaps, because he had not forgotten the face he had seen on stage.

Felix and women: they always respond. And not just Ileana and Marusja – servants both – or his beautiful mother. But elf-like creatures of seven or eight. Martina, who saw him for the very first time as a very young man when he ran into her in the open garden of the Evangelical church.

Selma Olafsen wore her shoulder bag criss-crossed over her left breast so both hands were free to hold paper bag and bottles. She was svelte, unselfconscious, and moved towards him with familiarity. A kinship. One that responded to Felix in simple, non-threatening ways. She mounted the tram laughing, and he helped her up first so she would not miss the step and then was fast behind her as the crowd had gathered and pushed him lightly. They were actors and theatre people glad to have finished the technical rehearsal of lights and God knows what, glad to get home or out into the green, like Felix and Selma. It was Sunday noon, late May.

Selma reached into her bag for the tram tickets, Felix holding lunch and bottles. Both were in a hilarious state, having found each other for the day without searching. They laughed, and everyone else felt spring in the air. Viennese, often silly, had an *esprit* of their own, everyone tuned in; including the *Schaffner* –

conductor, ticket-puncher, or whatever one calls them – who, mocking his own authority in Vienna-dialect, called out: "It is ready when I say it's ready," then pulled the tinkly bell and they were off.

Leaning back into the wooden comfort of the hard-backed seats, they were silent for a while, recuperating from a sudden decision, the nearness of the other, and dreaming a little without content. "It's another hour or so," she whispered to Felix, respecting everyone's quiet moment. Most of them she knew, if not by name, at least by sight. Across from her sat a young man who seemed older now, and another one whose face was still and inscrutable. Pointing in his direction, she said to Felix, "These are my two colleagues in the play. I'm the housekeeper and these are the two sons. We are rehearsing and changing things around."

It was *Exiles* by James Joyce, his only play, and Felix had seen it the week before. He had intended to go back to see it again, and had hoped Martina and her husband would join him. He fell silent now for a little while longer his absent toe twitched; a sharp pain moving over the vertebrae to the crown of his head. It was the thought of Martina, sharing her bed and body with a stranger. *I, who have loved her since she was sixteen.*

It had been some time since the "home-grown," the Czernowitz-native Germans left *Heim ins Reich.* By Christmas, 1939, they had all gone. Cattle in the fields, dogs in front of the door, left to grieve. They took what they could carry. Martina's mother, more "German" in the newly acquired image than all the others, left her husband, a righteous man of what she called "mixed blood." And it was just the local variety of Jews, Ukrainian and German. Just a few grandmothers, making to the newly acquired consciousness a strange difference. So Rosy packed her bags, fed her dreams of glory as any stage-mom would, took Martina her daughter, and left. Of course, a pastor's life was ascetic and poor. His wife's even more so, being watched and judged and living in glass houses. "I've seen her going to the movies –" Crime number one among true Lutherans. Moving pictures at the time being the devil incarnate. And she did go to the movies.

A Swabian girl from Rosch, married young to a theologian, true and evangelical, both mother and daughter had no easy life. So she ran *Heim ins Reich,* imbuing it with all the hopes she had hoarded and nurtured through the years. Worse was to come than she had ever known.

Felix's toe twitched as if alive. Martina. Forbidden thoughts. Loss. *She is still mine. Marrying does not change the past. She can never be anyone else's.* But he felt the absent knee. Brigands couldn't take it. Smiling at the thought, Felix remembered the splintering noise, the shot, the breaking of the bone. *If I can't lose a leg, how would I lose my love.*

He smiled again, turned imperceptibly to Selma, who said, "We're here, we have arrived," waking Felix from his non-sleep. But he had rested on her side, got up elegantly, hiding his stiff leg. She, in spite of wrong shoes – city shoes, a lightly elevated heel with a strap across – set the rhythm of the stride firmly. He fell into her step, as if he had always been there, not taking her arm, having to walk behind her in the single file furrow for a short time. But then a wide, well-travelled road opened up, lined on both sides with the young yet almost yellow-green he so loved. Vistas of a hilly land, rising as if in motion, made him sing to the step. Selma was familiar with his German folk song, marching song, and student-corps song, so good for truly stepping out, so she laughed and said, "Felix, you're a treasure, how do you know them all? Heavens! I had to know them," she said. "Not at my mother's knee, but I played with children and everyone else – and in the Nazi-time, well German folk song was the nationalistic thing to do. But you! You're a Jew, aren't you?"

"How do you know," Felix asked, "is it written all over my nose? Mine happens to be a totally non-*Streicher* nose, not bent by the weight of religion, just a tiny ridiculous straight nose I always disliked," Felix said. "Who knows why we dislike certain parts of our body? I just thought it did not fit into my face."

"It does fit very well, and it has nothing to do with noses, I just know a Jew if I see one."

Selma, knowing every pebble of this road, turned towards a clearing along a long line of *Waldrand* – a boundary sheltering the wanderer – holding the woods contained. It opened towards the southern sun, and they paused, having strained up a little to see the wide valley stretched before them. Busying themselves with opening the mineral water a little after having sat down in the grass, they both drank without a glass from the bottle, laughing and talking.

Felix, in his yellow shirt today, was young. He took one of those *Gänseblümchen* – a tiny daisy the Austrian hills are strewn with – to put it into a buttonhole and said to Selma, turning his face fully towards her, "Anybody ever told you how beautiful you are?"

"It's not about me today," she said. "By the way, many a man, woman, and child has done just that, and also my almost incestuous brother in the empty Swedish heartland – yes, they told me that, but today it is about you. Felix, how did you come out of that whole unimaginable thing?"

"Not easily," he said, "not easily. We had a family council around my mother's dinner table and it was decided I should run with the Russians. They had by then retreated, and most of the Jews, fearing the full German might against them – those only of course who felt the strength to run – had done so.

"I was late and slow by nature, not having ever been a young man of action," and he laughed a little. "Dreamy and pampered by my cultured mother, I was slow. But once the decision was taken and dinner was over they all rushed to make me go. Packed a rucksack, lined it with two twenty-dollar American bills in condoms, put in sausage, bread, and dried fruit, woollen socks, a sweater and heavy coat in the middle of summer – the first week of July perhaps. The year was 1941 – it's more than twenty years. And I walked out of my grandfather's house, to return just once for a fleeting visit. It had been after three years of running between both armies deep into Russia and back. But it is too long a story for a short May day, so please, Miss Olafsen, let's just live the day – let's *profiter du temps.*"

"Yes," she said, "just let's. Yes, I see you know that French *bergerette* from the seventeenth or eighteenth century perhaps, *'Jeune fillette profitez du temps.'* And she sang it with a slightly harsh northern sound. He knew it, but let her sing all the verses. He knew those French ditties. Mother and sister sang them. It was light, gentle, melancholy, about spring, the picking of the violet in season and all things passing. Making light of it and reducing it as only the French knew how, without taking the weight fully from your shoulders.

"Where will we have our lunch, here or down in the valley?"

"Here," he said, curious to see what she had chosen from the shop. One sandwich with a smoked fish, a *Bückling*, and one with

Viennese potted cheese, smelling of spring chives; they shared both, rested a little longer to stretch out after the meal, collected the wrapping, drank their mineral water, and started the descent. For today this was enough talk, until Selma said, "I love your yellow shirt, Felix, it looks like raw silk. Is it?"

"Yes, it is," he said, "it is my 'good-day' shirt, the one I wear when I do not think I might commit suicide."

"Pardon me," she said.

"Yes, this is right," he said. "I have another one with two pockets, two small buttons on it to keep them closed for a while, where I always carry Luminal in one and morphine in the other. Always. Of course, only since the day my father – well, from that day after dinner, when I left my grandfather's house forever."

"RUSSIA IS BIG and the Tsar is far indeed, Selma. One accepts all iniquities: no application for release, help, a parcel to receive, or to write a letter – which may lie a few years in the hand of guards. One day though, someone may hand you a bowl of soup and it may be his only ration. A grace that will make you weep and think of God and the man next to you. It happened to me," Felix said when he met Selma next Sunday noon in front of the Burg to take the tram again into the green somewhere. "*Grinzing* perhaps?"

"No," she said, "skies are threatening, it does not look promising for the day. We had a terrible performance last night, I forgot my lines, threw the whole thing – well, not totally, someone ad libbed and rescued me. We laughed like crazy afterwards, making jokes of the lower category like 'Next time Selma will forget to pee before performance, she'll do it all over the stage and we'll have to suddenly spill water or wine and say oh dear – to make it believable to the idiots out there.' But I cried all night because I felt my age and the jokes of my colleagues – much, much younger than I am – were directed right at me, and at my expense."

She pulled Felix across and they walked slowly, hand in hand this time, like old schoolmates, across the *Pflaster,* the pavement she knew so well, to the actors' hangout behind the Burg. Sunday. Just a few people. Sometimes Poldy closed on Sunday. Not today, a cloudy day, people not rushing to the outdoors. Greeting Selma Olafsen with that brotherly grin of many days together, Poldy – knowing her tears and triumphs – said, "So, *Liebling,* a much younger man now, are we there already?"

"Tell us what you have today – or just give us some of your *Brötchen* and a glass of wine, light please." Selma moved through the tables towards a dark corner, where mahogany wainscoting went half the up wall, with pictures of the Wessely family, Paula and the rest, young and not so young Hamlets above them. Felix had never been in that Sanctum Sanctorum; that witness to life on the boards – the most desirable boards on earth. It looked stable, respectable, and forever, but only those who had stood on these boards knew how they rotted under your very soles. Selma this Sunday noon felt her age. But looking into the sunny face of Felix, golden shirt, hair of a chestnut brown falling onto his neck, she felt youth returning, but did not dare think she was falling in love. Reaching across the table, she wanted just a touch of the other, but taking his full hand into hers did not let it go. A sudden longing for nearness made her move a little closer to the edge of the round table to inhale his breath.

"It is about you today," Felix said, sensing her readiness to give herself body and soul. "Speak, tell, where did you grow up? Why did you say 'incestuous' brother?"

"Because he was. We're from the open, inner cornfield land of Sweden, a land ripe with legend told by the old maids in the kitchen and the idle grandmother sleeping in the shed at the back of the barn, waiting for the children. Stories of mighty Swedish giants who make the corn grow, but only if we children are good. All this lies on our shoulders, and if we starve next winter it is because the corn did not grow and it is our fault. Candles snuffed out, we huddled together, we two, to listen, tremble, then rush into the cold linen to console one another. True love is love. We were brother and sister, twins, with parents of the prehistoric sort, good, hard-working, but in cold beds and barren after our birth. So we were one in the womb, and it was a thrill on winter days, when steady prayer, clouds hanging low and school made the days pass slowly, too long for our reunion. Yes, one bed of course. How many beds does a peasant need? We were lucky to have a room of our own. But the joyless life of our good parents and the life of our mother's mother in the back shed made us swear a blood bond to each other. And I scratched the skin around Johan's inner wrist and dipped my own red drop into it." And Selma brushed her bracelet away to reveal under the sleeve of her sweater small scars, healed but visible. "What else is there?"

"Nothing else, except hunger," Felix replied. "Except hunger."

"Enough for a Sunday morning, that will do." And she took her hand from his, seeing good old Poldy with *Brötchen*, wine glasses, and opened bottle, "To let it breathe," he said. He knew of course what she liked, and she said, looking at the spread, "Poldy, you have outdone yourself. Lox on pumpernickel, capers strewn across, the butter showing and Emmenthal, the true Swiss cheese on a *Stritzel* – the white, hard, crusted Viennese bun."

In that brown wooden corner, sheltered by the passing life, shelves ancient with paraphernalia of useless objects above their heads like a roof of the moment, they fell in love. Quiet couples around them filled Poldy's café more and more. A few coming in, colleagues perhaps, showing familiar smiles, asking with their eyes who the stranger across from her may be. Acknowledging their presence by a light turn of the head, she wanted to stay unapproached and separate, and the actors around her, sensitive to the strange turns life took, seemed to tone down their voices.

But it also was the end of their morning. Felix felt her rough night, saw it in her face, and said, "Go, sweetheart, have a shower and sleep. You can reach me at this address," and gave her a little written note, which she rewarded with a formal *Visitenkarte* of Miss Selma Olafsen. *Hofburgschauspielerin.* Touching each other's cheek lightly *à la française,* they parted.

TONIGHT HE WAS HAPPY

IT HAD BEEN A LONG TREK GOING EAST. FELIX RECALLED leaving the old house and Mary, Süssel's dog, would not let him go, had clung to him, following him down the steps, all three floors down, pulling her arthritic hind legs along. It was with his last look into Mary's eyes, that he closed the heavy gate calling back, "Go home, Mary. I know you love me. I know, don't cry, go home," as he went down the last four stone steps.

He had hugged his father, coming close to his warm brown face for the first time since childhood. And for the last time had heard the golden chain move, link against link, that light rustle, announcing it was time to come or to go, when father pulled his watch from the vest coat. A familiar, threatening sound. A ritual of the daily sort, ingrained with the meal, the hour of it, and the steaming terrine.

It tinkled now, this evening also, when he undressed. Chain and watch had not left him since Mother handed it to him from under her pillow a small moment before her death. A vestige now, an amulet almost, a way of asking to be forgiven. It was always with him. "I will wear it," he had said to Süssel on his mother's bed, "every day of my life." A penance for not having loved when there was still time.

Gold had a special sounding rustle, and Felix heard it as a coda to the past. He took watch and chain from the vest coat which he wore over his shirt, laid them tonight into a pattern of a curling snake, concentric circles moving as if alive; another night the gold would fall into geometrical squares, more abstract and unde-manding of sentiment. Today he was happy. He laid snakes out onto his night table, encircled the watch as was his habit. The dial showed nine o'clock, and he hummed to himself, able to face the memory of his father's house with greater ease.

He had kissed his sister, but always the last hug, tears mingling unashamedly, was for his mother. A unison so intense: of taste, of all things sensuous. A sleight of hand, a magic skill of laughing at the same joke, subtle sometimes, scatological another, mother and son in unison, held hands like lovers. He was fourteen.

Walking down the old staircase, they would turn away from the Gallows Hill, ignoring the legend, and up the wooded street behind the Evangelical church, chestnut-lined, changing in sea-son from bloom to fruit to barren branches. The two held hands, walking up the slightly hilly road and around the corner to the *Schillerpark*. After piano, Latin, and the rest, after having tutored his younger sister, which was a terrible nuisance because Felix felt her grasp to be good enough but not as fast as his, and calling her all names possible as only brothers can, he shouted to his mother, "It's enough already. Come for a walk or I'll go mad." They laughed, and she, his mother, ran with her son down all *her* father's staircase, to cross the street past the Ahi fountain, not lis-tening to the murmur of evil, the memories of the Turkish hench-man, retold by generations of maids and mothers.

He was young and adolescent on his mother's hand. Martina
he had seen for the first time on these walks, passing behind the
church gardens. Her elfin frame crouched in the grass, and she
looked up when they passed. He saw her eyes, black violets they
were, and melting into the green. His mother waved hello, having known Martina since birth, "This is a beautiful girl," mother
said. "Heavens, Felix, watch out!" Such memories.

Felix hung his yellow shirt a bit differently because it crumpled a little as *soie écrue* tended to do in such a tight closet. He let
it air, smiling at his linen shirt with the pockets full of stuff, glad
it was there and he not in need of it. He went out into the corridor to ask permission of his landlady and pay a few schillings for
a shower – hateful long corridors these were with doors leading
into stifling and badly lit bathrooms. Thinking of Martina's pala-
tial flat, gardens at the back and maids in the kitchen, he felt no
envy, smiled tonight at his cheap digs with landladies who know
all your hours, locked their toilets on you, and did it as if friendly.
Poor creatures, he thought, *caught in their dailiness, they have
smirks for smiles, knowing your underbelly. Inherited heavy
Biedermeyer furniture taking their last breath away, if there was one,
windows not opening for the fear of air or draught – they live by your
life.* And he made light of it, tonight – nothing mattered. He had
fallen in love.

Today he was happy. As if fourteen on his mother's hand, and
much before the steady flight from armed men, Russian or
German, the two had ran up the *Rothkirchgasse* in Czernowitz,
and on the highest point of the *Schillerpark*, behind the entrance,
sheltered by flowering hedges – yellow forsythia perhaps – they
had sat down. The village Rosch lay before them. Felix wanting
to kiss her, but, feeling it was wrong, he didn't, instead laid his

head on his mother's shoulder. He just let it lie there for a short moment of melancholy. Her stillness in reply, her holding back of herself, not reaching out to him, taught him he might not kiss her. And both were sad. But she sprang to her feet, laughter cascading from her lips like silver, as if there had not been a moment's shadow before. "Let's run down the hill where the cows are." And off they were.

Tonight he was happy. Like fourteen in some ways. Selma Olafsen's figure, by twenty or thirty years his senior, across from him, her gently touching his cheek on both sides when parting, made him feel that all was permitted, that he could kiss his mother without feeling a burst of guilt, of wrongdoing. It was nine o'clock. He looked again at the coiled snake on his night table, rushed into his vest coat that hung around the back of the chair to find her address. Whistled the Beethoven air between his teeth, *Ich liebe Dich sowie Du mich – I love you as you do love me.* Read the *Visitenkarte*, put his brown hair in order with an available comb under the blind mirror, and ran down the stairs before the *Hausmeister*'s ten o'clock closing of the gate. Feeling for the gate's key in his pant pocket, he hailed a cab from the open road, so anxious he was to see her face and not miss this night.

The friendly, elderly cabman knew exactly where she lived when Felix mentioned the address – Did he know her? *Of course not, he is just a sweet old man, seeing my ardour,* Felix thought. It was not too long a ride, and he searched in his trouser pocket for the right money, could not find it, paid handsomely, saying, "Keep the *Trinkgeld*," and found himself in front of a lovely old house in a district of Villas. It was almost ten o'clock, a Viennese night of spring, perfumed. A young woman stepped out on the arm of a man and he feared it was Selma. He rang her bell. She had heard the taxi stop and had repeatedly walked by the window since eight o'clock in the evening, hoping or almost knowing that he would come. She pulled him in, coming down the few steps towards the garden gate, one of those low iron gates, there not to protect, just to stake out property.

They almost ran to close the door behind them, and against that door they fell upon one another as if at the end of a search. They were not strangers. They seemed to have been lovers always. Her stocking and shoes flew from her feet and he giggled pulling his trousers down – a bane of a gesture for the very young, not knowing which way to turn to hide the buttons or the zip depending on the age – to be suddenly naked, without all obvious doing. None of it. Joyful and unashamed there was no time for viewing, and they saw one another only after they had come to rest. "Selma, it seems to me" – having caught his breath – "that I am running down the *Schillerpark,* having almost kissed my mother."

"Wonderful, wonderful," she replied, "I'm accustomed to incest."

"Well, no, not really kiss her. It's different with Jews, they don't let go of the law, it sits in there no matter what circumstance. No Vatican, no institution of whatever to enforce it, and there it is, like a stone in the stomach. So no, not really kiss her."

"Oh, dear Felix, what will I call you? Having never slept with a Jew or seen one undressed." Giggles, "We'll see. I know you and I have all sorts of private names for people. Early practice, I don't know yet. It seems to me I have also run through the waving corn on my brother's hand on all those days our feared giant was benevolent and the corn stood yellow and thick. It meant we had been good, guilty of nothing. Carefree and happy, we could be children. And like children all was private and hidden from the gloomy and burdened adults, who lived – it seemed to Johan and myself – up there above us a strange and censorious life. Alien. Our world was fear, too, but joyous and closed to them. Criminals, you could not beat the truth out of us. Not beat it and not beg it. We had faces of stone to this outer torture. We may have prayed silently, but words and address was of our making.

"It was I who invented this game. I found a hiding place in a cupboard with shelves ranged in sizes and depth and I crawled into the deepest, high up. It was dark and had a sweet old smell of dry heather. *Johan, Johan, come up there, I found my own church.* He was a little taller than I, not fitting as well, but ducked. We crouched into one another as we had done in the womb and Johan started with words of his making. They became our code, prayer, or oath, and seemed to be recalling long forgotten Gods, residing in our bloodstream. Memories of the far north. A chimney was our steeple and we looked from our cupboard into a Walhalla of Johan and Selma."

Felix on her breast and in her arm, somnolent from a day of search and find, turned to kiss her goodnight and said, "I have to leave by seven in the morning. I work for a living, not like my other friends," he said, not to be tempted again.

"What do you do?"

"I am a pharmacist, and have found work with other colleagues from my hometown, Czernowitz. It is not very lucrative, these are my old Vienna friends from student days who had opened the pharmacy in a district where Czernowitzers congregate, and they are not well to do. But it suits me to be with my own. It is in the ninth *Bezirk, Severingasse* adjoining *Brigittenau.*"

"It is not a very respectable part of town. Sort of poor, where one never knows whom one will meet next. Colourful but a little frightening too."

"It's where the *Ostjuden* find asylum. Vienna has to give shelter to its citizens from the east. Even in World War I, Czernowitzers used to come here, again, running from the Russian invasion in 1914–1915 to outlast the war. It has always been a district of poverty and working class. Suburban without its glamour or amenities. But I like it there."

"Why would you, if it's poor?"

"It's cozy, they're my own people. I feel at home. At home in the wine shops, with old dusty bottles on the shelves and no worry about aesthetics. Well, it offers a moment's rest for the working class. I like it."

Morning came sooner than imagined, and Felix hurried away with a wave of his hand.

IT WAS A JEWISH SHOP Felix had entered on his first day in Vienna, and refugees from all over the east congregated there. It was summer, 1951. Exiles looked for one another, strangers became friends with the first glass of wine. And stories of mass murder, personal accounts of rescue, as well as unimaginable images of cruelty coloured this first day and the joy of having reached Vienna; so the hope of re-conquering his youth or reviving his father's suffered a blow. And he took up residence where all his Czernowitzers were, not to be so utterly single and alien, in the *Währingerstrasse* first and then in the *Severingasse*. Emptied of the Jews by the Nazis, these tenements were now havens to the newcomers from the east. *Pensions* sprang up to house them. He had courageously entered one of the lower flats where a *pension*

with gourmet cuisine was advertised in one of its windows. He
had walked from the first *Bezirk*, as he had as a student in Vienna,
enchanted with its Austrian-ness, and its being so much bigger
and more formal than its smaller sister, Czernowitz, in the east.
But he was very tired now, older too, and a post-war mentality
had changed his wish to explore the town further. He wouldn't
stop in at the *Rathausstrasse* with its homogeneous, squarish, endless rows of newly built rental buildings. *How beautiful and how
distinguished is our* Rathausstrasse *in Czernowitz,* he thought.
*How varied, changing, and hilly, where occasional small parks and
the Catholic cathedral embellished it.* It was as if there was no air
here, no breath to be had between this uniformity of greystone,
and he had hurried away, ignoring the "reasonably-priced" *pensions* for rent, as their signs announced on their doors. He had
hurried away.

And Felix came, again and again to Selma. Stayed longer, for
talk, nearness, and for that poetic kinship he had felt when he first
had seen her on stage. So rich. It was as if they had never made
love before. He followed every criss-crossing line around her eyes
and the parallel ones above the brow along the hairline. He kissed
her mouth, open for his tongue, but didn't take it, and watched
her cheeks, vivid now with colour.

Selma thought he was or must be a sorcerer and that she
would likely pay for this bliss. *Yes, I will pay for it, there is no
escape. Too beautiful to leave, it may be my last encounter with youth.*
But she had seen a certain awkwardness, an unexpected turn of
his left leg. Unexpected, for a man as dextrous and graceful as
Felix. And she suddenly knew her friend had an artificial limb
and had learnt to hide it. It made him more desirable yet, a little
closer to herself and not so young.

Waiting for his next move, she let all her muscles distend, stripping them of motion, and noiselessly removed her remaining *culottes*. But he wouldn't acknowledge it, stayed where he was to follow her age, her life around throat and ear, her back, neckline, and slowly removed the golden ashes from it. And ashes they were. Greying, the gold was still with them, and he went with his right hand, lying on his left side, through the ashes. Thinking and speaking poetry. From his hometown poet, she did not know:

Your golden hair, Margarete,
Your ashen hair, Shulamith.

Paul Celan. Czernowitzers know one another, though Celan was younger than Felix. Celan, a poet, a tongue-magician, who turned our mother-German into bitterest pain. Yet honouring it.

Your golden hair, Margarete,
Your ashen hair, Shulamith.

And Felix's own lines rose to his tongue. The poetry of his Bucharest years before the falling of the Iron Curtain. Lines of longing and reinvented pain. Selma, who spoke the great texts of *Electra* and *Antigone*, knew how to listen. And he was grateful but, "No, not tonight," he said.

Selma

BELOVED LIAR

AND SELMA LET IT BE AS IT WAS, A MOTHER-SON, MOST intimate day. Waking early, he untangled himself gently from her limbs, to leave her in comfort, as if he hadn't gone. "Sorcerer," she thought. "Liar, beloved liar, dandy. Of course, I know you'll leave me. How would a mother not feel when her baby moves? Every one of your turns, silent or spoken I absorb, and will replay it like a record when you have left me – and you will. But not yet. I watch you dress – sock and shoe on one foot only – that is funny! How will your pants fit over it? Routine is born from day one! I watch my face so it will not break into smiles; I can fool him as he fools me. Or thinks he does. You never can trick a mother. She knows everything.

"I watch him: funny, almost feminine, small little panties; does he pull them down to pee, as we do? Oh, boys, how seriously you take your lives. I can swear there is no opening in front. But he has turned already. So I'll never know, has seated himself to put on his slim, utterly hugging trousers, got into them with a turn of a dancer's foot, as if in slippers and not in shoes with a slightly upped heel. He is not a tall man. To find vanity in my Felix, to find it in a heel I had not suspected. He is elegant and fast, in spite of his obvious handicap. Belt, no suspenders. The day is early, so colours do not show. But the shirt is golden copper that mingles with his darker hair, lying loose on an open collar. No tie, thank God. I hate them, they are the ugliest invention. He turns to my vanity mirror and I see, through half-opened eyes, his face in it. In this air of dawn, of swimming shades that almost erase all features, he is the adolescent God of my childhood dreams, he looks like or is Johan to me. Youth re-given. Through the slits of my eyes and holding all muscles in check I watch him comb his hair with my silver brush and comb set. He puts them back into their absolutely exact former position with a fussiness for order and law I had not guessed in him either. All soundless. My sweet now turns, takes his briefcase to go, stops for a second, opens it to remove a handful of pages and leaves them on the dining table on the way out. Turns again to look at me, tenderly, it seems, and leaves fast. Oh, he has left his vest coat, with watch and chain, around the back of the chair. I hear him return and fetch it. Businesslike. Hurried.

"I am left to have breakfast by myself. I put the kettle on and start to learn my part. But will not: I'll take it slower this morning, to rethink and savour. How old is he? I cannot tell. Forty-five, fifty, or twenty. Of course not twenty, after war, murder, and survival. The way he stood at my mirror, looking intensely, with his hands over his brow checking a receding hairline. No. It couldn't be. Just worried, peripherally. I open the door to find fresh *Brötchen* in one bag and *Kaisersemmel* in the other. I never had fresh white rolls in my childhood, but once in Vienna I loved those horse-drawn wagons, stopping in front of all houses with bread fresh from the oven. All Vienna is transfused with hope in the morning. I do not think people will murder one another before breakfast. Just not to miss coffee, heavenly rolls, and freshly beaten butter.

"The *Jokastha* script before me, *Brötchen* in a basket, my eyes fell on his tightly written pages on my table. No, I will not touch them before the joy of breakfast, for a little more lingering ease, unpressured, like lying in the fields near Johan, hand in hand or his on my not-yet breast.

Selma biting into the crusty roll with a dab of butter and marmalade on it, which was not orange, delighted in her morning. Long hours of nothing but feeling. She missed childhood's endlessness. So long to get to the next adult day. *Lying in the corn, high-standing corn, we found a bed and a roof above with giants roaming. As they do in the Scandinavian imagination.* And Selma smiled again, taking a sip of her rich, creamy chocolate. No coffee today. Cream came to the door, left by the milkman, and she decided against the kettle. She'd have hot chocolate, with whipped cream for the luxury of the moment, languid ease, and a sip of glory. She stretched her limbs into a *chaise longue,* as if in the corn, stubbly or rich with first growth. Johan and all the northern giants. They roamed and carried destiny, punishment for little children. *Johan loved to frighten me or to coax me with fear into the fields, and he called me Shushi, which he blew like a whistle through his teeth: "Sh – Sh – If you don't come the frost giant will come for you. He will rob you and throw you into the huge abyss, the one that has always been here, the original one."*

"Yes, I know who would throw me – Yes, yes, and we, certain of each other's protection – but I was counting on the sheltering giant who would stroll the land to find the fallen birds, the children, cradle them in arms so mighty, to hold all the young and weak. And I perfectly heard his footsteps, lying in the field, waiting for rescue, all clouds above me. Rescue from strappings of a leather belt by my father, whom I feared more than the frost giant. Because a child knows the real; she can tell when the leather hits the hide, if there are knots at the end. It would leave a wound that hurts into your seventieth year.

"We were forbidden to have pets. No cat or dog, no turtle, no goldfish. *Go and pray, Selma, my child,* my mother would say. But sometimes she would hold me so desperately close, that her kinship, her sisterhood, her being in want of me was overwhelming. She needed my wordless pity, my jumping into her lap when spotting her alone after work. As all little five-year-olds know, the dusky, stilled, early evening hours are so good in the arms of a mother, a maid, or a nurse grown old in the service of a household. There is where we little ones rush in. Mothers so in need of us, and we are so glad to give our meagre wealth."

Selma, sipping her creamy chocolate, let that last sweet taste linger on her tongue.

ALL THE RIVERS

Walking along the black Danube now, Felix felt the watery road was as dark as all the rivers in early morning hours. He did not go to work that day. Sitting on the banks of the Danube, he smiled, retreating to his thoughts, all of which concerning Woman led him to accept their superiority: a kind of grasp, the intelligence of the immediate, keeping life going, giving of themselves, yet never without a certain calculation. This was how they were. But he was older now, and thinning a little at the hairline, with deeper shadows leading up from his chin over his mouth, and crow's feet about his eyes tending to join a stern straight line between eyebrows.

The first time he saw that dividing line was when writing to Selma. He wrote to her how beautiful she was, how much he loved her aging body, her portrayal of Portia in *The Merchant of Venice,* her female humanity. He wrote in adoration of her sex. *They are a different race,* he thought. *Women. They are complete.* And he said so when writing his letter of goodbye to Selma. It was when his eyes had met a mirror opposite his desk that he suddenly saw, in the dulling electric light, the straight line on his forehead, almost halving it. It was frightening. *So, this is the way we go, being suddenly another: hair on collar and face divided.* But he let it happen, and said so to this beautiful northern specimen of the female race.

But he was contemplative and moody today, and saw his life as if it were an unstoppable, rolling film.

Having gone north coming from Georgia, where the world had a still human face in spite of the wars, he fell into German hands. He saw tanks and artillery against the horizon, moving over frozen ground but approaching faster than he had estimated. Felix went face down into an icy hollow, stepped on by a German boot. "A runaway miserable Jew," the German voice said, "we'll make *kurzen Prozess*." Felix, having understood, remained a stiff corpse, when he heard a commando voice to move faster. The boot removed itself, and he remained for an endless time, to the comfort of slowly freezing, a feeling of delight, a sweet hope for death to come soon. He woke next to a fire, lying on top of a hearth. It was south of Stalingrad. Heroic Russian women went out at night to do their Christian duty: to collect the frozen bodies, either to bury them and take their possessions, or feed them and warm them by their stoves. He could never forget that moment when his eyes fell onto a Russian woman, washing his face and calling to her mother, *We saved him. Slava Bohu.* Small incidents of goodness or cruelty springing up, mixing into the brew of daily living – all there, next to where to go for breakfast.

So he got up from his Danube bench, walked towards the village on the outskirts of Vienna, and found a café. Small, smoky, intimate, he seemed to have been here before but could not recall either when or how. The grumpy but good-natured old Vienna waiter brought him the daily paper, and he settled into his corner, coffee steaming, rolls and butter on the table, bit into a crunchy kaiser, when the waiter said: "What do you say to the *Ringstrasse* fire?" pointing to the headlines.

A sudden fear, sweat covering his forehead; it was Martina's neighbourhood. Paid and ran. Took a train and approached the damaged front. Martina and a dozen unknown persons were standing in front of the building. Martina holding her precious Klimt from above the liquor cabinet, and Annie was beside her, saying, "Don't worry, he'll come out of it, it's inhaled smoke and nothing else."

"And Gerhard – where is he?" Felix asked.

"You know the private hospital he worked in. He is there. Go and see, he may need help." Felix left the women to themselves, reluctantly. But he had grown to feel deeply for Gerhard, and left hoping that Annie would support Martina. *It is too much, it is just too much,* he thought while boarding the tram.

He entered the hospital and had to wait, Gerhard being in an oxygen tent. Allowed in finally, Felix never left Gerhard until he died. He sat at his bedside, Gerhard wanting desperately to speak, finally said quietly, "I have made a confession, and you'll find it in the drawer of my desk if it is still there." No smile visible, no muscle there, so burnt he was and bandaged in part. With his left hand he was able to remove the small band from his little finger, and dropping it into Felix's waiting hand, he said, "Stay with me while I rest."

DR *Gerhard Schneider*

THE WEDDING BAND

To Martina and Felix,
Where to begin? At the moment perhaps that I slipped the small gold band onto my little finger. Why here, why should such a small gesture have so momentous a weight? I have given it much thought, for it seems a small theft. We all do it as children. Coveting. Shiny black-silver revolvers rich friends had to play with, I was not allowed to own. So I stole them. Or perhaps, if to confess is to search one's heart where one never dared throw any light – this undistinguished gesture of noticing and putting the small golden object into my pocket, severed me from my roots. I tried to slip it upon my ring finger but it was too tiny and fitted barely the little one.

It is a wedding band, and in my dreams, which always are the same, recurring towards morning's waking hours, a very tiny, almost faceless Jewish woman comes to shake me, wagging her empty ring finger. Sometimes she is beautifully attired, a white wedding veil hiding her features, and sometimes she speaks. She always wakes me when she comes. Though she looks different from the woman I saw in the *Residenzgasse*. Because I did see her.

She was the owner of the house I think; it was a two-floor building. Wide windows opening towards the *Residenzgasse* revealed the Archbishop's Residence, and around the corner I saw the whole street as far as an old fountain.

We came in, with the *Einsatzgruppen*, motorized, often already high on Schnapps from the flat bottle on the belt, singing, storming the doors with rifles, and I was just – and perhaps for the first time – "one" with my peers. Having desired it, wanted to be part of the group, I saw it fulfilled. Stormed in, shot the men first in front of these houses. This was the third from the corner. We shot the men first to get the women without opposition. Not always, but this time we did. Not that we feared it much. Drunk with our twenty-plus youthful years, empowered with rifles, machine guns, and motorbikes, a collective madness took hold. Eliminated the men for fun and started at the women.

There, I suddenly stopped. The urge left me. My penis hung like an old rag within my military trousers. It was not for me. I couldn't. Tender in nature and a romantic in love, adoring frailty and elegance, the saintly other-worldliness of my mother, I was inexperienced; leant a little against the wall, saw the slim young woman whose ring was in my pocket. I heard my superior joking, and everyone else poking fun at me, as my schoolmasters had always done, as my father had done to chide my absent ways. My superior handing me now a bundled-up baby from the cradle, pushed me towards the window to throw it out. I threw it like playing ball.

Martina and Felix, you know the story that followed, that I ran from the scene, and having vomited, I went for fresh air. It had shaken me to the depths. There was another thing that added a strange fear, a truly terrible fear: for a young man to have shown impotence to his peers. My whole being had refused to be part of rape. I had become cold as ice to the tip of my nose and fingers. All blood rushing inward, towards the heart and leaving the body bereft. I ran out to find women.

The rest you know. The pastor, Martina's father, leading me out of the brothel, still in time to save the one hundred hostages from being shot.

Until the moment I slipped the Jewish woman's wedding band onto my little finger, until that moment I was another. A sweet boy, in fact. Doing what was expected of him, on the whole. A single child, a businessman-bureaucrat's son who was to fulfill his father's bourgeois hopes, but did not show a great deal of willingness, being dreamy and inclined to go to dress shops with his mother, or choose materials, texture, and colour for sofas and chairs. And the forbidden Art Nouveau! I drew well. Loved the Vienna turn-of-the-century scene. The unity of life and design. Chairs, straight-backed, glass flowers bringing nature into art and art towards nature. A kind of Judaic "God is One." Life and beauty inextricably intertwined.

I chose the pinstriped sofas, the chairs, the milky-flowered glass doors, bought them when I could afford them. Martina will remember, I chose them for her. She was made for it. When you, Martina, sat on our balcony, its wrought-iron woven into overgrown leaves, you looked like the flower in it growing from their root. A sculpture. But a living, passionate human being.

I will recall always your sparkling eyes and clapping of hands when you first laid eyes on my choices. You couldn't choose. You hadn't seen enough. Artistic but unformed, a pastor's daughter, and your mother – well, there are no words for Rosy, a villager with too much hate. And in total ignorance of your observant, poetic, inner nature. Truly lost when I met you. In dusty, small bookshops for a hunger pay, putting books in alphabetical order –

Yes, I did go to find you. I knew of your pilgrimage *Heim ins Reich* and the crossing of the Austrian border in preference to the inhospitable West Germans. Not that Vienna opened her arms: digs were poor, landladies rapacious. I fear Rosy died of resentment. Before this exile she hated Jews, whom she saw manipulating all levers, money and the like, but in a certain way Rosy just hated whomever she disliked, a collective hate. And when she found an object for it there were no limits.

So in the end it was Felix. You, my friend, with whom I have exchanged the *DU* with all my heart. You have become this object for her. She shouted, "You have taken Martina's innocence! Jews are worldly. They can't imagine a Holy Spirit. I know them from my childhood," she used to say. "They deal, have sticky fingers. Money does not roll, it sticks there. They look kind, but aren't. And they pray to their God in a tongue no one understands –" and so on. But she is no more, and I have mourned for the two of us, holding hands and sitting out there, at the pauper's cemetery, which is just as saintly and peaceful as lying next to the bourgeois.

But it took me a long time to truly court you, Martina. All through my medical studies I found excuses, thousands of them, not to court you, not to hold you too close, touch or kiss. I have to earn first, enough to offer you a home, I thought. I have no time for truly courting, going to the shops, flowers, books, and chocolates – a thousand excuses: she'll refuse me and I'll commit suicide over it. But my deep fears were true: what if I am truly impotent? I am a marked man. I wear a stolen, murdered woman's wedding ring with an inscription and a date on my lit-

tle finger. Why should she, Martina, with her childlike conscience, why should she be shackled to a branded man like me?
And so it went.

Yet I passed my exams, rented office space, and was in a very
short time highly successful. What made it that men, women, and
children flocked to my practice? Perhaps it was that day that
broke my life in two, a day in which I saw "man's ability to sink
to unfathomable depth" as my own, that made me extend my
heart to others, listen to their lives' pain, sleepless nights, or rage,
irrational and boundless. They came, brought their children who,
sitting on my lap, did not mind, and accepted an injection from
my hand trustingly. What made me a good doctor? Deep within
me I think it was this "one day."

So I took you shopping. *Kärtnerstrasse*. Shoe shops, hats and
scarves, Italian silk appearing in the window. No, no snake hand-
bags, shoes or belts. You are no hypocrite, you ate the flesh of animals, wore leather shoes, but to see God's design, the most intricate, ingenious, black-white-brown, almost moving skin, you
could not wear or see it all day. In the grass you want to see them.
Coiled in the green, unexpected, frightening you, and then
watching those crawling-on-their-bellies beings, pull themselves
the other way. My Martina! And you looked among Viennese
beauties – and there are some – the most stunning. Tall, transparent, as if made of no flesh, a head sitting like a barely opened
tulip on its stem, and eyes a searching intensity of undeterminable
colour! Either black, the pupil taking over, or disappearing within an ocean of green light. But black truly.

Sitting across from each other, or going to the museums, you
had only recently discovered we always went to see the same pictures: the Breughel rooms, happy skaters, brawling peasant feasts –

and you stood and said, How does a man do this! Or, the Rembrandt rooms with the Jewish Christ faces. Rembrandt did not live far from the Jewish quarters in Amsterdam, I said to you; he just goes in there and sketches his Christ face.

Or the painting of his mother; you cried before Rembrandt's mother's face. We all do if we want a good cry about what we have neglected to say or do, or what we could never turn the clock back to repair. We all stand there to look into this face, a mother's eyes rimmed in red. It talks to us, and we understand the language man speaks in pain or joy. Speaks it as if we're addressed directly and now. We talked of Rosy, and I of my own mother, when sitting in a little café, after such a visit.

It was early spring, daffodils were just budding or half-opened in small pots, lovers holding hands. It was late and we were happy to talk, when you, Martina, opened your handbag, the one I gave you, to take out a small note and hand it to me across. It read: Propose to me, I will accept, with all my heart. Sobs breaking my voice. When? Now, or soon as church or state permits. We stormed out of the café, paying fast, running like unruly children kissing for the first time, as if we were twenty and we were almost – well, you know, not twenty! We fell into one another's arms with no regrets or fears, on the sunniest of all my days. And yours perhaps too. You came to my flat that night; your digs were poor.

And the rest was full of wonderful times, especially the choosing of things for *our* house. Art Nouveau, a revelation to you, who are the embodiment of it. The Klimt picture, your wedding gift. And the wedding. It was then that I saw you, Felix. Martina, coming down the aisle, whispered when close to the altar: *Felix is here, in one of the last rows. I saw him distinctly in his yellow shirt.*

Felix – you know – Do not worry, I said to you; do not worry. We'll look after him.

Dear Felix, you are the only one to whom I unburdened my heart. But my love for Martina and the time it took to come to full bloom has also to do with her being of your tribe. She gave herself to you at so tender an age. Losing your child, and returning home to a reproachful bitter mother, her life was saved by the pastor. And I fear that neither you nor I had the overwhelming presence and power of her father. He looms between us. It is not easy to live with Martina, as she will grant you, because of this irradicable power. Evoked or not, he is there. I often felt her judging me against him.

The pastor. I owe him my life. He found me in scurrilous, bizarre surroundings down around the corner *Heine-Goethegasse,* and I've told you both this many a time. It is part of this crucial day. He found me, conscious by then, sitting in an armchair of the town prostitute Mitzi, with the madam Rebecca at her side. The women buttoned my buttons, brushed my coat, combed my hair, took me out of my chair, bubbling with the kind of noise that overcomes one's past hysteria. The pastor waited. On his hand, and the arms of Rebecca, I made it up the broken underground stairs to daylight. And to the German headquarters. He saved my life, but also took that hold on me that is a saviour's privilege. No exit. I felt as I did in early childhood, powerless in the hands of benevolent forces, but they are whimsical, unpredictable, and because of it perhaps savage.

Dear Martina, how was I to compete? I'm not a Lutheran, I'm not a Jew, and a Catholic *pro forma* – births and weddings, so to speak – and I wanted to please you. But how? And so I felt judged. Not cruelly, but observed at the breakfast table, when you would take cup and saucer out of my hand, just to turn the handle to the right, the way your father had held them. Oh, many things were expected of me which I can't name or even know exactly what they are. So I kissed you goodbye in the morning and left, to concern myself with others' lives. Easier.

Martina knows that in my drawer above the desk is my last will and testament. All I have is hers, of course.

After THE FIRE

THE ROOM LOOKED BLEAK WHEN WE WENT UP THE inner staircase. Her arm on mine this time heavy, so different from the first time I had come to Martina's and Gerhard's Viennese flat. I wore my yellow silk shirt then, with the pockets, thick with sodium barbiturate in one and morphine in the other. A singing, mommy's-boy I had been, to whom getting up in the morning meant hot water in a tub, steaming chocolate, and fresh rolls strewn with poppy seeds. Maids to take care of it. That kind of a boy. My mother coifed and beautiful only for dinner at one. Smiles all around me. No pains or sexual fears: my schooling was Ileana. Up among the drying linen in the attic of the old house. She just took me there. But when I saw Martina first, it was an imprint, a vision of the ideal. My mother, too, was stricken with that image.

We talked, sitting in the Evangelical gardens, and we watched Martina looking for stones, pebbles, or an unusual wild thing she hadn't seen before. She was innocent, but with an erotic heartbeat, ephemeral, unmade yet. I, a pharmacist, had no trouble in filling my pockets with this "chemical heaven," but I had never made use of it, not on the run, not in captivity, and not when my leg was shattered and the sunny boy had a wooden leg. I carried the stuff still in my two pockets of the yellow shirt when arriving at their flat. And seeing Martina with Gerhard, I nearly asked for that glass of water. But coming down the staircase I needed her strength.

So different now: she leant heavily on my arm, step by step.

The salon was covered with a dark dust; glass tables, pink-striped sofa and chair appeared as if lightly smeared. The air, of course, smelled of fire. But it was better than we had feared. Water damage here and there, and the stove in the kitchen, where it seemed to have started, was ashen with soot.

Annie came up, carrying the picture. Leaving it standing against the wall, she said in a pleasant, consoling tone, "There is no use crying over spilled milk; let's clean up the mess." And she busied herself with sponge, pail, and soap.

"Careful," Martina shouted, "what are you doing, Annie? This is not a kitchen floor! Gerhard would die if he saw you getting at it – oh, heavens!" And she stopped, ran to the bedroom to throw herself onto the bed, sobbing. "What now, what now?" Calling for Felix. "I won't be alone. I can't."

Felix found the room untouched by smoke, fire or water, the bedroom door having been shut had prevented all damage, and he sat down beside her.

The bedcover a shimmering gold, silver threads interwoven to cool the yellow with streams of blue water. Puffed by the down of the eider-hen as in the salon pillows, one sank as if into mother's womb. The balcony outside the bedroom windows and doors, hugging the corner, held the sky captive between the grown vines. Felix had never been inside their bedroom. By his own avoidance.

Not to be assailed by images that would spring at him from every ruffled cushion, suspenders on the back of a chair, cufflinks or diamond pins on night tables, and above everything, the books they would have read before putting the lights out. Now he looked and saw the book covers: Thomas Mann's *Joseph und seine Brüder. Who are my brothers?* To see his own Hebrew name thrown upon the floor, thrown probably from sleepy hands – He picked it up. *It's a big heavy book,* he thought. *Heavens I've read too little German. Mother encouraged the French.* Read Rimbaud, she had said, a poetry so fine it enters every unlit corner; to read the German novelists – you'll always find time for it, it's your mother tongue, it's accessible. And he looked at the shelves, right above the all-dominating bed. Franz Werfel, *The Forty Days of the Musa Dagh,* the tragic story of the Armenian deportation by the Turks in 1915 – no, not now, too much murder! Art books, lives of masters, small glass sculptures on either end, holding the books in place.

Martina's long and limpid limbs stretching, losing tension, let her fall into some rest, if not sleep. Felix, taking his shoes off, smiled as he saw how the brown velvet suede blended into the deer pelt at the foot of the bed. Only now he could see the stars in the stucco ceiling. A vaulted firmament it was, touching a horizon at its end. Not round, but seemingly so. Stars divined by a changing glimmer of red, disappeared if only just out of view. Felix had seen a sky like this one on an early Tbilisi evening, after a gruelling descent from the Caucasian mountains, when he had found a momentary respite at a rich Georgian home. Stars so similar at a time of terror and the unexpected opening of bliss.

Next to Martina the "What now, what now?" was not there. He allowed himself that moment, and he dared look at the woman on his side: evanescent almost, on her stomach, backside up, she had fallen asleep; right hand supporting her head a little, she hardly made an impression into the eiderdown cover, so ethereal, as if flesh were no flesh, and bone had no weight. She wore black patent-leather pumps; hanging over the bed, fashion heels slightly curved, stuck out, were enigmatic sculptures in themselves. But her skirt and blouse, crumpled and a little soiled, recalled the last day. Smoke rising from her hair kept the moment real. But sad.

Felix's particular consciousness of aroma, of myriad smells, judging, identifying them, was always teased in his schoolboy days. It's unmanly. It's women's territory. Women's noses keep life going – yes, this may be so. But women's things are Felix's: smells, tastes, colours, they are his life-leash, his easy access to them. Accomplices they were. He had shared an everyday bond with the maids in the cellar. Standing near big cauldrons of dye, they had helped Felix lift his shirts from boiling kettles, these maids, Marusja, Ileana, or whatever their names were, offering the adolescent a taste of the salty sweat from their armpits or lush bosoms, to – accidentally or not – brush by with giggles on all sides. For Felix, it had been an early schooling in companionship with the female sort. Or, having no business in the family kitchen, he stood by the big, blazing, ceramic hearth to put the finishing touches on the soup: more parsley, too much salt, a spoon of cream, it is too watery and perhaps a small amount of *sauce blanche* will save it – the women loved him. "Run," they said, "your mother is coming, don't let yourself be caught." And they hid him in the big cupboard; it had been too late to run.

He knew that cupboard well. A spicy air of cinnamon and cloves pervaded the space, and he did not mind being in the dark to inhale it. Felix thought of all the peppers still in his nostrils; a fine sharp perfume emanating from the pillow his head was resting on now startled him, brought the cupboard home: a distinct perfume of pepper and musk, and a childhood reinstated with all its comfort relaxed his muscles, made him smile, wonder about the incomprehensibility of it all, and he dozed off.

They had lain on that bed for countless hours. The day had descended into evening, when a fine movement or rustle in the silky cover and a breath of Martina's grazed his cheek. He did not move. And she came to him, as she had done when they were sixteen.

He had stolen into her bedroom from the back door of the rectory, up the staircase. Had dreamt of the lightness on his arm when she first had touched him and inadvertently had slipped her arm into his. It was her sixteenth birthday. He had rushed up the steps to her door, had stretched himself beside her on her narrow bed. Her linen, smelling of musk-moss and dry grasses, felt cool to his hot cheek. Pepper in the air. An array of peppers she had sorted and labelled early in the morning persisted, and he thought he'd remember it all his life. It struck again in this strange, Art Nouveau bedroom. A slightly sharp, a stinging perfume, it was Martina's own.

Now she was next to him, with a life in between to distance them, yet teenagers again. She rested against his face now as then, removing the strands of hair, sticky perhaps and in the way, and took her time. But a sudden violence, so unlike both of them, made them come closer and kiss. And slowly she took dominion, undoing the buttons of his shirt, putting her head on his chest and letting it rest, savouring the moment. And she whispered how long is it, how long, she went astride him to guide him into her.

He was totally still. Knew the sequence, her violent strokes, bursts of sound, the smell of sex, sour and a little noxious, mingling with the peppers, he knew them from the age of sixteen.

Rest. And the night with the stucco ceiling loosing its stars, tramway noises, strings of lights paling, permitted just so much that Felix could see her now. Veiled, her features lost all lines, the dim light erasing wrinkled corners and the years vanished between them, teenagers in each other's arms, crying and laughing to remember this or remember that – and no witness. No fear of inspection, or gagging, controlling eyes. No Rosy, no pastor, no Gerhard. Wild children on an island of their own.

"Look Martina, there is no use being over fifty when you have just reached the age of sixteen. A few weeks ago was our common birthday."

"Yes," she said, a little weary, "yes, newly born at sixteen is the right age."

There was not a moment of discord since that day and night. Just weariness, perhaps, having been so long at sea.

Martina decided to sell the flat, water- and fire-damaged as it was, salvaged what she could, the glass art, the slightly soiled, pink striped sofa, and the Biedermeyer desk that did not fit the décor but which she had loved for its singleness. Her hand reached into the silver cabinet and touched a glass tulip, tall, blown to perfection, yellow and orange petals alternating, playing with light as if alive on its greenish stem, having no other purpose than to be beautiful. And Martina sat down, tulip in hand, to shed her tears without pain. They just came. Not knowing why, and not knowing why here and now.

She sat for a while, tulip in hand, turning it gently from time to time to give the light a chance to transform it. Only a slight shift of angle would create a ship's sails flying, and looking into its heart, thoughts dark and ominous sprang from it. Now she cried over it. Couldn't move, and called Felix in despair to take over the house while she left with Annie. Just to go out and shop for fruits and greens and something of everyday. Not glass tulips and death. Something living. To get away from message bearing Art Nouveau, so artificial and true at the same time. But so artificial too, demanding of memory, reinstating Gerhard Schneider and a given love which was not hers to give.

It was Felix's. And his alone.

LETTING ANNIE SHOP in the butcher shop, she stood outside it, watching the crowd. She, Martina, was never at home here. A doctor's wife, she was expected to be one, that is to wear hat and gloves and give a Viennese *Jause* to other doctors' wives. She was not from here, did not fit into a *petit-bourgeois* world with pretence to the *grand-bourgeois*. She saw the stuck-up colleagues' wives in the shop, having just come from a Viennese hairdresser, and they all seemed alike, toothy smiles, and wondering what you wore. Disgusted, she looked for Annie, who made signs through the window to come and help her choose the veal chops, the butcher holding them out for her. *Make up your own mind.* Martina formed these words voicelessly, with body language to back them up. No, Martina did not handle meat. She wouldn't touch it. Its living surface, pink and humid, made her shiver. Cooked perhaps, with sauce to camouflage it, she would eat small amounts of it, but she would not touch raw flesh. "I can't," she had shouted once as a child to her mother. "I can't look at it. I beg you! Please, leave me alone, it hurts my innards. I'll vomit. I'll go to bed and never come to the table again." But Rosy, her mother, forced her to pluck a chicken, to sear its feathers after Rosy had killed it. "No, I won't do it. I'll kill myself if I have to do it. I'll throw myself into the Prut or from the steeple of our church."

But Rosy was adamant. Rosy did not allow what she called Martina's Jewish sensibilities. "She has learnt fancy behaviour from them," she had shouted, "with their special man killing the chickens, while talking devil-talk in Hebrew or some non-Christian abracadabra. Jews won't kill their animals. They'll have so-called religious people do it for them, praying while killing. Ha, ha. Hypocrites," Rosy shouted at her. "You, Martina, with Rachel Glasberg's milk in your veins – all your father's fault. I could have found a milk-nurse for you other than the one from the Jews. But no, your father insisted it should be the Jews from the Old House, across the fountain. And that Turkish fountain, with the infidel Turkish henchman built in, where you, Martina, sat on the rim with crazy stories coming out of its centre – this is what is happening to you. A devil's brood you have become, not mine." And so it went.

"My mother," Martina thought, "my poor mother, a butcher's daughter herself, who had to wash the blood off the floor then spread the sawdust all over before her father started work. She and her brothers, her uncles in Rosch, were butcher's children, hard working, cleaning their butcher's tools, axes, knives and saws for the bones of big animals, cleaning them early morning, before going to German school in Rosch for their eight grades. Oh, the poor souls." Martina had known the good people. They had come, hands full at harvest time with flour, potatoes, and green vegetables. Or at Christmas after slaughtering their pigs, with sausages, fresh or smoked to perfection, and the famous *Dauerwurst* heavily

peppered and spiced to hang on the kitchen wall to further dry
until one could cut it with the finest of knives. "We were the poor
relatives. A pastor, and one like my father – who worked for love
alone – made no money, could barely keep wife and child." So
they all came, our good relatives from Rosch, to share their
wealth.

"And I liked my cousins. For a day. And it was all of their harvest they stored in the cellar of the rectory when forced to leave
their ancient homestead, so my father, who refused to go, wouldn't
be hungry when the Russians took over. Of course, my mother
made me leave in September of 1939 with all the twenty thousand
or so Germans to go *Heim ins Reich.* An Odyssey of sadness. With
all my cousins and second cousins – all together in that train. Yet
everyone on his own. Through Poland first to find a night's sleep in
Polish beds. They all had fathers. Not me. My mother and I, leaving Czernowitz by train on that September day, we were even there
the poor relatives, being tolerated. Even there – but Rosy, proud
and resentful for all the hand-outs, couldn't bear it, and while all
our folk went to Augsburg or Bavaria somewhere, we succeeded in
entering Austria to get away from them. To be separate. A long
story. Why does it come to me – oh, every time I see, pass or enter
a butcher shop, the whole story will be there. Away, away."

Martina opened the door and called into the butcher shop as
she watched Annie paying her bill. "Annie, dear, go home, tell
Felix to do whatever he can to pack. I'll be a while out." She went
into the flower shop next door. With "Good day, *Frau Doktor,*
what can we do for you?" she rose out of her mother's life into the
Viennese smiles and jokes. She loved this making light of things.
Easy smiles and jokes, and the wife of a doctor was always *"Frau
Doktor,"* elevated into the heaven of a title here in Vienna. No one

would guess that she had lost her husband, or the freedom she now felt, from possessions, status, and all the phony trappings. But their smiles she liked, it took the friction from surface contact. Their stupid, degenerate anecdotes of the useless aristocracy, she liked. Marrying into one another's houses, without much power, Catholic, they remained the upper crust, kept their circles tight, to feel superior to the miserable lot around them. Martina did not mind them. She laughed at their Poldi-Rudi idiocies and pitied them *au fond. Oh, the poor things, still talking about the splendour of the Franz-Joseph court.*

So, she went to *Dehmel* for hot chocolate, whipping cream. and *Kipferl*, a rich hazelnut-vanilla smelling crescent. Small and heavenly. And there they all were at the glorious hour, four o'clock, two, three, and four around small tables, chatty, gossipy. The best moment of the day. *Poor things.*

"No, I am not from here," she thought, sitting at a side table by the glass entrance door to watch the crowd coming and going. "Here they were happy with their chocolate, mocha, light brown, dark roasted, or a *spritz* of cognac in their veins, lifted out of grey houses, hundred-year-old cat urine wafting; here they were lifted into coffee heaven for an hour. Not me, no, I am not from here, but I will miss that Viennese humanity, playing host to the world, trying to be K.u.K. – meaning *Kaiser und Königlich* – Royal and Imperial. Oh, touching, I'll miss them, and I'll miss the table with the doilies, the goodies of the Empire. And the wainscoting, warm brown mahogany, or red cherry, who knows? And the unchanging, reinvented past. Generations handing it down like a piece of jewellery. Oh, the freedom!"

A freedom so sudden, so exhilarating, that she smiled at the sweet thing in her stupid, white, starched head *coiffe* and apron bound stiffly in the back, smiled at this sweet Mitzi or Gretl when she came by to remove her cup or wipe the marble top. Smiled at her so endearingly, and got a huge grin back, as only women know how to communicate or share – so free and uninhibited, all strings severed; a moment of such deliverance she had never felt before. And she wanted to sit a while longer by her empty cup and watch that glass door close – having the slowly emptying shop a little longer to herself.

A young man, half her age perhaps, entered the café, *Spazierstock* in hand – a Viennese walking cane of a leisured gentleman – placing it carefully on the table next to hers, its carved double-eagle-head dark with age and polished by use, looking at Martina out of its shiny, bright, mother-of-pearl eyes. That young man sat down now, pushing his chair elegantly to face her. Served by the very same Mitzi or Gretl, who smiled at him just as sweetly as she had done to her – Martina, a little jealous thought, *Oh, you whorish Viennese* – the handsome young man shifted his chair a little and addressed Martina in a voice of a dark-honey timbre: *Would the lady mind if he'd joined her at her table?* Her inviting hand movement saying *Not at all*, he took his stick first from his table to place it on hers and seated himself comfortably across from her until Mitzi or Gretl brought his *café au lait* and a cognac on the side. Martina, now sixteen again, watched the beauty of youth. Harmonious, oiled joints, movements of the well-bred, who took his time to lift the fine coffee spoon from the saucer for one single stir, and then putting it back onto it, raised the cup to his lips for a slow swallow. Leaning back into his wicker-backed chair, he said in that absolutely irresistible fluid voice, "You are beautiful, and I hoped you would permit me to say so."

"But of course I would. I noticed you coming through the door, thinking there comes my son, my would-be or wanted-to-be son –" Smiles hanging in the air, picked up by both of them, changed into wit and repartee.

"I'm all for Oedipal complexes," he replied. "It helps one to see the world through a woman's eyes. Too much male thinking – a modern Oedipus can love and see without blinding himself, as your Greek gods would demand."

"Yes," she said, "But today is different, you wouldn't be in any danger of such tragedy because today I'm sixteen and could not have been your mother – as attractive as this may seem." She rose, thinking it is time, fearing if she didn't she would find herself in his arms, so free, unbridled, and sixteen she felt.

"Oh, let me accompany you," he said. He called Mitzi-Gretl by raising his *Spazierstock* a little – a known, old gesture – paid his bill, asked for permission with his eyes to pay hers, was denied, and followed her through the glass door. *Yes, I know who he is.* As he followed her through the glass door, he seemed anxious to fall into her step. The door closed shut with that glassy tremor of very old door frames. A light shiver, a goose flesh of a sound running down her back, Martina recognized Felix. When he took her on her maiden bed.

Or before, many years before – events now compressed themselves and stood close, landing on top of each other without time in between. How Felix lifted her out of the grass where she had sat, legs crossed, to wait for a lily of the valley to open. Certain that she could wait for it, she watched the closed bud, and saw it slightly open, or so she thought, when she felt herself pulled up, almost lifted into his arms, called the sweetest lily of the valley herself, a little bloom on a stem. He had been on a walk with his mother, this enormously tall, redheaded mother, whom Martina had seen many a time walking through or on the other side of the chestnut trees, alone or with Felix. He, not that tall yet, had held Martina up for a little and, putting her back onto her trembling legs, said schoolmasterly, "You should not crouch for hours."

"Why did you do this? I was just seeing the *Maiglöckchen* unfolding, opening its heart to me, when you interrupted it. You shouldn't do this either," she laughed and ran on her unsure legs, having had them in such a cramped position for hours – and when first he came up to her room under the steeple – all these things crammed, grafted themselves onto one another, topsy-turvy.

She always had sung. Inventions of her own, folksong, but not having a trained voice, she came late to it, in Vienna. It's the best place to learn the German Romantics: Schubert, Schumann, Brahms, Wolf. And today, this *Doppelgänger*. That melody had not left her since waking in Felix's arms. "Unattainable, my lover, I see him everywhere as Schubert does in his lonely longings, walking, the moon never left him; the moon, his double, mocking his suffering. Even in Felix's arms I fear treachery. Still," she thought, "always Felix, either with me or sought in others."

Oh yes, there were the two under-the-steeple rooms and a marvellous attic full of smelly books, Luther pictures, and wooden flutes. Luther flutes her father had called them. She loved blowing into those wooden things, to make the air vibrate.

When Felix came the first time, he came furtively. Thieves both, they knew one another in the break of a second. A touch of hand, a look of complicity, laughter, and they were ready for all things forbidden. Up in the attic, rummaging and finding locked boxes, secrets in all corners, and when he brushed his lips against her short hair and pulled one, she called him naughty. In all those childhood years, she had watched Felix grow and unfold, as layer upon layer fell from his pre-teen looks and a sculpted perfection emerged before her very eyes. She fell into his arms at sixteen. He was another suddenly, in his new, elongated, skeletal beauty and voice of amber. And so was she a total other. Someone wanting change, not to be talked to by anyone. Silent, moody to schoolmaster, pastor and Rosy alike, she waited for the step sounding at night on the rungs of the staircase. *Felix has felt on his soles, he breathes without noise and when he speaks I'll die,* she had thought then.

That other Martina had changed also, to reveal an impetuous will and a violence fully unexpected. It came in the spring of her sixteenth year, when she could not wait for him to shed shirt and trousers and had jumped astride him, afraid he might change his mind, God forbid, or not love her. And so it was – yesterday – when she took him as he stretched himself alongside her on the silver blanket of her marriage bed.

The young stranger walked in silence next to her, through the milling crowds on the *Kärntnerstrasse,* and they found themselves sitting on a bench to rest beside a lady with shopping bags who started immediately on this or that – but both sat in stony silence. Martina overwhelmed by thoughts. Felix. And she turned to the young man and she saw Felix, saw his image. His *Doppelgänger.* His Vienna double. A reality she had never suspected or thought possible. *No, it couldn't be,* she thought, *I am not superstitious.* But the intensity of his presence, the silence, the moving of his *Spazierstock* gently between the second to the fourth finger and thumb, brought Felix back: up in the attic, taking the piccolo from the wall and twirling it between his second and fourth finger and his thumb.

Finding a little more comfort, as the bag lady, unable to strike up a conversation, had left mumbling about the rudeness of people, the young man leant back a little, making room for Martina's handbag. He had turned his head into half profile, and Felix's Greek face, his melancholic air, and that smile of derision emerging made her blood run cold and she shivered. A true *Doppelgänger*. No escape. Two pairs of mother of pearl eagle eyes – the *Spazierstock* having shifted, lying loosely across his legs – staring her now in the face. Fearing her father's eyes and punishment, she rose with a light goodbye and heard his rich tenor sound: "Tomorrow at four. At Dehmel's. Please."

Annie and Felix were looking out for her on the balcony. She saw them from afar. Up the steps and into his arms: "Martina, where have you been? We were sick with worry."

"I was with you," she said, innocently. "All the time." Smiling a mysterious, blank smile, she lifted her right hand, taking the oath.

"There are three chairs left," Felix said, "The rest, sofa, footstool, loveseat, and your favourite straight-back, plum-purple, velvet chair have gone to the cleaners. Come sit down. No inquiry, no inquisition. Are you willing to tell me what took you so long? You left Annie in front of the butcher shop, sending her home to prepare the *Wiener Schnitzel* and it took you four hours to return."

"Yes," she said, and her face turned into that very earnest simple child's face with a pre-teen voice to match it. She said, "Yes, I was with you. It is something that has happened to me before. But today it was real. After I left Annie, Felix, I can't tell you the joy I felt: my youth returning. Vienna so beautiful, I beheld for the first time. I entered the florist. They had Japanese arrangements in small pots, all shades of grey-green, touch of purple mosses around miniature trees, not taller than your thumb."

"Yes," Felix said, "one arrived at the door an hour ago."

"Wonderful, wonderful! It makes it all real." Felix had put the small wonder onto the windowsill, and Martina saw it, clapping her hands. "I have not seen the stones at the base, that pebble path for little people like me. No *sans blague*, as you, Felix, like to put it. Seriously, I've never felt beauty so intensely. Narcissus in all shades spicing the shop, my head swooned and left me to catch my breath. Sixteen, Felix, sixteen. Right after that night. I thought Dehmel's and hot chocolate, *Schlagsahne,* and the air of leisure would be what I wanted. I sat down next to the door to watch the latest fashion come and go, when you entered the *Konditorei.* Seating yourself at the table next to mine, you put the *Spazierstock* with the *Doppeladler* of Imperial Austria across the table, and when you turned your face into half profile, I shivered. A certainty. Felix, I've sat next to your *Doppelgänger,* heard your voice twice, once when asking permission to join me at the table, which I allowed. Following me out of the Dehmel's glass door, we walked in silence; tiring we sat on one of those side-street benches for a little while, and when I rose to leave, I heard your voice for the second time. That honey-dark tongue of yours: *Tomorrow at four o'clock. Dehmel's. Please.*"

Annie shouting from the kitchen: Dinner is cold and I am going out for the evening. "That's fine, Annie," Felix said, "we are not hungry. Just leave a few morsels and we'll look after it."

"The kitchen looks halfway respectable. I've cleaned all surfaces. Help yourselves. I'll be gone for the week perhaps," she called, opening the salon door, looking at Felix and Martina on their chairs, two statues facing the balcony. "Be good, you two.

There is no use crying over anything. I'll be back Monday sometime. I may be on the *Semmering* helping out." She closed the door, and the two ancient lovers, looking at the fading day through not yet removed ash, smoke, and water stains, saw figures, landscape with moon above, on roads leading into themselves.

"You see them too," Martina said, "stones, rivers, and bridges across."

"Yes," Felix said, "I see them leading us back into that sixteenth year. Yours and mine."

"Yes, *you* entered the Dehmel's shop, and I saw the Luther pipes twirling between your fingers, the Adonis profile of my Felix, and I trembled, as I tremble now, watching the sun finding its way through the errant meandering of the water stains colouring the window."

"You're my Martina. If you thought it was me – so it was for you. You're mine. You're all my women. My mother, my sister. We sat around the *Bösendorfer* grand and sang and played Schubert. Page by page, through the book. Sweet melancholy, love and death. And the Viennese *Doppelgänger,* who mocks one's love and singleness, from whom one can't part and who follows your path. I know he was with you. In Vienna, *Winterreise* and *The Wanderer,* that joy in despair, lost love and pilgrimage, in Vienna this is real, to you and to me. My Martina."

She came to it late, Felix thought, *having lived unconscious of self, flowerlike. She woke to death, after her sixteenth year, giving birth to a son and losing him. Now she found the music of Franz Schubert. And she goes through all his houses, flats, or friends, sitting at her new piano, which Gerhard had given her, working her way through these pages that are with me from earlier days. Everything is real to her, the* Doppelgänger, *the poor organ grinder in a Vienna street, or the longing for the sunny land where mangoes and lemons bloom. All is real to her now. I let it be and do not contradict. There is no argument with fantasy. It takes over for a reason, for need perhaps, or healing. So I let it be. But it's ominous. Love and death, so truly one.*

Felix had put on his yellow silk Shantung shirt this morning, had touched his two bulging pockets and thought, *It is enough,* and then opened the buttons that held the packets secure, smiling at the temptation to call Annie for that glass of water. Weighing them for a short second in his hand, he rushed to the water closet to flush the contents down. Through over twenty years they had been with him: the comfort of his free will over torture or indignity. Sanctioned by his father on that last day around the dinner table before Felix ran from the Germans deep into Russia. He had his father's blessing and always felt his eyes on him every time Felix touched the bulging pockets: *Was the moment right, was it unbearable, had he sunk deep enough, is one allowed?* And he asked his father every time: would he approve? He didn't. But Felix, like every loving and rebellious son, played the game that comes with "death available" or the one children play with closed fists: yes-or-no, right-or-left, the what's-inside games. This morning he had decided it was time. And he let Martina come to her own "It is time."

They sat a little longer, watching the strings of light go on in the Vienna streets, only partly lighting up through the smeared window. Then Felix took her hand, helped her undress, watching her beautiful limbs, long and stretchy but slow with all that day lingering within them, and led her to their marriage bed. Removed the silver blanket, bedded Martina comfortably into cool linen, covered her with the weightless down, went to sit down for a little while, waiting for the stars to darken in the stucco ceiling. Took off his yellow shirt with the now open, flapping shirt pockets and buttoned them. Smiled as he undressed, went naked as he liked it onto the other side of the bed, set his wooden leg to one side, and slipped under the cover alongside Martina without touching her.

THE LITTLE GREY MAN

THE LITTLE GREY MAN BEHIND THE COUNTER, DUSTY with years and meanness, looked through his crooked glasses with just as crooked a smile at the elegant woman in a tailored suit of brown tweed, in hat, gloves, and shoes to match the lighter shades, entering his shop. He had seen her scrutinizing the windows for a little while, turning to the south side of the corner shop when he had lost her from view. This worried him, because he had never seen her before coming to his book auctions or browsing on the open shelf where manuscripts or cheaper editions were advertised for a reasonable price. As she reappeared at the door, which sounded the brass bell when opened, he had the distinct feeling of danger. Not that he had not seen elegant women before. They flocked to his specialty shop of manuscripts, imitations but respectable-looking nonetheless, or to the real thing at his auctions in the back room of the shop.

Aristocrats, or wanting to be that, Viennese women dressed with flair, walked in high-heeled shoes of snake- or crocodile-leather with the assurance of old wealth – or the memory of it. The little grey man had seen them before, had dealt and bargained with shrewd and simple minded ones. He knew when to ask for a price, when to spike it up, and sometimes let things go for less when they had been gathering dust on his shelves for too long.

Book dust was like no other dust. It made him grey and grow smaller. In time he resembled his shelves, as if grown into them. Indistinguishable. Nothing like book dust to cover a life. It affected your lungs, mites inhabited it, breath grew shorter as it bent the little grey man's back, which curved over the counter in front of his moneyed ladies and the gentlemen he greeted at the door. With *"Küss die Hand gnädige Frau,"* without kissing it, he would welcome the more important customers – often inherited from his father in a long line of cultured Vienna connoisseurs – and lead them to a corner chair, bid them to be seated, and remain standing in front of them.

He had grown up in his father's shop, dusting shelves for a few *schillings* as a little boy, and was taught order and the painstaking observance of Vienna do's and don'ts. All societal. The hump on his back, inflicted from his childhood, grew heavier with greying hair and changing, fearful times. Post-war Vienna. Jews reappearing everywhere. Demanding things. Account. A schoolmate he suddenly saw through his window, looking the other way in passing, not greeting him now, as he himself had done in 1938, on that stunning April day when all dreams seem to have come true and his hero drove in an open car by his father's shop. All flags were out, old and new, pride, and above all, love filled the young man's heart. To be someone of strength and beauty; he shouted his joy, linking arms with his equals. It freed his lungs from all his childhood years of obedience. An indelible day. Shouting and singing, boys and girls following their heroes in a cavalcade of power.

He was not old yet, perhaps late forties, but grey with shelf life; from his youth he looked ancient, or ageless, having landed old behind this counter. And today he felt a stab of age and fear. As if the sword of Damocles suspended, invisible to others, had moved a little closer, ready to sever his neck, and he almost heard the blade's metal moved in its sheath by the sound of the bell. He looked up to face a tall, commanding figure, a woman of elegance, of perfection, and he trembled.

"There was, a few weeks ago, a display of hand-signed first editions by Hugo von Hofmannsthal and others. Where are they?" She had interrupted his bowing and scraping of *Womit darf ich dienen?* – a servile *What may I do for you?* – coming straight to the point.

"They have been sold," was the reply.

And the lady: "I am taking you to court. The books were looted from my father-in-law's library. If you are, right now, willing to hand them over, I'll stay the proceedings." Martina put the list of books, manuscripts and first edition music on his desk and left without a word. All items, numbers, and dates of publication had been carefully registered.

He had known there was danger when he saw this woman through the window. She walked like a prosecutor.

A Christian she is. No Jew can be so haughty and self-assured; they're creeping vermin on the ground. Stalking. Now they're back, hiding in the skirts of the old aristocracy. Everyone for himself. Wanting to rob me of what is genuinely my own. I loved these books, especially *Florindo*, red leather bound, gold embossed, water-print drawings to enhance it. I loved it with a passion not experienced before I first put eyes upon it. No, I did not find or take them myself. It's a collector's dream! I did not! I'm a cultured man, can't lift a fist against another man, may he be deserving of it or not, it's not in me.

I'm a cultured man from way back. My ancestors were bookbinders in Bavaria near Augsburg. The great Mozart's folk. Cultured. Working people who teach their children how to handle beautiful things, how to cut, glue, bind the printed page. How to use leather, the finest Morocco leather, pliable like cloth, how to bind corners, folded under elegantly. We are booksellers for several generations now, but always taught the intimate art of binding. An inherited art. I can tell a book by holding it in my hand, the way it falls open, lies flat, or curls. We don't just sell books. They are our children. You don't sell children, you handle them gently, with wisdom.

No, it was not I. It was my friend Eberhard Weisgerber. We were stationed in the city of Czernowitz during the establishment of the ghetto, October, 1941, in charge of eggs and milk collection. The peasants had to bring them to the *Oberkommandatur* on the Central Square – the *Ringplatz*. It was business. I was in uniform. But it was business. Eberhard inventoried the *Residenzgasse* and said to me, one wine-filled November evening, "Come *Brunochen, ich zeig Dir was! Etwas für Dich, mein Kind!*" It was a crate full of treasure. An immeasurable treasure. I put my hands on *Florindo*. Red Morocco, gold embossed. The finest, signed, illustrated, waterprinted and signed by the illustrator whom I did not know. But I did know the author, Hugo von Hofmannsthal. A Jew himself or perhaps only half of one. Or a quarter. Somewhere an Austrian-Christian was in there. Mother or grandmother. Which accounts, of course, in my opinion, for this man's wonderful poetic work.

Jews are imitators. They can play other people's work on their fiddles but they can't create. They're not soil-bound. It does not nourish you if you pull up your stakes and wander; running always after greener pastures. They can't create. They are not fed by underground waters. The soil is hard under their feet. They do not take shovels in hand. They do not dig for inner worth. Imitators. I'm sure this is true for most of them. Hugo von Hofmannsthal had the source. Somewhere in his past there must have been Aryan blood. Richard Strauss, his great friend, for whom he wrote the *Rosenkavalier* libretto, et cetera, cried when he died. So enormous a loss it was for him and the world.

I trembled when I laid my hands on *Hölderlin*. Out of print. Not signed. An almost complete edition of his poems. I cried. And paintings. A magnificent garden scene – oil – mother and daughter at a tea table, dogs playing at their feet, by an Austrian 19th century painter whose name I have forgotten; it was taken from the frame and rolled up together with litho-prints signed or unsigned. "It's for you," Eberhard said. "I'll ship it out together with the eggs, which are also carefully crated. I have to send them inland," he said, "for distribution. It's for you, *Brunochen*. The war will be over soon. No one can stop us. No one. We're unbeatable, because we're armed, not by weapons alone, but by morale. We know who we are."

Yes, Eberhard, who gave his life for me, knew who he was. In fact, he died by an accidental bullet, or true sabotage – assassination exactly at the time *SS Führer* Heydrich died in Prague. Summer, 1942, I think there are connections. There are always connections, one just has to see them. We were the masters and we were hated. Mainly for that morale, mainly for what we stood for: a nation aware of itself. Young men like me for whom – never cowardly but simply unable to raise a fist – this was the greatest time of our lives. Never to be forgotten – when strength comes to you, from all around, from companions, books, words, leadership, the air breathes strength, the sun is brighter, you do not rise from your bed, you jump from it; there is spring in every muscle. You're so free to live your own life, so free you could almost fly. This is how I felt. And I could never and will never understand how we could lose the war. Where did it go all wrong? And so wrong. It could not have been our fault. Where it lies....

It took seven years from that November, 1941, it took a world to go up in flames until that crate, practically undamaged, would come into my possession. Mine. It was mine when I laid eyes on it in 1941. And no one else's. I kept it hidden under the shop. There is a *Falltüre* leading to the cellar. After work I would go down – ours is a true old book cellar. Lined with tarred paper and slate, the floor is protected from humidity. Controlled. The wall, thick with layers of oil paint, sports a water and a temperature gauge; some shelves are kept tightly under glass for the more perishable items. Music for instance. Old paper crumbles. Everything has to be watched.

I am a single man. Women? Oh, they may be pretty. But they're dangerous. They dominate your thinking. This is why war was so unspeakably wonderful. Such liberation. All men. Here and there a rotten apple. But to be among them lends you a certain power; men will share it with you, and your helplessness will vanish. I liked to watch them when they showered, back and front. I fell in love with them, when perhaps only fourteen, when playing soccer, or afterwards on the wooden benches, when panting and sweating, I tried to sit close and I would say to a young athlete, "I'll rub your back, hand me your towel." Such thrill. It's good to be among men. They share their power and do not rob you of it.

What good are memories? What are they for? It's better not to think. But what is a lonely man to do? He has to protect himself against invaders and robbers. So I keep things and thoughts to myself. But walls seem to move in steadily, and air is getting tight in my cellar under the counter. Emphysema – an antiquary's evil – is choking my throat, my eyes dim, and the printed letter shrinks on the page, disappears, and does not show up on darkening pages. So I run up the ladder from my underground vault, push the *Falltüre* open, which is right behind the counter, and fall into my swivel chair, trying to catch my breath.

And it was on such a day that I decided to take some of my hoard up. To look at it by daylight perhaps, or to escape the crushing walls in the cellar. Holding *Florindo* and some of the Nestroy editions in my hand, I started to think how nice it would be to display them in the window. For my own joy. Not even for money. But once out there I suddenly realized what it is I own: shivers of cold sweat run down my spine! Good Lord! How much is all this worth? And the paintings. Oil, old masters, perhaps I should really try to sell them. I don't need money, I make enough for my own needs. A single man, an only son, I have enough to last me a lifetime: dishes of porcelain, carefully packed, not even opened after my parents' death, silver, a house full of furniture locked in and covered with sheets of linen. Money? I make sufficient from my Catholic corner – press, bibles, new books all the time, and the devotional, beautiful objects; they are eternal and will always give you a piece of bread; because they are not subject to ridiculous worldly fashion, so the stock never gets outmoded. If it does not sell this year, it will the next. I have enough.

What devil, what evil inspiration pushed me to display, to show what I have? What fool am I to believe in the benevolence of others? Perhaps I behaved like I did as a seven-year-old, when I stole a cigarette lighter from the corner tobacco shop, played with it for a long time, cleaning, filling, lighting it. But one day I wanted to share my joy. Not with the boys, I feared some bullies; they would just punch me down and rob me. No, not the boys. I showed it to my mother, clicking it open, and the sudden flame frightened her. It was a huge to-do. Where, how – let's go to give it back, write a note of apology, pay for the loss of business, no supper, off to bed, and the strap from my father – here I am now in my middle years, being seven years old, and the punishment I fear will not be long in coming.

It started when I had lovingly displayed the books and one superbly crafted, 18th century Italian, seven-armed candlestick, that a man of my age perhaps, but much younger looking, upper-class *légère* walk, circled the corner of the shop repeatedly. A wild animal after its prey. I can tell a predator when I see one. After cruising several times, back and forth, as if he did not believe his eyes, he entered. To my question, how I could be of service, he looked a little around and then went straight to the Hugo von Hofmannsthal shelves and asked for *Florindo*. I do not remember what I said. Either, *It is not for sale,* or.... I sweated blood. I know, punishment is close. A seven year old should never show his lighter.

COURT PROCEEDINGS. The shop was sealed. The famous crate went into the custody of Justice. And they found the little grey man bleeding from his wrists in his parents' bathtub. He had not appeared when summoned, neighbours had not seen him for days, and the law took its course. No suicide note necessary: a lonely man dying in his bathtub is no special event worthy of attention. The ownership established, the contents of the crate went into the possession of the two surviving heirs of the Old House in the *Residenzgasse* from the city of Czernowitz, Bukovina.

Vienna Charm

ALL TREES BROKE INTO LEAVES. VIENNA. HUES OF PRE-green branches interwoven, of a more abundant green to come, imminent, but not yet there. Faces seemed friendlier, little girls in more pink and blue hustling through the parks, the wide avenues.

Felix stepped out onto the black wrought-iron balcony on the early Sunday morning to sit beside the glass table, and in that Art Nouveau summer chair he had sat on the first time he came in his yellow shirt, pockets full of death. Memories of his family dinner when he had to leave the old house, alone, with no destination in mind, but the abstract, absolute necessity of change was there. Fleeting thoughts, images always emerging.

The air was crisp with morning, no hint of life yet, twigs and branches heavy with buds nearly unfolding, looking as if they grew out of lampposts. Gates and windows drawn as if conceived by men in their search for the *just right,* the beautiful. This Vienna air of spring champagne this early morning made Felix lightly drunk. He had not slept much. Phantom pain made his knee pulsate, his missing big toe twitched as if stubbed, and there was no comfortable spot to be found for his non-existent leg.

"It knows everything," Felix thought. "It has a gut of its own, predicts, foresees, and recalls. Alive, as if there; no surgeon could sever it, though one did. With partisans from both sides of the warring factions: Oh heavens, I was lying in a marshy ditch, avoiding the Allies' bombs on the way to the oil fields of Ploeşti in Romania, and had thrown myself into that ditch, when fire from both sides of it splintered the bone from the knee down. Someone, rifle at the ready and smiling, pulled me to a waiting army truck and delivered me unconscious to a hospital. When I woke, I was told the leg could not be saved and had been amputated. But of course they could not take its soul. It has saved it all and more; it has memory, fear, knowledge of imminent danger, and will shoot up like lightning from the toe to the brain in an instant. It's a wooden leg now. I limp and try to hide it.

"To watch Martina's silent face next to me, may be to behold all the nights of my life. What will there be to long for, what other faces to infuse into hers, where the memory of that first narrow bed we shared when she bled but lightly? Ethereal as she was, it had surprised me, and we had giggled like schoolgirls, washing the spot in the small sink of her room under the steeple of the church. How will this be with Martina fully realized: bread and butter, toothbrush, bathroom sounds and smells? How will...?

"My leg, full of memory, hurt high up to the hip and I had to turn; not to wake her, I moved slowly. For the first time last night I remained next to her all of the night. How to move and not to wake her? Or does she not easily wake? Does she dream? She must. One always dreams shortly before waking. Does she? And does she turn, slowly or violently? I do not hear her —" Felix had felt her breath but did not hear it. "A very silent, still body, as if it were not she. Will she rise to pee like I do every two or three hours or is she not human? A plant life, like her mosses, a stunted Japanese tree, stones around it, such gentle soul and body. How will it be to wake next to her every morning?"

So Felix woke early from this sleepless night, and unaccustomed to her flat, in this bare, before morning light, he stumbled against the one easy chair, his fantasy leg hurting, beating alarm. Collected his wits, found the door to the bathroom, which was of course no bathroom but a toilet with a to-be-pulled-down handle attached to the ceiling. He had sat a while in that dark, windowless corner, had come out comforted, closed the door. Passing hall and the almost empty salon, Felix went out onto the balcony to a Vienna air of pre-morning spring. And life and youth returned with intensity. Stretching his happy leg into comfort, he seated himself onto a wicker chair. Night dew cooling the palm of his left hand, he waited for the morning.

A WINTER DAY. Such stillness. Light snowflakes, bodiless, as if carried by cruising winds. An unmoving, resting nature.

"I love winter," Felix thought, "I love these moments, open-ended on both sides, gentle stars frozen into perfection, not knowing direction and settling on a lamppost like the ones through my glass balcony door, looking now as if they were hooded hunchbacks. And the long lines of young beech trees, white or red – Or are they? – warm under the falling snow. I love a Vienna Sunday afternoon in January, when the coffee hour has passed and time takes on a winter slowness. Objects merge, the white taking the edge off things and the obligation to see or notice. Breath is slower, the need of air relents, and so does a pulsating heart and past passions. A chance to disengage, if not to justify. There was love when I erred through the streets. I stopped in front of the *Burgtheater* in search of Martina. Someone took my hand, led me to the theatre people's small coffee and wine shop.

"Selma. I left a few pages with her as I took my leave, but she had not answered. It was summer with her. Cherries were ripe at her windows. We had no winter with each other. Endless dark days are so much better than bursting spring or full, fruity summer. So much better for aging bodies. Hers. To view the creases, warts, hair in unusual places, folds, fat glands, and sudden bulges. I loved her aging body, and said so. But we had no winter with each other to live the slow hours, take time to find the new or cherish the known, the beauty of her even shoulder blades; symmetrical, strong, unfoldable wings."

Felix rose to turn to the sideboard, which had miraculously escaped fire and water, to pour himself a brandy. He cast a glance to the Klimt above, which so much suited his winter mood: the two figures as one, bound by the woman's hair at their ankles, a reassurance of love and eternity. Limping back toward the sofa, he put his drink beside him on the carpet, having decided to have no low coffee tables: "Oh, so good not to have all these cumbersome, low objects, glass or metal. They hit my leg wherever they can find it, and rob the carpet of its design." And he stretched himself on their new sofa, one without pretense to style, of Berlinese simplicity, meant for comfort and talk.

Night took over the streets: through his salon balcony doors he recognized Martina passing one of these lit, hunchback lampposts in white hoods, and he rose fast to receive her at the door before she rang the bell. Glad now to have his winter day come to its end, he took her fur coat from her shoulder and kissed her fresh, outdoor cheek.

"I'll write to Selma tomorrow," he said, pouring her a brandy.

"Do," she said. "Let's have things clean and honest." They seated themselves on the new sofa. Martina smiled in the dark, and in her lightly mocking tone said, "My Felix and his lovers. How many do you need?"

"It is only you, Martina. Faces change a little, circumstance too, or perhaps it is momentary fascination, another angle, a light falling onto a profile I had not guessed to be there. But it's you, Martina."

"Good," she says. "I will believe it, kiss me good night." She rose from his entangling arms, and turning back at the bedroom said, "Come when you are ready, sweetheart."

MARTINA ROSE LATE, towards midday. She avoided the morning hours, which even as a little girl had been a burden to her. Haunted by her proper, working-class mother from the village Rosch, she heard foul words, and she had pacified her mother by rising earlier than expected. Dressed in well-ironed, frilly cottons, she came down from her steeple room to face corn porridge, hot, sticky, and wonderful with milk from the village, and her father the pastor who was always there before her. Her ally. But being a powerless link in this tight triumvirate of daily ritual, he would run to help her down the last step, put his arm around her shoulder to lead her to her assigned chair at the kitchen table, and pull that chair out, leaving a comfortable space for the seven- eight- or nine-year-old young lady to straighten out her skirt before sitting down. "Are you at court?" Rosy asked once, looking jealously at

the two of them before adding, "you never hold my chair for me."
No reply. Just the usual.

These morning hours Martina avoided. And grey, snowy, winter days were not the comfort for her that they were for Felix. She
wanted colour and joy, Annie to wake her by midday with coffee,
hot milk, and fresh *Kaisersemmel.* They talked about household
things – the evening meal, shopping, workmen coming to the
house, new light fixtures for the bathroom and vestibule, which
was dark and dingy at the entrance with old, pervasive smells that
could not be helped. She wanted modern, milky light bulbs, that
might soften the memory of her first encounter with Gerhard
Schneider's flat. He had been solicitous at the time and she had
resisted.

"Come let's talk," he had said. "There are three floors up and
I have redone the apartment in an almost authentic Art Nouveau
style." But he had not touched the vestibule: dark black, almost
one-hundred-year-old mahogany to the ceiling. Entering for the
first time, she thought she could not take another step or the wall
would crush her. But it opened unexpectedly to the salon and the
glass doors across brought the *Ringstrasse* nearly in. All things
were new, bright, imaginative, pink and white, matching her
mood, and she fell into his arms, saying thank you. She had lived
in digs with rooming ladies of a variety only Vienna provides,
where a young woman could not wash a pair of stockings and
hang them to dry near the stove.

Whenever she could, she slept till noon or waited for Annie.
She loved a woman's chat, Annie's private life with yesterday's lover
or her visit to the cinema: *A stupid, slapstick comedy, pies flying
through the air, old tricks,* Annie said. Martina loved them too, but
would not go in; did not permit herself a fall in artistic standard,

for fear there might not be much of a distinction between a maid and herself. But she loved Annie's coarse account of her new lover's hand trying to squeeze her breast and her playing coy. "Well I let him have it for a while to make the wretch happy, after all he had paid for a meal – not the greatest by the way – and the cinema. Oh well, he is not a bad sort. But that is all he got last night. He has to shell out much more before I go to bed. Besides, I still have this ex-Count Herr von Neurath to get rid of. Or perhaps I won't for a while yet. He is easy to serve and really treats me like a lady. Not that he takes me out to fancy places or would be seen with me at Sacher's or in the streets, but when his wife is out, he sneaks me in through the servant's door on Sundays often. Kisses my hands when I enter. Just lovely. We rarely go to his bedroom. It's in the salon that he wants me. It's a few things I have to do for him. Well – he seats himself across from me and I bend down, to make him happy. Not a big deal. No, he does not want me naked, just the boobs showing, but he does not touch. He is easy to serve, my ex-Count. *Call me Franzerl,* he says, and I do. He is easy. He hands me his handkerchief, fancy, encrusted crown in the corner – No trouble."

Handkerchief. Martina's mind wandered. She let Annie chat on with the description of the salon in her ex-Count's villa: silver vases, silk flowers in cabinets, waxen fruit one can't eat in all colours on small tables under mirrors, just there to be pretty. And Martina's mind wandered to Othello's handkerchief with the strawberry in the corner. That fatal handkerchief that killed Desdemona. "I sat next to Gerhard in the *Burgtheater* when Iago showed the stolen handkerchief with the strawberry in the corner to Othello and I knew it is I who will be strangled. Gerhard heard the muffled sob, but was moved by it also and put his arm around my shoulder. The feeling passed, it was theatre. But an awareness that others can inhabit my soul took possession. It was theatre, and I stepped out, still Desdemona in all my being. It took a glass of wine at the small café around the corner, the artists' own, and the dear face of Gerhard, his silent understanding of my fear of death, to restore me. It was that night that I went for the first time to his flat."

And Annie's voice now resurrected itself bodily in her ear. "Oh – the salon, the goodies in the small crystal dishes, almonds in caramel, *Salzstangerl Mozartkugeln* and a few thousand *schillings* in an envelope! But Franzerl took the handkerchief from me before leaving –" *Ha, ha, ha.* Both women shook with laughter and complicity: the ephemeral beauty of Viennese society and the maid, partners in life, sharing, knowing about each other. She could say to Annie what she could not say to her man; she suspected Felix not to have any taste for the slightly yonder-world flavour of her experience: the meeting of a *Doppelgänger,* Felix's double, or the voices she heard or identified from early days, an old man's voice that she could swear she had heard sitting on the ruins of the Ahi fountain across from her father's church. That voice and face of the old man refashioned itself and met her in the streets of Vienna. She saw Rosy after her death, almost corporeal, giving advice on the ribbons or quality of straw for Martina's Easter bonnet, knowing everything better, annoying Martina to no end. The voice alone, carrying threats, revived childhood fears, and Martina brushed Rosy away. *Go away,* she said, *go away. It's enough, I'm a big girl now.* And the young milliner who had looked slightly askance at these words had frightened Martina. No, she could not talk to Felix about it. She had tried to tell him about the young man at Dehmel's, a true, live *Doppelgänger,* but had felt little response. So she decided to keep it from him. And

Martina wondered how would it be possible that a man of Felix's charm, intelligence, and above all learning, would not see something so real as – *Past life, alive for me, is still with me.* But not for him, where nothing is believed that can't be proven on his laboratory table. Yet simple Annie could. She listened. She heard the voices, saw the spirits, trembled at my childhood experience, held my hands and cried with me. A simple maid. She knew.

GERHARD SCHNEIDER'S WILL was found in one of the locked drawers of the desk Martina had chosen at an auction that was held not far from the *Theater an der Wien.* They had both gone there after what they called their "first night."

"Let's go and find a small desk, something antique, an old one with secrets, ghosts, old lives hidden in drawers, memories of others, to put our own in," he said, laughing, when they rose after that night.

Annie had been Gerhard Schneider's servant in his bachelor flat and had heard their giggles, warning each other not to wake her, had listened to the carefully inserted key into lock and silent closing. "They don't take their shoes off," Annie had thought, "so confident they are. But I do hear you, thievish lot." And it irked her because she had noticed Gerhard's returning later than usual, excusing himself from dinner, or leaving it without an excuse. She had become his mistress soon after he hired her three years ago. But when the first of a series of art objects arrived – a small sculpture of a reclining woman, which he moved – foolishly she thought – from one spot to the other to catch morning or evening light, she knew he would marry soon. "So, this is how it is now, the moment had come." And she knew Martina by her step, the furtive sound of her entering the flat. "She may not be such a lousy lout, lording it over me. Not by her step." And Annie feared her less. "But I have shared his bachelor days' meals, talked about weather, or what do we cook tomorrow kind of chatter," and she eyed Martina without much generosity.

But unexpectedly the women took to each other at first sight. A fast, intimate complicity, a response from the subconscious, unspoken but realized, made them both smile at Gerhard's introduction of Martina to Annie: "This is my bride, Miss Martina Rempel." Annie, without lowering her eyes, comparing Martina's height to her own, her airy, light appearance to her own swarthiness, minded it much less than she had feared. The bond of the underlings – the subverters of masters, fathers, uncles, or domineering mothers – was sealed with Martina's reply:

"And you are Annie! How will I compete with your perfection, dear Annie? I have heard so much about you. There is not a day that your name does not fall from Gerhard's lips."

Well, that was all she needed. A servant knows her place. She survives and profits, eats from all the plates, Rosenthal or gold, and does not shun the rest. No, not crumbs. Big chunks of steak left on the bone, the best of the cut, with herbed Hollandaise sauce, or just the Vichyssoise at the bottom of the bowl soaked up with a crust. No, these were no crumbs from the table. Annie had her pride, it was well deserved and her own. Servants know their masters, they know them, and not always with disgust. So often with pity and a little disdain. "Oh, the poor man, he works too hard, something plagues him, it must be love or a memory or something he regrets," Annie would speculate.

She would worry about Gerhard's melancholy, sitting by the hour watching the sun drift, not reading or listening to the radio.

But sometimes she would call him a pig, a womanizer, a pervert, and would raise her voice to him, her bread-giver, in full knowledge of his dependency. And she would go to his bed with the waggle of his little finger. Not out of pity, but out of love could she guess what he wanted: full comfort, a relaxed sex, an undressing without moving a muscle. Sitting in his chair, he would let her take off his unlaced slip-ons of calf leather, his knitted socks in grey and white, while reading a book, watching her sideways only to make sure the shoes were lined up with the socks in a certain order. Gerhard loved the thirties novels, Viennese or others. Jakob Wassermann's *Ulrike Woytich* and Franz Werfel's *The Forty Days of the Musa Dagh,* he read and reread. Redemptive reading perhaps, like Thomas Mann's *Joseph and His Brethren* – or *Tonio Kröger.* Annie proceeded silently but firmly, removing the book from his hand, as if it was mother saying, "It is time to go to bed, sweetie." And so it was. He let it happen. And she removed his shirt, jacket already hanging around the arms of the chair, murmuring, "It needs laundering," to remind herself to put it into the basket when she left. A true servant, self-effacing, stripping modestly in the dark and hurrying to stretch out beside her master. A loving servant, too. *He is beautiful,* she thought, *a baby really. So easy to make him happy with a little everyday.* Removing her left arm from under his neck after he had fallen asleep, she would slip out and into her servant quarters under the roof by two o'clock in the morning, taking the laundry along.

FELIX HAD MOVED INTO THE FLAT after Gerhard's death. But it was too soon, according to Annie's moral code. "Give Martina time to come to her senses, to feel the loss. I feel it. I grieve for the good man. He was so tender, did little things to make a woman happy. I did know him better than she did. Little things, like stretching his love to go a little further, to make sure I was happy also. Little things, as if I weren't a paid servant who washed his clothes and polished his shoes. And even after Martina came, he would never pass me without a light, not obvious touch and: 'The house is full of Annie's cooking, how wonderful! And what is it today?' It will be different now, and Felix should have given us time, Martina and myself. It would have been so good had Martina and I had a little grieving time. Just to hold hands and think about Gerhard. We'll still do it. I love my gentle mistress. I do not exactly understand what makes her so beautiful, neither do I really know her. But we all fall at her feet. Felix too. When he first came to the flat, I thought he was mad. Wild-eyed, silent, a voice of held-in anger asking for a glass of water. What for? I thought he was dangerous to Martina."

But she said, "No, no, he is only dangerous to himself. The glass of water is for the poison he carries in his shirt pockets, to dissolve it in. Be gentle, he has suffered, is homeless like me, and has loved me from the moment he saw me in the garden of my father's church. He loves me truly. Not better, but differently than Gerhard. I'm his, he thinks."

"Who would not adore her? But Felix moved in too soon. Maybe they won't stay here because this is Gerhard's house. Small things remind one of him. Unexpected cufflinks, cigar clippers, fountain pens inscribed G.S. turn up in odd places. Even after all that belonged to him – slippers, housecoats – had been given to the poor, and in spite of fire, smoke, and water there is still Gerhard floating in the air. I breathe it in everyday, recognize it, so I think they won't stay, they won't be able to bear it. New things have arrived, a few pieces of furniture. Ungainly, I think, useful but unattractive. The couch came from Berlin. The style, that is. Berlin-Bauhaus they call it. It does not fit in Vienna. We are different. Well now, the desk at least remains."

They started searching for the will. There were tens of little compartments, opening one into the other.

"I was not asked to help with the search, but I think I know where it is. They are impatient the two of them, or simply irritated or sad. They rummage and don't look, so they can't find anything. Now look at them, they sit hand in hand on that ugly Berlin sofa, staring through the glass doors, not seeing anything. At least Felix is not committing suicide every five minutes, because now he has my beautiful mistress by his side. Did she tell me that he was her first lover at sixteen, made her pregnant and she had to go to the big city to give birth? And where is that baby? Does she think of it still? Oh, look at them, two homeless orphans, from another time and place. I'm a working girl, but better off. I'm from here. I belong, but my heart goes out to them."

And Annie came in from the kitchen, making more noise than was called for, and said softly, "Come, Frau Martina. Come, I think I know in which secret compartment Gerhard had put the will." And Annie went straight to the spot, unhinged a few drawers, inserted the little key, and one sprang open.

"Dear Annie," Martina said. "Dear Annie."

It was more than Martina had expected. The will made her a very wealthy woman. And Gerhard had left it to her discretion to make decisions. The only stipulation was that perhaps a third of the property would go to a Jewish family whose name he did not know. It put a terrible burden on her shoulders. Of course, she knew of his sleepless nights. Being at his side, she woke to his repetitive nightmares, always returning at similar hours towards morning.

MARTINA, AT THE AGE OF SIX, had lost a dear schoolmate, the one she had walked hand in hand to school with through all her primary school years. She had asked her father where Kate had gone and received the enigmatic answer, "She is in heaven, darling – do not worry." But she did worry. The voice had gone. The physical touch of her hand had gone, the giggles, and always the voice. How, where? How could a voice come and go. No, she decided at this young age, it could not disappear once given sound. And she heard it when alone, sad, or in need of another self. And she heard it always distinctly. She also saw Kate many a time, walking by as another child. Or just as a fleeting voice she recognized, and she smiled. "Your daughter is crazy," Rosy had shouted to her husband the pastor. "She's out of her mind, she grins to herself or mutters under her breath. She is crazy, your daughter." And the pastor, calming the storm, had said, "Martina is spiritual. She feels things other people do not."

True, she thought. I feel things. A presence. The life in the other. A past life is not past. And even those around me, I see them in others. Hear them. Voices echo through others I encounter. They are always sounding. Perhaps my father's "spiritual" fits me. I need fewer words. I can get away with a smile and think my thoughts.

The second burden was all that property. A chemical plant and a publishing house from both his mother and father's heritage had come down to Gerhard, their only son. After the war he had disappointed his parents by leaving the management to experts and had gone to study medicine. An only son, many hopes were tied up with him, but he could not fulfill them. He kept an eye on it, putting in an appearance from time to time, and he did not interfere. But once. When, on his return from the war, he realized the chemical plant was run with Ukrainian prisoners of war, he was determined to free them. And did. To the annoyance and silent revolt of the people in charge. He told Martina, just in passing, that he would pay for labour or not have it. She loved him for it. But now it was in her lap and she was stunned. She had never owned anything or been responsible for the welfare of others, and she turned to Felix, a rich man's son.

Martina put aside the letter that accompanied the will. She needed a moment for reflection. I rarely have to act, she thought, smilingly. Somehow I was allowed to be beautiful in the eyes of others. I could grow and play with life as one would with coloured stones. Days came and went and I looked into a small mirror one day to behold an unexpected stranger. There were no mirrors in the church of my strict Lutheran ancestors. There was one on my mother's dresser, a silver set of comb, brush, and mirror she had received as a wedding present and had polished it eternally, and another mirror I had hidden. It was broken on one side and had lost its silvering, and I rarely looked at it. But when I pulled it out from under my carpet, which covered a secret box beneath a loose parquet board, I thought I'd faint. It was someone I had never laid eyes on. And my new "self" grew, independent of the world around me, free now of the mosses, violets, and little creatures that had been my companions. A self and a love of self I allowed to happen, not hearing my mother's voice shouting, "You're a no good, lazy, so-and-so," or a "Jew's brood," having been nursed on Rachel's breast. She would never forgive my love for the Jews in the Old House, or perhaps forgive herself for her empty breasts. But she loved me too in her petty ways, her only child. I became someone to be adored by others, and I liked it. I saw myself once in a darkening windowpane. A feeling of wonder, of completion, filled my heart. To be so perfect. Streaming pale hair braided or not. Waiting for the magic break of time, when the sun was just about to sink, darkening the window until it became a reflective mirror; I rejoiced in that sudden appearance. A goddess to come and to go and to teach you who you are.

On my bed on such a night, when I had dressed for my private viewing, had waited for the daily magic mirror in the windowpane, had opened my hair to fall over my shoulders – on such a night I gave myself to Felix. He was mine, too, since the moment I had lifted my eyes above the grasses and rose from my favourite crouching position inside the dew of mosses in the garden. He was mine, as our eyes met. And he often came by. I saw him running or just walking leisurely with his mother – and later without her. There was not much to say as we both knew now who we were and for whom. And I saw him everywhere. In others, in young men walking by. It was Felix; it was his voice. My mother, Rosy, beat me with the butt of an old broom when I confessed and nearly made me miscarry. But I did not, and she sent me off to Bucharest to distant relatives. It wasn't a good year. And I'm not good with children anyway. Well, who is to say…?

But life became real in September, 1939. With twenty kilograms to carry and sixty kilograms to follow by train, I had to leave to go *Heim ins Reich* by Hitler's orders, as if into the jungle. With mother. Relatives, peasant stock from Rosch, whom I never saw except at Christmas and Easter, strangers with a mother tongue, densely packed into the waiting trains. And it was past the Public Gardens, the northeast station, unfamiliar, ghostlike that I thought: I'll end this nonsense. I'll jump the train and throw myself under it before it rolls. But the engine sounded, and squeezed between strangers, life went on, as it has a habit of doing.

Clover Leaf

S HE WAS A WEALTHY WOMAN NOW. IT CHANGED HER. HER features hardened, her gait stiffened, she hurried her step. Martina took the reins of an empire Gerhard had left to his underlings into her hands. She now covered and protected her otherworldly second self with a façade of authority, and she applied an unexpected intelligence to tens of millions of *schillings*, as if she had been born to them. As such, they did not mean what they seemed. They did not alter what she loved, but power in her hands without the sermonizing memories of right or wrong freed her, and she fearlessly dismissed the inefficient, paid them off into retirement, and in one year she had sold the plant to the highest bidder. She ran a tight ship, and Felix looked at this tender, vulnerable violet with amazement. Annie, too, missed the girl-talks at noon in Martina's bedroom, as she rose at seven now, and left a menu and shopping list lying on the desk for Annie to pick up. "Pheasants and wild berries," she wrote down, "on Monday, apple and pear compote for dessert. I'll be back at seven o'clock in the evening." And so forth, for the whole week.

It was not only the weight of obligation to money and memory that changed Martina outwardly. It was one evening, when working at Gerhard's desk, that by an inadvertent movement of her hand Martina touched a button which made a drawer spring open. Densely written pages, in a childish fourth-grade-level hand, in-love sounds of *f-s,* baby talk, fell into her hands. It spoke of coded sex, the imagination of deep love, the body of the other, the sinking into oblivion of climax – in crude low-class fashion, but also as a *Heurigen* wine, that half-fermented, inebriating drink, and a dance in the cool of the night. *Fantasy? Have they gone dancing? Have they lived as lovers, true lovers, Annie and Gerhard?* Martina had no answers.

She saw Annie's despondency, her grieving, as if she were Gerhard's wedded wife, and Martina decided to part ways. But she had to think it through: how to do it without saying too much. How not to hurt – she saw Annie bewildered, missing her intimacy with Martina. She did her duty, and what was demanded of her, but felt suddenly excluded. Her Sunday love affairs remained unrecorded, with no one to hear them, and she grieved. Until one day Martina announced she had bought a villa outside of town, and Annie could come or not, as she wished.

The will had also endowed Annie handsomely. A pension guaranteed her old age, and the endowment was extraordinarily high and beyond anything a maid could expect of the finest master.

Why had Gerhard sought me out and married me? Martina, worried, asked herself. For redemption's sake? A paying of bills, feeling indebted to my father, the pastor, who had saved Gerhard from court-martial after he was found unconscious in a brothel! And she recalled, as well as she could, both their lives: Gerhard

Schneider, who had come back from the war laden with burdening guilt, had studied medicine to do good and, knowing of the pastor's wife and daughter in Vienna, wanted to help. He found us needy and grateful. And so he did his duty. Endowing Felix also. Heavens! But between those two Martina suspected a deeper brotherhood, a man-to-man commitment. Gerhard loved Felix, but then who wouldn't? He cleansed himself, perhaps.

And Martina was deeply convinced of that need, the need to pay, and she smiled. A ritual cleansing. It has been part of her inner habits, undisclosed and intimate, to always compare and think: What and how did they do it? And in the will was a stipulation that a small piece of land and one hundred thousand *schillings* were left for a family whose name Gerhard did not know. He had hoped and wished that we, his heirs, would find them. A *Residenzgasse* family in my own hometown, just a little up the street. Had he killed? Some? Left others alive? A Catholic, he needed absolution from morning until night.

Martina remembered well leaving Gerhard and Felix in the salon sitting on the pink pin-striped sofa, cognac glasses in hand. She had gone to bed to extricate herself from a strange, tri-fold clover leaf. Suspended into a dimming Vienna evening where time diminished invisibly, Felix and Gerhard were ready for each other. Confession and absolution on both sides. I'm not needed, she had thought that night, and had smiled at the thought of clover leaf having a rare fourth leaf: Annie. She rejected the thought, but it persisted all through the night.

The next day, Martina rose earlier, wouldn't wait to make menu plans with Annie, and greeted her in passing when walking by the kitchen on the way to the vestibule. With a nervous gesture she pulled her coat from the multi-armed coat hanger, flung it around her shoulders and left, calling "Too-de-loo" to Annie. The fourth leaf: Annie was a partner. The thought would not leave her: but to touch and unfold that letter had made it all real. At once. Annie was more than the fourth leaf in the clover, she might indeed be the stem and Gerhard's only love. So intricately spun into a past was all his life after that murderous day, that Gerhard's comfort and daily joy was to come home to Annie for sex, food, and love. And she gave him all that, until Martina entered their lives.

Felix, stunned by the endowment, had never suspected Gerhard to have come from such a Patrician family: inherited property, feudal estates outside Vienna, and the old connection of the Catholic aristocracy in charge of the Empire for hundreds of years. Gerhard had worn his heritage with elegance, discretion, and that particular superiority the clan could provide: doors opened by the sound of the name.

In Vienna one does know Jews. They're visible. They are in commerce and in the professions, and they write. Literate from the age of kindergarten, Gerhard loved his bookish companions. Did not think of them as *they* or *them*, had not heard it at home where a stately household, a mother in taffeta and silk, a father with a monocle who scarcely appeared except at dinner, assured the boy Gerhard of his uniqueness. Prejudices were hidden, civility and learning taught. Born to wealth, he saw his parents rarely. Church on Sunday, dinner at one o'clock: a bourgeois routine wrapped a cloak of comfort around him. Cooks and maids were his daily companions, and Gerhard avoided the boys: Women aren't dangerous; they smile, feed you, heal your bruised knees and tuck you in at night. For the rest, one is free to dream, do one's homework and grow slowly within that cocoon.

The first prostitute was a natural thing. Mother was not informed, but the maids knew. For the first time, Gerhard went out into the Vienna streets to show his independence. To himself mainly. But also to Claire, the youngest of the maids, who had offered herself, saying: "It would be time, Herr Gerhard, you are a young man now." He was sixteen, and had to show her he was in command and not to be bossed by servants. But he returned, never to go out there again. And after school or in free hours, he diligently mounted the steps to Claire's domestic quarters. Silently accepted by cook, janitor, and the *Stubenmädchen,* he was Claire's, who had fast climbed the ladder of any servant's ambition: to supervise cleanliness, the general running of things, table and bed linen, and all the needless accoutrements of a past age living out its days. *"Ah, der junge Herr ist hier"* – *Oh, my young Lord has come* – or something similar to that, she had said with smiling satisfaction when he first set foot in her neat little room, as if it were his right. These were his companions for love and daily needs. His mother was for museums, art shows, visits to galleries, or "Gerhard, do you think that dove-grey plush would be softer, more in spirit with modern times? I would like to take the red plush off the dining room windows to get away from old-fashioned, boring red. Do you think light dove-grey would please you?" And so forth. His taste was for change, discretion in design, and away from obviousness, as was Vienna's habit to parade her past.

Felix, too, was a man of woman made, and always seeking a refuge and sure to find it in her arms. Whoever she was. The two men, in their brief but profoundly intimate moments, the Austrian-Jew and the Austrian-Catholic, found themselves to be of the same tribe. They had a tongue in common, an aspiration to justice, a desire built into their daily lives to avoid assault, and they had an eye for beauty, the ability to see man's imagination transform the ordinary, elevate the daily grind. Heighten it. Made of the same stuff, they were brothers, if for such a short time.

And Felix mourned Gerhard, admired his courage. And his conviction grew that Gerhard's death was not totally accidental, that he had sought it, perhaps, and welcomed it. And that closeness of death was Felix's as well. But Felix had abandoned his yellow citron shirt with the two poison-filled pockets. A feeling of success or just physical joy made him empty them, but he never abandoned death as comfort, as close embrace.

Returning to civil life after all was over, Gerhard did all the right things: studied medicine, honoured his parents, buried them in style, married the pastor's daughter, and wrote the will. Death on his side. Gerhard's love for Felix was a regaining of freedom, a redemption, a hope of heaven.

The will made Felix free to give up the lab job he had held in Vienna, and made him contemplate buying a small pharmacy right in the city. He found it in the ninth *Bezirk*. Working behind a lab table was a solitary experience, even if shared projects would make it less so; he had missed the contact with people. His conciliatory ways, his simple listening, which were Felix's real genius, found response in as small a dealing as the selling of a headache pill. But he took his time.

His love for Martina had to adjust to a changed Martina. It was not fully unexpected. Thinking of her taking possession aggressively with the assurance of her sex when sixteen or seventeen, Felix knew that her otherworldly self had a tougher core. And she showed it now. With money and power in her hands, she made decisions, stuck to them, was not swayed by tears or human destinies, going straight to the heart of operations: dismissed workers, streamlined business, tightened her ship. Felix, having guessed that her female strength would not permit cruelty, was surprised that she paid redundant workers only to the limit of the law, without pretty words, a golden watch, an extra penny, or a smile. Felix interfered, and she said, "That's fine. You do it."

"No," he said. "It's not for me to consider." And the nights became loveless and money stopped being what money could be best: a recreation, an escape to a tropical island, or just a pair of crocodile shoes. It became a power lever, a hard, iron machine with laws of its own to be carefully gauged, observed, and acted upon in accordance.

Caught in a spiral, in a succession of events neither Martina nor Felix could foresee, they found themselves thrown into separate worlds. And did not seek each other. Neither for solace nor sex. Annie, often a bond, with a servant's know-how of avoiding confrontation, was let go by Martina in a sudden anger over the will and the betrayal she felt.

Felix and Martina drifted apart, having silent dinners, served by new, paid servants.

Two Sisters A PASTOR'S DAUGHTERS

FELIX LOOKED INTO THE FACE OF MARIA. SHE HAD entered the salon announced by the new servant as a relative from the country, wishing to see Martina. He had risen from his desk facing the Vienna streets, and turned at the sound of the servant's voice to behold his childhood fancy: a taller, slimmer, more wiry body, a face lit from the inside, an ephemeral, translucent skin, of eastern paleness. Hair drawn up and away accentuated her dancer's body. Startled, Felix, reassuring himself, thought, *No ghost of dreams gone by, no spirits reincarnate, yet.* He offered a chair to Maria and she took it gracefully, seating herself on a low footstool to look cheeringly up at her young companion, who remained standing at her side.

"This is my son, Alexander, and I am Maria Rempel," she said.

"Martina is at work," Felix, looking at the *Biedermeyer* clock, replied. "She'll be back in an hour or so."

"Oh good, that gives me a little time to talk to you. You are Felix? My mother, Anna Rempel, whom you know as Shainah, has often spoken of you." And turning to her son, she said, "Come, sit next to me, it is such a comfortable stool," and she moved a little to make room for her son. Felix, who was sensitive to the gait of others, saw the young man's infirmity and his trying to disguise it. *Oh, sweet little brother,* he thought. Felix's own absent foot struck like lightening, raced up to the crown of his head, and stayed, lodging there. His heart went out to that tender boy, and he rose from his desk chair, where he had seated himself again, having turned it around to face Maria. He took the young man's hand, gently pulling him towards himself, and heard Maria's voice saying: "Alexander understands everything but he does not bother speaking. He is an artist. A painter."

"Well, he does not need words anyway, they hide more than they reveal." Alexander's features showed delight, the pleasure of hearing his own thoughts, *Yes, they hide more....*

Maria looked around, but did not dare do it too openly, and Felix took over, explaining things to relieve embarrassed silences: "We had a small fire. Martina lost her husband. He had collected art, furniture from the turn of the century, sofas and chairs. Quite beautiful all of it, but she sold it. We thought at first to restore it for Martina's sake, the things he had given her, for memory's sake – but she decided to sell or give away what we could. So we do not have many things."

"Oh, that does not matter," Maria replied readily. To help Felix take the edge from the unexpected intrusion, she tried to reconnect, reweaving her own stories as if legends were coloured strands on the wrong side of the carpet. She clutched her handbag now, which she had laid on the oak floor, but decided not to divulge the true reason for her visit. *Too early,* she thought, suddenly conscious of the fact that he knew absolutely nothing about her existence, while she had relived her mother's rescue at Felix's hand many a time. *And not always in the same sequence,* she thought. *Stories do not seem to stay the same as first told; they change. People wandering in and out of them, coming to the fore in different mood or dress.* She smiled a little to herself, and Felix held on to Alexander as if he had won him as one would a teddy bear in a shooting booth at a fair and could lose him any minute. She smiled broadly now, lips apart, and Felix saw her sparkling teeth, a little too dense to be perfect: even her lower teeth, one grown over the other, were Martina's. *Heavens, I'm losing my mind or giving in to Martina's unworldly speculations. Doppelgänger,* ghosts returning to claim love or revenge on Viennese minds, fed on coffee and whipping cream at four o'clock in the afternoon.

Silence between the three of them was more comforting now. The silence of getting closer, finding one's way to the other, of touching the ground gently to free the path, removing barbed wire, everyone in their thoughts felt it with eyes open.

It is strange and a little unfair, Maria thought, to know about the other so much, while he is totally bewildered by my presence, and I wonder what it is that shook him when I entered the salon. I could not see his face well, because the light from the glass door to the balcony blinded me, but when he fully turned I saw his face, pale, astonished, truly bewildered. And there is no other word. He stood as if arrested, halted in his step by unseen spirits. It passed, of course, as would a veil when lifted, revealing his features. Felix. Whom I thought younger. Slim and elegant but drooping now in a paunchy way, just a wee bit. "Hair of chestnut brown," mother used to say, but it is mixed with silver now, still falling over his ears and barely touching the collar.

Stories change or we change them, either adding newly lived lives, perfecting future ones, or fulfilling wishes – but features do not change. I see Felix standing behind his pharmacy counter, people milling around him, serving them, talking in a firm, gentle voice to calm their fears. I see him with a young girl's eyes. My mother's. Sixteen at the time. I see him with *her* eyes, with that sudden imprint of love that took just a few, unnumbered days to last all her life. Yes, I could have called out his name, had I seen him in a crowd, no matter where. He moves now towards me, risen from his desk chair, gently takes his arm from Alexander's shoulders, and he truly limps and hides it like Alexander. He limps, or maybe it was that sudden bewilderment that I had noticed entering the salon that made him so ache he can hardly pull his leg. I could fall around his neck and shout *You're mine, you're mine as you were my mother's. You played with Martina's dolls I was told, setting the doll table for doll-tea. Oh, let me hug you –* And Maria jolted from her low stool onto her long legs, took one wide jump in Felix's direction, fell onto his neck, arms around it. "I love you Felix, now I have two limping –"

"Yes, you do," Felix said, removing her arms from around his neck to look into her mascara streaked face. "You are Martina's sister, and so you are mine." The ice had melted in the silence, words now tumbling from both their lips, she knowing, he assuming, both trying to match legends, inventions against memory first- or second-hand. So it went with laughter and tears, Alexander between them, trying to make sense, until Martina entered to join them, and they rose to greet her.

INTO THIS TIGHT, inextricable world, Maria appeared, Alexander at her side, as an angel of deliverance, someone heaven-made and simple. Maria had found work in the *Prater,* an old Vienna institution, a fair on grassy grounds, with Ferris wheels.

Small, independent theatre groups or clowns often played in the *Prater,* and Maria had been hired on first try. She was stunning, revealed a body of steel the moment she swung from a trapeze or leapt on a horse. And she opened her own show in a small tent for children a little off the *Prater* grounds. Teaching gymnastic skills for a token entrance fee, Maria found her vocation: children's bodies. She had seen them: tiny creatures mutilated, raw flesh at her mother's door, and had fled to avoid men who would make her give birth all over again. But children had been there all her early life, her grooming them daily, bathing them, or combing their hair; she used to put a ribbon in – no matter, boy or girl. She had heard them cry at night, had risen to change their linen, feed them, or take them to her own bed for their solace. She had seen it all, and love cannot change; it stays as the colour of your eyes does. And Maria turned to the little bodies now, to improve them, for a *schilling* or two.

Her trick-riding days were over; high-risk trapeze shows were for the younger ones. After once missing Giselle during a jump and hurting her own leg tendon, she never regained the immediacy, that ingrained know-how, when every muscle has a brain, acting on its own but for a common purpose. That was gone. And after parting from Dan and leaving him to his peasant girl-bride, she knew that a world had come to an end.

But she returned to the basic joy of the body: growing, moving in harmony, making joints fit and respond to the whole – to create a unit from crown to toe. She now went to Vienna gym shops to find books to learn from, and she discovered a world she had known in action, but had no name for. And without that there was no imparting it; of course one could show, demonstrate, but to truly teach, she went to learn. Swedish movements, with their own terms put upon laws she had obeyed from birth. And here they were in diagrams and designs. All named. Respectable. She called Alexander: Come, Raphael, come *Big A*, come see, everything is written out. And they laughed together, knowing it all; old practitioners of the art, finding their theory.

At first Maria had put up a tent. Circus people are never homeless. A roof can be stretched above one's head on any ground as long as there is a stake, a pole, and a piece of cloth. And Alexander painted double-jointed children, turning them in all directions with smiling, happy faces, saying in letters: Come to Alex's tent! *Big A* again, and find Maria, "Big M," for twenty *schillings,* for ten pennies, for no money if you haven't got any. And inside: The Body Beautiful. They had registered as refugees. And the police left them alone. Although for a while they had to go every day, and then only once a week, to the police station.

It was fine in the summer, but when the rains started Maria thought of permanency, or something that would enable her to send Alexander to a school for the mute. Vienna was the right place for it, she thought, with schools of all kinds, new, exciting for both.

In that mood of change to come, with a teenage boy at her side, she took the tram into town. It was a before fall mood, when trees turn, faces look more thoughtful, and a sense of the nearness of death softens the soul. People were friendlier, a little more courteous to Alexander, which was not always the case. Children, crippled to boot, were a nuisance in the eyes of adults who, oblivious to their own early plight, commanded them around and forbade them to sit when a holy adult came up the tram steps. But not today. Less rigorous, less selfish, young women passed up their seat for Alexander, which he refused smilingly, held his limping foot hidden while his good right arm gripped the leather strap that hung from the ceiling.

Was it his beauty, was it the aura of inner nobility? Was it that svelteness, attractive to men and women, which made them step back a little to let him pass? Or perhaps the presence of an artist who transforms what he sees, affecting those around him. All of that perhaps, and an endearing smile acknowledging a kindness. Without a sound. A little girl who moved slightly to make him more at ease, handed Alexander her doll to hold for a moment, and said: "She likes you, she wants to sit on your lap. You haven't heard her, only I can. She speaks to me because I've taught her all the words she knows. And she loves beautiful boys. Her name is Geraldine. Please, speak to her." But Alexander only smiled his tenderest thanks, held Geraldine lovingly as long as he was permitted.

The tram conductor seemed gentler. He asked Maria from which part of the Empire she had come, having detected a German less soft than street Viennese. And she said, "It's Eastern German you would not know. My parents are from the city called Czernowitz." And he laughed and said, replying in her own accent, "Isn't everyone from there!" It was a smaller city than Vienna but the spirit was the same, his parents, who had taken refuge here and stayed, had told him. "A few more stations," he said to her and then he helped both down the steps to the astonishment of the crowd because the conductor was discouraged from fraternization.

But no one could resist the big equalizer: fall in the air, all knowing our end. A shroud of colour and a changing light softening all the harsh edges, things looking rounder, trees in wild orange-gold telling us of our lives missed or still to be held on to.

People turned to each other in the tram, on its steps or at cross-roads to see if there was injury, or silently ask for pardon.

Such a good day for lovers, as were Maria and her son Raphael, his nickname since their departure from the Yugoslav island. Or *Big A*. Though at the time still so young, he had to grow into that *Big A*; taller now, Alexander had almost reached her height. They walked in a *légère* unison, in a harmony of rhythm with a slight offbeat syncopated accent; they savoured it, mocking it gently, for it was their very own and special bond. On a bench of the *Kärtnerstrasse* they sat down to eat their picnic lunch, an occa-sional flying beech leaf, red or yellowed, hitting them. Then, eyes closed, they rested, waiting for the right moment to rise and walk over to Martina's flat.

As she had not announced their coming, Maria hesitated to ring the caretaker. Streets were empty in the early afternoon and Maria and Alexander, looking up to the balcony, saw no move-ment anywhere. So she decided to walk leisurely to a *Kaffeehaus* called The Angel's Fountain, which she had spotted across the street, for hot chocolate, cream puffs, or a slice of *Kugelhupf*. Maria, entering the shop and looking for that fountain, found it leaning against the back wall, water spurting out of an angel's trumpet and falling back into a marble shell. "Come, Raphael," she said, "come look at this," and pulling Alexander into the direction of that baroque wonder, her eyes caught Martina's. She was thrilled to see her sister again.

Martina rose to greet Maria, arms wide open, measuring her-self against her own youthful reappearance. "Come sit by me. Alexander, join us! Waiter, table for three!" And she pulled Maria closer. An old Martina emerged out of that chic, Italian-cut, tai-lored suit, black velvet collar and white silk *jabot*. Grateful to find an opportunity to be her old, warm, simple self, she was alive for the first time since power in her hands had overwhelmed her. Sitting at a table now, near the half-open window where autumn-perfumed air softened fears and freed senses to deal with life, Martina, delivered almost, took her suit jacket off, hung it around the back of the chair, to be closer to Maria. A colour of youth rising up her neck, erasing all the years, lingered a moment longer. Giggling, she said, "Were I as beautiful as you are I would conquer the world!"

"But, heavens," Maria replied. "Don't make me blush –" They looked at each other, laughter rising from memories yet unlived. Alexander, mute, sat against the open window. Tall breezes played in his longish hair, which fell over ears and collar, and he brushed it away. The receding summer air illuminated his features, shining in bronze hues, and the two women turned to him at once almost, each taking one hand, and so they sat, skin to skin, a triangle, love flowing through all veins.

Steaming hot chocolate and pastry filled the table; hands retreated a little from one another, still staying close. The women found their own mirror image and each smiled at this stranger across the table. A stranger. Themselves. "I have to send Alexander to school," Maria started. "One that can help his particular need."

And Martina replied passionately, "Of course, right away. We'll go home and we'll see what we can think of."

"And there is one more thing," Maria added, "one that I did not want to talk about the first time we met at your apartment. I am anxious to fulfill my mission. I could not somehow talk about it then. Now, the time has come. Martina, you may know, or you may not, that our father saved a precious jewel for Felix's and Süssel's mother."

"Yes, they were living across from each other on the famous *Residenzgasse*. And of course I've known her from very, very young, and played in the old Jewish house. But I do not know about father holding jewellery in trust for them. You should know, Maria, that I left with my mother Rosy, in September of 1939 to go *Heim ins Reich*. And truly against my wishes. I had much rather liked to have stayed with father, who was of mixed parentage, and who absolutely refused to accept racial madness. Not so mother Rosy. She was German-German from the village of Rosch, and there was no holding her back when all the relatives left; she would not stay, and she made me leave. So I know very little about those terrible years. But Maria, Alexander, please do come up to the flat. Felix will soon be home. Dinner is served at seven o'clock and we have all night to talk." Martina paid the waiter, took her little sister by the arm, and pulled her resolutely out the door, followed by Maria's limping son.

It was a long night for the two women. After a dinner of *Paprika Knödel*, a chicken dish in a sweet burning, red paprika sauce, potatoes on the side, Martina commented, "We eat now what the servants like because I have no time anymore to plan meals or shop." With *Palatschinken* for dessert – a rolled up thin pancake filled with apricot and walnut – the day had run its course. Felix had sat between the sisters to make a little polite conversation. But very little. He was moved by their resemblance, his own love for Martina confronting a young woman bearing her traits. He ate quickly most of the time, looking for what the others wanted; Alexander, whose eyes, searching for salt and pepper or something spicy, Felix read, handed them across the table and received a broad smile. It was a quiet table. A mood of intimacy throughout. Felix grateful to see Martina relinquish her new, self-assured self to show a revived, if subdued, womanliness. And he wondered where he had gone awry or perhaps where she had faltered under the weight of money....

A glass of light wine, accompanying the paprika dish, drunk from Gerhard's crystal, sounded an A-flat when clinked, and they all giggled when Alexander's sounded a third down. There was no ice to break; they were a family at a square, portable, kind of card table – new furniture still not chosen or intentionally delayed – dining slowly. An evening autumn sun setting the air ashimmer, dissolving worries past or future. A family, as if it had never been apart or unaccustomed to one another. There was talk of good food and the glint in the glass of a refracted ray in the white-gold within. It was the first time for Alexander, and he liked it, drinking it a little too fast, not having yet learnt how to savour. Felix poured him a second glass to everyone's merriment. But no more. A *Stubenmädchen* called Milova, a Czech or Serb newly in Vienna, coming in to clear dishes and ask for the master's wishes, had not Annie's know-how but was eager to learn and please. Young, in traditional black dress, white apron and white headdress, she tried to put the lights on, but was asked not to. "And we'll do the rest, dear Milova," Martina said gently. "You're free for the night." With a giggle of thanks, the servant left. They were on their own. Slowly, they rose. Felix allowing the two sisters to seat themselves on the couch. Martina with a cognac, poured from the buffet under the Klimt painting. Maria saying, "No, no, no, heavens, not for me!"

Alexander and Felix both showed off their limp to one another and to the sisters, in an after dinner theatre mood. "You're a pair," Martina said. And for the first time for a while she came closer to Felix, hugging him before pouring her cognac. She kissed him fleetingly and said, "Felix, will you give us permission to leave you for the night?" *Us* meaning *us two girls.* "Please give Alexander the spare room, which is now my bureau. Find linen. Maybe you men also would like to find things to say to one another, whatever." Martina had come close, breasts brushing him slightly. *So, I haven't lost her,* he thought. *She is back.* But he nearly did not permit his joy to take hold, lest it vanish; he pulled Alexander by the hand to follow and implement Martina's orders, both mocking their limping limbs and laughing like ill-behaved Vienna street boys, two *Lausbuben*: wild, orphaned, wise street-kids with lice in hair and on body.

A SMALL LIGHT, diminished by a Hoffman shade, was just enough for Martina and Maria to cuddle into the cushions. They were on their own.

"Who was my father? What kind of man?" Maria asked, after night had fallen. The glass door to the balcony retained a fading glimmer, and the room, warmed only by the Klimt glow, hid its objects.

"And who was father to you?" Martina returned the question.

"He is what he was to my mother. What he was to her, what she thought he was, or," with a smile of forgiveness, "what she was prepared to let me know. So, I think he was different things. How could I unravel – a child born among Sisters of Mercy to a chaste nun – how could I come even close to imagine the real male-man-father-cleric figure he must have been? What was he to you, Martina? What was he to you, who physically knew him, day in, day out?"

It wasn't night yet. And the two sisters waited. To let the coming silence clear their minds. Slowly. To remove the day, its people, imaginings, and the need to act. Both took their time. A kind of homecoming. The Vienna world diminishing its noises, tired of itself, cars honking less and less, fiacres' horses' hoofs coming down to a trot, cooled all senses. Shedding the autumn warmth to prepare for the night, bodies stretched into whatever linen there was, and a dense, breathing world, spent in cubicles of stone, came to its rest. Maria, seeking that comfort on Martina's three-seater couch, pushed her sister gently to gain room, and both broke into laughter.

"How similar we are," Martina said, trying to arrange her own long legs into a favourable position. "We are the same, really bad girls! Looking for advantage wherever we could get it." But finding it now, they intertwined their limbs, and taking north and south ends with cushions for back support, they waited, full of the presence of the other. Night fell truly now. There was little light, a rare car flaring up to remind them of other nightly lives, when Martina started: "How to talk about this bygone world? Where to begin?"

"I want to know about my father, whom you have had, loved, shared mornings, nights, love and beatings!"

"No, no, not beatings. Not with a stick, a leather belt, or a flat hand. No, I feared him in other ways."

"What ways?"

"Inexplicable ways. Desperately wanting acceptance, in simple things. For him to say for instance, *How clever my child is,* or just *Well done,* and not always getting it. I feared his eyes. They showed a love beyond my comprehension. From three or four years old, I knew he loved me more than anyone would love me. But it wasn't a simple thing for a child, as a piece of chocolate or getting your dessert before meals would be. It was body and soul. Ownership. All of me. And I could not read him. Thank you, Maria, thank you for asking. It is time to look at my pushed-under-the-carpet youth and my escape, at sixteen, into the waiting arms of Felix."

As the night darkened fully now, the gold in the Klimt painting brightened. The two women saw one another through that veil of spun gold and black that falls from the rim of rich women's hats to take the edge off things. They saw each other as themselves. Bodies coming closer; a silk stocking against a naked leg. And Martina suddenly said, "Maria, you're barefoot."

"Yes," she answered, "My sandals are on the floor. I am always barefoot. My toes are clever, they behave like fingers. I've learned the art from Japanese circus people. I've taken a class once in Florence from a group of performers whose intertwining toes form poetic images of praying hands, sleeping heads, or running children. So I keep my toes bare, to move, to exercise, to remember really, as the body forgets." And Maria laughed. "Oh, terrible, terrible, how it forgets!"

And her sister Martina jumped up to strip herself of her silk stockings and night-coloured garters, threw them on the floor with Maria's sandals, and whispered, "Heavens, you're a breath of fresh air, Maria, you're me before I was other people's. They all owned me: tell me I'm beautiful, and I'm bought. It did change me. But there is something that is free still. How good it is to have you with me." And Martina went into her north corner, garter and stocking free. "I can talk to you and it amazes me," Martina said. "Perhaps because you are from my wildflower-self, and yet not entirely. A reminder of who I am or where I came from. Not to get lost. Yes, I will try to talk to you about our father."

"Thank you. To me, the pastor, my father, is just a story. Or a collection of stories. And they change over time. I thought I had heard one before, but somehow it took on new shape and I could not recognize it. Either my years changed my perception, my mother growing older changed it, or a story has no beginning at all. A seed it is, perhaps, or an event imbedded returns, showing itself in the light of our new eyes. Or it is not this specific event at all, but other people's lives suddenly growing into it, becoming part of it. Inseparably."

"And all of this now is my fiction," Martina said, "Because only your mother and I have lived his presence. So you'll get another story. Pain or joy, who knows?"

"Talk to me," Maria said. "It's a film. We can cut in a few more pictures. Coloured, they may not entirely be different from my mother's. Because, Martina, you may not know that my mother was still quite young when Felix brought her to father's church."

"No, I don't know anything about your Jewish mother. And this is what she was, is that right? Felix has told me the story of her rescue over and over again and sometimes I listen. But sometimes only." And she smiled at her own confession. "I have too little patience for other people's obsessions. I also should enjoy how the story changes, and how it suddenly gets a new character, who had not been around in the former versions. As he told me the stories, Marusja, the maid in the old Jewish house, had a hand in your mother's rescue."

"Well, stories change but I do know that she was young and grew up fast in the hands of the pastor, our father."

With a cascade of giggles, Martina added, "Anyone had to in his house. Unless you opposed him silently, did what you want, lied a little, if not outwardly, learned what he wanted of you and played the game. He was human after all!"

"Talk to me, tell me what it was to be his. I'll be silent and just listen. I want to make sense of things, of the absolute goodness of my mother, her chastity after my birth, and my own also, which perhaps is the same, who knows? We both have chosen to live without men. End of my story for the moment. I'll be good, won't interrupt, and perhaps fall asleep in my corner here."

"And so may I," Martina replied. "It had been a long day for me. Worries, dealings, and everyone wanting something. I had to dismiss two long-time employees and they threatened court action. It was a long day, but your coming and your astonishing beauty, and that you are my sister lifted me out of it. I may fall asleep in my corner, so tired am I. Besides, I hear no noises from the bedrooms. Alexander, true to his age, may have fallen asleep standing up."

A night different from all others, when childhood emerges in its almost hourly presence. *It is never past. Set in stone or broken into pebbles, one's life is built of it.* And Martina talks to herself, as to her other self in the dark, when features erase themselves and what matters arises. Martina, relaxed, free of propriety, saw her room under the steeple of the Evangelical church, her dolls aligned against the wall, her bed opposite in full view of them. And her father, the pastor, would come early in the morning, still dark at six-thirty; and it was his voice that woke her, his black silhouette just faintly guessed. She was five and six and seven and he stood there, already fully dressed, a pastor that early. As the summer days grew longer, she saw him better in the increasing light, and then the figure diminished again as winter set in. But the voice never changed. A soft voice, a warning built in, *Get up my child, I want to see you get up. No, take your shirt off first. Wash yourself. No, the water is not too cold.*

"And I went to the corner sink, where ice cold water, summer and winter, made me shiver. And my father, the pastor, would seat himself in front of my dolls, in the only chair there was, one with Rosy's cross-stitch doilies on its arms, and he would sit to watch me wash myself. *On all sides, under arms, lift your arms. Take soap. Make lather. Rinse. Dry. Good. Another towel for it.* Sometimes he would sponge bath my back. But not always. He would still linger a little, help me dress. Not always. Made sure my shoelaces were done, would bend down while I sat on my bed. An impish, wicked sense made me, one spring day, when he bent down in this humility – true or false, who knows? – or was it my innate meanness that made me lift my foot and with my big toe I stubbed his nose? It was intentional. I smiled wickedly inside, watching his total perplexity, and said, *Oh I'm sorry, forgive me Papa.* To which he replied in a voice removed of tone, *It is for God to forgive.* And so it stays with me, for he never forgave, and God is another matter.

"I would get ready for kindergarten, or school later on, and we always said the Lord's Prayer after that inspected washing ritual. Only when I heard Rosy, my mother, heating milk for me, grinding coffee beans, roasting them over the open fire in the oven for the two of them, did I come down the rounded staircase, sometimes with him holding me – what he perhaps thought was gently and I thought was firmly – for my breakfast. Both moved around me to see to it that I had enough bread, butter, and milk. Mother Rosy making my school lunch, which was again *Butterbrot,* perhaps a slice of ham in it if there was any, and an apple or the fruit of the season. A pear perhaps. But mainly an apple, the year-round fruit. Holding well over the winter, 'leather *reinettes*' were the last to be eaten of the year's apple harvest. And if we ran out of them, there were the winter fruit-and-vegetable shops up the Gallows Hill, just across from the Evangelical church, and up from the Ahi fountain. I was sent there to buy a kilogram or two sometimes, and I had to pass the many-armed Turkish fountain. I feared it terribly. The most horrific stories circulated about this hangman Ahi, who lived in the fountain and would grab little girls – especially with long blond hair – if they haven't been good, or if he just felt like it. So I avoided it. But I saw the Jewish kids who lived in the big old house, at the corner of the *Balschgasse*, I saw them sitting on the rim, dangling their legs, or playing hopscotch on the slate underneath their feet, which was full of polka dots or strange wiggles. Why were they not afraid of the Turkish henchman? Well, I knew Rachel Glasberg's family, my nurse-mother, and I never heard the story there. But maybe the maids – there were many maids in that rich house – they knew them, but kids did not believe and sat there anyway.

"So when sent to the small, winter vegetable merchants across from the church, I dared run up the Gallows Hill, and warned by both Rosy and the pastor not to go there, I did. But fast. Just a glimpse from the top of the hill. I saw a village below, my mother's village, Rosch, but nothing else struck me as dangerous. So I wondered about the adults and their crazy stories. Crazy or not, they stick, whatever else they do to you. Either they help channel your fears, freeing you, or they reinforce them, making you more suspicious of things and people. I think I had to take refuge from all of these legends, all these pictures crowding my mind.

"A little girl has to find solace somewhere. I could go into the garden, an enormous garden – it may not look as huge and wonderful to me now as it did then – to crouch in the grass. Almost covered by it and hidden, I would find my equals. Mushrooms mainly. Little people like myself, standing on one foot. A roof of sorts, holding the small fan-rooms underneath sheltered safely. Some mushrooms I would pick, asking forgiveness for ripping them, if gently, from their ground. Drying them, I watched them grow older and like people become wiser, creased and furrowed as my ancient village aunt was. *Tell me, tell me,* I would whisper to them, *where do you come from? Are you a princess? Bewitched perhaps for loving a lowly shepherd and changed into a stork to stand on one foot all your life? Did you fly in? From where? I can see your right foot hidden within your cap.* These were my friends. They did not talk back, did not shout at me, and did not teach me any morality lessons, Greek versus Christian, or Geography. I took refuge with my own.

"With my stones, too. They do not shout either or give you lessons. Except the ones who whisper stories only for you to hear. Right by the creek in the back garden. It may be just a gutter to drain the grounds but to me it was a real creek, with water flowing over grey-green and reddish-brown stones covered in moss, soft to touch, filling a little girl's hand. I took them up to my steeple room, gave them room on the shelf, sized them orderly. For species too."

"Yes, I know your steeple room. *It's Martina's room,* mother said. *I had Martina's room under the steeple, it looked out west, through long slit windows to the upper crenellations of the Archbishop's Residence. And the burning ball of the setting sun came through the slits at certain specific moments of the year. An astronomy of sorts, almost to partition the year as Druids would on Stonehenge,* Mother said. *I was punished,* she said, *by staring blue eyes for having found this book about ancient religions in the attic room, on top of the second staircase.*"

"Oh, you know about it? Did she tell you about this wonder of a staircase that wound itself around the first one? No one was allowed up there. Junk in heaps, old books, Lutheran, but also forbidden ones. Exorcised things of all kinds. Dust. The smell of it is still in my nostrils."

"Yes, mother told me how she stole into it when the pastor was away on his goodwill missions and she had the 'castle' to herself. *Sometimes castle, sometimes fortress or jail.* But I do know more about 'Martina's room.' Your dolls, your tea set, the wedding doll and…hidden letters and drawings inside the floor. My mother discovered the loose boards; stubbing her toes one day, she removed the ribboned letters and your diary, and read some of it. Clandestinely, of course, listening for the footsteps."

"So did I, who wrote it. Everyday. But I had to watch out for both their footsteps. My father's felt shoes, soft like his voice. But make no mistake about it, soft, but clearly understood by his congregants or people under his dominion."

Maria smiled. "Oh dear, I have heard that very word. Mother also said, *I was in his dominion.* But she said it with love. Though I could hear what she kept back. I understood that she tried to tread carefully. She had come from so different a world."

"What world?"

"A Jewish world. A tailor's world. Needles and pins to be collected, floors to be swept in the evening after a day's harvest of ends of cloths, threads left hanging, buttons to be sorted. A singing tailor's child, an only child my mother was to boot, with unmarried aunts, a grandmother or two, God knows! And of course her own mother also, treading the Singer sewing machine until midnight. And then the one who was to become my mother was ripped out of this hardworking but poetic world, where *God is everywhere* and praises are to be sung from daybreak to sundown…ripped from all these protective mothers, to face a night

of total abandonment. The night from the twelfth to the thirteenth of June, 1941. I heard this date all the time. Her running
through the Jewish quarter, her entering the pharmacy in the
Synagogengasse."

"Yes, Felix behind the counter. Midnight or so. People flooding in. It wasn't his father's pharmacy. He was sent there by the
Russians as punishment for being an owner's son. Felix talks
about this night. It's with him."

"And then my mother on Felix's hand – and it seems these
indelible pictures of the dark *Synagogengasse*, flashing lights, live
solid white shafts of light crossing the sky, revealing her own people on a truck surrounded by Russian uniformed men, would stay
with her forever. And small men, she had told me, with slit eyes,
Mongols on horses crushing the crowds towards the walls, to free
the narrow street –"

"Oh, the sweet thing, my heart goes out to her."

"But tell me, Martina. What was our father to you?"

"A master. A loving master."

"Yes, that is what mother said, a master. Caring, kind and
teaching. Strict also."

"Absolutely. He only had to look at you and you knew you had
overstepped the boundary he had set for you. He let me have my
Friday night candles, he let me be free to love Rachel, my nurse-
mother. He loved the Jews in the old house and said, *Be a good
Lutheran, but love God in all His ways.* Man's ways. My spirit was
free, I felt. But somehow my body wasn't. I had to be on time, I
had to wash and dress. He watched me. Praised and chided. For
regularity of the body. Asked me if I had been to the bathroom.
Wanted to hear things. I had to tell him everything. I assume it
was to help me grow up healthy and he felt responsible for it. But

it bound me. Made me fearful and only free among the stones and mosses. But no, there was the old house: the Jews, where things were absolutely disorderly, they worked hard, late into the night, but time was no straightjacket. Rachel's husband Carl was a grocer. There were no hours, when the barrels of herring arrived, they had to be brought in from the railway station. He had a village *"goy"* to help him, the husband of the *Hausmeister*. But he carried it also. You know, Maria, *goy* is not an ugly word. It just means gentile or stranger. But it has become that, so I should not use it.

"Anyway, the pastor, my father, or papa, allowed me a certain freedom to think or feel and I am grateful for it, but he was the master of my early youth. And now for a contrast: my mother Rosy was the absolute opposite. It was hard to grow up between the two of them."

"What do you mean opposite? Contradicted him or came from so different a background?

"Well, all of that. She let me live my life bodily, but perfectly haunted my soul. A butcher's daughter, from a righteous, hard-working lot. Her brothers, butchers in the village, living by ancient codes, hating everybody whose houses weren't as white-washed, whose windows weren't as spotless as theirs. *Filthy* a favourite word. Filthy Jews first. But filthy Ukrainians, peasants, they never wash their feet for fear the devil might enter through their clean soles. Filthy Romanians. All they want is wine, women, and do nothing. Filthy Gypsy is self-understood. But devout on Sunday. Clean white shirts, black trousers, hymn sing. Everybody sings while carving their carcasses. Good butchers, they knew their cuts, where to slice along the fibre or skeleton. She took me there as a child. I would not eat for a week after that visit. I resisted going again; but papa said, *Go with mother if she asks you.* So I went teeth clenched, silent. Rosy saying, *Martina, you don't love my people. Such good folk. Who pays for your bread and meat, dear, who? Your father? Ha! We would be hungry without them. He can do sermons, that's what he can do. A days' work? Never!* But she let me be a child, have a child's body. Didn't harass me for dirty black nails. Yes, my earth-filled nails she called a *Trauerrand,* or mourning-edges. Made me cut them and use a hard brush to get them clean, when wanting to dress me into frilly things, all hand-me-downs from her richer cousins. Things like that.

"While papa at least let me love whom I wanted, the Jews in the old house, my mossy-mushy stones, or dolls in wedding dress. But as for the body – well, this is another story. And I fear it is not a pretty one. What did your mother tell you?"

"Hard to put a finger on," Maria said. "Nothing, except wonderful things. But slowly, as I grew older, the stories changed. The same story, which is always simply told, got an edge. She would say, *Did I cry! The Greek gods for instance. I learned them all, diligently. But I mixed them up. A Jewish girl with one great God, who is everywhere, what were these Gods to me? Jealous Gods, unjust Gods, pleasing themselves. What where they to me? But your father loved the Greek myths. And I had to know or else.* What was the "else" I used to ask, and mother said, *He nearly hit me, and he left,* she said, *without a word.* Was not seen until the next morning. *When he came,* she told me, *he had picked wild violets in the garden.* And still wet with night dew, he put them upon her pillow. When she woke up, she was so touched. Tears coming to her throat, she sprang from her bed, fell upon his neck, kissed both cheeks, tears flowing now freely, and he said: *It's fine my child. We both were naughty.* And she said: *I will forever remember the goddess*

Athena sprang fully armoured from Zeus' head – forever. So, your father and mine wasn't only a Lutheran minister, he was also a scholar of antiquity, looking at Jesus historically: a man-God in his time, a Jew among Jews. *The people you stem from, Shainah,* he used to say to my mother to hearten her. So you see, Martina, I have so many different pictures in my head. As I grew up and learnt about men, everything that was good and simple became clouded or had a dark side to it, slowly showing itself. This is why I thank you, Martina. So I can come to grips with a storybook father seen now, more and more, *through a glass darkly."*

"And mine," Martina responded, "being just as complex but becoming lighter in spots. But I had to run from them both. Watching Felix and his mother, lighthearted, talking, walking, sitting on the stone benches in our Evangelical church gardens, I wondered about other people's happiness. I saw it as a rescue. Scenario after scenario, I saw it as a flight into their arms. At twelve or thirteen, my father's dominion slightly waned. Either by my rejection or because his love is for the little ones. So I thought, in any case that *I'm a big girl now, I'll soon be a young lady.* Which means…you know what! Well, menstruating. And I felt his turning from me more. Fetters loosened. He came fewer and fewer times to the morning ritual washing. Finally it stopped. And I went to sleep crying at night, missing it now. Then fantasizing about Felix and about his redhead mother whose daughter-in-law I would be, who would lift the veil from my eyes on my wedding day. And it came differently. I ran, fell into his arms long before such things may have been possible. Mounted him perfectly as if I knew something about my own sex. I didn't much, but he let me be the aggressor. Felix coming furtively up that staircase to my steeple room when all was still, stretched out onto my slim bed and waited. I went on top, legs apart. It did not work very well, I must say. He could not break the hymen. But we turned and it did. I cannot explain my joy – I knew I was rescued. I had gone away. I was out of prison. Jubilation. Conquest over both my jailers. Sorry to talk so badly of them. I am talking to you as if I wrote a confession. And perhaps it is. But they did love me with all they had, yet it was alien to me; a double bind. At sixteen I ran. And it takes a lifetime to forgive."

"We all run. You in a double bind – I in a multiple. An unreal, multiple straightjacket. With *Love* and *God Is Everywhere*, where to go? With many lives thrown at your door, every one a story of pain and wrongdoing, and the legend of the pastor, my father, all crowding my mind. How to know who one is, let alone where to go. Surrounded by Merciful Sisters, each of them a story, silently told or untold, and my mother, called Anna now, a reluctant Lutheran, born Shainah, a little Jewish person. A maze. How to find my way?"

"How?" Martina asked.

"To the circus, of course! Where else? Who would take you, unschooled, young? The circus would, if you're good at what you do. And I am, or was. I trained in the gym of my school every free moment. I'm simply endowed with joints and muscles that almost talk to each other. I am born a bundle of nerves, tendons, and muscles; as I grew older I was the school's champion. I flew through the rings from the horse up on the rope ladders against the wall and back. Designed my shows in my mind before going to sleep at night and on paper the next morning. Alexander drew them for me with colours on brown paper when he was three or four. I showed them in school. The gym teacher pasted them all over the entrance hall and he named Alexander *The Big A*. He was very tiny then, you know, the one foot even more deformed than it is now, and he was even then mute. When the teacher asked me to bring this child, he stood in front of his paintings which, stuck to a panel five or six times his own size, were touching the ceiling. Everybody cried and hugged him. So he too grew up in a world of the unspoken story. Of course, the circus, I was born for it.

"Let's cuddle a little, hold onto the night a moment longer," Maria said. Leaving their north-south positions, the sisters sat a little while arm in arm, as teenagers do going for a walk. Kissed and said *Good night*. Martina bedding Maria on the sofa, cushion under head, plaid tucked in, and with a last pat on Maria's head, she joined Felix in their bedroom. It was three o'clock in the morning.

OUT OF THIS CONFESSIONAL NIGHT grew a new day. For all of them. Felix found his Martina gentler, less judgmental, and she woke after only four hours sleep, seeking his warm morning body for the first time since the death of Gerhard, and took him as she had liked it from the first day. Wanting her sex her way, but holding his head in both her hands, kissing his mouth, and covering his body with hers. "Stay with me, do not leave me. Thank you for your patience," she said. Changed position, turned together like one. Giggled, made love like schoolmates on their first date.

All four around the breakfast table had come home. Felix had arrived home the moment he saw her in her bridal gown coming down the aisle on Gerhard's side. It mattered, but it also did not. He had seen her alive after all his errant wanderings. Had seen her imprint in every woman's face or body. In Bunin's even: in this Russian rustic stalk of maize he saw his delicate violet.

Everywhere. Not really seeking it. There was no need for it. As if
born at the same hour, she was his; as if opening his eyes to the
world, they had fallen upon her. Indelibly. And all his roads led
to her. Errant, wayward, distracted as they might be. Seeing her
in the *Karlskirche* in ivory satin, camellias in her hair, had the dag-
ger pain of homecoming, that melancholy of loss of youth perhaps, of wind, rain, and where to sleep the night. That sweet
melancholy that made Felix drive for an hour or two around
Vienna, talk to the taxi man, not wanting to face his own four
walls, afraid he might ask his landlady for a glass of water, which
had achieved mythical dimension. The one glass of water in
which he would dissolve his soluble barbiturate, always present in
his buttoned-down shirt pocket. But he had come home, just
having seen that svelte, tall figure that moved in the waist as an
upright blade of grass would in the evening breeze, a waist indented
above the hip, pliable, but held up by a column of vertebrae to
the small of the head. His Martina.

The sisters found each other at the bathroom door after only
a few hours sleep, embracing and giggling as they bumped into
each other. "It is strange to have come home to a place you have
never been in before," Maria said. The sisters had come home,
jumping time to fall into each other's arms. A sudden shelter of
the familiar: a like, a dislike, a taste for salt or sugar, the morbid
or hilarious, the seeking of solitude or the wide whirl of society, it
was with the immediacy of recognition that the sisters found
themselves at home. Looking alike. They went into the kitchen to
find the coffee beans before breakfast – the maids were out –
Martina in silky kimono, Maria in her undies, and they bent over
with laughter, not knowing almost who was who. They stood
against the doorpost, measuring their height. Maria, perhaps

shorter by two centimetres, and so much younger, was just a little broader in the shoulders. But the fine swan neck, gently tilted, carrying a sculpted human head, was both theirs. Bumping into each other in search of breakfast things, finding the butter and not finding the butter knife, everything was good enough for bursts of laughter. A joy. A release. "I think you're rounder on the hip," Maria said, turning Martina round. "Definitely. You're a little different."

"No," Martina said, "absolutely not. Have you heard of gravity? It just settles there. A little rounder hip won't kill anyone." Maria could not look enough at her sister; she was a woman's woman. And she knew it. Guarded against it, too. Flashing images of Claudette, she rejected fast. This was her sister. But she allowed herself that heightened state, just being close to a woman so unspeakably beautiful. And Martina knew it, performed for it, was silly, giggly, teenagerish, felt easy and comfortable. Two children they were whose father, a fine pastor, had gone out on his goodwill missions, and they were ready for their nonsense. Girls now, behaving as unruly children would, they succeeded in assembling all the breakfast things available on a glass tray.

They ran to the door together, having heard the baker's boy with the daily *Brötchen*, fresh Kaisers, or long crusty *Stritzel*; and with coffee cups, saucers, sugar and cream, and a few jams in crystal on a tray, they pushed the salon door open shouting, "Where are you, lazy bones!" Alex and Felix appeared instantly, in their pajamas, hands and faces washed. The tray landed on the side buffet with a clang under the Klimt, and Martina set the table for breakfast. Coffee poured, the crunch of *Brötchen*, and Felix, dropping his butter knife, looked around. There were no words, but he took the hands of his people into his own, one after the other.

A grace-saying, having found one another one morning; and they fell upon their coffee, *Brötchen*, bread and butter, as if they had never had any before.

It was a beginning.

Goodbye TO VIENNA

F ELIX FELT WHAT EVERY *Ost Jude* ENCOUNTERED IN THESE
post-war years in Vienna. What Paul Celan must have felt
coming there: a triumph in part that a goal, a destiny, had been
reached. But Vienna remained the unachievable, *das Unerreichbare.*
In the words of Ingeborg Bachmann, who came there from the
west at that time, "Full of impatience and expectations I arrived
in Vienna, which had been unattainable in my imagination." And
this is what it remained for the *Ost Juden,* for Jews from the east
with a German mother tongue of the eastern tone scale. The
German in Felix's ear was of a Jewish descent, harking back to the
Rhine of the Middle Ages, yet purified, ennobled in a way, by the
Latin construction of a Luther sentence. The music came from
that polyglottal mixture of the *Habsburg Symphony.* It came from
Vienna, from Prague and Budapest to the Jewish world: to an
anxious, ready, and turbulent world; and added to it the Austrian
sound – a lilting, seductive, and lighter-in-weight quality than the
western one. Refugees found one another by its familiar childhood sound; the uttered word did it. Over the telephone now,
also. Not every household had one because of the extra expense,

and an inborn tendency not to change one's habits. But it was too wonderfully convenient. And no one could resist its charms. So Czernowitzers found one another long distance.

Sasha called. Sasha! He was in Paris. The year was 1968, and refugees joined the students and workers of Paris, gathering in the streets. Carried by the revolutionary mood of '68, he was in a state of rediscovered juvenile exhilaration, and called Felix to join him in Paris.

"Come to Paris, it is where we always wanted to be."

Memories resurged, and Sasha and Felix sang to one another over the telephone. The songs of their Russian time, rousing *Budyonny*, cavalry songs, marching songs, needing the rhythm to propel them forward when on seemingly endless treks across Russia. Or simply *Ochi chornia* – *"Oh these black eyes, beautiful black eyes."* They sang now as then, when they got drunk if there was vodka. Mainly songs of youth; journeymen on the road from village to village. Ancient intervals of the wanderer, the fortune seeker, or the one fleeing the law. German, in the major key, but also the melancholy parting songs of leaving one's sweetheart with never-kept promises of return. *Wann-i-komm, wann-i-wiederum komm* – *"I'll return to you."* They sang over the telephone to one another.

And it was in the early morning one Sunday that Felix was wakened by the ring of the telephone and the frightened Czernowitzer sound of Sasha's voice, "Paris is in flames."

"But Sasha, it is early morning."

"Oh, dear. But to whom should I talk, they are all strangers?" And Felix, using his most mellow tones of comfort, quieted Sasha, as he had often done. Sasha had learnt to be tough and aggressively fearless in an immediate confrontation: "My life first." But he could fall into despairing moods, not wanting one more step. He simply had refused one day to walk any further. And it had been south of Kharkov, when he had seen village after village burn and the land was barren and hunger pangs became so intense that his strength failed. So he had crawled into a small cave and had fallen into a torpid sleep. Felix remained by his friend, stretching out by his side, and ancient prayers, praising the Lord for his abundant goodness, found their way to his lips. Covering his friend with the camouflaging spindly green, whatever grew there, and not knowing exactly where he was, he foraged out in the crouching position first, and then a little more upright – to establish where the Germans were, in front, behind, or north of them. He was afraid to go too far, lest he fail to find Sasha again on his return, so he arranged stones he found in certain patterns to mark the site. But, having walked just a short distance, he spotted a small crowd resting, in what Felix judged to be the north. It was a group of women and old men carrying children, obviously Jews on the run, and code words of the faith as the *Shema – Listen, O Israel* – identified him, and they let him sit with them and shared some of their bread with him.

BUT TELEPHONE CONVERSATIONS were expensive and, everyday life taking over, they became rarer. Martina had resisted installing one. "Oh, Felix," she complained, "now we have the monster indoors, it will ring at all hours. Where to put it, what colour to suit the décor – oh, it definitely will interrupt our lives." But then, there it was. One couldn't stop it. As one couldn't stop the flying airplanes. "Yes," Martina said, "the noise overhead, the whirring about of grey metal in the sky – I hate it already," she said. But people loved it, and no one could stop anything. And it was convenient and very exciting.

"Look," Felix said, in one of these decision making days, "look, the world is open. We can go across an ocean in hours, instead of weeks, and the world lies in patterns underneath you, as if on a map for you to see." She shook her head but submitted to the telephone. And it became a marvellous tool of unification.

His sister Süssel had called after the Red Cross had found Felix for her, urging him in her impetuous, passionate pleading, which always had been her trademark, to join her in Canada. It had to be her way, and there was little reasoning possible. But the heart understood many things reason doesn't, as Blaise Pascal so exquisitely put it, Felix thought, *Le coeur a ses raisons, que la raison ne connaît point.* And in the abundance of crisis in their lives, the fast decision making, the taking of the right or left road – it was her heart that found the way. Yes, Felix thought, she was selfless when it came to love. And when it came to music, she was all there. At all hours, the evening hours in our teen years, I played for her and she sang for me. Her voice was of the middle range with good upper notes, but it was that middle, that mezzo, which showed her passion. It was always structured, and held by her artistry to do justice to the composer; she was a joy to accompany on the piano. And on the telephone she sang a Schubert line that made him weep. It was a simple tune, so right for strangers in someone else's land. The voice was lower yet, and he longed to see her.

And so it was over the telephone that all Czernowitz came calling. For addresses, for digs, for connections: Have you seen? Have you heard? – and so forth. And Vienna became a rallying point –

in front of the university on benches sheltered by the elderly for-
sythias showing yellow blooms.

Vienna was the eternal remaking of one's youth. The
Burgtheater was so much grander than the Czernowitz Opera
Theatre but it was of a similar layout and majesty and brought
back the first experience of the great plays, be it *The Virgin of
Orléans* by Schiller or a *Romeo and Juliet* by Shakespeare. Vienna
had always been the aspiration, the longing to emulate it if not
imitate, to rise to its level of artistry.

Czernowitzers, homeless now, sitting on these benches, with a
sandwich or an apple in their laps in front of the university or in
its halls, were being chased from the main stairway – the one with
the famous Klimt ceiling above, where they liked to congregate to
find one another. These Czernowitzers, dreaming back to the days
of a benevolent emperor and the Habsburg monarchy, did not
find a return possible in post-Second-World-War Vienna. It was a
hurried place. A desperate rebuilding frenzy took over, a counting
of one's losses – many of their own sons having fallen in frozen
fields by Stalingrad or Moscow. Yet there was very little memory
of Vienna's own murderous behaviour: chasing the Jews out of
their houses, occupying them, eating from their plates, and forgetting all about it. So there was hardly any willingness to accom-
modate new Jews from the east.

And not just Jews, but Germans who had been made to go
home into the *Reich*. And having come to settle in Catholic Austria
and Bavaria, Protestants to boot, they found just as little welcome
or interest. As it was with Martina and Rosy. But Vienna had been
preferable in spite of it all. It was more accessible, the language was
closer to home, buildings looked alike in their late 19th century pre-
tensions, streets sounded the bell of home, being called *Herrengasse*,

and *Rathausstrasse*, and *Ring* – like the main square in Czernowitz. And after all the tears and cruelty there were the jokes, the laughter, the bringing-down of holy cows, a bit of the Jewish survival genius mixed with the self-irony of the Viennese, which lightened the texture, the fabric of daily life, and made it possible to live.

Paul Celan had been here – the poet of "the Meridian," as he called Czernowitz and its surrounding nature – whose powerful, imaged German tongue sang of region, time, and murder. He had been in Vienna a short time; had come after the war as all of them came, drawn by this inexplicable longing for Imperial Vienna. He couldn't stay. He didn't find it there; they were too self-obsessed to have an ear for others, and they had none for Jews. Celan left for Paris, and so did others.

Felix nearly went, having an intense love of the French from his youth. All his Caucasus companions were in Paris, friends from Bucharest times, the Romanian connections. Even old anti-Semites were there, great writers somehow reformed who had been caught up at the time in the fervent waves of Romanian nationalism. French was easier for Romanian speakers. A Latin tongue at the root, with Slavic sounds built in and double references – so Romanians flocked to their big Latin sister out west. But Felix did not go. Not even to visit. He felt his time curtailing itself. With Süssel's letters of memory and welcome and with her insistence: *Canada is a vast, endless land and new, where there is work to be done, for you and me.*

But he suddenly felt how Viennese he had become, and not just in his habit of coffee houses, mocha, whipping cream, daily chat with its waiters and the little people in the streets. But truly Viennese. After closing the pharmacy gate at night and hanging out the night service sign on the door, he strolled through the town, aware of every step. Haydn, Mozart, Beethoven, Schubert, Brahms – the idols of his youth – had paced these stones. Tunes that came from every doorway, either whistled or sung, he sang. And he thought of his father in Austrian uniform: sword at his side, gloves in hand, tall officer's hat, and stripes on epaulettes and armband. Memories were so vivid that he came home to Martina on one of these days, saying, "I don't know if I can leave." It was his father's love of Vienna, the turn-of-the-century music scene, Gustav Mahler reigning at the Opera House – it was all that charmed world of which he was a part that held him captive.

Felix in his fifties was suddenly conscious of a mellowing of pace, a desire for the essential values he had learned at home. "Look for beauty," his mother had said to him when he left at eighteen for the dream-city Vienna. "Look for beauty and thought. Look for Vienna's music, it will nourish you all your life."

And now that time had become shorter, with an unsuspected end, a calendar type of end where the hours suddenly counted. They had to be filled with Vienna, to be remembered, imprinted. And what love and longing had been for the impatient, young Felix arriving in Vienna at eighteen, in 1934, fulfilled itself now. Laden with admonitions from his father at the time: "Learn your trade well, it is science that will answer the problems of the world. Find your place, a man's strength lies in his work, yes!" He had also added, "Well, go to the theatre and opera, but do not indulge; it leads you astray." And he had been right, of course; it does lead you astray. It does because art reveals humankind, in its intricate variety and with its intertwining of thought and feeling. And Felix, twenty then, setting foot on those holy cobblestones and derelict Vienna houses, was stunned by the sudden appearances of a plate with the inscription: *Beethoven lived here.* It arrested his step and made him touch the handle of the gate with reverence.

Twenty was a time of utopia, implemented and lived. Hallowed names, which were with him from the age of three when he had put his fingers on the keys of a concert *Bösendorfer* for the first time, sprang to life from every corner of Vienna. Nourished by a Czernowitz adoration of culture, industry, and the arts, Felix, as a young man taking a corner where the *Ringstrasse* bends to face the parliament building, was unprepared for its Greek grandeur. He had walked for the first time – after renting student quarters in the *Berggasse*, not, but almost, across from Freud's famous dispensary – he had walked all the way to the *"Ring"* along the treed open space. Striding along it, his dreams fulfilled themselves at every step, because these mighty buildings did not face each other to compete for sight, air, and sun, but looked towards the *Ring;* each in their enclave they were separated by parks but united by the Avenue. It carried you from one to the other in a continuous movement yet led you suddenly to different empires. Felix loved it. Exhilaration of youth, health, and money from home transfused him, and he, walking that day along the circular street, all along budding trees on his right hand, he saw the *Rathaus,* Vienna's City Hall, with its fine Gothic spires, all striving upward. "Different," he thought, "from our Czernowitz City Hall on the *Ringplatz,* with it's one middle tower," and he didn't cross to see it closer, but went along the Avenue until he faced the *Burgtheater* in its massive baroque style. A dream had come true. His father too had talked about it: "Go see the Klimt paintings on the ceiling over the grand staircase." And Felix did then. It depicted the history of the theatre, with scenes from Shakespeare's *Romeo and Juliet,* wealthy patrons of the arts, aristocracy, or society watching it, even the mistress of the emperor Franz Joseph II, Miss Schratt, was there. But it was the ensemble of his parents' memories and urgings and his own presence in those halls that overwhelmed him.

To the University, in its sprawling Renaissance elegance he went another day, to register, meet all Czernowitzers, desirable or less so; he was arrogant when young, inclined not to mix with the lesser folk, but of course that was then. Life teaches you other lessons. Many a young man has come to the *Ringstrasse* with awe implanted into him by his father. The turn of the century with the great liberal victory over the powerful forces of the anti-Semitic right, made Jewish students, artists and scientists flock to Vienna. That a young man called Adolf Hitler would also stand in awe in the *Ringstrasse* one day, like any other young man would, no one could foresee.

It had been a charmed time, and it was not all illusion or his father's memories. What Felix felt for Vienna is what the world feels: a belonging. As Shakespeare's *Hamlet* or *King Lear* play on the Vienna stages, so Haydn symphonies and Mozart operas, Beethoven and Schubert, are heard in every corner of the world. Vienna rises above the dirt of politics to take its place and be revered for what it has nurtured.

And now he went to the *Burgtheater* on his own, to say goodbye.

But to the "green ring" of Vienna he took Martina, as almost any tramway would lead you into the lush green of its surroundings. He wanted to celebrate: the *Grinzing* for its wine or the *Semmering* for a few days of walks on wooded paths. They both, Felix and Martina, liked to forget the city with its modern changes and fast pace of life. The world had come home to them more to disturb than to comfort. *Fernsehn* – the television of *To see from afar* – seemed to fascinate the Viennese with its immediacy of events. One lived suddenly the lives of others with an undercurrent of intimacy. A Vienna everyday petit-bourgeois existence, where curtains were hung from every kitchen and bedroom window to exclude the other, had become public display. And murder in its banality of statistics, reduced to the little screen, lost its enormity intruding into homes. Yet true historic events made a greater, deeply incisive impact, when the Viennese, as did all the world, viewed on the 22nd of November 1963 the assassination of JFK. Television could not be resisted any more. Expensive still, people went to neighbours to watch. They watched the private lives of anonymous suffering and the sudden fall of the great. They went to see Jackie Kennedy in her widow's weeds, her two children at her side – and Martina and Felix would not any more intrude into their neighbour's privacy and bought a small screen but delegated it to the kitchen. "I'm afraid of it," Martina had said, "it makes terrible noises, we'll be victimized by other people's misery." And Felix and Martina fled to the *Semmering*. "We're refugees from the *Fernsehn*" was the current joke. But there was no escape, and an unexpected bonus: Vienna's music transmitted and the players seen as if in concert. Schubert's *Lieder*, a Brahm's lullaby, Wagner's *Tristan und Isolde*, this love-death duet, so close to their own transfiguration, made them both accept it. But grudgingly so. And they went more often to the Vienna's woods, which, circling the city, reminded them of their birthplace, of the springy forest floor renewing itself by rotting underfoot.

These were good times. Vienna – having nurtured and attracted the greatest in music: Beethoven came from Bonn, Brahms from

Hamburg, Wagner, Richard Strauss – Vienna was irresistible. Martina joined Felix now. Every free evening, they went to the theatre, and not just the *Burgtheater* but the *Theater an der Wien,* for lighter fare and talk with the ordinary people in town. "Either I'm more tolerant now or –" Felix saw the charm, the courtesy, and a sudden generosity he had denied them.

WALKING BY THE CORNER BOOKSHOP one day, Felix saw it sealed by Government order and he suddenly felt he had caused the death of the shopkeeper – an officially meaningless death, anonymous, hardly reported in the press. He felt he had done it, having spotted his father's *Florindo* in the window of this man's shop. Events had rolled on their own from that moment on: Martina saying one day, "I will not permit it. It's yours. I will not let criminals enjoy the spoils. I have seen the books as a child, the paintings on the wall, racing in and out as children do, in your father's flat on the third floor of the Old House. It's your sister's, it's yours, I won't permit it." And she had gone into action, produced witnesses, unearthed papers, and what she could not find, they both, Martina and Felix, declared on oath. The crate was opened, inventoried and published.

His sister had called. It was an immeasurable joy, a bridge to his own teenage years. The dance hall where he chaperoned her, her willful, wild ways, an image of his mother but more unpredictable – all came back with her voice, it had an unchanged ring. A shade darker, a singing voice with built-in intervals rising; a fast paced voice. He never could catch up with her in singing duets, trios, or quartets with whomever was around the *Bösendorfer.* Felix asked Süssel, his sister, what to do with all that property and she said: "I want one thing only, the garden scene, tea time at the table. One thing. I have received the violin-shaped silver ladle and the Rosenthal terrine, it was returned to me, and I do not want so much memory. You keep what you want and sell the rest in open auction. My part in any case, and donate the proceeds to a refugee cause. Jewish or other, since one suffering, one homelessness is like another."

It felt right. He was thrilled with Süssel's decision. But he could not part with *Florindo. What permanence childhood has,* he thought. All the faces crowding your mind, school friends, old servants, and first love. One runs from it to escape, wings spread, to find oneself returned full circle to stay. As if one had never gone anywhere. The voice of a sister, a Morocco leather-bound poetic play from behind the glass of your father's bookcase will bring you home inescapably.

Almost three hundred thousand *schillings* were the result of the auction, and Felix handed it over to different organizations, churches, and Jewish people to distribute to the needy still flooding in from the east. But *Florindo* he kept. Its outer shell a brownish carton, sun-bleached, a little torn at the back, showed its sufferings, but the book fell out of it in absolute perfection. Water prints as good as new.

All things completed, they sat down to dinner that night, *Florindo* in lonely grandeur on the sideboard to be seen and handled for a little while longer. Another winter had passed, and the four of them now, the two sisters, The *Big A,* a young man overnight – almost at his mother's and aunt's height – and Felix, assuming headship at the table, sat down to dinner on a late April evening. Hyacinths and tulips had come and gone, lilac was in the air. All the bushes were in bloom, from the almost white to the deep purple in single or triple petals around the stem.

"I'll hate to leave the lilac," Martina said. "I left it once with tears in my eyes. The Evangelical gardens of my father were heavy with perfume. They bloom in the east just a little later than here in Vienna. They stood next to the chestnut trees and started to fade when the pink and white blooms of the chestnut lit the sky. Chestnuts, I do not see them here."

"Yes," Maria said, "mother told me. The air was so heavy with it that eyes and noses…"

"Yes," Martina said. "Yes, it is true. I choked. A schoolmate of mine died when her throat swelled with what you call today an allergy. Then it had no name. Just running noses."

After the auction was over, Felix looked at the glowing face of Alexander and both his Martinas, as he called the sisters jokingly; they were together every free minute. Alike and totally diverse, they fitted where alike, and completed one another where they were different. They laughed when they rose and laughed at night. Exchanged Maria's second-hand tales against Martina's memories. Maria said one day, "You had black boy's shoes as high as the ankles, laced around hooks, and your coat had a fur collar. I've seen them. My mother wore them when she fled. The Russians were just to occupy the city of Czernowitz and she ran down to the train station in the hope of catching one of the last trains going south."

"Heavens!" Martina said. "So long ago. Yes, a lovely beaver collar. Oh, the things you know about me. I loved this coat. It was reversible, lengthened by Rosy as I grew out of it, I would not give it up. So it has served well. And those boyish shoes. Perhaps inherited from richer cousins in Rosch."

"Mother said she wore all your things. It was war, shops were looted, and one made do with what one had. Father hid and protected her. Jews were hunted. Your room was a fairy castle, a dream world with turrets and staircases winding around themselves, hidden treasures, secrets in all corners and under the wooden floor."

Felix listened to the sisters as they chatted about a common past, imagined by the one or reconstructed by the other, unreal memories all. He said, "I too, of course, have lived in that room, slept on that bed, and know every one of your dolls, Martina. What they wore, how they sat or stood –"

"Yes," she said, "of course, Felix," and Alexander smiled at all of that. He understood or did not, but what he knew was that this was his family talking about their common roots; undoing intertwined ones to clear debris and see them better.

Felix, *pater familias,* around the table, let them chat and laugh, but then he poured himself a glass of wine and said simply, "What are we going to do?"

And Martina: "Would you go to America and Canada where your sister lives if Maria and Alexander were for it?"

Felix replied, "With all my heart."

"We'll sell the publishing firm, dispose of the rest of the assets," Martina said. "And we'll set out as Felix and the three Rempels."

EVERYONE ACCEPTED the telephone as a modern reality. A daily convenience to use, in spite of the soaring price, all of Europe connected displaced people; homeless wanderers found one another. So all of the east. Messages flew across this dismantled continent. Germany, in a passionate attempt to rebuild, installed them faster than any other country. And Romania certainly did.

And *God is Everywhere* had modernized also; had freed itself from the institutional church – as Communism took over and

God became dangerous. But there was an underground network of support for homeless young mothers – no questions asked – who could find shelter and give birth under safe conditions. Doctors worked for free, and nurses and cleaning personnel, even being paid minimum wages, flooded the gates. And Shainah-Anna had done it. A feat, under a regime that prided itself in taking God out of the vocabulary. She had done it with perseverance and a tradition of a Judaic *morale* that was inbred and not traceable. But there, "One does what one has to do to please God." So she just lived according to rules she could not name. "Call them Christian if you wish," she liked to joke.

But finally the hallowed word "God" had to go for her work to survive. Pragmatically, as she had handled her life, she justified it all by doing what was demanded of her; as she had justified her acceptance of the Sisters of Mercy. "Christian is Christian," she had said when she – first a Jew then a Lutheran – knelt down and made the sign of the cross. "Christian is Christian. I do it for my baby. The sisters are good to us." That was Shainah-Anna. So "God" had to go. "It is a word, just a word," she argued, in her fashion. "The essence will stay untouched. He will be everywhere." And she officially changed the name to *Shainah-Anna's Home for Women*. She got permission to hire workers and run a kind of maternity home. Amazing, indeed, for that time of tumult and take-over by the powerful Soviet forces.

Cleanliness, the washing of hands at the door – Judaic as it is – was law. A derelict warehouse was refurbished, and of course with the help of the telephone everything was easy. Or easier in times that hard!

And one day in *Shainah-Anna's Home for Women*, that telephone rang. Maria, Felix fighting to speak first. "We're going to

Canada." And the mother, just hearing the voice of her daughter, had to sit down, overwhelmed. But she collected her wits as was her way, and her joy rang through.

"Write to me in detail. This phone call costs you a fortune."

"No worry," was the reply. "We can pay for it." That was Felix. And Maria now said to her mother, "We will let you know about absolutely everything, and if all falls into place and we find work, perhaps you will…"

"We'll see," the mother said. "Watch out for yourselves. We'll see, a step at a time."

A few more messages back and forth about the new *Shainah-Anna Home*. No politics, but, "How is our Alexander?"

And last, Maria said quietly, "We will very soon deliver all to Felix and his bride Martina, what you, dear mother, have entrusted to me." Hugs and kisses, the conversation was over. A silence followed; of satisfaction at having reached the other, but also of a certain melancholy at leaving her and the old world for the new unknown.

A RAINY APRIL EVENING, dark, comfortable, and reassuring of the love within. But Alexander stood at his drawing board for a few more hours. He had sat and listened very attentively. Had to concentrate on the German. Felix's and Martina's mother tongue and Maria's by adoption, it had come to him in crumbs and morsels thrown in between the prevalent Romanian when he was very young, but since their arrival in Vienna it came directly. Not having to speak it freed him; he could infer meaning, or sense it by other means, feel moods in harmonies, descending or upwards moving intervals. He would smile when no one else would or, overcome by tears, swallowed hard, so as not to show that he had seen things that were irreversible. He had felt Felix's restlessness for his father's *Florindo,* which stood now for all to see in its splendour on the side board. *Just a book,* he thought, but it stood for something. It must. A symbol for all these childish, unconscious imprints young eyes will take along through life and cannot do without.

Alexander painted roses. And they weren't roses. He had stood once near a long-stemmed rose, looked deep into its unfolding heart: leaf on imbedded leaf in shading-down reds he watched, he a five-year-old who ran out every morning to see it change, fade, dry, and not die. But just change colour, its heart growing tighter and less luminous or visible inside. And with thick chalks he drew his first rose on derelict papers. And roses were with him. He still drew them, hid the world in them, and no one knew they were roses. They had become folded-in shapes, forms that fit, sometimes angular ones perfectly bedded into one another; he had solved, without any theories at his disposal, a complicated packaging problem. Geometrical answers to old problems. Economically using space and form with elegant folded roses. Sometimes a line would tangentially touch them, unite them on an axis and he would smile and think in words: *Aren't they beautiful, my roses, even without colour. Oh, the laid-open rose.* And he wondered about his new friend Felix. What worries him? What is it he wants?

Was it for God? Was it for beauty? *You can transform things,* Alexander thought. *You do not have to have* Florindo, *staying there. You can draw it with a finger on this dusty surface, without it being there. But perhaps people who speak with tongues and words cannot do what I do, they have to touch and hold an object. It must be so for*

Felix or he would not have to run after it; Martina joining him, being of that same world.

But Alexander felt his stomach heave with pain. As if a hole had been punched into the middle of his being, his heart, or all his innards. What others who have words would call omens, he just felt as death. Too much anger in the air, dinner conversations tense with actions planned. Against. Against this, against that. Against robbery, the past, the erring about, the homelessness. The intense railing against injustice. Everywhere. Martina's words one day, "I will not permit it," struck Alexander deeply. He knew what no one knew: he saw the little grey man condemned, he saw him paying for all the murder of "the innocents." Just a little man. Alexander did not see him in his red bathtub, but he saw his death come and waited for it. Day after day, trembling, a hole in his stomach. It was irreversible. And when the picture came, wrists slashed, red colour all around, he could not cry. He had done so for days. But his family was stricken. With silence. Tongueless like him. And then came a haste of decision making. One could not remain on this old earth. Too haunted, too many memories of the indescribable. Away, away.

So Alexander stood that night at his drawing board. Such a fancy, glorious thing. A light above, clamped on, it was just enough; shaded, framed, it lit the pages without blinding him. Instruments of all sorts, angles and circles, which he did not think he needed or wanted, were nonetheless wonderful to contemplate. Concentric circles he could take apart and redesign for his rose-packing problems. To learn from perfection. All geometric forms in front of him from the simple line, partitionable to the nth degree, to the many-many-angled, the polygons. But his soul was heavy with the decision making of the others.

And he started very slowly to work. A stem, a branch, a leaf, but there was no heart in it. Yet he persisted. *Let's see what comes of a bitter rose!* And she was dark. A female figure. Tall, contained, arms folded within the garment. It started to be the Klimt figure above the sideboard. Now he sat down and cried. Sat and cried on his moveable desk chair, when he felt Felix's hand on his back, who said, handing him a handkerchief, "This is a beautifully folding desk. You can take it apart and put it together anywhere. It's yours. And wherever we are, there you will be."

OF WOMAN BORN. To be born of her, fed, guided, and led. To always return, take your dusty shoes off, stretch beside her and sleep. To be assured of a bed, that luxurious home in the wilderness. From Tiflis, across the vastness of Russia, Felix had many a time opened his shirt pockets, not wanting to walk another mile. Not endure another hungry or soaked-to-the bone day. But a woman would button his pockets down again, give him her son's pair of shoes when his soles had been worn through, wash his feet, feed him sour milk and sticky bread, and smile at him. Of woman born and to return. An end-feeling, delicious, gently bitter.

And he went back to the *Burgtheater*. To say goodbye to Selma, without speaking to her. To see her aging body as Queen Gertrude. Too old for the part. Much too old for a youngish Hamlet – she had to replace an ailing actress – Selma was a glowing, beautiful temptress to her almost grandson Prince of Denmark. Perversely attractive she was to the youth in her timeless queenly garb, to that youth who buried his face in her lap. It was a leave taking of love. As it had been so for Felix one day. She had sat on her *chaise longue* against the tree-filled window. Both had risen early and he dressed to leave. He had thrown a few pages of love and life onto the table for her to glance at – then he had turned back and saw her in her open black robe, face in tears, against the window.

Today a true goodbye again. It was for him alone, or so he felt. After all was over, Felix did not go backstage but went around the corner to the actors' café where they had their first encounter and a glass of wine. Poldi was there, of course; nothing changes in Vienna *Kaffeehauses* or small restaurants. And Felix said: "We'll be back tomorrow for the evening meal, the four of us. There is no stove left to cook a meal! We'll miss you, Poldi. We'll miss your wine and your great Poldi-Rudi jokes. But there is a time…." And it was goodbye.

They came back the next day to sit at the corner table, sheltered by ancient wainscoting. A silent family. Ordered a few things: goulash with dumplings, a bottle of red wine to share. Alexander's eyes a little questioning, but delighted with the silence. It was on that rainy April night, after decisions had been made, that they sat a little longer before parting for the night. Everyone now in his thoughts. No plans. What is there to know on crossroads? Realities are of yesterday, and they all were silent.

Maria then bent down to her bag, opened it, unfastened a safety pin from the bottom of that handbag, and laid the velvet pouch onto the table. She drank the last drop of wine from her crystal glass and wordlessly untied the string, took the jewellery out of the pouch and laid it out, eighteen diamonds encrusted in a gold oval, concentrically moving up in size to the centre, single diamond. Gold chain around it.

There was a gasp from Felix's lips. "Maria, I know it well, Grandmother Esther wore it when she was young. She wore it pinned down," and indeed there was a pin on the verso-side, "always on her blouse, right within the frill."

"Yes, it is for you and Süssel. The pastor, our father, Martina's and mine, had gone to the ghetto clandestinely, late October or early November 1941, to see how he could be of help – as you know much better than I ever could through all the stories I've heard – and your mother handed him her family heirloom for safekeeping. He saw all that misery, that stupid bizarre, senseless displacement, looked into their bewildered eyes, but couldn't do much more for fear of being caught with bulky things on his body.

"Mother said he went often with food, carrying messages, or finding children separated from their mothers. It's too long a story. My mother found the precious thing in a shoebox with a string around it, next to her fake birth certificate – she still does not know exactly how old she is – and a letter telling her that this piece of jewellery belonged to your mother, Felix, and would have to be returned."

Stunned, they passed it around the table. Alexander asking in mute behaviour: "Why eighteen diamonds?"

"It's the letter *Hai*. In Hebrew it means *Life* as well as the number eighteen. A good luck idea. I do not think it means more than that."

"A magnificent piece of goldsmithing. An old cut of the stone. Not so multi-faceted, a little on the amber side. Something from late eighteenth or early nineteenth century, I think," Martina said, handing it back to Felix. He held it then a little longer in his hand, and said in a somewhat hoarser or graver voice than he had hoped he would, "Dear Maria, thank you. But I think it has to be Süssel's. By right. She would have worn it on her blouse after our mother's death."

Passing it back to Maria, he said quietly, "We'll say goodbye to Old Europe. We'll all cross the big pond and you, Maria, will hand the heirloom to her. I hope you'll agree. Süssel has written, there is room for us. She has built a house on the model of the Old House, our grandfather's house. She built it on a river, and her adopted children are around her. She is a scientist like me, and she said I'll find work. Let me read a few lines from her letter:

The land is vast. Endless. The prairie stretches from sky to sky. A dome above the firmament is – it receives us beech-country children, river children, shelters us. It is a home, albeit a demanding one. Elemental, winters do not seem to end, and summers burst upon us with the sudden ferocity of a furious sun at five o'clock in the morning. But as the day descends there is a night to come, and we feel it approach. A welcome of fragrant air, the sky cooling to its greens, envelops us. I sit on the doorstep of my house – which I've built three stories high, as our grandfather's was – and watch that river mirror the sky. It blackens slowly until dark as a velvet band, then I lift my eyes and that dome is aglitter. Truly like nowhere else. Perhaps Safed or Jerusalem will show the heavens the way a prairie night does, and you'll find that river that brings you home.

And home is where red beeches grow and our torrential river Prut breaks out of the Carpathians. You and I, Felix, have swum on high-water days, knowing full well that it was explicitly forbidden, and have walked knee deep in its sands along the lower bank. This brings you home. The river does it. A wide, shiny surface, a blue band, clouds moving in it. It looks almost complacent, but it can't be trusted, fast and violent underneath, one cannot resist its power when caught. I am a stupid, romantic soul and behave as if I were sixteen. I've built my house right here where I can sit on its threshold and watch the river flow while the sun descends.

Dear brother, bring me the pastor's daughters and his grandson. I have a tribe around me. We all work. Life's good. Come.

THERE WAS LITTLE MORE TO DO. Another day tomorrow, different and unforeseeable. Not much left. All things packed. The Klimt painting, in a special case to be carried by Martina, stood against the wall on which it still had hung two days ago. No words, just a few hugs. The sisters and Felix said good night to Alexander, who remained a little longer at his desk.

He lingered, couldn't part, looked once more lovingly at the precision tools, his circles and angles – undid the clamped-on lamp to be safely packed the next day. Then he rose, but stepping inadvertently upon his poor left foot was taken by surprise how well he held his balance. This was new, wonderful, and so totally unexpected. It gave him a sudden awareness of his own youth, and made him think:

"It is a good beginning…"

ACKNOWLEDGEMENTS

MANY THANKS TO COTEAU BOOKS FOR PUBLISHING *The Apothecary*, as it is close to my heart. It took a few years to write, but it is almost consistently the natural completion to *The Walnut Tree*. It covers three decades, and leads my characters into the critical adjustment period of the "after-war world."

Thank you to Duncan Campbell, designer at Coteau, for the stunning cover of the book. It is an artistic pleasure to hold it in one's hands.

And now a very big thank you to Geoffrey Ursell, a fiction writer, playwright, poet, and editor. Geoffrey is a tremendous asset to any writer who can get his editorial collaboration. He gave the book structure and saw its inconsistencies, while heightening its relevancy. I am truly grateful to him, and I hope he will help me again as I continue at what I have set out to do – to bear witness to the past, the passing, and the lives caught in these tumultuous historic times.

To Margaret Kyle, my right-hand helper, many thanks. From the first pages of *The Walnut Tree* to *Children of Paper* to different essays to *The Apothecary,* she diligently worked from my handwriting to keyboard and correct the text.

To my friends Anton Kuerti, Irene N. Watts, Mavor Moore, Henry and Susan Woolf, Ian C. Nelson, Silke Faulkner, and Rabbi Roger Pavey, my most heartfelt thanks for their erudition and willingness to help in answering my interminable questions and sustaining my morale.

And I thank my daughter, Irene, as always, for her love and encouragement, as well as for her scholarship, corrections, reading, and rereading of the book, and the occasional French passage. Thank you.

I have consulted two good books. One is *Paul Celan: A Biography of His Youth,* by a friend of mine (now deceased), Israel Chalfen. The other is *Fin de siècle Vienna,* by Carl E. Schorske. I owe them the reinforcement of my memory as well as some new artistic and political information about Vienna. The aspiration of Czernowitz, until almost World War II, was to emulate its counterpart, Vienna, and to be part of its cultural heritage. And in many ways, even in exile, this allegiance is deeply felt.

MARTHA BLUM was born in Czernowitz (now Chernivtsi, in southwestern Ukraine) in 1913. Her novel *The Walnut Tree*, set during World War II, won two Saskatchewan Book Awards and was nominated for the Canadian Booksellers Association's Libris Award. Her short story collection, *Children of Paper*, portrayed the vibrant and compelling world of a small Jewish *shtetl* in Ukraine in the early 1900s.

A student of pharmacy, languages and music at universities in Prague, Strasbourg and Paris, Martha Blum has lived in Saskatoon since 1954, working as a pharmacist and teaching musical interpretation. In 1998, Martha received the Universal Declaration of Human Rights Award from Human Rights Canada, recognizing her contribution to the cultural life of Canada.

Also by Martha Blum:

 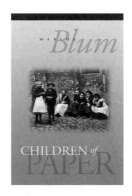

The Walnut Tree
ISBN: 1-55050-154-2
Coteau Books, 1999

Children of Paper
ISBN : 1-55050-208-5
Coteau Books, 2002